O. M. [illegible]
Perkinsville.
Vermont.

ALEK & ERYCINA

BOSTON: PHILLIPS, SAMPSON & CO.

WOLFSDEN:

AN AUTHENTIC ACCOUNT OF

Things There and Thereunto Pertaining

AS THEY ARE AND HAVE BEEN.

BY J. B.

An' clever chiels, an' bonnie-hizzies,
Are bred in sic a way as this is.
BURNS.

BOSTON:
PHILLIPS, SAMPSON AND COMPANY,
13 WINTER STREET.
1856.

Stereotyped by
HOBART & ROBBINS,
New England Type and Stereotype Foundery,
BOSTON.

To

MY SISTER,

WHOSE GOOD WORKS HAVE SHAMED MY IDLENESS AND PROVOKED ME TO EMULATION, AND FROM WHOSE VIRTUES I HAVE ENDEAVORED TO DRAW ATTRACTIVE PICTURES OF GOODNESS, I DEDICATE WHATEVER IN THIS VOLUME HER JUDGMENT OR PARTIALITY MAY APPROVE.

WOLFSDEN.

P. F.

Midnight has passed. Morning dawns. The fading stars twinkle idly in their blue depths, or melt from view in the spreading light. The fringed clouds glow in the eastern sky like the bright wings of Apollo's steeds, ascending their star-paved way. The god of Day — of the golden harp and silver bow — appears. His swift arrows pierce and illuminate the misty morning. They glance from ocean's breast and gild its surging foam. The iceberg's towering pinnacles receive and scatter his million shafts. The arctic shores, cold and desolate, where the waves dash their congealing spray, where the white bear snatches the unwary seal from his lurking-place; the snow-piled mountains, receding far, and resting in the majesty of desolation against the northern sky; the wide-extended plains, tracked with the footprints and echoing with the howls of the gaunt fox and famished wolf; the dark and dwarfed forests of fir, where the reindeer gathers his mossy food, — all the inhospitable realms of Winter's despotic reign greet with grim defiance the god of the bright bow and golden song. Yet upward ascend his coursers, bearing the bright banners of morning — smiling in victory upon the sullen array.

New England's shores catch and reflect the glowing smile. Here Winter rules his divided empire with a gentler hand. Like a stern father, — stern, but beneficent, — he blesses even while he frowns. His severe lessons teach us wisdom, prompt us to effort, compel us to industry. He hardens our frames, and stimulates our energies. He reminds us of the duties of mutual kindness and benevolence. He gives occasions of social intercourse, diffusing enjoyment and promoting improvement. He nerves the enterprising will. He inspires the generous thought. He gives vigor to the active frame. He is the father of New England character, as the Summer is the genial mother. Though we better love the warm lap of our smiling mother, let us no less thank the sterner father for the discipline of manly virtue.

Morning dawns in Wolfsden. It is time. The night has been long. The beasts in the stall have consumed their nightly fodder, and chewed the cud of patience, while the frost has silvered their hoary brows, and hung with icicles their whiskered cheeks. The silly sheep torpidly wait the morning, each with his nose buried in the woolly warmth of close-crowded mates. The feathered brood, cramped upon their high perch, have counted with unerring instinct the last hour of night, and their high-crested lord wakes the morning with a cottage-rousing crow.

Awake, Alek! Arouse thee! Come from the land of dreams! Arise from the slumberous pillow! A new day dawns, bringing duties, cares, and enjoyments. The golden moments of youth's treasury are gliding away. Up! count, secure them!

Alek needs no second call. The bounce of his elastic feet upon the floor echoes to the last note of chanticleer. With the iron-bound bucket he has drawn a copious cosmetic from the deep well, and dashed his ruddy cheeks and youthful limbs in unsparing profusion. His frame glows with intenser life.

The fire smokes, and snaps, and sparkles, and roars, in the ample kitchen chimney. The red light reflects from the frosty window-panes, from the polished platters ranged upon the dressers, from the gilded figures and round-visaged moon upon the tall and venerable clock, and sends cheerful gleams abroad upon the snowy landscape.

Shaggy Lion, with his big paws and depending ears, his wide mouth and ivory teeth, is awake, and ready for the fights and the frolics of the day. Tabby mews from the cellar, where she has guarded the public weal from stealthy mice and marauding rats. Alek answers their greetings, and hastens to his expectant subjects in the barn. From the high mow he pitches huge heaps of hay before the hungry herd. The bleating sheep, the lowing kine, and the whinnying horses, are bountifully supplied. Down from their high roost fly a various brood, — cackling hens, gobbling turkeys, and screaming pintadids mingle their various language in one unanimous call for food. Alek scatters corn with liberal hand, and they hasten with eagerness to fill their crops.

Here come Billy and Tommy, racing and shouting through the snow, barefooted, barenecked, with only their trousers buttoned about their waists, as if playing among new-mown hay in sultry June.

"Back to your beds, you young dogs!" roared Alek, "or I'll duck you in the watering-trough. Hurry, or I'll set Lion on you, you ragamuffins!"

Billy and Tommy are not much terrified with Alek's

threats, but their tingling toes incline them to obedience, and they retreat to the kitchen fire, to the disappointment of Lion, who had already joined their frolic in the snow, and wonders why they should so soon leave the sport.

A mighty wood-pile rises in substantial dignity, and bounds the door-yard on the east. The solid trunks of tall trees, only lately towering in their native forest, now lie ready for the axe. Well can Alek wield the keen axe, and sever the knotted boughs, and rive the huge logs.

Billy and Tommy again appear, now dressed, buskined, capped, and mittened, for work. On their hand-sled they heap the severed and rifted wood, and with merry gambols draw it to the shed, where, piled in compact tiers, it will slowly season for future use.

What bright picture of the morning appears in the open doorway? O, Frances! beautiful amid your clustering locks of gold, sending radiance from your soul-speaking eyes of blue, cheering every heart with your sweet voice, how welcome the summons to breakfast from lips like yours! Alek answers the invitation ere her voice can reach him; he buries the axe deep in the massive log, clasps his sister in his arms, and, with a fond kiss, tosses her to the kitchen. Here is spread the bountiful table. Ever may such a table be surrounded by hearts as good and kind, and faces as bright with pleasant thoughts, as these! How various their characters, and yet all how good! The father and mother, slowly verging toward old age, rich in the experience and reflections of well-spent years; rich in the respect and love of devoted children; richer than all in the hope and full assurance of a better home beyond this mortal life. Long have they brought their spirits into subordination and union with the spirit of peace and love. Long have they taught by their example the excellence of their faith.

Helen, — fair, placid, sedate, good Helen, — why is she the last one noticed? Is it because she is always so exactly where she should be and what she should be, and her presence so essential, that, like the blue sky and the pleasant sunshine, we think of her only when we miss her? Helen, mild and calm as a summer's morning, seldom speaking, yet ever expressing good and wise thoughts through your soul-fraught countenance! O, if all were not so good, you would be the best of all!

Pour the steaming coffee! Spread the brown toast! Slice the wheaten loaf! Plenty reigns.

O, love-encircled and love-breathing family! how blessed with all that gives health to the body and joy to the soul is your cheerful board!

Thus far had I proceeded, when an inquisitive face came peering over the page; and soon a remonstrating voice exclaimed,

"Why, brother, is this the way you begin your long-promised history of Wolfsden? Here you have already put in the whole of Deacon Arbor's family, with not the slightest account of who they are, or where they live, or when they were born, or any other of the proper beginnings of a story! If you set out in this prancing, curveting style, when will you get to your story's end, and who can follow you, or guess where you are going?"

"Dear sister," said I, "it 's the very thing I do not want you to guess. I am preparing pleasant surprises, unexpected results, astonishing developments, and astounding catastrophes, — for what else do readers care for, in these days of wonderment ? "

" Poh, brother ! there are common-sense folks, now-a-days, as many as ever, though book-makers seem to forget them. Write a plain, straight-forward, common-sense history of Wolfsden, with a genealogy of all the inhabitants, and then every family in town will subscribe for a copy, and you will be famous."

" Dear sister mine, your words are inspired with wisdom. Go and borrow every family register in Wolfsden, and in the mean time I will begin at the beginning, and our town shall be chronicled according to rule."

" That 's a sensible brother," said my sisterly critic ; " but it would be a pity to throw away what you have already written. Can't you alter it a little, and let it stand for the preface ? You know that nobody ever reads the preface ; so it may as well be nonsense as anything else."

" Sister," said I, a little piqued, " I will have it printed where it *shall* be read. Let me tell you," said I, holding up the sheet, " that this is very fine writing, only a little too high-flown for your understanding. I will have it for the first chapter in the book ; — and, since I must make another beginning, I will call this the Preliminary Flourish, and mark it P. F."

" Dear brother," said the kind creature, " print it where you will. There must be something in every book, as you say, that nobody can understand. I have always found it so ; and it may as well be at the beginning as elsewhere, for then we can the easier skip it. So I 'll go and borrow the genealogies, and you may begin the beginning."

THE BEGINNING.

WOLFSDEN is a quiet nook among the mountains in Maine, where the sun delights to prop himself among the tall trees, while he peeps down the green valleys, and sees his face reflected in many a winding stream and placid lake. Toward the south and east the view extends to a far-distant horizon, where, aided by a telescope, you may see the sky shut down upon the ocean.

Toward the north and west the high and rugged hills of Wolfsden are surmounted by higher hills beyond, which grow more and more wild and savage as they approach the White Hills, whose vast and lofty chain seems, at this distance, but as the highest step in a series of ascending mountains, which, beginning far toward the east, rise by regular gradation to the clouds.

Scenes of rural beauty are more delightful when contrasted with the sublime and terrible. Along the base of those high and desert mountains are scattered the cultivated farms of a happy and well-instructed people. Primitive and plain in their habits, and moderate in their aspirations, they pass their time chiefly in providing things convenient for the present life, and in preparation for the life to come.

2

There is no strong dividing line separating people into classes. Each family owns a farm of a hundred or two of acres, divided into fields, pastures, and wood-lot, with house, barn, orchard, garden, and other improvements, of which the greater or less apparent perfection is the chief external sign of abundance or deficiency in worldly goods.

I dwell in mind amidst those scenes of my early days, for there my eyes first saw the light and my first ideas were awakened. I knew the sweets of home affection; of a mother's love and sister's fondness. There I found friendships around me, and became conscious of the emotions which beauty can inspire. There were genial minds, and kind hearts, and loving eyes, among my school companions; and when lessons were learned, what else was left to the ever-busy mind of childhood, but mischief, or merriment, or love? But, under the birchen rule of a country schoolmaster, mischief and merriment are dangerous resources, while love — quiet, deferential, unspoken love — has nothing of danger, and yet fills the void of the earnest heart, and gives fleetness to the wings of weary time.

I am to speak little of myself in this story, — little of myself, and nothing of my love. It was unspoken, and so it shall remain. The sweet idea of her soul-revealing eyes as she met my admiring look; how happy I was to see her enter the school-house; how I knew her neat and pretty hood among the flock, as I saw afar off their merry coming; how a grace and excellence seemed to surround and separate her from all others; her mild, and yet intellectual look; her rosy, and yet reserved and unapproachable lips; her agile, and yet gentle and graceful motion; her knowing that I loved her, and yet minding it so little, while my soul was swelling with the magnitude of its emotion!

Ah, the beautiful spring of life is past! Its lovely blossoms are perished, and there is no fruit to glad my autumn. Yet I cherish the fragrance of their memory. I will not speak of our pleasant times, when the boys and girls of our neighborhood assembled to spend a winter evening, how I managed to be near her; and when the apples were named, that in eating them we might know by the number of the seeds our present feelings and future relations to each other, how happy I was when some one would give my name to her apple, and the seeds would come out plump, and read, "He loves, she loves, both love;" and how, when another name instead of my own was so blessed, I pretended to care nothing about it. And when we separated, how eager was I to be ready with my arm to escort her home before another should usurp my place!

Nor how I sought occasion to be by her side when studying her lesson; and when she was puzzled with a sum, to take the pencil from her dear fingers, or perchance from her sweet lips, and, first putting it to my own, which she would not notice, proceed to put down the figures as they should be, and whisper arithmetical explanations, while tenderer words were trembling on my tongue.

Why should I speak of this; or how, when roses were in bloom, and strawberries were ripe, I found the fairest and picked the ripest ever by her side; or how I watched her in meeting, and forgot the text; and at singing-school heard no melody but hers; and — but I am determined to say nothing about it. Thirty summers have passed away since those bright spring-days of my life. I hear and feel the blasts of autumn, and Frances Arbor is gone where she should be, — where spring, and youth, and loveliness, are perpetual.

Every one has noticed that, even in the most rustic population, some families seem endowed with a natural refinement of character, extending not only to personal manners, but to sentiments and feelings; and that even in the same family some individuals will excel others in these respects. This was strikingly shown in the family of Deacon Arbor. Frances was as graceful as the sparrow which flitted around her sunny head, and agile as the pet lamb which delighted to frisk about her path; while Alexander, or Alek, as we called her eldest brother, was as awkward as his two-year-old steers which he exercised daily in trying to "break," and which, as if conscious of their master's awkwardness, acted as if determined to break him. Alek, however, was victorious; the steers became docile, well-behaved oxen, while Alek grew up, as far as externals go, an awkward, lubberly, left-handed blunderhead.

But Alek had solid qualities of heart and mind, as well as of person. He was four years older than Frances, and two years more than myself, and was one of the most successful competitors in the athletic and often boisterous games and exercises of our school-intermissions and half-holidays. I owe to his good-will and strong arm much of my exemption from the tyranny and violence which my imprudence often provoked, and my strength could not repel. It might be that I won his partiality by the frequent assistance which I bestowed upon his "sums" and other lessons; but I loved to refer it to a more flattering motive, — the kind partiality of Frances, whom he loved as such a sister should be loved.

Ah, Alek! genial, generous and warm-hearted bear, in your

shaggy coat! How shall I describe you, that others may love you as I did, in spite of your rough and rustic garb? And yet you were not so awkward, after all, only when you had on your Sunday coat, and gay vest, and shining hat and boots, and no place where to put your great, brown hands, and no way to apply your great, ox-like strength. A whale or a porpoise is ungraceful when out of water, but in his native element he is quite at home. So with Alek. Who could swing the axe in the forest or at the wood-pile, or the scythe in the meadow, with better grace than he? Or who could guide the plough or handle the hoe with more dexterity? Or, if we come to good looks, who had redder cheeks, or brighter eyes, or whiter teeth, or curlier hair, or a more eternally good-natured, half charitable, half self-complacent laugh, like one who thinks pretty well of everybody, and very well of himself? For, however diffident, and deferential, and even self-depreciating, his deportment might appear abroad, and in his Sunday suit, yet, when at home and in his working dress, — or undress, for his coat was always off, and generally his vest and hat, — he appeared sufficiently confident of himself, and much as one born to command, not oxen merely, but men, — that is, workmen, the only kind of men with whom he really cared to have anything to do.

And then, too, though unskilled in ready and graceful speech, Alek could feel and cherish the emotions of a great heart, — a heart seemingly formed by nature in a rustic workshop, but where, as everywhere else in this rustic region, there was an abundance of material, of the soundest and best quality. As he went forth at early dawn with axe, or hoe, or scythe, or with whip beside his team, to the business of the day, attended perhaps by a hired man or his boy-brothers, or only by his constant companion, the heavy, shaggy, half-Indian and half-Newfoundland dog, Lion, who everybody said was like his master in knowing more than he could tell — wherever Alek might be, and however employed, the sense of an ever-present and all-seeing Power was ever with him; not a terror or restraint, but a high companion and friend, — a friend possessing every power but that of injustice or unkindness; one with whom he might happily and profitably commune at any moment and all the time, or whom he might neglect and turn his thoughts away from at any time, without giving offence, though with great loss to himself. He saw in the dewy grass, in the fresh morning flowers, in the merry birds flitting among the branches, in the brisk squirrel, who, secure in his lofty perch, chattered a defiant reply to the big and shaggy Lion barking a good-natured good-morning beneath his tree, — in all these, and in everything around and beyond him, Alek saw the unfailing goodness and the persevering workmanship of his great and unseen, but not unknown, companion and friend. And he felt that, in the companionship of nature's God, there could be no want of society; and with the evidences of His works everywhere about him, it was a noble business to WORK. And as he thought of this great Companion, and how his own comprehension was enlarged by communing with him, and increased knowledge gave increased power of comprehension, he thought how excellent it was to gain much knowledge and enlarge the resources and the power of thought; and he resolved to know all that he could learn from nature, or men, or books. He did not wish to change his pursuits or position in life, for he was content with both, and had not thought that there might be a worthier or happier. The germ of restless worldly ambition had not yet begun to develop itself within him.

But yet he knew well that there was a busy and ambitious, an exciting and magnificent world, afar off, beyond his humble and happy sphere. Beyond the hills of his father's farm, and the higher hills of neighboring farms, successively swelling to mountains toward the north, arose the vast chain whose dark, forest-clad sides ascended and blended with the gray mist and the blue sky, till their white tops were lost in the clouds. Beyond these, he knew that the road through the "Notch" led to the busy tumult of a very different kind of life, — to gay and populous towns, and proud and wealthy cities, filled with the commerce and fed with the riches which the St. Lawrence receives from opposite sides of the great world.

The Saco, too, rolls its impetuous waters from amidst those mountains on the hither side, now winding its dark and devious way through trackless forests, undisturbed by man or animal, except by the leaping of the salmon, or the smaller fry of the finny tribe, or by the plash of their fierce and cunning pursuers, the otter, or mink, or hawk, or by the rush of the timorous deer from the gaunt pursuing wolf, or the crossing of the prowling bear or stately moose, — unfrequented by man or animal, except by the wild beast or Indian, — ever rushing, and eddying, and rolling over its rocky or sandy bed, now dashing over an opposing precipice, now leaping and chafing in white foam down a long and rocky descent, now seeming to pause a moment in the peaceful bosom of a dark-fringed and white-shored, quiet lake, — yet ever through deep forests, or over opposing precipices, or down steep rapids, or through quiet lakes, or amid green meadows, rolling its waters to the ocean.

As Alek would sometimes visit its summer solitude, or skate upon its wintry expanse of ice, he would think to what strange scenes and agitating pursuits this river's course, or yonder mountain-pass, might lead him, and how, perhaps, his sagacity to discern, and perseverance to strive, and strength to do, might find or force a path to distinction among the striving crowd; for Alek, as has been intimated, was not of a disposition to distrust his own powers, but, on the contrary, had much of that feeling of capability which vigorous youth and rustic inexperience usually inspire even in the most unassuming persons. Yet he felt no temptation to engage in the world's strife; he clung to his quiet home, to the peace and plenty of his paternal roof, to the constant and careful love of his honored and venerated parents, the watchful affection of his elder sister, the endearing fondness of Frances, whom everybody loved, and to the boys, Billy and Tommy, who, whatever others might think, looked upon Alek as their all-endowed and all-accomplished leader and instructor.

We will not further describe the different members of the family to the reader, until they have occasion to appear in the coming incidents of this history. There was nothing very peculiar in the others. Frances was chiefly remarkable for her grace and loveliness; and Alek chiefly so, at least to the generality of people, for his awkwardness and homeliness, although nature had given him a form and features which art might rejoice to train and polish, and place among the favorites of fashion.

In every New England town there is a place where its influence and fashion centre. It is generally near the territorial centre, and is known as "The Village," "The Corner," or sometimes "The Meeting-house;" this latter appellation being derived from its church edifice, which is the chief architectural ornament of the town, and always on Sundays and holidays the great centre to which all worthy people converge for worship and social reünion. The town-house, with the selectmen's and town-clerk's office, and generally a tavern, a store or two, where all varieties of merchandise are sold, a few mechanics' shops and houses, a physician's, and perhaps a lawyer's office, sometimes a high school, and a few houses of the more wealthy or aspiring class, combine to give it an air of magnificence in the eyes of home-born and home-staying townsmen. Here, of course, is to be found whatever pretension of gentility the town affords. There is enough of society for emulation, and comparison, and criticism, and whatever else of good or evil grows out of social proximity. Here the singers meet for a weekly concert. Here is the quarterly military training, and here the annual speeches and guns in honor of our glorious independence are fired off, and the occasional ball, or "sociable," is held. To each town this central village is what the capital is to the state, — a place which all regard with a blended feeling of pride, jealousy, and admiration.

Our neighborhood was somewhat remote from the centre of the town, so that we generally rode, when business, or recreation, or devotion, called us thither. In winter, Alek would delight to harness his favorite colts — a spirited and well-matched pair — to the big "pung," and, filling it with all the younger members of the family, and smuggling in, when possible, a fair cousin or two, give loose rein, and scamper away through clouds of snow, and perilous drifts, with boys, girls, horses, and the faithful Lion, all equally zealous and eager in the duty of Sunday devotions, and quite outrunning the zeal of the father and mother, the staid deacon and his placid wife, and the serious mare that followed soberly behind. Yet often in such cases it might be seen how zeal outruns discretion, verifying the maxim, "the more haste the worse speed," as when a pair of high-mettled steeds are harnessed to a "pung" filled with not too serious boys and girls, and driven by a Jehu who fears a snow-bank as a pig fears a clover-field. Were there not some smashings, and some overturnings, and some premature buryings, and some unexpected resurrections? And did not Alek always find a plausible reason for such disasters, though the others declared he did it on purpose? There are many reminiscences of that sort, which we, surviving relics of those giddy days, recall to each others' recollection in our sober meetings.

We always noticed that these accidents never happened when Margaret Murray was of our party. She was the only daughter of a neighbor, distantly related, who lived about a mile from Deacon Arbor's, in the direction opposite from the meeting-house. She would sometimes visit her cousin Frances of a Saturday, and pass the night, and would, of course, be one of the party to fill the "pung," and share the perils of the Sunday pilgrimage of devotion. At such times, though the colts would prance as proudly and fly as swiftly through the snow as ever, yet the pung would keep right-side up, and bring its lively freight safe to the meeting-house steps; so that, by oft-repeated observation, it came to be understood that the pung would not tip over when Margaret Murray was in it. Alek always had a reason, but the girls said that the pung would not hear to reason, except when Margaret was there.

But every rule has its exceptions, and the pung once forgot to be reasonable, although the fair Margaret *was* on board. It happened on this wise :

An old lady from Portland was making a visitation in our neighborhood, taking turns at every eligible house where a claim of acquaintance or hospitality could gain admittance for her. The slightest invitation which civility, in such a neighborhood, requires to be bestowed on even a disagreeable acquaintance, was construed by her into an earnest wish for at least a week's sojourn ; during which time she would manage to pry into every one's affairs, and make herself as meddlesome and disagreeable as possible. She had great claims to "gentility," upon which she plumed herself, and upon the grounds of which she, as a matter of course, seemed to expect, as she certainly managed to get, a great share of deference and attention. Reverence to age, and respect for even its caprices and weaknesses, are traits of New England character; and old Mrs. Simperkins had no delicate scruples about stretching the chain of toleration to its utmost tension. So that, although ignorant, conceited, vulgar-minded, and mischievous, she managed to command the best attentions and hospitalities of our town for two mortal months, of which two weeks were divided between Major Murray's and Deacon Arbor's, where her affectations and pretensions, her shallowness and conceit, had pretty nearly neutralized the natural respect and welcome accorded to aged womanhood. Not that this feeling found utterance even in private, though every one felt that it would be a relief to be free from her society. It may be mentioned that she claimed to be "a hinglish lady," and to have been "heducated hin the 'ighest horder hof society," and to be quite conversant with "duchesses, countesses, and hall the 'igh life hof Lunnun." The probability is, that she had been employed in some cockney milliner's establishment, this being her occupation in Portland, where she had temporarily shut up shop to come upon her mission among us.

Alek, although so tolerant of everybody, and especially deferential to the claims of age and womanhood, was quite disgusted with the old lady's character; especially with the shallow hypocrisy which she wore, like her ribbons and ruffles, as the advertisement of her trade. But the chief annoyance was her constant claim to be present in all the social gatherings of the young people, where her society was always felt to be superfluous.

It happened that Margaret Murray came on the Saturday of Mrs. Simperkins' week at the deacon's, and that three or four other young friends "happened in," which made as near an approach to a "party" as might be allowable at a deacon's on a Saturday evening. A fire was built in the "fore-room," and there was a cheerful time. We had tea, and toast, and doughnuts, and pies, and all the plenty of a substantial farmhouse supper, where people eat as they do everything else,— in earnest. We had conversation and sober amusements, as usual, till the "old folks" had retired to their room, which they always did in season to allow an hour or two of livelier play to the young; and then we were as merry as we could very well be, though all were secretly annoyed at Mrs. Simperkins' presence, who not only remained, but assumed, as usual, to be the important personage of the company. We boys, including Alek, were not only vexed by her presence, but that the girls should show so much deference to her pretensions, and so perversely decline ours; which vexation, however, we swallowed with our supper; and, with the apples and nuts, and a stolen kiss or two, we made ourselves about as happy as usual.

Next morning, after breakfast, Alek had the colts harnessed to the pung a little earlier than usual, as he was careful to do whenever Margaret was to be one of the party; for it had happened sometimes that the major and his wife, who had to pass by the deacon's on the way to meeting, had come along and had called to take Margaret along with them, much to our dissatisfaction. I suppose we had all a secret presentiment of Mrs. Simperkins' society; though nothing was said till the pung was brought to the door, when, there she stood, with her bland and malicious smile, the first one ready, and evidently prepared to take the first place in our conveyance. This was bearing pretty hard on Alek's patience, and he ventured gently to suggest that she had better ride with the old folks; that the pung was not so comfortable as the sleigh; that the colts were very wild, and the roads much drifted, and we were almost sure to be upset. But Mrs. Simperkins, who had, doubtless, learned that the pung never upset with Margaret in it, was deaf to all remonstrances; and, being supported by the girls, who apparently enjoyed our vexation, although sharing in it themselves, she crowded herself into the party. It was very remarkable that the colts, which, being well trained, were generally very quiet during the process of loading, now, in spite of Alek's reining and scolding them, and snapping the whip, or perhaps having some secret divination of their master's present mood, were uncommonly restive and unaccommodating, starting backwards and forwards as the girls were crowding into their places, and pitching them in every direction; and especially when Mrs. Simperkins was clambering into her seat they gave a sudden start, which, but for the girls around her, would have tumbled her over; but, as if to make amends, they were very quiet when Margaret, who got in last, was taking her seat. Sagacious colts they were!

But after all this difficulty we started off in fine style, and I could see, by a pleased twinkle in Alek's eye, that there was fun of some kind ahead. The colts scampered, the snow flew, the girls screamed alternately with excitement or terror, as we dashed along through the blinding drifts, until, about half-way to the meeting-house, a tremendous bank of snow loomed up directly in the road, presenting an apparently impassable barrier. We knew very well that Alek could guide us by it, or through it, or shipwreck us in it, at his option; and, but for Margaret's presence, should have expected the latter, which indeed I began to suspect would be our lot, at any rate. This suspicion was soon confirmed, when, as we neared the drift, Alek quickly placed one foot outside the box, and one hand under an arm of Margaret, who sat very near, and, giving the reins a shake and a jerk, in an instant we saw him spring, with Margaret on his arm, from the right side of the pung, and at the same moment we were all floundering over head and ears in the snow-bank on the opposite side, while the horses were plunging, almost completely buried in the snow. As we struggled out of our awkward positions, we saw Alek disentangling and backing the horses out of their difficulty, and Margaret standing in a smooth, hard place, entirely untouched by the disaster, but looking with great sympathy upon our distress; though, being bundled and bound up in wrappers, cloaks, shawls, and furs, she could scarcely move to give the least assistance. However, we struggled bravely, helping each other to a perpendicular position as fast as possible; and Alek, having relieved and righted the team, and put Margaret in the pung, soon came to our assistance. He was full of apologies and explanations; but he evidently felt like a man who had begun the day very well. He was over-profuse in his aid and sympathy for poor Mrs. Simperkins, whose crushed bonnet, and draggled ribbons, and general derangement of millinery, gave good color of justice to the anger of her countenance. I think that a sense of having over-punished the old lady reäcted upon his generous nature, so as really to kindle a flame of kindness toward her; for he was very careful to soothe her fears, and convey her safely the rest of the way, and upon our return urged her to ride back with us, assuring her there would be no danger of another overturn. She would not, however, venture herself with us again, but rode with the old folks; and, what was sadder still, we had to part with Margaret, who, as usual, returned home with her father and mother. However, we all went home in good spirits, especially Alek, who looked as though he had gained much good from Parson Boreman's sermon, and had acquired a stock of charity and good-humor sufficient to outlast the visitations of a dozen Mrs. Simperkinses.

CHAPTER II.

Dear images of early days, when life was full of freshness, when the glad young blood bounded through elastic veins, and an overflowing vitality supplied the nerves with energy, and the heart with abundant feeling! Sweet were our daily dutiés, dear were our ever-recurring social enjoyments, and bright our anticipations. Or, if a pang of disappointment, of jealousy, or some fancied injury, pierced our sensitive bosoms, how soon was the wound healed, and the pain forgotten!

Of all the models of propriety, of quiet, unassuming dignity, softened with gentleness, — of all the daughter-like and wife-like and mother-like qualities which go to make up a perfect woman, — I have seen none surpassing my remembrance of Helen Arbor. She was the elder sister of Alek, and, like most elder sisters, the best-instructed, best-dispositioned, and best-qualified member of the family. The father might be tardy, but Helen was always prompt. The mother might forget, but Helen always remembered. Alek might blunder, but Helen did everything rightly. Even sweet Frances might sometimes be wayward or mischievous, or in some way betray her descent from Eve; but Helen might have been born free from all original sin (if such a thing had been possible in her father's creed), as she certainly grew up and lived without any visible faults of her own. Helen was not strikingly beautiful, though everybody allowed that she was good-looking; and the girls, especially those who had pretensions of their own to beauty, all declared that she was full as handsome as Frances.

But, though thus endowed and graced with all the excellences which would have made her a treasure of a wife, to a man worthy of her, Helen was now twenty-five, and still single, and even without the reputation of ever having had a suitor. I know not how it was, but there was something so mind-like in her countenance, so much apparent depth of judgment, and power of discernment, that the most presumptuous spark had never ventured an approach to flirtation; and more serious suitors, if they had ever appeared, had been quietly dismissed, and the world was none the wiser.

It may here be recorded that Helen's maternal ancestry were of Quaker descent. Mrs. Arbor, generally called "Aunt Deborah," as everybody likes to call so good a woman, was the grand-daughter of Mathew Purington, a prominent Friend before and during the Revolution, and who, living near Boston in those troubled times, had "borne testimony" against the violence of both sides, to both General Washington and General Howe, in a manner characteristic of his faith. Aunt Deborah spent her childhood and formed her early associations among the descendants of the old Quaker, who are now numerous, and form a considerable portion of the "meeting" still flourishing near its original locality, which is now the heart of a city famous all over the United States for its manufacture of shoes.

Aunt Deborah was not born a member of the sect, her

mother having been "read out of meeting" for choosing a husband who was not a member thereof; but she honored and perhaps prided herself in her Quaker ancestry, and, besides practising their common virtues, she retained many of their peculiar sentiments, especially a faith in the "inward light," which, being cherished and followed, she believed to be a sure guide, not only in spiritual, but also in worldly affairs; and that warnings and revelations of things important to be avoided or to be done were thus communicated to the spiritually minded. This undoubted faith of Aunt Deborah was confirmed, not only by early teachings and the really remarkable experiences of early Friends, but also by her own experience in frequent cases, one of which came under my own observation, and is so impressed on my memory that I can hardly proceed without telling it.

It happened that Alek and I went one day to a distant part of the town, to give to a poor man, who had been disabled by accident, a day's work in harvesting. Among a few others who were gathered for the same purpose was Josiah Brown, a strong, active, and generally good-natured fellow enough, but of a violent temper when provoked. A difficulty arose between him and Alek, about a matter which was afterwards explained, but which produced much ill-feeling and harsh language between them at the time, and which, but for the presence of others, might have ended in blows; for Josiah was very violent, and Alek, though averse to a quarrel, had hardly enough of his brave Quaker ancestor's blood or spirit to bear violence without retaliation. However, they parted without anything more serious than hard words and hard thoughts, which, to Alek's peaceful mind, were an unpleasant burthen, though it seemed to be pretty much worn off and forgotten before we reached home. Alek attended to his out-door affairs, and went in to supper with his usual good-natured look; but his quick eye noticed that his mother looked graver than usual. He knew that she could not have heard of the quarrel, for it had taken place just before he started for home, and no one came before him, or could have passed him on the road, or could have any motive to tell his mother of so trifling but unpleasant a matter. But, when the family were out of the room, to his great surprise she said to him, "My son, have you had a quarrel with anybody this afternoon?"

"A quarrel!" said Alek, forcing a laugh; "with whom, and for what? You know I am no quarreller. You might as well think of your grandfather Purington's quarrelling."

"Yes; but, Alek," continued his mother, "I feel impressed to ask you if you have quarrelled with anybody, — with Josiah Brown, for instance, or anybody else?"

Alek saw that evasion was out of the question, and replied, "Well, mother, I did talk to Josiah Brown rather plain, perhaps, but I said nothing but what was true and right."

"My son," said his mother, "you doubtless said what was *true*, but what was not *right* to say, at least in the spirit of anger. Now, my son, you think that Josiah Brown has done you some wrong, and I will tell you how to get the advantage of him. Will you take my counsel?"

"Yes, mother, I always take your counsel."

"Well, Alek, in the first place forgive in your heart whatever injury Josiah may have done you; then examine candidly whether you have not done him some wrong, in his feelings or otherwise, which ought to be confessed; and, whether you have or not, go to him at the first opportunity, and be reconciled."

"I will, mother. But who told you anything about it?"

"No one, my son: it was *impressed* on me about an hour before you came home."

"Well, mother, that was just the time I had the words with Josiah."

Alek told me, the next day, of this conversation with his mother, adding that he believed she knew his very thoughts, and that it was of no use to keep any secret from her.

"In that case," said I, "you are well guarded, for you have both God and your mother watching you. I think you 'll go pretty straight."

"Well, I mean to do just that very thing," said Alek.

Ah, Alek! trust not thus in your own strength; for it is spiritual as well as carnal pride which goeth before destruction, and a self-righteous as well as a haughty spirit before a fall! And yet Alek's moral strength and firmness might seem reliable. It had already been often proved, and the very next evening, after his day's work, he rode over to Job Brown's, found Josiah, and, offering his hand, said, "I was wrong yesterday — let us overlook the affair."

"O, no, I was wrong," said Josiah, melting at once; "I am sorry you came to me in this way — I mean I wish I had gone to you; but I had n't spunk enough to do it, although I found out, soon after you went away, that I was entirely in the wrong — it was all my mistake. But how can you say you were wrong, when you know you were entirely in the right?"

"I mean," said Alek, "that I was wrong in losing my temper, and using hard language; but it is none of my merit finding that out, and coming to own it. It 's all mother's doings; and you may be sure when I do anything right, or mend anything wrong, that mother has a hand in it."

"Well," said Josiah, "you have mended your wrong, if you did any, and left me no chance to mend mine, and that I call getting the advantage of me. Now, I only ask you, when you see me play the blackguard again, just give me a good kicking, and I 'll take it kindly, and thank you into the bargain."

Alek laughed, and, after going into the house and chatting with the family a while, went homewards feeling quite comfortable, reflecting what a mother he had to give good advice, and especially thinking of the remarkable coincidence of language in his mother's counsel, and Josiah's confession that he had *got the advantage of him.*

"There is something," said Alek, "in this 'inward light,' that is wonderful. Mother says we may all have it by attending to it; but I think it won't come easy to any of us, except Helen. She 's got it, safe enough, though she says nothing about it."

Thus meditated Alek, while his colt, with loose rein and at his own pace, bore him quickly home.

"All right, mother!" said Alek, exultingly, as he came into the kitchen.

"Yes, all right, my son," said his mother, just as if she knew where he had been, and all about it.

Josiah Brown told me, a good while after, about Alek's coming to reconcile the matter. "And," said he, "that just cut me the worst kind. But there is one comfort, — he gave his mother credit for it, and it 's my mind them Arbors would n't be so much better than everybody else, if it was n't for their mother. It does a fellow more good to have her just speak to him, than to hear Parson Boreman preach seven years."

Alek's mother had once reproved Josiah, when a boy, for swearing at his horse, and with such good effect that folks said he went home and asked pardon of his horse, on his knees. That might not be true, but it is a fact that he broke himself of the habit of swearing.

People everywhere admitted Aunt Deborah's excellence, and that Helen was just like her; and thought it a pity that she should not marry, and bring up just such another family, instead of living and dying an old maid, as she was likely to do. From this latter destiny there could be no doubt many a nice young man would be glad to save her, if he had only the courage to "propose;" but, for want of it, or some other cause, the prospects in that direction looked rather blank.

But it takes everybody to know everything. The world is a prying, inquisitive medley of all sorts of folks, having all sorts of notions, and finding out and guessing all sorts of things; and yet it often happens that some quiet, simple-seeming, grave-looking old gentleman or lady knows a thing or two, of which the slightest whisper would set the same shrewd, prying, self-conceited world a wondering for a week, and buzzing for a month. For instance, if Aunt Deborah should tell all that was thought, said, and done, when she, and Helen, and the deacon, visited Uncle Lemuel's family, at Saco, three years ago this winter;—how Cousin Hezekiah, the schoolmaster, at first eyed her as keenly as if he thought she might in some way belong to him, and then so timidly spoke and shook hands with her as if he feared she might belong to somebody else,—and then was so anxious, and inquisitive, and communicative, as if that question must be settled soon in one way or another; and how he invited Helen to his school, and introduced her to all his favorite scholars among the girls and young women, but not to one of the boys or young men; and how he carried her home from school alone, forgetting to invite the girls to jump in and fill up the sleigh, as usual; and how flustered and fidgety, and yet how very happy, he seemed, all the time of her visit; and how very grave and pathetic he looked when they came away; and how he put a large hot stone in the bottom of the sleigh, and tucked the buffalo-robe about her, as though he supposed she might be some tender vegetable, very suitable to be cooked over a hot stone, but not hardy enough to be exposed to the frost; and how he shook hands with her at parting four times as long as was necessary and proper; and how, since that time, Aunt Nabby, *his* mother, had written to Aunt Deborah, *her* mother, every three months, enclosing a letter directed, in a nice, schoolmaster hand, to Miss Helen Arbor; — all these things, which Aunt Deborah often talked over with the deacon, and sometimes with Helen, what if she had hinted to some sagacious secret-finder for the wonder-loving world? How would the wonder-loving world have stared, and buzzed, and looked wise for a month! Ah, busy world, be not too impatient! Everything shall be known in due time. In the warm and mellow mould of all bounteous earth seeds of mysterious organization lie hid and unsuspected. Yet not too long shall they remain in their secret hiding-places, for the genial season comes on apace, when they shall burst their dark coverings, and bear the glossy leaves, the bright flowers, and the fragrance of their destiny. So from the dark unknown do we arise to light and life. We are nourished in weakness, imbecility is taught to reason, and the low instincts give place to high aims, until the soul aspires to a destiny which only the hereafter can reveal.

Deacon Arbor held, with unswerving steadfastness, the creed of New England doctrine, as stamped and moulded into the consciences of their own and succeeding generations by the Pilgrim Fathers. He knew, indeed, that it had been disputed and strongly controverted; and perhaps his own meditative mind had been disquieted with doubts about doctrines which religious consistency required him to hold fast. But his doubts had never disturbed his faith in the goodness of God, in the truth of his Redeemer, and the blessed salvation which he felt assured he should attain, by direct communion with him, even though the Westminster Catechism should err.

In Helen's mind were blended, in finer and softer texture, yet with equal strength, the elements of her father's faith and the mysterious "inward light" inherited from her mother. If she meditated less upon the "plan" unfolded in the catechism and creed of her paternal church, she received them with perhaps a more undoubting faith from their very incomprehensibility, and drew richer consolations and higher motives to holiness from the depth of doctrines too divine to be subjected to the scrutiny of human investigation, or to be questioned by human reason. In her were manifest the results of that vital piety which, independent of the garb of doctrines surrounding it, penetrates and finds its congenial home, and makes its sanctuary, in the sincere and earnest heart. And though she declined to dispute about matters too high for her, and took no part in the doctrinal discussions which kindled the zeal of neighborly disputants, she well knew how to take the shortest way to the surest knowledge, for she trusted the "true light which lighteth every man that cometh into the world," and that "whoso doeth his will shall know of the doctrine." And therefore her life became, not only the most successful pupilage, but also the best exemplification of Christian truth.

But still more in the gentle and lovely Frances, whom we generally called Fanny, did piety present its most attractive grace. She seemed born to put to its hardest trial the stern dogma which declares the total depravity of all mankind, and that every descendant of Adam is a child of wrath. A stumbling-block in the Calvinistic believer's path, even from her mother's womb, she grew up a child of grace, recalling to every beholder's mind, as each germ of her nature unfolded, the sweet words of him who said, "Of such is the kingdom of heaven." The open, unaffected, childlike, and perfectly natural form of her piety, was a puzzle to those to whom the garb of peculiar solemnity and peculiar phrase seemed essential to religion. She thought and spoke of the Saviour, not as of an awful and mystical being, unapproachable except through prescribed forms, which the initiated must regulate, nor yet as the still more unnatural object of ecstatic adulation and rapturous adoration, but rather as the sure and faithful friend in heaven, to whom she might always turn in confidence as to her earthly father, and to whose arms she would run, if now on earth, with full assurance of the same welcome reception that he gave to the little children of Judea.

Yet if Fanny was a puzzle to believers in the creed of total depravity, Alek, on the contrary, was an exemplification of its truth. He was often alluded to as showing how the natural man might possess all the amiable qualities of natural goodness, and yet be destitute of saving grace.

"There is Alek Arbor," they would say; "everybody knows

that he is perfectly honest and faithful, and would go further out of his way to do a good turn to a poor person, or to atone for a wrong action, than some Christians that could be named; and yet, after all, everybody knows that he is not a Christian; for, though he understands the Bible very well, — at least, the letter thereof, — and keeps the Sabbath outwardly, yet he has never 'experienced religion,' nor even 'been under conviction.' We must regard him as a child of the devil under the law, and therefore under the curse; for what saith the Scriptures? — 'He that is not with me is against me, and he that gathereth not with me, scattereth;' by which we are to understand that we should gather ourselves into the church, or we shall be scattered as the chaff." This clear and conclusive exposition of Scripture of course completely defined Alek's case.

And yet, of these devout neighbors, who so confidently and conscientiously settled Alek's spiritual condition, not one would hesitate to grasp his hand in warm friendship, or give him the most hearty welcome to the festivities of his fireside. Even Major Murray, the most reliable, or at least the most unyielding, of the champions of the faith, seemed by no means alarmed at the possible contingency of having this child of the devil for a son-in-law — a contingency which neighborly gossip could not fail to convey to his ears, even if his eyes had failed to discern the signs of the times. But this was only a thing in the common course of the faith, which permits the deacon's progeny and the devil's progeny, like the wheat and tares of Scripture, to grow together till the harvest. Besides, who could know that Alek might not yet be plucked as a brand from the burning?

CHAPTER III.

Now — look out — for a — Snowstorm. — Farmer's Almanac.

Stern Winter holds his ancient reign. The cold constellations, who watch his empire from their high places, sparkle with keener lustre. The winds awaken and gather their forces from the valleys and mountain-tops. Their voices roar in wild disorder through the leafless forests, and blend in solemn harmony over wide, dismantled plains, while they fling their fleecy tribute in his path. The night of the busy year! He brings sleep to a million eyes. The insect tribes hide in the rough bark of trees, or in the gray moss at their roots, or bind their silken drapery to the fluttering leaf, and wait in dreamless slumber the vernal breath which shall renew their life. The humble hibernating and amphibious animals make their beds in fissures of the rocks, or dens of the earth, or beneath still waters. Half of nature's life waits in torpid repose the coming spring. But man and the nobler beasts rejoice in the stern, sinew-bracing blasts of winter. To the New England farmer the season comes with welcome. The cares of summer and the bounties of autumn are supplied with a purpose and a use by the requirements of winter. The fleeces of his flock, transformed to comely garments, protect and adorn his family. His well-filled granary and cellar supply the solid nutriment and savory cheer which generous life and liberal hospitality love. From his mows of fragrant hay he spreads their welcome food before the lowing cattle, and answers the whinnying welcome of his horse with a heaped measure of oats from the bin. From the towering wood-pile huge logs are supplied to the ample chimney, which sends ruddy heat through the capacious kitchen, where the experienced mother, and her neat daughters, pursue their domestic affairs, while the younger fry clamor in their various sports.

Such was now the cheerful, busy scene in Deacon Arbor's kitchen. There has been even a more than common diligence there for a few days past, attended with an air of mystery portending the coming of more than common events. Baskets of apples have been brought from the cellar, peeled, and consigned to the chopping-tray, compounding a delicious mass, which yonder long row of pastry-covered plates shall soon receive and bear to the hot oven. The voracious mouth of that hot oven ! What interminable plates of various pies,— what pots of pork and beans, — what pans of various puddings, and deep platters of chicken pasties, — what swollen loaves of bread, the white and the brown, enter the capacious cavern at the end of this busy week ! Yes, it is the end of the week, and the month, and the year. To-morrow is Sunday, and New Year's Day. It is well to welcome the birth of the new year with ample cheer. May it be a happy year, such even as the last ! It promises to be so, and is welcomed with abundant bounty. It is welcomed with complacent grace by the benignant parents, with beaming smiles by the expectant daughters, and with the glad and noisy mirth of the uproarious boys, Billy and Tommy, who often press the compliant Alek into their wild sport. He tosses them into the drifting snow. They scream with mingled indignation and delight, and pelt him with snow-balls. Now at once they clasp and entangle his legs, and tumble him into the drift, and strive to keep him down and bury him before he can regain his feet. He struggles and recovers, in spite of their combined efforts. They turn and scamper away, to escape the coming retribution. Billy succeeds, and gains the sanctuary of the kitchen, where he is safe, and where, O, lucky Billy! a mighty pan of doughnuts, hot and smoking from the fatty caldron, greets his sparkling eyes, and invites his watering mouth. He seizes one, and is about to make a general onset. Helen, who presides with the ladle, tells him to be off. She will not have her doughnuts eaten while she is cooking them. Billy insists, but compromises for one more, with which he again ventures forth, in time to learn the fate of Tommy. Luckless Tommy! Alek caught him just as he had gained the door-stone, and threw him into a deep bank of snow, and then wallowed off, with long strides, to visit the cattle in the barn. Tommy had just extricated himself from the smothering bank, and, all white with snow, and panting with exertion, reproaches Billy with having, in the heat of the conflict, made so cowardly a flight, quite forgetful that he had himself joined in it, and only lost the race by chance, when overtaken. Billy mollifies him with his extra doughnut, and they hasten to the barn, where Alek promises them sport in breaking out the roads, as a recompense for their defeat.

It has snowed all the night, and now the morning has far advanced, and still it snows. Abroad, far as can be seen, over the broad fields, in the deep valleys, upon the hills' steep sides, is spread the deep and still-accumulating wintry store. The fences disappear, the shrubs and bushes vanish from the landscape. The river's winding track is hidden. The trees of the orchard, and the long rows that border the lane on either side, seemingly shortened in their trunks, struggle to raise their over-burthened branches above the overwhelming snow. From up in the sky still come down the exhaustless stores. Looking upward, how dark and murky seem those winged messengers of the clouds! Looking downward and abroad, how sublimely they tell their silent part of the great story of earth and heaven! How awful the aspect to him who sees in the storm the hand of Him who directs it! How dreadful to the misguided or improvident wanderer, who has no shelter from its unpitying rigor! Yet how cheerful the contrast of its out-door inclemency renders the bright and busy kitchen, where the blazing fire sends forth its radiant heat, blended with the music of the kettle and the fragrance of the coming feast!

So dark and threatening seems the storm without, so pleasant and promising the scene within. There the drifts swell higher and higher with the cold, driving snow. Here the fire blazes higher and higher, and higher swell the piles of good cheer. The inhospitalities of the storm without are more than compensated by the hospitality within. Our garrison is supplied with provision and stored with ammunition to withstand the siege of winter, till the tardy April sun shall come to the rescue. And full are we, every mother's son and daughter too, of the spirit and bravery which dares to sally forth and defy the storm.

Yes, it is even so; we will not be enclosed and pent up here. Why, the roads are piled above the fences with impassable drifts, and still the snow is coming down and heaping up! Shall the elements be so active without, and we idle within? And see, — a flock of snow-birds come as if from the clouds, and hop from spray to spray, and from limb to limb of the bare lilacs and plum-trees in the garden. Their quick and lively chirp foretells the coming of friends. Other omens have indicated as much. The kettle sings the sleigh-bell tune; brands fall from the fire, and stand on end in the corner; two strangers were seen in Helen's cup of tea, last evening; a cricket hopped across the floor, and the cat has twice leaped up in a chair to look out at the window. The good mother has carefully noted all these signs, and even Helen, generally incredulous, seems to believe them; while Fanny, with a roguish dimple, says she guesses that the letter which came last Saturday evening, and which she was not permitted to read, was the thing which inclined mother and Helen to put so much faith in signs.

But there is evidently too much expectation and energy to brook confinement. Alek and the boys have returned from the barn all agreed upon the necessity of breaking out the roads, and the deacon says he guesses it may be as well to do so. The deacon is district surveyor this year, and, therefore, his decree is the law of the road. Alek had a whisper with his mother this morning, and gave a nod in reply, such as are often the seeds of mighty resolves and deeds. A hasty and ample meal soon spreads the table, and is as quickly despatched.

And now the four strong oxen are brought from the barn, and ranged in their yokes in due order, with Alek by their side to lead the way. Onward they move, now wallowing along, and forcing their unwieldy weight through the yielding snow; now floundering inextricably in a drift which buries them to their backs; now, again, partly uncovered by the quick aid of a dozen snow-shovels, — for several men and boys, notified by Alek's prudent foresight, have arrived, — they struggle onwards with a vigor and perseverance which never fails to force the most formidable intrenchments of winter, and to keep open the lines of communication between beleaguered villages. Through drifts and banks, with cheers and shouts, they force their way onward to the village, gathering reinforcements from every farm-house which they pass.

Colonel Bowler's was the first house on the way. The old colonel — the father and grandfather of a throng of Bowler men, and Bowler women, and Bowler boys, and Bowler girls, the former already in the snow-subduing party, and the latter peeping from every window — was as lively as any of them. With his old military spirit, the spirit of '76, as he jocosely said, though with no claim of revolutionary honors, for he was but a boy in those days, but because his own age now approached that ever-honored date, he gave out his orders, and marshalled his reinforcement.

"Isaac, yoke old Brown and Turk, and put them ahead; put Star and Bright behind, and the steers in the middle; hitch 'em to the logging-sled, and fasten the bob-sled behind; roll on two of the mill-logs, and let the butts drag behind. Old Brown and Turk will show you where the road ought to be, and the logs will make some little marks, so you 'll know it. Tom, Harry, Jim, and the rest of you, put ahead with your shovels, and clear the drifts. Adjutant, my boy, must *you* go? Well, tell your mother to tie your cap over your ears, and pull a pair of stockings over your shoes."

Sammy was the youngest of the boys, only seven years old, and the colonel called him his adjutant. The colonel was fond of his grandson, and loved to use his old military terms and phrases.

"I am getting to be old," he would say, "but I don't need the old man's staff, and I don't think I shall, so long as I can keep up my military staff. The adjutant is a brave soldier; he puts away my chapeau" (so the colonel called his raccoon-cap), "and brings my slippers, and reads me a chapter in the Testament, and two pages of Weems' Life of Washington, every night. And a brave fellow, too, he is with his rations. Don't he know how to forage for apples and doughnuts? He beats Johnny Horner with his Christmas pie, and stows away a bowl of pudding and milk in no time; — but he is a sad dog to sleep in the morning, — next winter we shall teach him the tune of 'early to rise.' We shall beat the *reveille* in his ears at day-break. But, adjutant, bring a mug of cider, and you, girls, go and draw it for him; the oxen are ready, and we 'll have a fair start." The colonel never forgot anything, especially the cider.

Refreshed with rest and cider, and reinforced with men, and boys, and oxen, and steers, away, shouting, and plunging, and wallowing, now shovelling a passage through a huge drift in advance of the oxen, now gathering together on the sleds to crush down the snow, they work their way over the ridge, and down the hill, and through the woods. Old Brown and Turk plod perseveringly on. They are the colonel's boast; the biggest oxen in town by four inches in their girth; the heartiest at a pull, and the surest on the road. The colonel evidently mixes up the merit of the oxen with his own, and, with true military justice, appropriates to himself the laurels won by the prowess of his host.

And so, plodding, and pushing, and plunging, they work

their way ahead. The colonel maintains his post on the long logging-sled, touching up the hinder cattle, and directing the efforts of the boys. Ike keeps by the heads of Turk and Brown, and Alek with his team lags behind, prepared to take their place again in front, when Turk and Brown shall need relief. Alek has pride in his team, but he will not dispute the palm with the colonel. If it were only Ike, it would be quite another thing. On the other hand, Alek takes undisputed precedence in the matter of colts, which the colonel affects to think quite beneath the dignity of men, though he allows Alek's to be pretty nags enough.

"But what a waste of time to drive them! Old Turk and Brown will take him once a week to the village, for his newspaper, and take a load of wood, besides. Oxen are the only reliable cavalry for the farmer. What are colts good for?"

Thus arguing the superiority of his team, and directing the general force, the colonel gets over the ridge, and down the valley, and through the wood. Just beyond the wood, near "Bragly's Corner," are the cheerless-looking, dilapidated house and hovel and shop of Bang Barker, the thriftless, broken-down blacksmith. In the house is his lean, discontented, much-abused, and equally abusive wife. She was born with some of woman's blood in her veins, and some of the wolf's. Circumstances have suppressed the woman, and developed the wolf. Romulus and Remus would have found in her a famous nurse; but she would have made Arabs of them, instead of Romans, — at least, such her own progeny have proved. Four darling boys had she brought forth, and brought up, who, with precocious genius, had successively beaten their mother, set fire to the hay-rick, stolen 'Siah Brown's donkey, robbed widow Bowler's turkey-pen, and done numberless other mischiefs, before running away and going to sea, as they had all done before the age of fifteen. One hopeful boy, not yet eleven, and another, "a girl more young than he," as the ballad says, remained. Whether they shall emulate the spirit of their elder brethren, remains yet to be seen. It all depends upon themselves; there is no lack of like education.

Bang Barker was a broken-down blacksmith. Rum broke him down. Folks say that when he began at Bragly's Corner, twenty years ago, there was not a better prospect for a man in twenty miles. He was then twenty-five, a giant in strength, and a good workman. Even now, there was not a surer hand at giving the right temper to an axe, if he were only drunk enough; or a quicker workman to shoe a yoke of oxen, if he could only be caught sober enough. But he seldom shoes oxen or tempers axes now. The uncertainty of finding him in a right mood for either operation has driven custom another way. When a neighbor came with an axe to temper, he was not drunk enough, and the customer must get a pint at Bragly's for an eye-opener; and when oxen came to be shod, the pint from Bragly's had shut the Cyclops' eyes. A big, bushy-headed, black-bearded, broad-chested, bullying sort of a Cyclops, was Bang. He could throw a barrel of cider over his head, and had knocked down an ox with his fist. His arms were as strong as ever, but his legs tottered under his burly body with uncertain steps, to which not even Bragly's rum could give steadiness.

In the little slab-covered hovel back of the house stood an old cow, munching some sorry-looking husks and poorly-made hay; and a few forlorn fowls divided themselves between the hovel and the perch, while a discontented pig, who seemed to complain that he was not fat enough to be killed, and put out of this sad and starving world, into a comfortable pork-barrel, hasted from hovel to porch, and from porch to hovel, seeking something which was not to be found.

In the shop, nearer the road, stood the cold, deserted anvil, by the black, frozen water-trough. There was no coal, nor was there need of any, for iron or steel there was none, save a few outworn ox-shoes and broken links of chain, and a cracked kettle, sent last summer for a hoop, and a skillet with a hole in the bottom, which some old lady, believing in the omnipotence of iron, had sent to be mended; and the fragments of a glass bottle, which accident had dashed, with its precious contents, upon the floor, when last the Vulcan of this forge urged the wheezing bellows, and smote the ringing anvil. All around was the desolation and destitution of improvidence and vice. But yet there was something indicating a recent slight attempt at improvement; for some new panes of glass had recently taken the place of old hats and bundles of rags, which generally stuffed the windows; and some strips of board had been nailed over cracks which the fallen clapboards had long ago exposed, and which had for successive seasons admitted the storms. At sight of those slender signs of improvement, Isaac, who had stopped to give Alek an opportunity to bring his oxen ahead, and take his turn in front, remarked, with a knowing wink, that he guessed Santa Claus had been doing a good chore thereabouts; to which Alek, with an intelligent nod, merely replied, "I guess so."

Let us now hasten on; for the snow is deep and the drifts are high, and there is yet a long way before us. Little help shall we get from the house of Bang, and it is not worth while to call for any. But look, — the door opens, and out comes young Ax. A big stocking-leg is drawn upon his head for a cap. The remnants of some bigger body's frock are comfortably enough secured around his lank yet strong and active frame, and a pair of coarse new boots, drawn ostentatiously above his trousers, encase his legs and feet. Ike glanced at the new boots, and winked at Alek, who nodded again, and then started his team in the direction of the pathless road, and Ax joined the jolly group of snowy boys behind.

CHAPTER IV

Muse, who from the floating filaments of transient memory spinnest the thread of faithful history, let thy description be brief, lest thy lagging tale tire the courteous reader.

Away through the deep, obstructing snow, bursting the barricades which the wild mob of warring winds raised, the hardy company are ploughing their way. They now ascend the hill whose summit is distinguished by the proud mansion of Parson Boreman, in front of which four tall Lombardy poplars, like so many posted sentinels, rear their stiff, martial forms, and wave their tall plumes.

At Bragly's they did not stop; for when did any help of public good come from Bragly's? Pitiful dribbler of drams, and picker of small coppers and small coins! Little-souled barterer of execrable tea and poisonous tobacco, for eggs of nobler hens and pelts of honest lambs; sneaking measurer of penny tapes and four-penny ribbons; paltry retailer of clay pipes and long-nine cigars; scanty weigher of thin salt-fish, and consumptive pickled mackerel! Let me, while the indignant winds howl around your dwelling, preach you a sermon as we pass. To what purpose is your miserable life, already verging upon three-score? What spot of earth is greener for your existence? What noble ambition have you ever prompted in another's breast? What generous emotion have you ever felt in your own? Cowering in the encasement of your own selfishness, spinning around yourself, like the nobler worm, the shroud of your ignoble end, what inscription of infamy shall we scratch upon your grave, to point the contempt of your race? But we will not anticipate. Your epitaph will be worthily written.

Away from Bragly's let us hasten. Our company have reached the top of the hill by the stately mansion of Parson Boreman, and here they pause. The minister has a noble yoke of oxen, and a sprightly pair of steers, and a strong hired man. They are summoned to aid the struggling band, and soon come forth and are placed in the van. Onward again they drive, not without strong invitations to renew their strength by the cheer of the parson's kitchen.

While they drive onward, shall we pause at the parson's? It is with some misgivings that we invite the reader to a nearer survey. What with the elegant mansion on the top of the hill, and the tall poplar-trees in front, the fine oxen and steers and their prompt and stalwart driver, and the generously-proffered hospitalities of the kitchen, we must have raised grand ideas of the parson and his dwelling, which closer observation may abate. Not that decent competence and respectability were not there, but that outside show exceeded inward reality.

A vague idea of sham, and hollowness, and constraint, lurks in the mind of the distant observer, and becomes stronger as observation becomes closer. The grandeur of the house is but the grandeur of needless dimensions, useless clattering window-blinds, faded paint, a veranda with loose and weedy pavement, precarious pillars, and decayed cornices.

A lawn fenced with painted palings, swayed and propped from falling by extempore braces; gates of light material, but ambitiously massive proportions, which, refusing to swing upon their loosened hinges, either in or out, are kept by rope or leathern strap in a position obstructing, yet not totally preventing, entrance and exit. A front door so far removed from the family that the huge brass knocker, though it might be used as a battering-ram to force an entrance, could by no means summon an answer from within. An end door — the usual entrance — from which the granite steps seem preparing to step forth on some excursion of their own, having moved each a few inches from its original position, and with different angles of departure. Let us enter.

The good old parson comes forward to meet us. He is good; for he is a minister. He bids us welcome, and insists that we take off our outward garments. The air of the room feels not too warm. The fire seems to have been not long burning; but we comply. We wish we were boys, and could go into the kitchen, where we suspect there is more comfort, and less gentility. The impression of *sham* makes us feel chilly. The parson sits in his study-chair, not far removed from his study-table, on which big volumes are piled. These are the tokens of study. Why should they betoken *sham?*

The parson commences conversation concerning the storm. The topic is soon exhausted. Local news lasts a little longer. He is trying your mind, and taking observations of its drift. It is proper that a parson should presume a religious bias in his visitors. He throws out a religious remark. The current drifts another way. Politics, — he has not hit it. Literature, — uncertain; but the topic is a safe one, and the parson fancies himself at home there. He has been composing a dissertation on the "lost tribes," and their relation to our aborigines. He favors you with his views, fortified by some passages from his manuscript, which is always conveniently near on such occasions. He asks your views on the subject. Of course you know nothing about it. He has you there. He has taken the gauge of your mind, while you are trying to think of something besides *sham.*

A rather spruce, good-looking matron comes in from the kitchen. She is Mrs. Boreman, the wife. You try to get rid of your impression of *sham.* A good-looking old lady is always antagonistic to that idea. Still you do not quite succeed. Another door opens. A spruce, good-looking young lady comes in. That is Miss Boreman, the daughter. You make a desperate effort to throw off the impression of *sham.* A good-looking young lady should be a perfect antidote. But *sham* torments you like the nightmare. Miss B. has long since passed her bread-and-butter days; she has passed the days of indiscretion and coquetry; she has passed the days of timid apprehension and reservedness, and she has arrived at that interesting, though uncertain age, when damsels solicitous to please and to ensnare put forth all their attractions. What generous, manly heart but beats responsive to that sentiment, and smothers the thought of *sham!*

Lucy was she christened; but, from her early teens, — perhaps from her first sigh over her first novel, — her name has been Lucinda. Her altitude is not great, nor is her circumference large; in fact, it seems painfully slender. Nature was not wholly in fault, for whalebone and stays have contracted the limits which nature would have allowed. A thought crosses your mind that the improvement should have been the other way; but you repress naughty thoughts in a presence so divine. The freshness of long-cultivated youthfulness charms you; the elaborate and shining ringlets, dependent in regular order over either cheek, fascinate you; the slender neck and gentle bosom, bounded by delicate lace, enchant you; the graceful ankle and taper foot captivate you. Why should the miserly thought of *sham* mar your satisfied admiration?

A pretty table, with a nice work-basket filled with the appropriate implements of female industry, is drawn nearer the fire, and soon those fair fingers and bright eyes commence their proper and practised task. She is apparently netting a silken purse. *Sham.* The purse has been netting a long time. Every stitch has been taken in the presence of admiring visitors, whose eyes have watched the dextrous movements of those fair fingers with an interest, perhaps, equal with your own. A deeper purpose pervades that gentle heart, and guides those delicate fingers, than that netted purse explains.

A showy annual lies by her basket, and invites your attention. By way of introducing conversation, you ask permission, and examine it. It is the Religious Souvenir. You commend its binding and engravings. It has pretty sentimental sonnets, and scraps of semi-religious romance. Many of them are pencil-marked in the margin; and so you learn that Miss Lucinda is poetic and sentimental, religious and romantic. What less could you expect? You already knew her to be pretty, and engaging, and diligent. What more could you desire?

She asks if you like botany, and brings her herbarium. Of course you like botany; but you blunder about corollas and calyxes, and staminas and stigmas. Lucinda sets you right, and you see that she knows botany. A pretty album follows the herbarium. Miss Lucinda must have had a host of devoted friends, some day, whose "hearts lie buried here." What lots of sublimated sentiments! Friendship, first born of heaven! Platonic love! Remembered regrets! Swelling sighs and eternal farewells! It is evident that Lucinda's lights are fled, her garlands dead, and all but you departed.

Thank Heaven, you are here at home, and quite competent to the occasion; so you prepare your pencil, which she observing, produces pen and ink, and, under a broken tombstone, you inscribe a complimentary sentiment, in impromptu verse, which you have already written in a score of albums, but too far off to be detected; and so you subscribe your initials, while conscience retorts upon you, "*Sham!*"

We are invited to remain to dinner. Let us remain. We feel that some little preparation has been made from the beginning, in that anticipation. It shall not be disappointed. It is worth while to study a little longer those features of society which, though rather commonplace, are not wholly uninstructive. It is fair, also, and perhaps not wholly unpleasant, to be studied in turn by those who pay us the compliment of thinking it worth their while.

From albums and herbariums to politics the transition seems rather abrupt; but it becomes a necessity, for rural affairs are out of season in mid-winter, and the legislature and congress are in session, and men's minds tend to public affairs. The parson is non-committal; and, therefore, however decided and strong our predilections, we also are non-commital; and in this mock-neutral spirit we proceed to discuss the merits of our governmental administration, the qualities of our public men, the chances of prominent political aspirants, the character and spirit of messages, speeches, reports, and other national and state proceedings, till dinner is announced.

However we may have relished the feast of reason and the flow of soul, and all the elaborate elegances of the parson's parlor, we are happy to change the scene and the subject for the genial and welcome-looking kitchen, the ample and well-spread table, and the good and substantial dinner. It is all that it should be, and well worth the complacent parson's devout and dignified thanks and blessing. Fat ribs of beef and a dainty shoulder of pork smoke from the boiling pot, and sweat big tears of shining fat, as if yet panting from their fiery trial. Around them, ranged in due order, is a bounteous vegetable store; potatoes bursting with internal heat, white turnips, — mimic spheres, flattened at the poles, — beets, parsnips, carrots, and cabbage, prove by their size and flavor that the parson has not been unmindful of his own garden while weeding the sins of his parish. Bread, — brown and white, — butter and cheese, such as only a farmer's wife, emulous of good works, can produce; pudding, pies, and doughnuts, which you hope the fair Lucinda helped to flavor, all combine to convince you that, wherever else hollowness and sham prevail, the country kitchen is the last retreat and most impregnable castle of honest, generous life.

We feel an instinctive reverence for the good parson, whom Heaven blesses with so bountiful a board; and the gentle impression comes upon our minds that there might be a worse mistake than to take the fair Lucinda and settle down somewhere in the midst of so much rural abundance and happiness. Blessed be the benign influences which lie latent in well-packed barrels of pork and beef, and well-filled bins of potatoes and turnips, waiting only the alchemy of the kitchen to expand the frame and the heart of man with healthful strength and generous emotion!

We are invited to pass the evening, and should like to do so; but other affairs press, and now we must go.

"Please to come again."

"Certainly; we shall not fail to do so."

It is now too late to visit the village. Our company have returned an hour since. But they must break off at Bragly's, to track the road to the school-house. We shall overtake them before they get home. We *do* overtake them at Colonel Bowler's. Alek has stopped there a few moments. He generally stops there when passing; if he did not, some tears would fall from a bright pair of young eyes. A little girl there calls him uncle. He is not her uncle, nor of kin in any other degree; but there is no name of kindred too dear for her to apply to him. She calls him her dear uncle. He calls her his dear daughter. Well may she call him her dear uncle; — she owes him her life. Well may he call her dear daughter; — it was he who rescued her from a terrible death. This is a tie of love as sacred as that of a father, or at least as sweet. He feels all the luxury of loving the child whose life he has saved; she feels all the gratitude and confiding affection with which a loving child clings to a tender father. The story is now an old one; it happened three years ago. She was then but six years old. But we may as well repeat it now. Alek and the boys have yet to take care of the oxen's dinner and their own. Alek embraces the dear daughter, and promises, for the hundredth time, to take her home to live with him, when he gets a house, and a wife, and a pony; and she — the little Amy — verily believes in that good time coming, and dreams golden dreams.

CHAPTER V.

SINCE we must stop at Colonel Bowler's to tell our story, propriety requires us to introduce the family. You have seen the old colonel before. He calls himself old, and we will not refuse him the compliment. He is only sixty-seven ; but he speaks of verging to seventy-six. This, however, is in reference to that glorious era of the Revolution.

Three solid sciences the colonel knows: arithmetic, agriculture and history. Arithmetic from Daboll, agriculture from experience, and history from Weems' Life of Washington. Three lighter arts amuse his leisure: military tactics, poetry, and music. Military from Steuben's Manual Exercise, and poetry from the calendar pages of the Farmers' Almanac. The hymns of Watts come not in this department, but in that of music, being made for singing ; but the ballad of the Major's only Son and Barbara Allen's Cruelty complete the poetical library. The music is psalmody, and came by nature. A noble bass the colonel sings ; he has always led the bass in Parson Boreman's choir. Once there was trouble about the bass-viol, which Major Murray objected to ; he would not hear the "big fiddle" in the house of the Lord. It was played one or two Sundays before he found it out ; for the major had no ear for music, — could n't tell the filing of a saw from a jewsharp; — but he saw the colonel bringing in the big fiddle, one day, and made up his mind what to do about it. When the choir commenced the first hymn, he took his hat and marched out of the meeting-house. It was plain he had determined to bear no part in the profanation, and meant everybody should know it. The colonel understood it, and, choosing to remove the stumbling-block from the major's path, brought out the viol ostentatiously when the morning service was closed, and sent it home. The major was comfortable that afternoon, and for a dozen Sundays following, though the viol, which the colonel had secretly restored, was regularly played. Some mischief-maker at last told the major. He was full of indignation, and said that if he heard it again he should quit the meeting-house. The colonel heard of the threat, and removed the viol. Next Sunday the major came with ears and conscience wide awake to detect the sinful sound. The hymn was given out, and the colonel sounded the key-note in his deepest tone, imitating the bass-viol as nearly as possible. The major, proud of the quickness of his ear and the promptitude of his principles, immediately marched out of the meeting-house. He stood reverently on the steps in prayer-time, and, after the second singing, returned to hear the sermon. After service the colonel walked up to the major, and asked why he left the house in singing time.

"Because," he replied, "you made it a fiddling-time. Did n't I hear your big fiddle? You can't cheat me! — I can tell it as fur off as I can hear my black bull; and it sounds just like him!"

The colonel assured him that there had been no bass-viol, nor any black bull, in the meeting-house that day, adding that his own voice was a little hoarse, which probably caused the mistake. The major was convinced that he could not trust his own ears in that matter, and said no more upon the subject, though the viol was restored to its place in the choir.

A hale, hearty, self-opinionated, and yet very manageable, stern-spoken, and yet very tender-hearted, frugal, yet generous old man, is the colonel. His wife, a cheery, blue-eyed, round-featured, double-chinned, close-capped matron, is a dozen years younger than the colonel, and looking younger still. Always busy, but never tired; always scolding, but never cross; always cooking up all sorts of good things for everybody, but always choosing the plainest food for herself; never sick, but with a whole garret-full of herbs and chest-full of medicines for others' sickness; never going abroad, but always ready to "fix up" and start off the family on visiting excursions. In short, assuming and governing as mistress of all, and yet making herself servant of all.

Samuel, the oldest boy, married Job Brown's daughter Betsey, sister of Josiah. A good wife was she; but Samuel died within the year, soon after little Samuel, the colonel's "adjutant," was born. Jacob married Samuel's widow, and now resides in a part of his father's house till he can finish his own. The colonel made the last match,—the only one he ever made, except his own,—and both were good ones. The widow, his daughter-in-law, was the favorite of Aunt Jane, and the adjutant was indispensable to his grandfather. Perhaps the colonel and his wife had talked it over; at any rate, it was the colonel who, as he said, broke the ice. "Jacob," said he, one day, when they were alone, "Jacob, it 's time for you to be doing something for yourself. Go over to Job Brown's, and get Betsey. Your mother wants her nearer; I want Sammy;

and you want a good wife, and the Morgan farm, that your poor brother bought, but did not live to enjoy. I have pretty much paid for it, and you and she may have it. The old house on it is good for nothing, but we 'll build a new one, and you and Betsey may have our end parlor, and we 'll all eat together till it 's done."

Jacob blushed, but wisely said nothing. Upon such a matter, a man should think twice before he speaks, even to his father. He afterwards said that he never was "so struck up in a heap" in his life. But he thought of it. The next day his father asked if he had done the thing mentioned yesterday — just as if it was a thing to be done in a hurry. Jacob replied, "Not quite yet, father."

"Well, you mean to, I suppose?"

"Why, it don't look bad, father, if nobody objects."

"Why, nobody objects, of course, till they are asked; so you 'd better be about it before it 's too late. Such a girl as she need n't wait long for such a lubber as can't speak."

"Thank you, father, for the compliment; but, I 'm thinking that as you have begun the business so well, it will be best for you to carry it through. Perhaps you 'll go over and introduce the matter."

"Why, han't I introduced the matter? Who but me put it into your head? I 've done my part. However, if you han't the pluck, get your mother to go for you; or rather go and invite Betsey to bring Sammy and pay a visit, and we 'll talk it over here."

This last device suited Jacob well; it turned out well, and all were happy ever after.

Isaac was next to Jacob. Their names had got reversed from Scripture order. He was about Alek's age.

George, one of the twins, was younger. A good fellow, he, and a droll one — the wag of the family. They said he became so by sitting on the dye-pot when little. The dye-pot, in which woollen yarn is colored, generally stands covered with a board, in one corner of the capacious fireplace, and whoever sits on the dye-pot grows witty. George was full of fun, odd jokes, quick repartees, and raillery, ridiculous representations of others' acts, or of his own; full of laughter and merriment, yet serious at times — more serious than anybody else.

Music was his passion. He could draw music from a corn-stalk fiddle, or a pumpkin-vine trombone. At twelve years he played the fife for the Wolfsden Light Infantry; and lively were the tunes he played. At thirteen, with an old fiddle, he made many a husking and apple-paring merry. Nobody so popular, and so much sought after, as George. The colonel was gratified, but dissatisfied. He was pleased with his son's genius, but predicted his ruin. "But," said he, "it 's no use to interfere. We 'll give him good counsel, and trust Providence." The result proved the resolution good. George threw away his fiddle, and everything of the sort, before he was eighteen. "Too boyish," he said.

James, his brother, was a more retiring, pensive boy. We will not say much about James. Perhaps the reader may get some notion of him as we proceed.

Of the girls, Ann is the oldest. Everybody allows that she is a good and good-looking girl. Josiah Brown evidently admires her. People joke her about it. She says Josiah Brown is nothing to her; "he comes over to see his sister, and it 's well enough to talk with him; he is Betsey's brother, and a civil, respectable person enough. She wishes to be civil to everybody." Very discreet and very considerate of you, Miss Ann! Have courage, Josiah! To be civil and respectable, and Betsey's brother, is a good beginning.

Hannah comes next — younger than Ann. A good girl, and good singer. Hers are the truest tones in the choir; and, being willing to sing anywhere, — at the foot as at the head, — she escapes the jealousy and trouble about precedence which vex the others.

Amy is the youngest. She it is of whom we promised the story, and for whose sake chiefly we have introduced the others. Amy is only nine years old, and small at that. Three years ago she was only six, and smaller still. A little, fairy-like pet, dark eyes, bright hair and complexion, generally sprightly, yet often thoughtful, and almost sad. She is indulged in everything, yet not spoiled by indulgence. She seems to have an intuitive perception of right, and never asks anything wrong; or, if she takes a whim for anything judged inexpedient, she never insists. Some tempers are so amiable that love seems their proper discipline, the atmosphere where they thrive best. Perhaps that discipline and atmosphere would suit more than have a chance to benefit by it. Amy grew up in it; everybody loved her, and she loved everybody.

Three years ago last haying-time, Amy was six years old. Haying was pretty much done, at home; but, since Samuel's death, the colonel had also to manage the "Morgan farm." All the force of the farm, with an extra hand or two, was now employed in getting the hay down there. They went early, and generally returned at sunset, taking home a load with them. Blueberries were ripe, and very plenty. The road down to the Morgan farm was retired — not a public road only a cross road, but very pleasant. Tall pines grew occasionally along the way. In some places a grove of young trees offered a cool resting-place — a smooth, soft surface, and a grateful, fragrant shade. Here and there, also, a spreading beech gave a dense shadow, where, when the frost comes and opens the burrs, the clean, sweet beechnuts strew the ground, and attract eager children. Now that the sweeter blueberries bordered the road on both sides, Amy came every day and filled her little basket. Nobody picked such sweet berries as Amy.

It was but half a mile to the Morgan place. Amy often went there in company with her sisters, but not alone. She only went a little way, perhaps a third of the distance, to fill her basket; but, as they were haying down there, she ventured a little further — so far that she could see them away down in the field, there, mowing and tossing about the hay, and old Turk and Brown yoked and lying down by the cart, ready to draw it home at night. Next day she ventured further. Isaac was loading the cart, and the colonel was on it, stowing the load. George and James were raking. They saw Amy in the distance, and called her. She was glad to go and see them rake the hay, and show them her berries.

When the load was finished, Isaac lifted her up to ride home with her father. Old Turk and Brown did not mind the additional load, but jogged lazily home, no way disposed to give unnecessary jolts. Delightful ride was that upon the hay to Amy! No splendid coach in Broadway ever bore a happier freight.

The next day she went again. She filled her basket sooner than before, and was in the field before the time of loading up for home. After talking and playing a few moments with George and James, who were too busy to be detained long, she returned to heap her basket a little higher, and pick some wild-flowers to put into her little vase.

She did not return to the field; but that caused no alarm. They supposed she had returned home. The road was plain, and almost the whole way in sight, either of the field where they were at work, or of her home. In one place it diverged a little way into the woods, along the border of which it ran, but soon returned. There was no getting out of it, for no other roads led from it; and, besides, being so recently travelled with heavy loads of hay, it was as plain as the turnpike.

But Amy did not return home. As they were not expecting her till the men should return with the load, they could not be alarmed, and the hours passed on.

But where was Amy?

When she returned to the road, she heaped up her little basket as long as the berries would lie, and then she sat down her basket by a little tree, and looked for flowers for her bouquet. The summer sun had dried up most of the pretty flowers, but here and there might be found a tall yellow lily, or a bunch of columbines, or an oxeye daisy, — gaudy, but scentless flowers. But she gathered the fairest she could find, and in her hands they looked fair enough; and still she wandered on, looking for more and prettier. She was pursuing the direction opposite from home, as she knew well enough, but meant to return to her basket in a few minutes; and so she went on a little further, and a little further still.

In the edge of the woods, a very little way, she saw a bunch of beautiful flowers, crimson and gold. Country people call the plant celandine, and children call the flowers lady's eardrops. Amy ran in and gathered them. There were a good many. They grew around and among some stones which were partly covered with white moss. She filled both hands, and then ran to find where she had placed her basket. She returned to the road, and ran along in it, not doubting that she was returning. Her little brain was confused, — "turned round," as they say, — she was going the wrong way — still away from home. Her little cape-bonnet covered her face, as she ran along with her eyes upon the ground, but once in a while looking up to see the tree where she had deposited her basket. She ran a good way, then she walked a good way; still she could not see the tree — not *that* tree; there were a good many trees, and they grew more and more plenty. They grew on both sides of the road; she had not marked that before; she wondered that she had come so far without knowing it: and then she ran again; she ran a good way; the trees grew thicker; the road became more obscure. In one or two places other paths diverged to the right or left. She was tired with running, and so she walked again; but she walked fast. The road became less distinct. Little bushes grew up in the middle of it; then it turned out of its direction, to pass round some great trees; on the other side of the great trees she could see hardly any road at all, and then she began to fear that she was lost — lost in the woods, like the little babes. The terror of the thought thrilled her little frame, and nerved her with new strength. She ran along in the direction which looked most like the road. She ran hard, and ran a good way; and, as the terror pursued her, she ran still the harder, as if to escape from it. She panted for breath; she stumbled, and fell. It did not hurt her much; if it had hurt her more, she would not have minded it now.

She regained her feet, and would have run again, but she could see no road. There was none. Then she knew she was lost. She thought she would return and find the road where it went round the great clump of trees. She looked for the great clump of trees, and thought she saw them; but they appeared to be in the wrong direction. There was a clump of trees in the other direction, but they looked differently. In other directions were other great clumps of trees, and she knew not which to go to. She thought she would go to them all, till she found the road; but when she got to the first, there was no road, but other clumps of trees on every side; and then she knew that she was lost — lost like the babes in the wood.

She thought she would pray to God; and then she doubted whether God could hear her in the dark woods, where the tall trees shut out the heavens where he lives. She knew he could hear her in her little bedroom at home; for there her mother had taught her to pray, and there her mother and her sisters prayed, and God knew the place; but did he know that she was lost in those lone woods? Had he seen her come there? Could he hear her there? May be he could. And so she prayed that God would come and show her the way back, and carry her back, for she was very tired, — only carry her back to her little basket, and then her father would take her home on the hay; and she prayed that he would not let the bears and wolves get her.

And then she sat down, and waited for God to come. She waited a good while, but she knew heaven was a good way off, and she resolved to be patient.

The road to the Morgan place turned off from the main road a little north of Colonel Bowler's. It was but a cross or private road, and not a public way. The entrance was generally closed by a gate. It was a good smooth road down as far as the Morgan place; beyond that it was little used in summer, and in the winter only to draw wood homeward, and timber to the river. The river, in that direction, is two miles off. In a more northerly direction it is nearer, but southwardly it diverges further. The road is good in winter, but, not being used in summer, is scarcely distinguishable, except for perhaps half a mile beyond the Morgan place.

Amy was now more than two miles off; for she had diverged towards the south, and was still far from the river. In one short hour she had gone all that weary way, and now she sat among the leaves at the foot of a tall old maple, waiting for God to come and help her. A little ribbon which bound her hair was found under the tree the next day, by which it was known where she rested; and she afterwards told that when she prayed to God she heard it thunder a good way off, and thought may be it was God speaking to her. The thunder was heard in the haying-field about an hour after little Amy had left.

While Amy sat under the tall old maple far away in the boundless forest, waiting for God to come, her father and brothers were diligently completing their day's work in the haying-field, and her mother and sisters were busy at home, little suspecting the peril of their beloved one.

The slight thread of mystery, which runs through so many of the incidents of this story, as traced in my memory, here again makes its appearance. It shall not be suppressed; for trifles often serve as indications of the sublimest truths.

That afternoon, a little before the thunder was heard, as Aunt Deborah Arbor was about her household affairs, she became suddenly *impressed* with the idea of trouble and misfortune at Colonel Bowler's. She tried to turn it off, and kept about her work; but the impression grew too strong for her quiet. The afternoon was warm, and the distant thunder might forbode a shower; but she resolved to obey the voice within, and, telling Helen to send Alek after her, if she should be detained, she put on her sun-bonnet, took an umbrella, and departed. It was nearly half a mile, but she walked fast, and was soon there. Her first words were an inquiry after Amy. They told her that she was with her father and brothers in the haying-field. After resting a few moments, she said that she would go down to the place. It seemed a strange proposition, that warm afternoon, after so long a walk; but Ann and Hannah immediately offered to accompany her. Aunt Deborah accepted Ann's company, but told Hannah to remain at home, and help her mother. On the way she made several inquiries of Ann about Amy, — when she went, &c., — but without a word of explanation. When they arrived in sight of the hay-field, the men and boys were loading and raking; but Amy was not in sight. "Run and find Amy!" exclaimed Aunt Deborah, pale with excitement. Ann, alarmed at her manner, flew across the field, calling, as she approached her brothers, for Amy.

"Why, she went home two hours ago," exclaimed they all.

The alarm was instantly communicated. Hasty and frantic inquiries were made. The boys threw down their rakes, the colonel leaped from the load, Isaac detached the pin which fastened the oxen to the cart, and, in less than a minute, all were in the road, running, calling, shouting, exploring the woods in various directions, and making every effort which the agony of terror or the suggestions of hope could inspire.

They soon found the little basket, filled with berries, which she had left under the tree. Unfortunately this happened to be by a little path, which went into the woods toward the north, at a right angle with the road which she had pursued; and they inferred that she had taken that path, especially as it led to a grove of sugar-maples, where was a little hut used in the sugar season, and where the sap-troughs and other conveniences were kept. She had been led there once to see these wonders, and was much delighted with them; — all therefore turned to explore the woods in that direction, and tired the echoes with their frantic calls, while Amy was waiting under the old maple, two miles away, for God to come and take her.

Meanwhile Aunt Deborah hurried back to the house alone; for Ann could not be kept back from joining in the search. Alek had come after his mother in the wagon, and all were instantly informed of the terrible truth. Aunt Deborah hastened home with the horse and wagon to summon the family, and Alek flew to join in the search.

In an hour, all the men within two miles were in the woods, and women in wagons hurrying for more help. The search was kept up all that night. In the morning, before sunrise, hundreds of men and boys, from every direction, were collected at Colonel Bowler's, ready to follow any orders from him. By the advice of Deacon Arbor, horns were sounded as a signal for the men in the woods to return, and a council of proceedings was held. It was pretty clear that the missing one was not in the direction where they had been searching, for the whole woods on that side had now been explored for miles.

A systematic plan of thorough search was now speedily

adopted. The whole company formed in a line, extending more than two miles, the individuals being within hailing distance. All were directed to march in silence, except that every minute the word *March* was passed along the line. The silence was required to listen for any sound; and the frequent shout of *march*, not only to attract the attention of the lost one, if in hearing, but also to give such individuals as could not see the others proper indications of course and distance.

In this way they extended themselves, and took up their march toward the river, from a little beyond where Amy left her basket; and if she had but remained where we left her, under the old maple-tree, they would soon have found her. Every rod of ground was explored, as they passed; and long before noon the ribbon which bound her hair was found under the old maple, and immediately sent to the house, to communicate the encouraging presage of success, and also to show that search in other directions was not needed; for the search was still being pursued, by women and others, in the direction of the maple-grove, and elsewhere.

Refreshments of bread, cheese, beer, and water, were brought, and passed along the line, without intermitting the search; but no further indications of their object were discovered that day. Before night they had explored the whole ground swept by their line of march to the river, being nine or ten square miles, besides their previous search. When they arrived at the river, another council was held. The company divided, and two lines were formed, each extending from the river as far towards their first point of starting as their number would allow, and which was far enough to sweep all the ground that the fugitive could in any likelihood have passed.

In the same order as before, one wing moved down the river, and the other moved up. The wing moving down the river was longest, extending nearly two miles back; on the other side, the course of the river made a less extensive line sufficient to cover the ground. The upper wing had also but about two miles ahead, before coming to a county road, which, of course, must terminate their search in that direction. The route of the lower line was, in one sense, interminable, for the forest stretched south and west to an indefinite distance; but there were streams running into the main river, some of which, within a few miles, were broad and deep enough to prevent the child's crossing.

The upper wing swept the whole ground in their line of march before dark; they reached the main road, which, if the fugitive had found, she would have kept, and it soon led to houses in either direction. They, therefore, turned to aid the down-river wing, on the extremity of which they formed themselves, so as to extend the line still further from the river. This arrangement must have been infallibly successful, but for a most extraordinary cause of failure; for they were now sweeping all the ground remaining unexplored which she could possibly pass.

While thus moving onward in regular order, and exploring every foot of the way, and in perfect silence, except that the word *march* was regularly passed along the line, the approach of night delayed their progress. In those dark old woods, shut in by thick branches overhead, and, for the most part, obstructed by thick-tangled growth beneath, the light faded fast with the declining sun; but they had advanced some three or four miles from their last point of starting, and had swept nearly all the ground where the child could have strayed. For, but a mile or two further on, their progress would be stopped by a broad, deep, sluggish stream, known as "The Dead Brook," which extended back from the main river many miles. By this time, also, the conviction prevailed that their search would be fruitless, and that they should see the child no more. She had probably made her way to the river and fallen from its high banks, to be swept away by its current; or, still more dreadful to be imagined, had been carried off by some wild beast. Bears and wolves, as well as more harmless animals, frequented these woods; and though the wolves, retreating to the mountains, were seldom seen here except in winter, yet the bears were said to be numerous. They were not considered fierce and dangerous at this season of the year, when berries and other sweet vegetables were plenty, but yet would, perhaps, destroy a child.

However, though with little hope, the party still proceeded to explore the remaining ground; but, when they came to the Dead Brook without finding any further trace of the object of their search, all the company seemed to yield to the conviction that their duty was done. Most of them, indeed, were exhausted from fatigue and want of accustomed food and rest; for they had not ceased a moment in their effort since called from their beds long before morning, and had taken no refreshment except such as could be passed from hand to hand along the line. It was now late and very dark, and there were evident signs of rain. The whole company gradually gathered toward the left extremity of the line, at the confluence of the Dead Brook with the main river. They had all, in passing down the Dead Brook, explored it thoroughly, and all agreed that there was no point where the child could possibly have crossed it. It was broad, deep, and impassable, for many miles back. Much was said about a place called Beaver Dam, about two miles up the stream ; but several men of reliable judgment had examined this, the only supposed place of crossing, and had found it, beyond all question, impossible to be passed by a child. Hope had deserted every heart, and the colonel, with pale and haggard features, worn with fatigue and anxiety, and with a trembling voice, thanked them for their kindness, and dismissed them to their homes.

It was now near midnight, very dark, and beginning to rain. They had long before provided themselves with torches to pursue their search ; and, as the large company departed and separated themselves into different groups, extending for miles in different directions, the woods seemed as if illuminated by a vast army. But all did not depart. The colonel and his sons, Deacon Arbor and Alek, Job Brown and Josiah, with about twenty others, remained on the ground, some with a vague impression that something might yet be done; besides, some were too much exhausted to return without refreshment and rest. A large fire was kindled, and food, which had been forwarded from the contributions of many houses during the day, was brought; boughs and leaves were collected, old garments spread down, and the colonel and deacon, with a few others, were persuaded to lie down and rest.

But Alek, though he had been one of the most active during the day, and had been searching the woods the whole night before, showed no signs of fatigue. After brief refreshment, and seeing his father and the colonel as comfortably disposed of as circumstances would permit, he declared his determination of examining the beaver-dam himself. This, as has been mentioned, was two miles up the Dead Brook. Some ten or twelve volunteered to accompany him, and, preparing their torches, they departed.

It now began to rain fast, but their pitch-wood torches flamed brightly, and they moved swiftly. In half an hour they were at the beaver-dam. The first glance gave no encouragement. The old dam consisted of a mass of decayed wood sunk in the stream, and on the further side reaching to the surface of the water, forming an eddy above, covered with floating sticks and leaves; the dam, which was evidently the work of beavers some years since, was decayed and washed away on the hither side, leaving a space of clear, deep water, of six or eight feet breadth, between the dam and the shore, so that the stream was clearly impassable.

But the searching eyes of Alek noticed that from the hither end of the dam a loose and rotten log of wood swung down stream, and vibrated in the slow current, its upper end still attached to the end of the dam. It appeared, from the lightness with which it floated, that it could not have been in the water long. Measuring it with his eye, he judged that it would about span the space between the shore and the dam. The thought flashed in his mind that such had been its position till very lately, and that some slight cause had displaced it, and caused it to float to its present position. That slight cause might be the foot of little Amy. If so, she might have crossed, or, more likely, might be sleeping in the dark waters beneath them.

This last supposition seemed most likely, when Alek's dog

Lion, who had been the active companion of his master in all the search, now, after rapidly snuffing the ground near where the loose end of the log might have been attached, and putting his fore-paws into the stream, as if to search it, uttered a long and melancholy howl. Alek was then convinced that Amy had been there. She was probably there now, or had been carried a little distance down the slow stream. But she might possibly have gained the other side, and be still living. He determined to seek the living child before searching the water for the dead.

The water was deep, but Alek could swim. His clothes were already wet with rain, and therefore he did not take them off. In a minute he was on the other side, and Lion, who could swim as well as his master, was there too. After a moment's snuffing, Lion sprang about, wild with excitement. He had evidently made a discovery. He would run a few steps into the bushes, dart back, take a circuit, and make off again, and then return and look wistfully at his master, as if anxious that he should accompany him. Alek shouted for the others to come over; a stick was found strong enough to bridge the chasm, and in a few moments the whole party were exploring the other shore with their torches.

Lion led his master, in a line diverging from the stream, downward toward the main river. Some of the party followed; others beat the ground in various directions. Lion kept on in a circuitous course, but far ahead, occasionally with a low bark, as if to give his master indication of his course. Alek hurried on in the direction of the sound. After some fifteen minutes, the loud, sharp bark of the dog followed by a long-protracted howl, gave Alek notice that

Lion had found the object of his pursuit; and that it was probably the child — dead!

With palpitating heart and wild haste, he hurried on. A thick growth of low bushes opposed his progress, but he rushed resistlessly on, holding aloft his torch. In a few minutes his excited apprehensions were ended. There was Lion; a slender, white object lay upon the ground before him, which he was eagerly licking, all the time uttering a low, whimpering cry. Alek threw down the torch, and, carefully taking up the insensible child, pressed her to his breast. He thought she was dead; but she was not quite cold. He put his ear to her side; he could perceive the beating of her heart.

"FOUND! FOUND!" he cried, at the top of his voice.

"FOUND! FOUND!" was shouted by the companions of his search, scattered in various directions, and some of them not far off.

"FOUND! FOUND!" reëchoed the woods far and wide, to the loudest of human voices.

They were nearer the party which they had left an hour ago than when they crossed the stream; but they must still be more than a mile off. Yet soon from the far distance they heard the combined shout of many voices, "Found! found!"

"*Found! found!*" was again replied by Alek's party, who were now fast hurrying toward him.

"FOUND! FOUND!" reëchoed the woods far and wide.

In a few moments, the deep sound from the distance was again heard. It was the tone of inquiry, "ALIVE? — ALIVE?"

"ALIVE! ALIVE!" shouted Alek.

"ALIVE! ALIVE!" shouted his approaching companions.

"ALIVE! ALIVE!" reëchoed the woods far and wide.

"*March!* march!" was again heard from the deep distance. It was a signal that the distant party were coming.

It is impossible to describe the excitement of the party left behind, when roused by the shout, *Found! found!* To cross the Dead Brook, and hasten in the direction of the sound, was the irresistible impulse. Luckily there were plenty of light logs, branches, and drift-wood, along the banks, from which a rude raft was in a few minutes constructed, and, three or four at a time, they were quickly on the other side of the stream. "MARCH! MARCH!" was again shouted, and answered, at intervals, to direct their course.

In the mean time, Alek's companions had gathered brushwood, and other combustibles, and kindled a great fire. Little Amy, closely embraced by Alek, felt its reviving warmth, and her little limbs shivered. Alek chafed her body; others heated portions of their dripping garments, and successively wrapped them around her feet; others, making their hands hot by the fire, pressed hers between them. Lion, eager to assert his claims, pressed his nose to her wet garments; and soon all had the satisfaction of hearing the indistinct murmur of her voice.

"Amy, dear Amy!" said Alek, in her ear; for Alek still held her, as having the first right, although her brothers stood around.

"*Father!*" whispered the unconscious child. She thought it was her father's voice.

"Dear daughter!" replied Alek, with tears in his eyes. He has always called her "dear daughter," since.

Words cannot describe the agony of joy shown by the

father, when he again beheld his child. With streaming eyes and lifted hands, he uttered thanksgivings to God. He had never before been known to utter words of devotion in presence of others, though believed to pray habitually in secret. But now what to him though a thousand stood around? He saw only his child; and he felt that a present God had restored her. Never before or since has the inspiration of fervent piety struck me as on this occasion. From this I could imagine how David looked, when he cried, "O, Absalom! my son, my son!" But his was the inspiration of grief. This was the inspiration of gratitude and joy.

We have purposely omitted to speak of the agony of terror and suspense which agitated the anguished mother and distracted sisters, during all this dreadful interval. We shall not attempt to describe their joy in the restoration of the lost one. With what deep feeling the mother thanked Alek, when the whole story was told her; and how the daughters overwhelmed and embarrassed him with their gratitude. Is it a wonder that Amy loves Alek, and calls him dear uncle, and that he calls her his dear daughter?

The town was soon made aware of the good news. The next Sunday, Parson Boreman improved the occasion with a most eloquent sermon. Everybody thought it eloquent, and a committee was appointed to solicit a copy for the press. It was given, and an enormous edition of five hundred copies printed, from which every family in town, and many elsewhere, were supplied. The colonel reads the sermon annually, every Thanksgiving Day, with tears. I have looked it over lately to make some extracts with which to close this chapter; but find nothing particularly appropriate, and rather suspect that its chief merit at the time was, that it touched a subject in which his congregation were interested.

CHAPTER VI.

THE storm has passed. The bright sun looks from behind his cloudy curtains to behold mother earth decked like a bride in her drapery of flowery white, to welcome the new approaching year. How virgin fair and pure she looks! Her ample robe spreads its undulations far as the eye can reach. The woody hills are rounded and softened in their outlines by the superincumbent snow, spread as a veil of white over their bending tops. Yet less lovely now is the earth in her splendor than she shall soon appear when night shall display her softer charms, and the silver moon, and the sparkling stars, and the deep-blue sky, shall spread their glorious canopy over her head.

Let us now go back to Deacon Arbor's. Alek has returned, and has brought good news; not unexpected, and not unprepared for. Two sleigh-loads of company are coming;—Uncle Jotham driving Aunt Nabby in one sleigh, and a young dandy driving a rustic schoolmaster in the other. Helen turned her head a little the other way, at this last intelligence; and Frances asked, archly, whom the young dandy had come for,—just as if she already knew the schoolmaster's intentions.

"Not you, sister," said Alek.

"O, no; the schoolmaster 's after me and Helen," replied she, just as if that were to be a triple affair.

They had stopped a little while at the village, at Captain Boynton's. Captain Boynton was the rich old revolutionary soldier at the village, and the young dandy was his grand-nephew. The young dandy's name was Harry Boynton. His father was a planter in North Carolina, and his uncle a merchant in New York, and his aunt was no other than Aunt Nabby; but she was a maternal aunt, not a Boynton.

Harry was a Harvard University student, and proficient in the sciences and accomplishments often very successfully pursued there. He was not one of those few unexceptionable and indefatigable young men, who, late and early, pore over crabbed characters in dusty tomes, and from the commencement of a term to its close keep the college honors full in view. His mathematical pursuits were more practical than theoretical; and he described his curves and angles upon a billiard-table, with the white and red balls, aided by the dextrous use of the cue, which he substituted for the more complex instruments of his shagreen case. Of all the great personages of history, he most fancied the four popular kings and queens whose portraits so often draw admiring connoisseurs about the card-table. In the diplomacy of shuffling he was an adept, but his practice involved rather an unprofitable familiarity with the knaves. In astronomical studies, he by no means neglected the theatrical "stars." The bowling-alley balls demonstrated the movements of the spheres; and he explored through opera-glasses the constellations which sparkled in the deep concave of the dress-circles. Botany often solaced his leisure, with tobacco-leaves rolled in the form of cigars. The wine-merchant's bills were regarded by him as free translations of Anacreon, though not always happily rendered. His opinion was always authoritative in questions of port, madeira, and champagne. But these laudable and brilliant attainments, indicating the fastest improvement of his time, so far from winning the approbation, only excited the jealousy, of the grave and reverend professors of dull, dry, collegiate study; which was carried so far, that, at an official meeting of the faculty, they voted him a polite but somewhat peremptory permission to recruit his mental health, and renovate his moral habits, by a temporary rustication.

By this kind consideration of the college faculty, and at the suggestion of his uncle in New York, he improved the period of his rustication by making a visit to his aunt in Saco. There he made himself generally agreeable, as indeed he did everywhere; for he had natural good qualities, which dissipation had not wholly eradicated. When the visit to Wolfsden was spoken of, he proposed to be one of the party; and his Aunt Nabby, who had received a confidential letter from his uncle, commending his health and habits to her own and Uncle Lemuel's especial watchfulness, approved the proposition.

At Wolfsden village, Harry must needs pay his first respects to his grand-uncle. Aunt Nabby, who considered that her duty of watchfulness could be best performed by keeping him in sight, concluded to call and pay her respects, too; particularly as the horses really needed breath, for they had travelled fast, notwithstanding the snow. Harry had driven, though not so fast as he would have done but for Hezekiah's mild remonstrance.

"If I have a genius for anything, it is for driving," said Harry.

Though Harry made no pretensions to superior talents in a general way, he had a habit of claiming a peculiar "genius" for whatever business happened to be in hand; so that his piecemeal pretensions, if added up, would have excelled those of the Admirable Crichton himself.

Captain Boynton was a gentleman. He was the only gentleman by profession in Wolfsden. There were other gentlemanly men, but no others who made that business their exclusive pursuit.

He was an old gentleman, and a gentleman of the old school, and of the old habits of the old school. He gave them all a warm welcome, and brought out his decanter of old Jamaica, to give them warm toddy. Aunt Nabby declined the toddy, as did the others. Perhaps Harry might not have declined, but for the others' presence; but he had too much grace to violate their example while he was their guest. "My genius lies in the cold-water line," said Harry.

Captain Boynton chose to maintain the ceremonies of the old school, notwithstanding the degeneracy of these cold-water days; and so he drank the toddy to their health, and ordered cake and tea for their better refreshment, and proceeded to fight the battle of Trenton for their edification. Captain Boynton, it was evident, had done important service at Trenton, though Weems, in his "Life of Washington," had neglected to record it. He then proceeded to Princeton, and, after the fall of General Mercer, rallied the retreating regiment, and won the battle, — a circumstance also forgotten by Weems. The captain was indefatigable, and, going backwards in the generally-received order of events, he proposed the storming of Ticonderoga and Crown Point; but his auditors were now tired of battles, their horses were rested, and they took their leave, Harry promising soon to rejoin his uncle for another campaign.

Hezekiah permitted Harry to drive as fast as he chose, the rest of the way. He had become impatient of the captain's achievements. He had no taste for war; his inclinations drew strongly in another direction. But Harry drove provokingly slow.

"A merciful man is merciful to his beast," said Harry. "Slow and sure, wins the race."

But the distance was short, and soon they arrived at Deacon Arbor's, and met a hearty welcome. Harry, though a stranger, was equally welcome for the other's sake, and he soon made himself welcome for his own.

It had been arranged to invite a few additional friends, — in short, to have a "party," as much as might be allowable, without scandal, on a Saturday evening. Margaret Murray was already there, in pursuance of previous understanding. She rode over on one of the ox-sleds, which came from that direction, to break out the roads. The Bowler boys and girls, including Amy and the adjutant, came after dark. Josiah Brown was with them, and looked very well pleased. Helen, glancing at him, whispered the fact to Ann; and she replied that they were all happy on her account, glancing at Hezekiah. Very well turned off, Miss Ann!

We were all very happy, and Helen appeared as tranquil and as easy as if it were the most natural thing to have a lover. — She, who had no experience in that way, and whom, for her old-maidish ways, everybody had marked down as a predestined old maid, though yet but twenty-five!

Hezekiah, too, was evidently happy; — staid and quiet in his happiness, yet luminously happy. I mean that the light of his happiness shone through his eyes and features.

We were all glad to be there, and glad to see each other there. The great kitchen fireplace glowed with the lasting heat of solid maple logs. The sitting-room and parlor were illuminated with brighter fires. Their polished hearths and painted floors reflected the ruddy blaze. How fresh, and nice, and new, seemed the furniture, in its maturity of forty years! Years had ever fallen softly upon all that house.

Besides the company enumerated, there is one more to be mentioned; the new schoolmaster, — not a very new man, though, for he is forty-five, at least; but he is new to us, for this is his first winter in Wolfsden. A quiet, unobtrusive, silent sort of a man he seems; but we will not overlook him, for he is still a great man even here, and at the school-house greater still, — the monarch of all he surveys, but a very good, just, and benignant monarch.

There is a saying, that there is a skeleton in every house; meaning that, however fair external signs may be, yet some open or secret trouble lurks everywhere. But surely there is no skeleton here. No; there is none. But look!

What spectre is that emerging from the corner bedroom? It *is* a skeleton! The face grins with a leer of sepulchral satisfaction, beneath a double row of crisp, short curls of false hair, surmounted by a crisp, crimped, double-bordered cap, surmounted higher still by bunches of gaudy ribbons, overtopped in their turn by a short, waving feather. Is it the skeleton of some squaw, decked for her wedding, and seeking for her lost "*brave*"?

Around her yellow neck is a crisp, crimped double-ruff, disposed so as to show a row of yellow gold beads just above it, and a golden chain, attached to a yellow shining ring, attached to some yellow shining trinkets, just below it.

Below her tight waist spread far and wide the rustling folds of her silken dress. She moves forward with a bobbing curtsey. It is! O, goodness! it is ——!

Let us turn around and walk into the sitting-room. There is no skeleton there. There are bright, welcome faces, instead. Margaret Murray, hazel-eyed, dark-haired, fair-browed, cherry-lipped creature of self-conscious beauty, let me introduce the impatient reader to a nearer view of your charms. Ah, how prepared are those sparkling eyes for the compliment, and how prompt that musical tongue in appropriate reply! Will you address her a few words, no matter how commonplace? — in a few moments you will be delighted at your newly-discovered powers of conversation. Though cold and dull as the black steel of the tinder-box, if there be fire in you, she will strike it out. But you must not engross her; Alek is near, and envies your happy chance. Another stands at little distance, and looks on admiringly. Can it be that he envies, too? O, no! it is the light-hearted, thoughtless Harry Boynton. He is evidently surprised to see so much beauty, grace, and vivacity, in a place so remote from city life. But he is too familiar with the attractions of polished society to be very deeply impressed with the graces of a country maiden, even if capable of deep impressions at all; and yet he looks more earnest and thoughtful than is his wont. Is it possible that he has a heart, and is just finding it out?

And now let me introduce you to ——. But look! the skeleton of millinery is in the doorway, advancing with a bobbing curtsey. Let us retreat into the kitchen.

Ah, genial sight! With what ample and tempting cheer that long-extended damask-covered table is spread — food for fifty, and we are but a score. The big turkey is there; he justly claims his honored place at the feast — such was his destiny. For this he lived, for this he was worthy to die. The brown, savory spare-rib is there. For this the reluctant sovereign of the sty yielded his life. In yon deep, broad pasty lies a flock of imprisoned chickens, waiting, as once in their parent egg they waited, to burst their brittle covering. And on yonder dressers see what puddings and pies, and wonderful works of pastry, stand ready. But we will not tire the reader with details of what his appetite may desire, but which, perchance, his fate may deny. But look! Ah, look the *other* way! The skeleton approaches, glittering in millinery, rustling in silks, and bobbing her curtseys. Let us turn and face the spectre. Mrs. Simperkins! Your old acquaintance, Mrs. Simperkins.

How came she here? How, indeed! How came she everywhere? How came the maggot in the cheese? How came sin into the world? How came it that each pleasure has its poison too, and every sweet a *sour?* Let us turn to pleasanter themes — to any other theme.

In yon obscure corner sits the schoolmaster. He is talking with Ike. Ike is interested in his communication. We cannot hear what he says, but Ike answers aloud, "He *shall* be encouraged! The rest have gone to destruction, but we 'll save him if it can be done." They are speaking of Ax Barker.

The schoolmaster has been here only a week. He was sent

for from a distance, to keep our school this winter, for his fame as a successful teacher had reached us. Well does he seem likely to justify it. He has already engaged the interest of every pupil; all respect him, and try to do their best.

He "boards round." The school-money would last but two months if the master's board were paid from it. To make it three months, a dozen families of the district volunteer to board the master each a week or more. This has been the week at the deacon's house, and he has proved an agreeable guest. They invite and persuade him to stay another week, thinking that Hezekiah, also a schoolmaster, may be the better entertained, — just as if Hezekiah cared about any entertainment but Helen!

Supper is ready; but let us skip the supper, since we cannot partake of it. Aunt Jane Bowler says it does her as much good to see others eat as to eat herself. Others may not have that "genius," as Harry says.

Supper ended, the plays begin. The old folks and grave folks appropriate the parlor, leaving the sitting-room and kitchen for the young folks and gay folks. In the parlor are the deacon and his wife, the schoolmaster and Hezekiah, and also Helen. In sitting-room and kitchen are distributed the others. Mrs. Simperkins wavers between parlor and sitting-room, as if uncertain of her position; till, urged by the serious-looking but mischievous Margaret, she settles down in the sitting-room with the young and gay.

Harry Boynton, seeing Margaret's attention to the old charmer, took it for granted that she was her especial favorite; and, as Margaret seemed coy of his perhaps too marked attentions, he deemed it politic to patronize the millinery establishment.

He thought her, perhaps, an elderly aunt or grandmother of Margaret, and made his addresses accordingly. The Simperkins was flattered. She had already found out that he was son to a Carolina planter, nephew to a New York merchant and to Aunt Nabby, grand-nephew to Capt. Boynton, and student at college. She supposed him to be studying for the ministry, and bent her conversation accordingly. He inferred that she was a particularly religious lady, and answered in the same strain; for it is his genius to conform to his company, to be all things to all men, and women too; besides, it was now his policy. Their conversation was edifying. If it were the major whom he wished to win, instead of his daughter, that conversation, could he have overheard it, would have done the business.

Not that any pious pretensions were made on Harry's part; he only gave general assent to the merits of favorite ministers and doctrinal tenets praised by her, and declared his charity for all sects (by which she understood evangelical sects), when she deprecatingly informed him that she belonged to the "church of Hingland" (supposing him a Congregationalist); but his eloquent declamations about the wisdom and wonders of Providence confirmed her in her estimate of the sacredness of his calling.

When she changed the subject to college life, it was wonderful with what eloquence and fervor he expatiated upon the snares set there, and thereabouts, for the unwary; how he condemned the corruptions of society, and deplored the vices to which the young are exposed. It was wonderful, too, that so discreet a young man should be so well acquainted with all the details of what he so earnestly condemned; for, in his zeal, — his thoughts, and his eyes being mostly elsewhere, his tongue ran at random, and he rattled off the slang of the billiard-saloon, the bowling-alley, the gambling-table, &c., — told how they gulled the flats, green-horns, pigeons, and outsiders, till his language became unintelligible to the Simperkins' understanding, though not the less gratifying for that. It was all Latin and Greek to her; but it was not surprising that a divinity student should talk Latin and Greek, and she was proud to be thought worthy to hear it.

Meantime, Harry's thoughts and eyes were wandering among the gay and lively company. One bright particular star attracted them. It was a star of strong attraction. His soul newly magnetized, turned and trembled under its mysterious power. Harry was in love! He who had whirled so lightly through the mazes of fashion, whom the bright eyes that so often attracted had never been able to subdue, and who had come heart-free to his twentieth year, now yielded at the first summons of the bright-eyed country maiden.

Yet, though his freedom and the lightness of his heart were gone, emotions far more animating thrilled his frame. They gave a new impulse to the beating of his heart; they gave intensity to the glance of his eye, and new animation and expression to his countenance. He lived now in a new element, a new atmosphere. It might be as illusory as the atmosphere of frivolity, where he had so long lived; but it was new, and it gave him new life.

As his eyes still furtively pursued their object, he felt rather than saw that her eyes were once or twice turned upon him. "It is my destiny," thought he; and thoughts and visions floated in his imagination, as thickly and confusedly as the storm, through which he had all day driven, filled the sky

To him Mrs. Simperkins was a lucky resource. He had

poured oceans of information into her greedy ears, and it was now his turn to get information. He inquired, firstly, about distant matters — the minister of the parish, especially. (Discreet Harry!) Then, cutting short the too long account about Parson Boreman, he asked about the schoolmaster, — "Was he pious? Deacon Arbor, — was he a friend to missions? Mrs. Arbor, — did she enjoy good health? These young gentlemen, — were they all her sons?" (Cautious Harry!) "These young ladies, — were they all her daughters?" (Sly Harry!) The young lady who just passed, and who urged her to remain in the room, — "Her niece, he presumed." (False Harry!)

Miss Simperkins informed him upon all the topics; indeed, she was entirely too prolix, and he hurried her on successively till they came to the last, and *then* she told him too much, too much for his comfort, for she told him, in a long history, including the major and his family, their relations to the church, &c., that Margaret was engaged to Mr. Alek Arbor. She said it as quietly as the engineer lights the match of the mine beneath the castle of the beleaguered city. Its effects were as fatal — Harry's castle was blown into mid-air.

When the insane, unreasoning power of love takes possession of the heart, other kindred, absurd fantasies come in to share the dominion. Honor, that will not take advantage of opportune circumstances to invade others' rights. Self-respect, that would scorn to accept advantages so won. Conscience, which forbids the enjoyment of dishonorable success. Sympathy, which disturbs the pleasures of self with the pains of others. He who writes for the present world must class all these, and kindred sentiments, as fantasies. People of primitive days counted them realities. To them these shadows indicated substance. Our age has weighed them in the banker's scales, which give standard weight, and find they "won't pay."

But these fantasies were now ruling sentiments with Harry. Love had upset his understanding, and honor and self-respect had entered the breach. He could not violate, with treacherous designs, the hospitality he was receiving. He would not employ his superior position and advantages to entice away the affections already bestowed, or promised, to another. He would not even accept a heart which could be so enticed. Some romantic notions of pure, disinterested, undivided love, confused his calculations.

On the other hand, he was now under the control of a power he could not throw off. He had never resisted his inclinations, and therefore they were irresistible.

But what should he do about it? He asked this question himself, and walked to a secluded window to meditate. The moon rode among the fleecy clouds in her silvery brightness. The stars sparkled like gems in the deep-blue firmament. The distant forest stretched an obscure, interminable shadow. The grandeur of nature's solitude soothed the tumult of his soul.

And so he meditated. But his meditations came to nothing, except a resolve to be quiet; "For," said he, "I 'm cornered." Strange that he should be cornered where room is so plenty! He came back from the window, but not to Miss Simperkins.

The plays were progressing. Blind-man's-buff had already been performed in the kitchen, till all were panting with the excitement. "Button, button, who 's got the button?" passed round in a new circle formed in the sitting-room. Harry was in it. Mrs. Simperkins was a little astonished; but, upon the whole, concluded that a divinity student might go *so* far, since he had preferred her conversation to blind-man's-buff. The company would like for *her* to go further; but she would not go at all. There she sat like an owl damping the spirits of sportive chickens, or, like the nightmare, spoiling their pulses' healthful play.

Forfeits are a part of the play of Button. Alek and Ike were in it. When Alek and Ike were together, something might be expected. Ike had to redeem a forfeit; he appointed Alek to judge him. "Kiss every lady in the room," said Alek.

"Oldest first!" shouted Ike, bounding from his chair towards Mrs. Simperkins. She held up both hands, with severe dignity, to repel the profanation. She had better submitted in silence. Ike burst through all barriers of fists, elbows, shoulders, plumes, ribbons, caps, and curls, hugged her round the neck, and smacked, or pretended to smack, her heartily. Her plume was draggled, her crimped ruffles were crumpled, her false curls were displaced, and all her millinery deranged; crippled in all her rigging, like some over-matched privateer, she moved off to refit, and the coast was clear for the present. And all this before the divinity student! Poor Mrs. Simperkins!

One more forfeit must be mentioned. It was lost by Harry. He was adjudged by Ann. He must make a speech to Margaret, take her hand, and give her a kiss. The words "Spirit of Louis, ascend to heaven!" when uttered by the abbé to the King of France upon the scaffold, could not have thrilled the monarch more. The prospect of heaven is pleasant; but timorous mortals stand and shrink, and fear to launch away.

Harry had resolved to be quiet. When people resolve to be quiet, they should make an exceptional proviso for volcanoes, earthquakes, tornadoes, avalanches, and such outside influences. Harry did not feel quiet just now; and yet this thought was not new to him. To take Margaret's hand, make a speech, and give her a kiss, was among the sublimest of the fancies that floated amid the commotions of his brain, half an hour since.

But there was no retreat, nor time to think about it; so he marched across the circle, and took her unresisting hand. It was white and cold; the blood had retreated to her fluttering heart. Her other hand covered her face. That, too, looked pale and cold; and so did her face, so far as it could be seen. "Forgive me," he whispered. This was an evasion of his sentence; — an oration, and aloud, was meant. He kissed her hand; — another evasion; her cheek was meant; but it was permitted to pass.

Margaret removed her hand from her face; there was redness enough then. She forced a cough, that she might use a kerchief. It was a slight cough, as if something could not be swallowed; it compelled her to turn her head and hide her face, while the kerchief was applied to her eyes; but she was soon composed. The cough did not return.

Why should so many words be written about so slight an affair? But who can tell what affairs are slight? Often the most seemingly trivial become the turning-points of our fate, — perhaps even of the fate of nations. This slight matter, for instance, though it made no impression upon the circle, left an abiding one, an ineffaceable one, upon three persons in it: — Harry, Margaret, Alek. Harry saw or felt that his deep passion was not unperceived, perhaps not unappreciated, by its object. Margaret had found a new era in her existence, marked by emotions which she had deemed but the idle dreams of romance; and Alek saw the foundations of the house which his long-cherished fancies had built, and where he had stored his choicest hopes, sink in the faithless sand. His eyes, sharpened by interest, had not failed to see and interpret the omens so fatal to his hopes.

His heart throbbed with repressed agony. He rose and walked to the secluded window, and looked forth. The silvery moon still held her way among the fleecy clouds. The far expanse of glittering landscape blended with the sky. The distant forest stretched its obscure, interminable shadow. The grandeur of nature's solitude soothed the tumult of his soul; he swallowed down the grief which rose to choke him; he folded his arms with mingled resignation and resolution, and then unfolded and suffered them to fall by his side, while he meditated. He came to the conclusion that it was best to be quiet, and so he resolved to be; "For," said he, "I 've run against a stump." Strange that he should run against stumps, when they were so deeply covered with snow! In his resolution to be quiet, he made no exceptional proviso for earthquakes, tornadoes, and avalanches. No need. Either, or all, would now have been a relief. Suddenly two little hands clasped one of his great ones. They were Amy's. With childish instinct and childish sympathy she saw that he was troubled, and wished to comfort him. He took her in his arms; she was slender and light, — a small burden in his arms, not enough to counterbalance the burthen upon his heart; yet she seemed to relieve it. She put her little arms around his neck, and pressed her lips to his cheek, then to each of his eyes, then to his cheek again. His view overlooked the woods where she was lost, and where he had rescued her; and she thought he was thinking of that, and of her. The subject was so important, and so constant in her mind, she thought it equally so in his. She failed to read aright his troubled mind; but her remedy was not the less salutary. He pressed her to his breast, returned her sweet kisses, and felt relieved.

Alek's discomposure had escaped every eye but Amy's. He returned to the sitting-room with his usual aspect. Margaret was just retiring to the kitchen. Each appeared perfectly composed, and smiled with accustomed greeting; each sought only to evade the other's scrutiny.

Margaret went to the secluded window. The silvery moon, the fleecy clouds, the sparkling stars, the snow-clad mountains and far-reaching forest, still performed their silent part in nature's grand mystery; and she repressed the throbbings of her heart. She recalled her maiden pride, and, resolving to be quiet, returned to join the merry company. Strange that, of all that merry company, the only unquiet ones were they who were so strongly resolved to be quiet.

The various round of trivial plays successively diverted the company, and then the "Match Stories" began. Some, who are unacquainted with the amusements of Wolfsden, and the region thereabout, may ask what "Match Stories" are.

Match Stories are invented and told by the company in pairs, in this manner: One commences a story, and proceeds to the midst of the narrative or plot, and then appoints another to finish it. These stories are assumed to be extempore, and often are so; though it is allowable to concert and make previous preparation, which is generally done. On this occasion, several stories were told in this manner, which we will put in the next chapter, as specimens of the inventive faculties of the untrained youth of Maine.

CHAPTER VII.

Life has two grand divisions: the time when we seize and enjoy our own enjoyments, and the time when we provide and enjoy the enjoyments of others. The first is that of youth; the second is that of maturity. The dividing line is not sharp; the divisions blend into each other, yet these are their distinguishing features. Happy are they who partake the benefits of the first; happier they who fulfil the duties of the last.

Happy, therefore, are Deacon Arbor and his wife, and all whose destinies they influence!

The whole company, of old and young, are now assembled to hear the Match Stories. The younger take their first turn. Perhaps they have been assisted in preparation by the older; but most of the invention, and all the credit, is their own.

Grave people, who think it undignified to laugh at childish sports, may skip the whole of this chapter.

MATCH STORIES.

Story First (begun by Amy the pensive, and ended by George the wag).

(*Amy.*) "There was once a very pretty and pleasant couple lived in a pretty little house, in a pleasant field, a little way from the road. The man and wife were both young; and very neat; and they had six children, all very pretty. There were five girls and one boy; but the boy was as good and pretty as his sisters. They were all about nine years old, except one, and that was a baby, — a very pretty baby, with curly hair, and blue eyes, and a pink frock, and red shoes, and a little wagon to draw him out in. And there was a nice garden on one side of the house, with walks all through it, and all kinds of flowers by the walks, and cherry-trees, and plum-trees, and currant-bushes, and gooseberries that were ripe every month in the year — only in the winter. And there was a row of maple-trees each side of the lane going down to the road; and the children played, and drew the little baby in the wagon, under the shade of the maple-trees; and their father tapped the trees, and they got plenty of sweet sap when they were thirsty. And they had a gentle cow, that would not kick, but gave plenty of new milk; and a pig to eat up the skim-milk; and some chickens, and ducks, and young turkeys; but no geese. And their mother made pudding and milk, and sometimes porridge, for supper; and she made plenty of pies and pancakes, and they had plenty of sweet apples baked to eat in their milk. And they went to school every day but Saturday afternoons, and Sunday they rode in a nice carriage to meeting. And the schoolmistress was not cross, but very good; and they always carried her flowers, and plums, and some nice cake, and that 's all I know about it. — O yes! the girls were all very industrious and studious, and so their mother bought them beautiful dolls that would roll their eyes. And George may tell the rest of the story, but must not spoil it."

(*George.*) "Well, this nice pretty young couple, after a

while, grew old and homely; and the five little girls, all of sister Amy's age, grew up, too, and went into a nunnery, and became nuns; and the little baby wore out his pink frock, and lost his red shoes, and grew up barefooted to be a great boy; and his name was Robinson Crusoe; and he ran away and went to sea, and was left on a desert island, and kept goats, and caught a savage and named him Friday; and I have his picture and whole history in a nice book, which you may all come over to our house and read. And, as for the old folks, the longer they lived the older they grew; and their house grew old too, and they became poor, for many thieves infested that pleasant country, and stole all their property, till there was nothing left but the pig, that eat all the skim-milk. And their cow was stolen; and they had to kill all their chickens and ducks and pigeons, and sit up nights to eat them, to prevent their being stolen. And when these were all gone, they wished they had some geese; but sister Amy would not let them have geese, because she is afraid of the gander.

"And so they began to be hungry, and one day the old man said to his wife, 'We 'll kill the pig and have him to eat; for *he* has nothing to eat, and has not eaten anything for six weeks.' And so they killed the pig, and pulled off his wool, and took out his tallow, and hung him up in the wood-house to dry. And after they had gone to bed, the old woman said to the old man, 'We 'll get up and put the pig under the bed, lest the thieves steal him;' and they did so. And after they had gone to bed again, they talked about what they would do with the pig to-morrow; and they concluded to roast his spare-ribs for Thanksgiving, and salt his shoulders for pork, and bake his head for Fast-day, and smoke his hams for bacon, and save his lard to fry doughnuts, and send his tail to the minister for a present. And there were two thieves came along, and listened under the window, and found they had a pig, and resolved to steal him. And they waited till the old folks were gone to sleep; and they tried the door, but it was fastened; and one said he would crawl down chimney. And he got on the house and crawled down most to the fireplace, and he could get no further, for the chimney was so narrow. And the old man and woman waked up and heard him, and got up, and saw his legs hanging down in the fireplace, and each caught hold of a leg and held him fast. And then the old man tied the great brass kettle, which was full of potatoes, to one leg, and the old woman tied the great iron pot, which was full of turnips, to the other leg, and left him dangling till morning.

"Then the old man went to the door, and before he opened it, the thief outside heard him, and thought it to be his fellow-thief, and asked him if he was bringing the pig; and the old man said, 'No;' and that he must come in at the window and help him, for it was so heavy. So the thief went round back of the house to get in at the window; and the old man told him to put up his feet, and he would pull him in; and he put in his feet, and the old man seized one foot and the old woman the other, and shut down the sash and held him fast. And the old man tied the wash-tub, which was full of suds, to one foot, and the old woman tied the churn, which was full of butter-milk, to the other, and left him till morning. And in the morning they got the sheriff to come and take them all to jail; and they kept their pig, and had plenty of spare-ribs, and pork, and bacon, and doughnuts, which lasted just as long as they lived; and they sent the tail to the minister, and it was put in the contribution-box for the heathen. And this is the history of all three, the old man, and old woman, and thieves, and little piggy-wiggee."

All laughed as George rattled off and ended his rigmarole; but Amy said, "That 's just the way George always spoils my stories!"

The next story was begun by James, and finished by Fanny. James loved Fanny. He had loved her from childhood; he loved her while she lived. He still loves her; time is transitory, but love is eternal. Fanny loved him, — it was the love of a sweet sister for a kind brother. His affection was more ardent. It was the idolatry of fond, heart-filling, yet unspoken love. He was of a thoughtful, retiring turn. She was mildness and goodness personified.

MATCH STORY. — II.

(*James.*) "There is a broad, boundless ocean, which rolls its waves upon a smooth and sandy shore, which borders the eastern side of a lovely island. The island is lovely on that side; in other parts its features are more forbidding. The waves generally roll softly there, over smooth, white sand; in other parts, they beat boisterously against rugged rocks.

"A Genie came out of the ocean at early dawn, and sat upon the shore. He took some fine sand and clay, and rolled them into figures of a curious form, and left them to warm in the beams of the rising sun. And soon the sun warmed them, and they began to move, for they received life from the sun. So they rose up and walked side by side; and they seemed two pleasant children, a boy and a girl, and they loved each other as brother and sister, for the Genie had formed them to love each other. The little maiden was beautiful and good, and the boy was loving and kind. And they walked along the smooth shore, and the waves rippled over their tiny feet, and they chased each other, and chased the rippling waves.

"So they walked along, and gathered beautiful shells and corals, and built gay houses and mimic gardens upon the sandy shore; but soon the waves came and washed them away; but they were not sorry, for they saw a fair lawn, with beautiful flowers upon the banks, beyond the shore, and they ascended and played upon the soft turf, and gathered roses and lilies, and sweet strawberries, and made little houses from branches of the bushes which grew there. And they sang sweet songs, and repeated pleasant stories, and sometimes they sat in silence, and inquired in their thoughts how they came to be there, and if they were to live so happily there forever.

"Then the Genie came up out of the sea, and looked upon them, and they wondered; but they were not afraid, for he looked kindly upon them, and they asked him many questions, and he told them that his name was WISDOM, and he would instruct them by and by.

"And soon the sun rose higher, and sent stronger rays of heat, and seared the green turf where they played, and dried the beautiful flowers, and withered the boughs of which they had builded mimic houses. But yet they did not grieve, for they saw upon the side of the ascending hill tall trees, which cast a pleasant shade and bore delicious fruits, while lambs and kids frisked among the fallen leaves, and birds flew about. And they made friends of the kids, and lambs, and birds, and all they saw, and were well pleased with all, and especially with each other; and if they wandered apart, they soon returned, for they were happier together than when separated, and they inquired in their thoughts whether they should always live together, and if they might still remain in this pleasant spot, and call it their home.

"And the Genie came to instruct them as he had promised, for now they were old enough to learn; and Fanny may tell the words he said, and what else came to pass."

Fanny proceeded, with a soft and even voice, slow, but without hesitation, thus:

"The Genie told them all that they were capable of understanding, concerning the mystery of their being; — that their outward forms were not made to last forever, and were not in reality an essential part of their being; and that they should look upon their hands, and heads, and bodies, as but sand and clay, which they must soon lay aside for other and better forms; and that the spirit within was alone their true and essential selves, which would live and learn forever.

"He told them, too, that they might not long remain in this pleasant spot, for he had another and far more beautiful home prepared for them, to which they must arrive through various ways, some of which would be smooth, but some would be rough; and then he pointed out to them distant mountains, whose tops reached above the clouds, beyond which he said was their permanent and happy home; and that there was a safe though sometimes toilsome path over the mountains, through which all, who followed his directions, safely found their way to the happy home beyond.

"He told them, too, that perhaps they must soon be separated for a while, till they should arrive at their journey's end; for that he had a shorter and easier passage upon the ocean, on which he conveyed those who were too weak to travel over the distant mountains; and that if he should take the maiden in that way, still he would not leave the boy to pursue his path alone, but would send Faith and Hope, who were two loving Genies, to show him the way, and help him.

"When the young companions heard the Genie speak of separating them, they were sad; but soon they reflected that their separation would be transient, but their union eternal, and they considered that the good Genie, who had already given them so many pleasant things, and who had told them so many true things, which they could not otherwise have known, would still do what was best for their happiness, and they were comforted. And they asked him to make them acquainted with Faith and Hope; and he summoned them, and they came, soaring on bright wings; and they looked so pleasant, and uttered such sweet words, that the children felt assured that in such society they could pass whatever period of separation the Genie, whose name was Wisdom, should appoint."

"And this," said Fanny, "is the best place where I can end the story."

A sadness, like that which the Genie's children felt when he spoke of their separation, passed upon the spirit of James, for he associated himself and Fanny in those forms of his imagination.

The schoolmaster was next requested to commence a story, to which he assented, premising that, not being very imaginative, he should tell them a true story, which, however, they might finish as fancifully as they chose; and said that, as most of the company probably knew something of the facts, he would suggest that one of the gentlemen from abroad should finish the story. Hezekiah nominated Harry, who assented; and the schoolmaster, whose story was from what took place in his own school in the past week, proceeded.

MATCH STORY. — III.

(*Schoolmaster.*) "One cold, snowy December morning, a flock of country boys and girls assembled at a school-house, which was just large enough for the district, and where they had made a wood-pile just as large as the school-house. The boys had made an early fire, and the girls had swept the room, and everything was prepared in expectation of the master, whom none of them yet had ever seen. Pretty soon an oldish, homely-looking man was seen coming, whom, as he was a stranger, they supposed to be the master. As he came they saw the end of a ruler projecting from his great-coat pocket, and then they knew it was the master.

"He walked in and took his place behind the desk, upon which he gave three loud raps with his ruler, and the boys and girls took their places. The back part of the room was furnished with writing-seats. A portion of the space in front had forms, or benches, for pupils who did not write, and which were mostly occupied by the smaller pupils.

"The pupils and their books generally presented as good an appearance as might fairly be expected, except that upon one of the forms not furnished with writing-benches sat a boy whose appearance was an exception to the general tidiness of the school. He was larger than others who did not sit at writing-benches; was poorly clad, especially about the feet; and had only a tattered Webster's spelling-book, which he held open at the lesson beginning with '*baker.*'

"The master asked his name, and, without looking up, he said Ax. The school tittered; the master was puzzled, but asked his other name. The boy, confused, hesitated, as if trying to think, and then lowly muttered, 'Jotham.' The younger scholars again tittered, and the master was still more puzzled. Telling the school, in a stern voice, to mind their lessons, he then told the boy to pronounce his whole name aloud. After some consideration, he spoke hesitatingly, as if not quite certain about it, 'Jotham Barker.' 'What did you say Ax for?' ''Cause the boys all call me Ax.' 'That must not be permitted. No boys of this school shall give you, or any of the pupils, nicknames.'

"Then, looking at his tattered book, the master asked him where was his lesson. The boy pointed at '*baker*.' 'And have you no other books?' He had none. The master asked him how he came to be so backward. He did n't know. 'Have you not always come to school with the other boys?' 'Yes,' he replied. 'Then you must have been an idle boy,' said the master; and the boy, by his silence, assented. 'Have you parents?' 'Yes,' said the boy. 'And what do they think of your backwardness?' The boy did n't know, and therefore did n't say. 'Suppose,' said the master, 'your father should come in to see the school, and find his boy the only idle and ignorant one, how do you think he would feel?' The boy appeared more cast down. The thoughtless children tittered, for the idea of *that* boy's father, a miserable drunkard, called, in derision, Bang, coming to inspect the school, was altogether too amusing. The master looked sternly upon them, and then at the boy more closely. He saw that there was some mystery in the matter; and, telling the boy to prepare his lesson, proceeded to organize the school.

"In the afternoon, the master having examined the case

of the backward boy more thoroughly, and without finding any natural deficiency or disability in him, told him to stop after school, and he would talk with him. When the scholars had all gone, the master sat down by the boy, and soon learned all his story. His father was a drunkard, — all the time drunk, — he did n't have good clothes, like the other boys; and so they 'looked down' upon him, and he had n't anybody to give him books, and nobody cared about him to teach him; but he wanted to learn, like the rest of the boys, and not be an idle boy, and wished his father was not a drunkard.

"The master, therefore, spoke encouraging words to the boy; told him that he was his friend, and that he meant to make a good scholar of him. 'Do your duty,' said he, 'and before the school is done the scholars will not look down upon you, — perhaps some of them will look up to you.' The boy brightened up at this thought, and the master dismissed him, telling him that they would turn over a new leaf to-morrow; by which the boy thought he was to leave 'baker' behind, which would indeed be a bold step.

"The master provided a new spelling-book, writing-book, and slate; and when Ax came, next morning, bright with expectation, he was advanced to a seat with a writing-bench, and put upon a course of exercises adapted to his age. His first attempts were awkward enough; but the master was patient, and was rewarded by seeing the encouraging progress of his pupil. He also called the attention of one or two neighbors to the case, and soon the boy appeared with a new pair of boots, and several other external improvements. Which is all I can tell of the story."

Harry, who had listened, meditating how to finish it, proceeded in a light and punning strain:

(*Harry.*) "This little Ax, being thus handled, became quite a different instrument; and soon became as sharp as he had before been dull. Being no longer cut by his companions, his temper improved, and people began to see that he was made of the 'right stuff.' Whoever attempted to impose upon him, found him a hard customer; and when disputes arose, he could use knock-down arguments. After leaving 'baker,' he struck boldly at the tree of knowledge; what he did n't know, he axed about, and soon got to know everything.

"He was famous in mathematics, especially conic sections, division, and fractions. He learned to chop logic, and could split hairs in metaphysics. Those who had heretofore looked down upon him, and abused him, found it best to be careful how they handled edged tools; and those whose trade it was to grind the faces of the poor found it best not to grind him too much. After quitting school, he became a merchant; and, by cutting down his prices, he cut out all competitors, and soon was able to cut a great figure. He was no longer the hatchet-faced 'baker' boy of the school. He became a politician, and struck a bold stroke for Congress. When elected, he proved himself a patriot as inflexible as iron, and true as steel. It was encouraging to hear what hard knocks he gave to the hollow-hearted government, and what trimmings to the underbrush of the political forest. After that, he became judge, and decided causes with the wisdom of Solomon, — and after his manner, too, for he always split the difference, and compelled quarrelsome litigants to bury the hatchet. The longer he lived, the more edge he got; and finally, after making a good deal of noise in the world, as became the son of Bang, he left his mark upon his generation, and then died, or, as might be expressed, cut stick. His estate cut up rich, and a handsome portion of it he bequeathed to the schoolmaster, who had brightened up his faculties, and sharpened his wits. And this is the end of the last chapter of Ax."

Alek was appointed to commence the next story, and Margaret to finish it. The young people had associated Margaret with Alek, and the arrangement was natural. In the present case, both would be glad to be excused, but each had too much spirit to decline.

MATCH STORY. — IV.

(*Alek.*) "There is a country of considerable, but indefinite extent, inhabited by an incomprehensible people. The country is called the Land of Change, — not with reference to the currency, but to the instability of its affairs. The people are sometimes called the Fools of Chance, — not wholly in reference to their inaptitude to learn, but because their sagest conclusions are often based upon some fatal error. The country is pleasant enough, and the people, being accustomed to its instabilities, seem not much concerned about them, but proceed in all their calculations and business just as if everything were firm and reliable. There prevails a peculiar delusion among the people, that each one seems to consider his own condition and calculations safe and reliable, while each sees that his neighbor is at the mercy of demon Chance.

"In this region dwelt a young man, who, having never been anywhere else, thought it the finest country in the world. He owned a considerable territory, embracing some beautiful views to be seen from his dwelling. It is uncertain whether he owned the property by inheritance, or discovery, or possession. Everything is uncertain in that country; and he did not scrutinize his title very closely, perhaps from a vague apprehension that he might find a flaw in it; for he was so charmed with his possessions that he could not bear to raise a doubt about their permanence. So, taking the validity of his title for granted, he proceeded to build a castle worthy of such valuable possessions, and such fine prospects.

"He laid the foundations of his castle on the spot which commanded the best and loveliest view upon his estate. He did not dig very deep for his foundations, for he thought chiefly about the superstructure, and he soon raised and completed it to his fancy. The front was of white marble, with spacious windows, from which he viewed with delight the lovely scenery before him. The rear and end walls were of hard granite, with massive buttresses, intended by their strength to protect the slighter structure of the front. Everything within and around was arranged in the most perfect order for convenience and taste; for he had employed two famous artists of exceeding skill, whose names were FANCY and HOPE; and, under their superintendence, everything was admirably planned.

"When all was finished to the satisfaction of the proprietor, he took great delight in looking from his spacious windows upon the prospects beyond. His happiness would have been perfect, but for occasional misgivings about his title, and regrets that he had not dug deeper for his foundation.

"One day, a stranger came, with whom the proprietor was much pleased, and who seemed very much to admire the beautiful prospect from the windows of the castle. The proprietor left him looking from the windows, while he himself slept for a while.

"When he awoke, he saw, from his window, that the stranger had taken a spade and dug a trench in front of his castle, so that it was impossible to pass out to his beautiful prospect beyond; and, though he could still see and admire it from his window, it gave him pain, instead of pleasure, because it was inaccessible.

"He saw, also, that the trench was dug so near his castle, that the front was already undermined, and was sinking to its fall; for, the foundation not being deep, it was easily overthrown. And when he knew that the stranger had a better title than his own to the land, and the beautiful prospects before his castle, and saw the impending destruction of all his possessions, he threw himself from his castle windows into the trench which the stranger had dug, and the walls fell immediately, with a tremendous crash, and buried him beneath their ruins. And this is the end, so far as I know anything about it."

As Alek proceeded in his story, Margaret perceived its hidden meaning, and that Alek had not failed to observe and interpret her emotion. Her heart beat with troublesome throbs. The surroundings of whalebone and steel, which, in polished society, confine, contract, or obliterate that important organ, were unknown in Wolfsden, and the hearts of women as of men, beat freely where rustic nature placed them.

But, before Alek had ended, Margaret had composed her thoughts, and she thus proceeded:

(*Margaret.*) "When the noise of the fall had subsided, the proprietor opened his eyes, and, looking round, found that nothing had fallen but a slight vase of flowers, and that he had been all the time dreaming; for there still sat the stranger, as sleepy as himself, and quite unaware of all the imaginary trouble of which he had been made the instrument. But, though the castle-builder was glad to awake and find himself whole and safe, he was impressed with the warning of his dream. He reflected upon the folly of building upon insecure foundations, and over-valuing prospects which he did not own. He remembered that in that fickle country the liability to change was an element which should be considered in every project; and that, as this could not be guarded against, it must impair the value of every possession, and leave less cause to regret its loss. He considered, also, that what was so insecure might also, in other respects, be less desirable than he had supposed; for, as he had not travelled, he knew not what valuable possessions might be unappropriated elsewhere, and to which he might obtain a better title. In short, growing still more doubtful and dissatisfied with his present position, he concluded to survey his castle anew. He found many things about it which, now that the glare of novelty was worn off, seemed misplaced, inconvenient, and even absurd. The castle was constructed in violation of all just proportions and good taste; the foundation was even more insecure than he had feared, so that he considered it unsafe even to return to waken the stranger whom he had left sleeping in the window. He then resolved to abandon his fancied possession without regret. 'I am young,' said he, 'the world is wide,—I will explore it further, and will only fix my habitation when I have skill to choose wisely, and can be well assured of my title.' And so he departed, wiser and far more happy than before; for fortune had in store for him choicer things than he had imagined, but of which I am not informed, and therefore end the story here."

All applauded the story and its obvious moral, though Alek and Margaret were the only ones who felt its particular application.

Isaac was next called upon for his story. Ike was humorous, loved burlesque, and paid little attention to the probabilities or the moral of his stories, and therefore generally ran into wild extravagance. In the present case the appointment fell upon Ann to finish the story.

MATCH STORY. — V.

(*Isaac.*) "An old man and old woman, and their daughter, lived together in a castle. — A castle is as cheap to put in a story as a cottage; so we 'll give them a castle, for they had not much else. The old man was a shoemaker, and his wife was a witch, and the daughter employed her time in making nets for cabbage-heads, and fishing for gudgeons in a pond hard by.

"The country about the castle was pleasant enough, though rather wild, and there were many very reputable and good people scattered about; but many of the inhabitants were ignorant, and some were bad and cunning, for the ignorant and bad often become cunning, just as the good and well-instructed often become wise. Of these the worst and most ignorant were witches and fortune-tellers, like the old woman in the castle. The old man was ignorant and bad, and also cunning; and, thinking it easier to get his living by his cunning than by industry, he went about to his neighbors and promised to bring them shoes, by and by, if they would give him food, and clothes, and money, now. So they gave him what he asked for, and he and his wife and his daughter ate heartily, and dressed finely, while the good things lasted.

"But the old man did not make the shoes which he promised; and when they had eaten up and worn out all they had, they were very poor; for the neighbors, who had been cheated once, would not trust them again; but still they could not be made to understand that honesty is better than cunning.

"So they concluded to practise the black art, which the daughter had already partly learned from the old witch, her mother, and by which they hoped to gain much money; and they went about in unfrequented places, and caught foxes, cats, snakes, and lizards, and gathered thistle-tops, and buttercups; and the old woman boiled them and made a kettle full of broth, and they spread the cats' skins for a table-cloth, and sipped the broth for many days, until they had acquired the nature of its ingredients, and were smooth, deceitful, ungrateful, and poisonous.

"When they had acquired all these fine accomplishments, they supposed that they should do very well, as they could now transform themselves into the shapes of all those odious creatures, and could return to their own forms when they chose, by which tricks they hoped to make their fortunes.

"Then the old woman told her daughter, whose name was Mewy, to curl her hair in little snaky tresses, and put some bright buttercup ribbons round her neck, and put on a pair of green lizard-skin shoes, and sit in the door, and purr like a cat, and look sly like a fox; and when a nice young man should pass by, he would stop and ask her to marry him.

"So she dressed herself as directed, and sat in the door, and purred like a cat, and looked sly like a fox. And a good many nice young men came by, and some of them stopped and heard her purr, and admired her sly looks; but none of them asked her to marry.

"At last, a nice young man came by when she was purring her prettiest, and looking her slyest, and he asked her to marry him. And she said yes, and gave her hand to the young man; and it felt soft and smooth as velvet; the sharp claws were drawn in.

"Pretty soon the old man came in, and, finding that his daughter had entrapped a nice young man, he spoke very civilly to him, and asked to borrow his watch, which the young man willingly lent, and went home very happy without it; for he was in love with the daughter, and he dreamed that night that he was lucky as Whittington, who became Lord Mayor by means of a cat.

"The next day being rainy, he took his umbrella and came and sat by Mewy, and listened to her purring, and took her soft, velvety hand, and admired her sly looks, and snaky curls, and lizard shoes. And the old man came in and borrowed his umbrella; and the nice young man went home and dreamed that he had been a voyage with Sinbad the Sailor, and had found a great many diamonds in the valley of snakes.

"The next day was muddy, and he put on his overshoes and went, and was entertained as before. And the old man came in and borrowed his overshoes, and he went home in his slippers; and that night he dreamed of King Midas, who wore asses' ears; and he was much puzzled and a little alarmed about its meaning, for the dream had been sent by his good genius to give him warning.

"So he went the next day to get back his watch, and umbrella, and overshoes. But Mewy had hidden them; and when he went to search for them she flew at him and squalled like a mad cat, and thrust out her sharp claws, so that he was glad to escape without watch, umbrella, or overshoes. And he dreamed that night about Christian and Hopeful, who escaped from the den of the Giant Despair; and he came no more to see Mewy.

"But there lived back in the mountains a countryman named Bruin. He lived there so long alone that he became very rustic and clownish, and, as he killed and ate many bears, he became much like a bear in manners and disposition; and, when he was tired of living alone, he came down out of the mountains, and asked Mewy to marry him. And she said yes, and looked sly, and purred softly; and he gave her a hug, like a bear; for he liked her very much, and knew nothing of her sharp claws; or, if he knew, he did not care, for his skin was tough.

"After a while the old man came in, and, seeing that Bruin was in love, and was also very fat, he begged to borrow some fat. But Bruin answered, roughly, that he had no fat to lend; and after a while Bruin went home, and dreamed that he had found a bee-hive, which, on trial, yielded no honey, but proved to be a wasps' nest. This dream was sent by his good genius, but Bruin paid no attention to it.

"When Bruin came again he gave Mewy another hug, and heard her purr, and was more delighted than ever. And the old man came in and begged to borrow his bear-skin coat; but Bruin answered, with a growl, that he chose to keep his coat for his own use.

"When he was gone the family had a consultation whether Mewy should marry Bruin. The old man thought it would not pay; for Bruin was too wise, and meant to keep his good things to himself. But the old woman was in favor of the match; for Mewy was getting old, and might not have another offer; and she thought that when Mewy was married to Bruin they might be able to borrow, or beg, or steal fat, and fur, and other good things, from him.

"But Mewy said she would not make up her mind just then, but would keep Bruin along, as she could marry him at any time; but, if she should have any better offer, she would dismiss him. So Bruin came frequently, and would hug Mewy, and she would purr and look sly, but would not name a day to marry him; for she still hoped for a better offer. And this is all I can say about it."

(*Anne*). "In another part of the country was a place called 'Happy Home.' It was a pleasant cottage by the bank of a beautiful stream, with green meadows, and fruitful fields, and shady trees, and cows, and sheep, and everything delightful.

"In the cottage lived a brother and sister, whose names were Manalone and Maralone; and the sister had two beautiful children, and they all four lived very happily in the cottage, and took care of their grounds, and had plenty of milk, and butter, and wool, and a fine garden, where grew all varieties of fruit. And the sister was a wise woman, and taught her children properly, so that love and contentment prevailed in Happy Home.

"But the brother one day had occasion to travel; and he saddled his pony and rode all day, and towards night he passed by a castle, and saw a woman with curls, and ribbons, and green lizard-skin shoes, and asked of her the way. And she looked very demure and amiable, and invited him to stop and rest. And the old man came out and urged him to tarry; and, being tired, he consented to remain all night. And the woman, whose name was Mewy, looked sly, and purred, and tried to appear amiable; but Manalone said he was tired, and went to bed.

"While he slept the family held a consultation. And the old woman said that she had heard much about Manalone; that he was generous, and gave away a great many things, and if Mewy should marry him they would all get a good living from him. And the old man said the same, and Mewy said she would try to get him.

"In the morning, when Manalone got up, they all pretended to like him very much, and gave him breakfast, and invited him to come and see them again. And he thought they were very nice people, and asked them to come and see him and Maralone at Happy Home. Mewy said she would certainly come, and then Manalone returned home.

"After a time, Mewy dressed herself in her best, and curled her hair, and put on her ribbons and her lizard-skin shoes, and commenced her journey. She walked fast all day, and at night arrived at Happy Home. Manalone and his sister were glad to see her, for they thought she was as good as she appeared.

"And she remained many days, and helped Maralone take care of the children, and pretended to love them. And Manalone thought she would be a pleasant companion to him and his sister; and he asked her to marry him, and she said yes. And he went and told his sister that Mewy had promised to marry him, and live with them.

"But his sister felt sad when she heard it; for she loved her brother and their happy home, and she feared that any alteration might lessen their happiness. And, besides, she had begun to fear that Mewy was not quite so good as she seemed;

for Maralone was wiser than her brother, and had learned to look more deeply into character. But when she knew that he had promised to marry Mewy, she did not oppose it, but hoped for the best.

"That night Manalone dreamed that he went a voyage with Sinbad the Sailor, and came to a desert island, and the Old Man of the Sea came and got on his shoulders, and he could not get him off. This dream was sent by his good genius to give him warning; but Manalone was too much infatuated to understand it, and pretty soon he married Mewy.

"When Mewy was established in Happy Home, she soon showed her real character; for, though put in possession of all the pleasant things she had coveted, she was not content to enjoy them in peaceful partnership, but was like the fox, of whose nature she partook, which, though fed bounteously, instinctively carries away his food and hides it, to eat in solitude. So Mewy sought by stealth, or violence, to obtain exclusive possession of the benefits provided for all. To this end, her first efforts were to drive Maralone from Happy Home; and she soon succeeded in making her position so unpleasant that she was compelled to go, with her two children, to another house.

"Manalone was unhappy when he found that he had brought trouble to Happy Home. He visited his sister often, and tried to comfort her. And Maralone talked with him, and told him it was best to bear their trials patiently; for there was another house building for them on the other side of the river, which they would soon be permitted to dwell in, and where no wicked person could come to trouble them.

"And Maralone appeared very bright and cheerful when

she spoke of this, although she soon grew pale and feeble; and after a while she told her brother that her house was ready on the other side of the river, and that she had great riches stored there, and also some dear friends were there expecting her, who had provided everything to make her happy.

"She also told her brother to get ready to follow soon; and then, being quite prepared, she went down to the river, and her brother went with her to the shore, and she stepped cheerfully in, and was soon out of sight; for there was a mist hung over the river, so that her brother could not see across it; but he knew that she had gone to another happy home, of which she could not be deprived; and, though he felt lonely, he rejoiced that she had passed away from her sorrows.

"And after that Manalone walked often by the river, and tried to look across it, but the thick mist prevented. Yet, as he grew old, and his face grew thin, and his hair grew white, his sight became clearer; and sometimes, as he walked by the river, he thought he could see sweet fields and beautiful dwellings, and many very happy people; and among others his sister Maralone, and others dear to them both, and *one* loved dearer than all, and that they were beckoning him to come; and he resolved that he would prepare to go as soon as possible."

Hezekiah was next invited to take his turn, to which he assented, premising that whatever interest they might find in his story must not be credited to his imagination, as he should only repeat the beginning of a manuscript story, long preserved in his family, and which Helen, having heard their grandmother repeat, was qualified to finish. With this preface, he began.

MATCH STORY. — VI.

(*Hezekiah.*) "The mysteries of the Salem witchcraft are such that time cannot solve them, till we know more of the spiritual world, and of our relations to it. Much of it was doubtless imposture, and this fact gave currency to the belief that it was wholly so; but there are circumstances which cannot be so interpreted without disregarding the strongest evidence to the contrary. The story which I am about to give could be supported by such proof as would be difficult, at least, to explain away, if any benefit could be anticipated from the verification of such wonders. But it seems useless to pursue investigation into the truth of facts, which, when established, cannot be understood, or employed for any useful purpose.

"There lived in Salem village — now Danvers — during the Andros administration of the colonial government of Massachusetts, a gentleman of the name of Levering, of high social position, and supposed to be very wealthy. He held some office, which required occasional attendance at the seat of government; at other times, and, indeed, most of the time, he resided at home.

"His house was an aristocratic mansion, situated upon a rising ground, and surrounded by a walled park, through which were various avenues, smoothly gravelled and bordered by box and other evergreens. The ample grounds, so well arranged, and neatly kept, the elegant carriage and horses, the costly style and furniture of the mansion, all bespoke the owner's affluence and taste.

"The appearance of the proprietor was in keeping with his estate. His air and manners indicated habitual superiority, though there was nothing arrogant or offensive in his deportment to those about him, who were generally willing enough to yield the deference which wealth and power claim from the humble.

"His wife, though seldom seen, was well known to be a lady of remarkable gentleness and sweetness of disposition, and possessed of that peculiar kind of piety which tends to humility and good works. She was regarded, therefore, with as much real reverence and love as her lord was with apparent deference and submission. Both, however, were known to belong to the Episcopal party, and were supposed to be church communicants; which, in that Puritan community, much impaired the influence they might have possessed.

"Apart, and at some distance from the elegant estate, dwelt Goodman Hobart, a plain farmer, of simple habits, but strong character, and highly valued by Mr. Levering as neighbor and friend.

"Goody Hobart, the good man's wife, was a quiet-looking, motherly sort of a woman, of a remarkable knack at keeping her house in good order. She had lost her two elder children, but her youngest, a fine boy of about six years, was enough to employ a mother's care and solicitude; and well he repaid it, for even at that age he could read the 'New England Primer,' answer the easy questions (by which is meant those with brief answers) in the catechism, and repeat the 'Dialogue of Christ, Youth, and the Devil.'

"Goody Hobart was more familiar at the 'mansion' than her husband, for the lady not only frequently sent for her under pretence of asking advice about domestic affairs, which was always followed by a cup of tea, — a rare treat in those days, — but would often come over to the farmhouse and spend an hour, taking great interest in the dairy, chickens, &c., which Goody was only too well pleased to show to so pleasant a lady. She also frequently invited young Azariah, and made him more familiar with the mansion than anybody else.

"After a time these visits ceased on the lady's part, but Goody's became more frequent; and, after a little longer time, Goody had the good news to tell that the lady had a fine little daughter; but soon after the good news was saddened with the addition that the lady was very low, that it was feared she was declining; and, after a few weeks, the fears were confirmed, — the lady was dead. Great was her husband's grief, for great was his loss. Goody Hobart was entreated to take the superintendence of his daughter into her own hands, which she willingly assented to.

"During the following three years, the infant Jane — for so she was named — grew and improved in every childish grace. At the end of three years Mr. Levering announced to Goody Hobart his approaching second marriage, and in less than a month brought his new bride to his old mansion.

"When Goody Hobart saw the bride he had brought to take the place of the favorite lady, and to be the mother to the child whom she had cherished so long, she felt an instinctive dread and aversion towards her, without knowing why. The new lady was tall and elegant in her person and manners, with a smile sufficiently condescending, and a self-possession and promptitude of action which indicated sufficient capability. Little Jane shrunk from her at first; but, being told by her father that it was her new mamma, came confidingly to her, for she had been taught sweet associations with that word. The mansion was again inhabited, Jane was installed by her father's desire in her mother's favorite chamber, and things were returned to their old order. But in their old order they did not long remain. The new lady chose to signalize her accession by innovations of no slight character. Painting, gilding, costly hangings, and rich and showy furniture, changed its former elegant but unostentatious aspect. Soon the old housekeeper and gardener were discharged, the number of servants largely increased, some of them put in livery, and all the modes of vulgar-minded display were adopted by which wealth may be made to excite envy, hatred, or contempt.

"By the lady's persuasion, her husband was induced to take a great share in some moonshine speculation then rife, in which great gains were promised to adventurers; and this, with the lavish expenditures of his lady, so embarrassed Levering's affairs, that he was driven into bankruptcy.

"He bore his misfortune with magnanimity, but its effects upon the lady were marked and violent. She was no way subdued or disheartened by the misfortune, but provoked to stronger and worse manifestations of energy. Her first efforts were to abstract and conceal as large a portion of the property as possible; and then to dispute, inch by inch, the creditors' claim to what remained.

"When the available effects were sold, and the establishment reduced to reasonable limits, enough still remained, with the income of his office, for decent support; but not enough to satisfy, or even mollify, the lady, who had not been content when in possession of the whole. She constantly beset her husband with complaints, reproaches, predictions of utter destitution, and assurances of the present contempt of all his acquaintances; for she could have no idea of respectability apart from riches, and since her husband had lost his wealth she had lost even the semblance of respect for him. In her harangues she urgently advised him to bestir himself and retrieve their fortune, giving numerous instances of others' success, and suggesting various schemes of her own, some of them absurd, and others of still worse character. Mr. Levering, lacking energy to repel these assaults, and tired of their perpetual din, took refuge in the bottle, to which, since his last marriage, he had become accustomed.

"His former intimacy with his neighbor Hobart had nearly come to an end. Neither the good man nor his wife were seen at the mansion; but Azariah, a tall, smart lad, of ten or eleven years, was a favorite with Mr. Levering, and especially with little Jane, who visited Goody Hobart's house with unrestrained liberty, where she was always gladly welcomed.

"Mr. Jeremiah Raven, a young clergyman, of solemn deportment and much zeal, recently ordained, and particularly recommended by the Rev. Increase Mather, President of Harvard College, as a young man of godly spirit and great promise, was at that time resident with Mr. Parris, then minister of Salem village. Mr. Raven frequently visited Goodman Hobart, and took a great liking to little Jane, which he manifested by much serious instruction and counsel, and by hearing frequently her recitations in the catechism. Azariah also shared the admonitions and instructions of the earnest young minister.

"About that time was frequently seen in that vicinity a stranger, whose appearance excited much attention and remark, because no one knew or could obtain any account of him. He was first met by some children in a retired lane, at a little distance from the village. He was a tall, well-formed person, of quick motion, though uneven gait. He wore a large-brimmed hat, not looped up in the fashion of the time, but flapping. His outer garment resembled the cassock worn by priests, and was of such length as to touch the ground. One of the children got a glimpse of his face, and described it as pale and thin, with a hooked nose, and a terrible sharp eye.

"After this he was often seen in various places, always alone, and walking quickly, but never far from the village; and never by more than one or two at a time, except when he was first met by the children. Sometimes his sudden appearance was extraordinary; for persons affirmed that when travelling the road, with no one in sight, suddenly the stranger would appear within a few yards, and pass without greeting, and, after passing, would disappear as quickly. It was also remarked that he was never seen, except at a distance, by either of the ministers, or other men of reliable standing in the church; but frequently by women, children, and the lighter sort of young men.

"Soon after, it was found that the mysterious stranger was an acquaintance, or had formed an acquaintance, with the lady at the mansion. It was not known whether he visited there; but he was seen walking and conversing with the lady in the dusk of the evening, at some distance from the house, and sometimes in the twilight, in places so retired as would have excited scandal, but for their extremely serious deportment; and it was observed that the lady became more gloomy and discontented than ever. It was also noticed that her formerly rather handsome countenance had become prematurely changed to an ugly and peculiarly unpleasant aspect; and her complexion became of a blighted yellow color, with innumerable small wrinkles, like those upon leaves exposed to a scorching heat, while her eyes, never remarkable for frankness of expression, were now always turned aside, with a suspicious glance. This was talked of more freely afterward, but noticed by several at that time.

"Mr. Levering, when at home, sat sometimes in the parlor with his bottle, sometimes in the library with his books, and sometimes with his daughter in her chamber, or in the garden. Since his loss of fortune the old housekeeper had been restored by Mr. Levering's influence, and she was now specially commissioned with the care of Jane.

"Little Jane's chamber was, as has been observed, that which was formerly her mother's, and in which the daughter was born. In the late renovation of the house, this room, by Mr. Levering's express command, had been left undisturbed. Everything remained as when her mother lived and died. Her favorite books lay upon her dressing-case; her work-basket, with its light implements, stood upon the toilet-table; the mirror which had reflected her fair form, and the portrait painted in her bridal bloom, still hung against the wall. Here Jane slept; here she said her morning and evening prayers; and here her father spent many pleasant hours with her, notwithstanding the untoward circumstances around, and notwithstanding his degenerating habits. Into this room the stepmother never came. Mrs. Jenkins' room was on another floor, a few steps lower, but nearly adjoining.

"A few days after the stranger spoken of was seen conversing with the lady, it happened that two young men of the village, Dick Furlong and Harry Wilder, being near the mansion, one evening, a little after dusk, saw a heavy wagon, drawn by four small black horses, stop suddenly in front of the avenue leading up to the house; several men, small of stature, but of wonderful activity and strength, commenced unloading heavy bales and boxes, throwing them with reckless violence over the way, and against the iron gate. The articles were of various sizes, but all evidently of great weight; yet the men handled and tossed them, one over another, as if they were bags of feathers. This they did with the most extravagant feats of activity, — vaulting, throwing somersets, leaping over one another's heads, all the time shouting and screaming in the most uproarious manner. One little fellow, with red hair and enormous whiskers, seized an iron-bound chest of twice his size, and threw it from the wagon sheer over the gate upon the gravelled walk beyond, where it imbedded itself deeply in the solid earth. There were many boxes and bales; some square, some like enormous iron kettles, some like coffins, and some bound about as if with the hides of animals; but all were believed to be filled with silver coin, and other valuables. The men were but a few moments unloading, though the load was large; and all this time their extravagance of behavior increased. One outlandish fellow, with large silver earrings, and with his hair braided behind in an enormous pigtail, seized a coffin-shaped box, and, placing it perpendicularly upon his head, marched up to the gate, and leaping over it with an unearthly shout, ran up the avenue to the house, where, with a toss of the head, he deposited it upon the door-stone, still in an upright position. Another, following his example, crowned himself with a huge kettle, and danced up the avenue in the same style, followed in like manner by the others. In returning for the remaining bales, they threw somersets over each other's heads, ran rapidly upon all fours, or upon their hands with their heels elevated in the air, and all the time laughing and shouting and uttering uncouth sounds, like words of some unknown language. The door was seen to be opened by the lady herself, and the strange porters, with their strange loads, disappeared within the house in the same manner. Meantime, the horses were impatiently pawing and neighing in the street, while a cloud of smoke ascended from their nostrils, and their eyes gleamed with strange brightness.

"After a few moments, during which, tremendous blows and crashing sounds, mixed with shouts and laughter, were heard in the house, the men returned, rushing down the avenue like bedlam broke loose, leaping and screaming as before, till, reaching their wagon, they sprang into it, and drove off with reckless speed, scattering a shower of fire from the clattering hoofs of their steeds, till they disappeared in the darkness.

"The main circumstances of this story were afterward verified by examination of the ground, where the deep indentations made by the wagon-wheels, the horses' hoofs, and the heavy boxes, long remained visible. Nor was the probability of the story at all lessened by the fact that the extraordinary shouts and noises described by the young men were not heard by others who might be supposed within ear-shot; neither at Goodman Hobart's, nor even by the housekeepers, or others in the mansion itself; for this only proved the diabolical nature of the whole transaction, as it was well known, and afterwards frequently proved, that the arch enemy can control the laws of sound when it suits his purposes. Further insight, amounting in many minds to a perfect explanation of the matter, was derived from the lady's immediately launching out into all her former extravagance, scattering money with ostentatious profusion. But it was notorious that those who received her money were not able to retain it long; it having the same tendency to fly lightly away as was shown when tossed through the air by the demon porters.

"At this time, Mr. Raven, having become acquainted with Mr. Levering through the medium of his child, occasionally called at the mansion. Walking in, one day, unannounced, he overheard the lady, in loud tones, urging her husband to sign some writing, against which he, though with apparent irresolution, objected. As Mr. Raven came in sight, the lady suddenly retreated; but he could see, notwithstanding her efforts to conceal it, that she carried away a large red book, with brass clasps. Mr. Levering welcomed him with evident gladness, as if suddenly relieved from something disagreeable, but gave no intimation of the temptation with which, in Mr. Raven's opinion, he had been assailed. Once or twice, indeed, he seemed as if about to speak on some weighty topic, and then suddenly changed his mind. Mr. Raven was deeply impressed with forebodings of some impending calamity to the house; but, as he could obtain no clue to the subject, he discharged his duty by earnest conversation with Mr. Levering concerning the value of the soul, winding up with the text, 'Resist the devil, and he will flee from you.' Mr. Levering heard with attention, but with no sign of that deep impression which Mr. Raven hoped to make.

"This was in the autumn, and soon afterward Mr. Raven returned to Cambridge for the winter, where he enjoyed the instructions of the reverend president, and also much of the companionship of his son, the Rev. Cotton Mather, then colleague with his father in the ministry of the North Church, in Boston. The encouragement and guidance of these learned and godly ministers was of the utmost benefit to him in preparing him for the trials and conflicts with the devil, which he was shortly to encounter. The 'Remarkable Providences' of the elder Mather, giving full accounts and proofs of many cases of witchcraft, was then a work of standard authority; to which the son had recently added his book of 'Memorable Providences,' relating to the same subject; both of which Mr. Raven studied faithfully.

"No events of note occurred at Salem village during that winter, except that the mysterious stranger was several times seen near the mansion. But in the following spring, when Mr. Raven returned and renewed his visits to Mr. Levering, he was struck with the great change in his manner, being much more reserved and gloomy than formerly; from which Mr. Raven inferred that the lady had prevailed upon him to sign the 'Red Book with Brazen Clasps,' the diabolical character of which he no longer doubted. Mr. Levering's uneasiness and impatience, when the subject was approached, was ample confirmation of those fears.

"One day, when Mr. Raven was passing into the library of Mr. Levering, he heard loud talking in an adjoining room; and, the door being slightly ajar, he saw the mysterious stranger, whom he had never before seen but at a distance, now in earnest conversation with the lady; the earnestness, however, being mostly on her part, he seeming to be quite *cool*, especially when we consider his probable character. It was only a part of the conversation he heard, yet sufficient to give a clue to the whole. 'I tell you,' said the lady, ''t was for twenty years — for twenty years, that I signed the contract.' 'And I tell you,' said the diabolical gentleman, 'that it is twenty months only; of which ten are already past. You may look for yourself,' said he, producing the identical 'Red Book.' The lady glanced at a page, and immediately assumed an attitude of horror and despair. The diabolical gentleman calmly reminded her that it was no use to fret about what could n't be helped. 'Besides,' said he, 'we can compromise the matter; — only get me a couple more good signatures, and I will extend the bond to twenty years.'

"But the lady sat fixed in stony rigidity, as though she heard him not. Then, springing from the sofa with a piercing shriek, she exclaimed, 'O, wretched woman! O, vile cheat!' intermingling her lamentations with the fiercest denunciations, and all the time springing about the room with hysterical and superhuman energy, so that her head nearly struck against the ceiling at every bound.

"While thus employed, the diabolical gentleman looked calmly on, with malignant satisfaction, until, the lady's energy being exhausted, she sat upon the floor sobbing convulsively, when he again renewed the conversation, telling her there was no need of so much fuss; the case was not so bad, after all; he was willing to be reasonable; concluding by telling her to get two more signatures, and the writing should be made to read her own way. The lady reminded him that she had already got one signature; to which he assented, but said he wanted two more. The conversation then subsided, so that the reverend listener could only hear disconnected words; from which he inferred that the contract, whatever it was, was being remodelled; and, hearing the word 'children,' among others, he easily divined the nature of the new conditions, which he piously resolved to prevent, knowing that his warfare with the 'Prince of Darkness' was now approaching a crisis.

"On passing into the library, he found Mr. Levering quietly engaged in reading; and, on inquiry, found that he had been no way alarmed, having not even heard the din and uproar in the room so nearly adjoining; of which being informed, he went quickly into the lady's chamber, but found no one there, save the lady herself, quietly sewing. The supernatural character of the event was thus proved, as also the fact that Satan can prevent the transmission of sounds, to suit his purposes, except to clerical ears, which are privileged to hear, in spite of Satan; for which, also, Mr. Raven found warrant in the text, 'He that hath ears *to hear*, let him hear;' which he interpreted to mean, 'purged or ordained ears.'

"It was well that Mr. Raven was thus put upon guard against the plots for entrapping the souls of the two children; for he was enabled, that very evening, to rescue young Azariah from a terrible danger. His father having sent him on an errand to a remote part of the farm, Mr. Raven, who was sitting in an open window, soon heard screams and cries proceeding from that quarter; upon which, taking a Bible under one arm, and a staff in his hand, he proceeded with haste in that direction. He found Azariah quite alone. Upon being questioned about the sounds, he had not heard them, nor seen any one; but Mr. Raven had seen a shadowy female form gliding through some bushes near a fence, which quickly appeared to change into a black animal, with a very long body, but extremely short legs, keeping in the shadows till it disappeared. Mr. Raven was fully convinced that his timely appearance had saved the boy from a dangerous, if not fatal temptation. The matter was laid before Mr. Parris, who agreed that it required active care and watchfulness, until some decisive measures could be adopted. Mr. Levering was also warned of all the circumstances; and, though affecting to disbelieve their diabolical character, and solemnly averring his own innocence of any engagement with the devil, in confirmation of which he repeated perfectly the Lord's prayer, which no one who has signed the devil's book can do, yet he engaged to watch carefully all proceedings in his own house, and especially to keep little Jane always in his sight, except when in the charge of the trusty Mrs. Jenkins, or when sleeping in her sainted mother's chamber, from which the lady always kept away.

"The lady and her associates, in league with the powers of darkness, are supposed at this time to have arranged their plan of proceedings on a larger scale; her first effort being doubtless to obtain the two signatures, which were partly overheard by Mr. Raven to be the condition of prolonging her own term to twenty years.

"It was on a gloomy evening, in the latter part of March, about a week after the last-mentioned affair, that Mr. Raven, who had been all day pondering upon these events, while sitting in the house of Mr. Parris, had occasion to go to the outer door. It was very dark; it had been snowing or raining most of the day, and a thick fog had settled down with nightfall into an Egyptian gloom. Suddenly, while standing in the door, he heard piercing screams and cries of distress proceeding from a northerly direction, and seemingly at no great distance. Returning immediately to the house, he armed himself with his Bible and staff, as before, and, without waiting for a lantern, hurried in the direction whence the sounds proceeded. Immediately he felt himself partly raised from the ground by an invisible power, and borne in the direction of the sound at a rapid rate. Although it had been perfectly calm when he started, the wind now blew in his face with great force, but not at all impeding his progress. His feet, as he successively raised them in his eager haste, appeared to span many rods of ground at each step, and always came down, though in perfect darkness, upon smooth and solid ground, though he knew he was passing where no road led, and though the ground was everywhere, at that season, rough with dissolving ice and snow, or soft and miry; and he afterwards observed that, while thus impetuously borne along, the text revolved in his mind as applicable to his case, 'And in their hands they shall bear thee up, lest at any time thou dash thy foot against a stone.'

"After being thus rapidly borne, or rather impelled along, for the space of an hour, the invisible power left him standing in a wild and solitary place, where a wonderful and terrific sight was spread before him. A large space, covering an acre or more, was lighted up by what seemed to be the mouths of innumerable ovens, from which murky and sulphurous flames, with clouds of smoke, were belched forth. Around, in a wide circle, irregularly enclosing the whole ground, stood giant forms, waving their arms, and brandishing strange weapons. These appeared to be the sentinels of the infernal camp. Enclosed within their magic circle were innumerable lesser demons, many of grotesque deformity and low stature, and of a dark color, but evidently of amazing strength, all still and silent, and waiting as if for some word of command. In scattered groups were others, all of like infernal aspect, engaged, some in feeding the sulphurous ovens, or pouring fluids into huge seething caldrons, and others employed in strange and obscene rites. Near the centre was elevated an altar, on which were spread instruments of incantation, intermixed with various vessels, filled, no doubt, with the deadly compounds of sorcery; and among all was seen the Red Book with Brazen Clasps. Yet no sounds proceeded from this strange assemblage, except now and then low mutterings, which doubtless were the secret forms and ceremonies of sorcery. Near the altar the most prominent in this scene of horrors, a monstrous figure was seen. Its form could not be clearly discerned. It seemed in a recumbent or prostrate position, like a huge dragon, of which the head and shoulders were uplifted, while the body lay extended for a great distance in the obscure darkness. Snaky heads arose on twisted and spiral necks from its huge shoulders, with arms and claws diverging on every side. It seemed that the Prince of Darkness had taken this horrible form for some more than common infernal purpose; or, perhaps, this was the very gate of hell, and this the Evil One in his accustomed form, and this his altar where his worshippers serve him with impious rites. But who can describe the terror that curdled the blood of the man of God, as he saw, dimly indeed, yet so plainly that, by spiritual aid, he could clearly make them out, a group, composed of the diabolical gentleman already so well known, with the wretched lady of the mansion, and the two children, Azariah and Jane, whom their devilish arts had inveigled, or their supernatural power (permitted for a time for wise purposes) had brought hither.

"Mr. Raven now understood the purpose for which, in this wonderful manner, he was brought hither. Single-handed and alone, he was appointed to confront and overthrow the camp of hell, intrenched upon their chosen ground, and in the moment of their triumph. The peril of the children admitted of no delay. 'Should such a man as I flee?' thought he. Looking upwards, he uttered a short and fervent prayer. Raising his Bible aloft in one hand, and his staff in the other, he rushed forward, exclaiming aloud, in the solemn form of adjuration, which, when thus authoritatively spoken, the powers of hell can never resist, 'IN NOMINE PATRIS, FILII ET SPIRITUS SANCTI, ADJURO VOS, O SATANAS, ET OMNES DIABOLI, ABSCEDITE.'

"At the sound, the infernal assembly were struck with a divine terror; and, as the hosts of the Midianites fled when the son of Joash and the three companies of valiant men shouted 'The sword of the Lord and of Gideon' (Judges 7: 20), this demoniac host shrank back in terror, and started in the very act of flight; when, either through his own fault, in not taking heed to his way, or, more likely, from the machinations of the Enemy, his feet stumbled, and he fell.

"He was sorely wounded and stunned by his fall, his Bible and staff fell from his hands, and the Enemy, taking advantage of his unarmed condition, seized him, to work all manner of afflictions upon him, even as they were permitted to use power over the holy Job, not touching his life.

"Four strong demons seized him, and bound him with thongs to a sort of bier, in a position of intolerable pain, so that he could not move, while hundreds, nay, thousands, of infernal creatures danced around, with exulting outcries and horrible grimaces. Overcome with pain and terror, he fell into insensibility; and, when again restored to consciousness, he found himself elevated upon a throne, and covered, in blasphemous mockery, with the impious vestments of the Pope, that whore of Babylon, while infernal devotees stood around; some offering a mock worship, and others holding aloft censers of burning incense, and idolatrously bowing toward a pyx, which they called the *host*, and pretended to adore; while others, at the head of a confused procession, bore on their shoulders images of a woman and child, which they called the Blessed Virgin, while they chanted songs of praise and worship to the senseless idols.

"He attempted to shout in rebuke of this blasphemous idolatry, but his tongue clove to the roof of his mouth. Determined to bear no part, however forced and involuntary, in these diabolical rites, he heard a voice speaking in his ear, 'Come out of her, my people, that ye be not partakers of her sins, and that ye receive not her plagues' (Rev. 18: 4). Thus warned, he sprang from his throne, and dashed through the surrounding legions toward a mountain which he saw afar off, and which he knew to be the mountain of the Lord. As he ran, the whole infernal company, determined not to suffer him to escape, pursued him with terrific yells; and, though they were not permitted to prevent his flight, yet they had power to distract, terrify, and mislead him. His course lay through a tangled wilderness, filled with thorns and poisonous plants, and infested by venomous reptiles and winged serpents, which filled the air and covered the ground. Doleful groans and shrieks resounded on every side, and the soil seemed like sulphurous, scorching lava beneath his feet. Creatures of human form, but of strange, distorted countenances, were driven hither and thither, crossing his path at every step, and pursued by malignant fiends, with whips of scorpions. An intolerable thirst was raging within him, and in all that dreary region no cooling water might be found;

but ever and anon a malignant demon at his side tempted him to drink of a cup which was filled with the wine of abominations and the blood of martyrs (Rev. 17 : 6). Long and tedious was the flight, and fierce and unrelenting the pursuit. At length, from the opening ground fierce blasts of *mingled fire and* smoke belched forth, blinding his eyes and suffocating his breath; and he felt himself lifted and borne aloft amid rolling and sulphurous clouds, from which dim lightnings flashed forth, to show the interminable horrors of the scene. He felt that this was the hour of the Prince of the Power of the Air, and that he himself was now roaming through the regions of despair, from which he saw no way of escape. Soon he felt himself cast into a deep labyrinth of perplexed and devious paths, where, at great distances, in each he could see a dazzling light, while around him was utter darkness. Yet, as he attempted to follow the light, it fled before him, and other lights in other paths tempted him to new pursuits, each flying and deluding him with fruitless toil.

"Suddenly he felt himself immerged in a lake of slimy water, offensive and revolting. He could feel no bottom with his feet; yet he was borne up in it. He attempted to struggle through it, but monsters beneath held his limbs with firm grasp. A brooding darkness overspread him, and he felt that the power of death was upon him. Long was the time, yet not measured by days or weeks; for in that dreary region there is no sun, that there should be days, and no blessed Sabbath, that there should be weeks.

"At length, ere he was aware, he found himself upon a strange and desolate shore. Ripe clusters of golden fruits hung pendent from over-spreading scathed and scraggy branches, and lay scattered upon the flinty sand. Yet when he gathered and tasted, he found only ashes in his mouth; they were the fruits of the land of Sodom and Gomorrah. Beyond these were steep and flinty mountains, where were the ruins of the dwellings of the Edomites, whose bones still lay bleaching in the sun; yet no living beast, or bird, or creeping thing, passed over it — all was utter desolation. Long and dreary was his journeying among these barren mountains, and amid these valleys of dry bones. He felt that he himself was but a walking skeleton, and that the dry bones, the fleshless jaws and eyeless skulls, were his companions; yet, when he would converse with them, they answered him but with uncouth sounds and unmeaning words, — for they were people of a strange language.

"Then he fell into a deep sleep; and when he awaked the power of evil enchantments had passed away, and he found himself, how conveyed he knew not, lying upon the bed in his chamber, in the house of his hospitable friend, the Rev. Mr. Parris, weak and emaciated, but surrounded by the familiar faces of anxious friends.

"It shows the wonderful and inconceivable power which evil spirits are sometimes permitted to exercise, that these guardian friends, including the Rev. Mr. Parris himself, were all unaware of the perils, and wanderings, and fiery trials, to which their poor friend had been exposed, and from which he had come off victorious, though sorely wounded and weakened; but believed him to have been for many weeks under their care, in the delirium of a fever. His form was doubtless simulated by the Father of Lies, while he himself was thus subjected to the infernal power.

"The end of this series of horrible events was now approaching. Mr. Raven had been for several weeks convalescent, and the summer was far advanced, with the approaching end of the twenty months which was the limit of the wretched lady's bond, which she could only have extended by betraying new victims to Satan's power, and which she had been prevented from doing by the providential interference of Mr. Raven. It might therefore be expected that the diabolical gentleman would soon claim his own; and so it fell out.

"It was a sultry day in August, when the lady, who had all the summer been gloomy and reserved, ordered the coach for a distant ride. She was doubtless aware of the impossibility of escaping her impending fate, and her pride dictated that the scene of her humiliation and woe should be remote from the scenes of former triumph and enjoyment. As the carriage was descending a hill in the north part of the town, a thick mass of clouds rolled over the sky, darkening the sun, and involving all nature in awful gloom. The howling winds were let loose, and the forests rocked beneath their terrible rage. Sheeted lightnings filled the murky vault of heaven with awful brightness, subsiding anon into ten-fold gloom. The thunder was heard, now remote and now nearer, like chariot-wheels of divine wrath. A fierce torrent of driving rain poured from the windows of heaven; the beasts of the field and the birds of the air fled for covert from the tempest.

"In the midst of this awful scene, when all nature seemed about to dissolve in ruin, there was a crash, as if all the artillery of heaven and hell had burst in simultaneous outroar. Looking towards the north, the villagers beheld, coming with frightful speed, the terrified horses, dragging the pole and a portion of the carriage in which the ill-fated lady had rode forth. Hastening in the direction of the hill, — for now the storm had passed away, — they beheld an awful sight. The coachman was thrown beside the way, sorely bruised, and bewailing his condition. A little beyond, the blackened corse of the lady was seen. The fires of heaven or of hell had blasted her form, and in one hour her great riches were come to naught (Rev. 18 : 17). 'And they arose and took up her body, and carried it forth to her own house; and great fear fell upon the church, and upon as many as heard these things' (Acts 5 : 11). And the matter was improved to great edification by the preaching of the Rev. Mr. Parris, aided by the Rev. Mr. Raven, whose experience in the affair had been so wonderful. But many Sadducees mocked and reviled thereat, for which they afterward suffered grievous punishments; and some, being convicted of witchcraft, were justly condemned. And to God be all the praise. Amen."

"This being the end of the story, according to the manuscript, Cousin Helen will have to supply her part from other sources."

(*Helen.*) "The closing part of the story, as given by Cousin Hezekiah, speaks of the Sadducees who derided the account. Those who disbelieved in witchcraft at that time were called *Sadducees*, by the Mathers and other believers, in reference to the Sadducees spoken of in the New Testament, who believed neither in the resurrection, nor angels, nor spirits.

"The manuscript from which the story is taken is accompanied with a written envelope of a somewhat later date, from which it is ascertained that the Rev. Mr. Raven was considered to have partly deranged his mind by too close attention to the mysterious subjects of which he treats; and, though an ordained minister, and considered a fine writer and earnest speaker, he was never intrusted with the care of a parish, but finally fell into obscurity.

"Those who attempted to account for his discoveries and statements in a common way, suppose that the conversation between the lady of the mansion and the diabolical gentleman referred only to worldly business; and that the diabolical gentleman was not really an infernal being, but only an attorney intrusted with the management of some bonds, or other legal papers.

"The lady's extraordinary calisthenic exercises were probably exaggerated by Mr. Raven's excited imagination, aided by his imperfect vision through the crack of a door, or possibly a keyhole; and the extraordinary noises and screams, heard on that and other occasions by himself only, were probably disturbances in his own brain. The story of Dick Furlong and Harry Wilder, concerning the demon porters and their load, was received with some grains of allowance, even at the time, on account of their known propensity to a certain license in narrative called 'drawing the long bow.'

"Concerning the extraordinary meeting of witches and devils, it is stated that a few people were quietly engaged in the process of making maple-sugar in a grove, when Mr. Raven suddenly burst among them in the manner described. The giant sentinels might have been trees seen imperfectly in the darkness. The shapeless and silent demons were stumps and bushes; the sulphurous ovens and seething caldrons were the sap-kettles and fires beneath them; the altar, with its infernal furniture, was a rude table with a few dishes; the extended dragon, with upraised snaky heads and claws, was the upturned roots and body of an overblown tree; and the book, with brazen clasps, but an addition of the imagination.

"When Mr. Raven stumbled and fell, as he described, he was recognized, and borne senseless to the house of his protector, nearly two miles, where he lay for many weeks in a delirious fever, the consequence of his exposure and fall, acting upon a frame already weakened and deranged by strong nervous excitement.

"The lady's fate was much as he described it, for she was either struck by the lightning, or thrown from the carriage and killed from the fright of the horses by the flash; but the coincidence of the twenty months is subject to the suspicion of all prophecy which is recorded only after its fulfilment. At any rate, the grounds for supposing the lady a witch are much narrowed by a close review of all the circumstances; and the most reliable fact of the whole story is that Azariah and Jane grew up, loved each other, were married, and inherited the old mansion many years, and in the lapse of time became the great-grandparents of Cousin Hezekiah and many other Hobarts."

Mrs. Simperkins, being almost the only juvenile who had not contributed to the round of stories, was next called upon; and, being suitably urged, and her diffidence suitably overcome, and especially being prompted by an encouraging word from the divinity student, commenced her relation. She proceeded to vex our ears with her old story of how, when a resident of London, in her youthful days (about ten years ago), she became the victim of misplaced confidence in a certain somewhat unscrupulous though exceeding high-bred COUNT FLIPPERTON, who adroitly obtained possession of property belonging to her employer, and left in her care, and also of a very valuable bracelet belonging to herself. We have scruples about appropriating the story, which is still her chief capital in the line of anecdote, lest we also should share the odium which Count Flipperton's conduct so justly merits; but, if her consent can be obtained, the story will be given in the appendix.

Meantime it may promote the ends of justice to give her description of the stolen bracelet. 'Hit was ha werry waluable hunique," being made of gold and diamonds, with a central brilliant, or star, of a single diamond, with rays of different costly gems, pointed with diamonds.*

While Mrs. Simperkins was going on with her story, the girls, who had heard it half a dozen times before, were preparing for departure; and Ann having whispered to Ike and Alek, they and Josiah Brown had silently withdrawn to prepare the sleighs, and soon all were jingling merrily at the door. The company were soon cloaked and hooded, all but Amy and the adjutant, both of whom had been asleep an hour, and were now snugly stowed away;—the adjutant to occupy the space between Billy and Tommy in their bed, and Amy to nestle by the side of Fanny. Josiah Brown evidently did not think the departure a very sad one, perhaps because he had secured the privilege of taking Ann to her home in his sleigh. In fact, nobody seemed sad;—it was a merry night, though the last of the year. Merrily pranced the horses through the snow. Merrily jingled the bells. Merrily laughed the light-hearted group. Merrily twinkled the stars, looking out, from their bright heaven above, upon the bright earth below.

* Any reader who may obtain information of a jewel of this description, or of Count Flipperton, may communicate with the author through the publishers, or by a line directed to J. B., care of Alexander Arbor, Esq., Wolfsden. And if this should meet the eyes of Count Flipperton, he is requested to return the property, as above, and no questions will be asked.

CHAPTER VIII.

Sleep rests upon the peaceful dwelling of the deacon's family, and all the house is still, save the measured and stately ticking of the ancient clock, which counts off in solemn numberings the last steps of the departing year. The cricket, too, trills forth its claim to a place in the list of living things. The deserted kitchen still glows with hospitable warmth and soft light, shed from the solid mass of living coals, into which the huge logs have subsided. Beneath the table lies the shaggy Lion, dreaming of sports and battles past, and often moving his feet in imaginary chase. Near his side, in long-tried companionship, purrs the confiding cat. Peace and sleep rest upon all the house.

In their snug bed, with their fair foreheads just discernible above the folded blankets, little Amy nestles in the arms of Fanny, as the bud nestles by the side of the opening rose. Lovely incarnations of beauty and goodness, thus ever in the protecting embrace of love and happiness may ye grow and ripen to your destined immortality! Tommy, and Billy, and the adjutant, are sleeping recklessly and determinedly, as if each were resolved to outdo the other. Each has a half-defiant brow, and a fist half closed; and each, by his earnest breathing, seems half provoked to burst into a snore.

Alek had invited the schoolmaster to share his bed. So many visitors require some doubling, and the cold night also favors it. The schoolmaster composed himself tranquilly, but Alek's pillow was not so easy. Thoughts which serve no purpose of thinking, broken, confused, tumultuous, undefined yet intense, swift yet coming to no conclusion, excited and harassed his brain. In vain he invoked his firm will, and commanded his distracting thoughts to peace. His very efforts at self-command awakened to more activity the busy machinery of the brain. The excited current of his blood rushed through all the channels of thought, and drove in rapid evolutions the wheels of the mind. He commanded his eyelids to close, and they obeyed; yet he was cheated of his will, for the eyeballs swelled and threw off their accustomed covering.

If he were alone, he would arise and escape from his confinement. If he could now, in the bright moonlight, plunge through the snow into the forest, with Lion for his company, how welcome would be the effort to his excited mood! If he could change the conflict within to a war with the elements, or with the bears and wolves without, there would be relief in that. But he could not escape, for he would not disturb his bedfellow, or allow his inquietude to be suspected. And so he lay in resolute silence.

He fixed his eyes upon the window, where the curdling frost had marked its fantastic tracery, now glittering in the silver light of the moon. In fancy he saw there the allegorical panorama of his life. He gave fancy the rein, and followed her visionary flight. She guided him through dense forests, bright with dazzling but uncertain light. His path led along a precipitous and dangerous way, into unknown scenes. A city rose around him. Magnificent and busy streets crossed each other in endless confusion. Rivers, parks, villages, and splendid mansions, filled the back-ground. An ocean, speckled with islands and adorned with tall-masted ships, stretched beyond. On the hither side, near his primitive forest, was a falling castle. It recalled to his mind his own story, and Margaret's veiled advice in its conclusion, and he mentally repeated it. "I will explore, and only fix my habitation when I have skill to choose wisely, and can be well assured of my title."

How still and cold shines the moon upon the glittering tracery of the frosty windows! How slow and solemn the distant ticking clock measures off the steps of the departing year! Peace and sleep rest not on all, even in the deacon's quiet dwelling.

In the parlor chamber, devoted through successive generations to ostentatious neatness and elegance, where a carpet woven of variegated list and yarn covers all the centre of the floor, and approaches to the walls, — where the painted chairs, and shining chest of drawers, and gilded looking-glass, reflect the brightness, but show not the rust, of their fifty years, — there, in the high-post bed, surrounded by snow-white curtains, rest Hezekiah and Harry. To them, who unite the claims of scholarship and strangerhood, is this dainty chamber appropriated; and very well do they seem to enjoy it. Hezekiah has already subsided into a calm and happy slumber. The course of his true love runs smooth. It needs not watching, — well and peacefully may he sleep.

But Harry seems not to care for sleep. He can dream without the aid of sleep, and dreaming is now his delight. He dreams that he is in the house where angels dwell. The brightness of one is reflected upon the others, and all are angels. He feels it reflected upon himself, and he partakes of the angelhood. How easy in such society to become angelic! He will henceforth discard the grossness and folly of earthly life, and commence now, in the brightness of his youth, a life of transcendental aspirations and enjoyments.

His eyes are fixed on the window where the bright moon silvers the frosty tracery. How fantastic, and yet how regular and beautiful, are the outlines sculptured there! Castles and cathedrals with pointed turrets, churches with tall spires, landscapes stretching in interminable perspective, oceans with opposing navies, islands with enchanting groves, — groves where love and innocence might wander hand in hand, where a bower might be built in which an angel might reside, where domestic bliss might give new interest to the loveliness of the scenery.

Only with restrained and guarded thoughts let us approach the chamber where sleep the beloved of those whom we now leave and commend to rest. Side by side, in quiet innocence, Helen and Margaret repose. Helen lies in profound sleep. Gently and scarce perceptibly rises and falls the drapery of her pure and peaceful breast. Gently, with even and tranquil beat, her pulse measures off the moments of her well-employed and happy life. The course of her true life and true love runs smooth. Peaceful and sweet be her sleep!

But why does that other heart beat less tranquilly? And why, as if compelling sleep to her eyes, does she compress their fringed lids till tears distil upon her pillow? She lies in seeming quiet; yet her mind rests not. Conflicting emotions disturb her peace. She is fighting the battle of life. She calls up every worthy resolve, and determines to conquer herself. Could she arise and go forth, that her body might share the struggle of her thoughts, it would be a relief; but she is constrained to stillness and silence, for her emotion must not be suspected. She opens her eyes and gazes upon the frosty window. Its figured outlines seem to represent the path of life. Here mountains rise in forbidding grandeur, and oppose insurmountable barriers; there yawning precipices wait for unwary feet; a cold, stern, and rough acclivity stretches between into the interminable and unknown distance, — interminable and unknown, perhaps solitary and sad. Yet it is the path where pride and duty and prudence point; and it is the path she will pursue. Sleep and peace rest not upon all, even in this tranquil home.

Yet the night wanes on; the stately clock measures off, in solemn numberings, the last steps of the departing year. Soon the hammer strikes its measured strokes upon the clear, ringing bell.

Departed year, adieu! the last,
  Last sand that measured thy career
Is gone; the records of the past
  Alone are thine, departed year!

CHAPTER IX.

SLOWLY moves the mighty panorama across the silent sky. The constellations which gem the brow of night decline in the west, for a dawning glory glimmers in the east, and the morning star heralds the day. From his high perch Chanticleer sends forth his morning summons. Soon from the chimney-top ascends a wreathed column to the sky, and from the kitchen windows the red light of the blazing fire within throws its glare over the snowy landscape. The long row of patient cattle, lying in their stalls, lazily uprise and stretch their strong limbs, as they hear the approaching feet, and the opening of doors by the hand that feeds them. The horses whinny their welcome, and expect their reward. Down from their perches fly the feathered flock. All claim their share from the abundant granary, and have their claim allowed. Around the cheerful fires come, from their deserted beds, by ones, by twos, and by threes, the sleepers of the preceding night; the rising sun finds no sluggard there. It was the mother's maxim that the Sabbath's true rest is not a self-indulgent sluggishness, but a permitted refreshment to the body, that the mind may arise to its higher exercises of thought and devotion, to favor which domestic cares and duties must be promptly and seasonably discharged, that all may share in Sabbath benefits to their full extent.

Bright and cheerful were the morning faces of the family circle, and kind and true the greetings of the happy new year. If there were troubled and anxious hearts beneath any of those smiling and cordial countenances, their secret burthens were unknown to others, for every face seemed radiant with happy content. Noble and generous hearts diffuse their own cheerfulness, but suppress and conceal their sorrows and fears.

Harry had determined upon a line of conduct at once generous, sentimental, and discreet. He will not betray, even in thought, the kind hospitality he enjoys; but will substitute friendship, warm and earnest, but unaspiring, for love. His heart, enlarged and filled with tender enthusiasm, reflects its light on every object, and sees beauty, goodness, and worth, in every face. Even in Mrs. Simperkins' self-complacent smirks and affectations he sees only an amiable desire to please, where the motive should excuse the mistakes. Towards Alek his friendship particularly expands, partly because he sees and feels his worth, partly in atonement for the involuntary injury which he feels half conscious of having inflicted, and partly because in loving Margaret, as he now represented to himself, with a pure platonic love, he must needs love those most nearly allied to her. Thus, though agitated by a deep emotion, which might otherwise have manifested itself to observant eyes, he managed to preserve the balance of his mind and the propriety of his conduct, and confirm the good impressions he had already made. Alek was the first and the most earnest to praise the noble endowments of the young visitor, whom he had so little reason to thank for coming; but Alek had already determined to yield to his adverse fate with the good grace which his manly pride demanded. His heart was sore, but that was good reason why he should compel it to rest. His self-appreciating thought suggested the desire to gain for himself the cultivation which gave Harry such advantages. His former good opinion of his own merits was very much unsettled; but his confidence in what he might *become* was strong. Appreciating and admiring his successful rival, he was very ready to receive and reciprocate his friendship; so that, actuated by different motives, and neither understanding the other, they became fast friends.

Poor Margaret seemed the chief probable sufferer by this new interchange of affinities. The capricious power, which binds and loosens the fetters of the soul at his will, had severed the early and long-accustomed ties which bound one manly heart to do her homage, while the one who could have repaid the desertion with far more welcome devotion was withheld, by honorable respect for the other's superior claims, from making advances. But she had schooled her mind to the strict discipline of maidenly reserve, and if she threw a veil over her deeper emotions, we have no right to remove it.

The schoolmaster held conversation with Harry, and was pleased with his diversity of knowledge, propriety of sentiment, and elegance of expression; for Harry knew how to acquit himself creditably when in contact with well-informed minds, as he knew how to shine among the volatile and frivolous. To the latter society he had been too much addicted; but now his feelings, and the current of his mind, ran in more serious and reflective mood, and added a thoughtful dignity to his manner and conversation.

Mrs. Simperkins was all respect, reverence, and obsequiousness, towards the "divinity student," whose good looks and polite behavior, in preferring her conversation, and talking Latin and Greek to her, rather than to others, had so perfectly proved his piety and discrimination. Uncle Lemuel and Aunt Nabby were well pleased with his popularity, and glad that they had brought so acceptable an addition to their society, though they hardly knew how to reply to Mrs. Simperkins' earnest assurances of his wonderful piety and spiritual gifts. The younger fry, with whom, and Alek, he had already visited the barn, and there delighted them with some practical jokes and gymnastic feats, had voted him a jolly fellow, and earnestly invited him to stay all winter, with glowing promises of infinite fun in sliding down hill and skating upon the ice; so that Harry was now, as usual, on the high tide of popular favor.

Breakfast ended, family worship was performed, as usual. The members of the family, including visitors, read the Scriptures, which the deacon occasionally explained. In prayer, the deacon knelt with such members of his family, and such visitors, as professed religion; while others were expected to stand in reverent silence. Such is the custom in Wolfsden, and all that region; so that to kneel in prayer-time is equivalent to a profession of religion. Harry, whose religious training had been Episcopalian, with whom all, whether saints or sinners, kneel and respond, was quite unaware of this distinction, and therefore knelt with the deacon; and, at the close of his prayer, innocently responded *amen*. He intended only good manners, but was at once set down by all the family as a professor of religion, and therefore entitled to be treated with more gravity than a mere worldling. Billy and Tommy, remembering his funny feats in the barn, and that, too, of a

Sabbath morning, thought it a new sort of religion; and as it came enforced by so good authority, and was much more in conformity with their sentiments than the Sabbath strictness which they had been compelled to keep, they concluded to recommend the change to their father, as a manifest improvement.

The hymn for the occasion was a new one, written by the schoolmaster at Fanny's request. All united in singing; but Harry's well-cultivated voice, naturally melodious and strong, though beautifully blending with the others, elevated its music beyond its usual character. Fanny was delighted with the success of her hymn; and Alek, who took some small interest in the "Philharmonic band," engaged Harry's assistance in the choir for the day.

There was quite a turn-out of teams from the deacon's, that day; but Alek was not careful, as at other times when Margaret had been one of the company, to have all in readiness so early as to anticipate the major's arrival. The major's family sleigh came along while Alek was still busy in harnessing the colts, so that Margaret went with her father and mother. Mrs. Simperkins, who had a motive to secure a proper reception of the divinity student at church, and thereby magnify her own importance, proposed to go in the major's sleigh; to which none objected. Once on the way, she expatiated to the major on the arrival of the divinity student, whose piety, and learning, and Orthodox standing, she vouched for, and expressed a decided opinion that Mr. Boreman should be prepared for so unusual a hearer. Major Murray inclined to the opinion that the parson should be prepared for so distinguished an arrival, and therefore urged his horse to unwonted speed. Dobbin demurred, but the major insisted, and they arrived fully five minutes before Alek's party came in sight.

Events were auspicious. They met the parson in the porch, and explained the affair. The group waited in the porch till the deacon's family arrived. Harry was then formally introduced, by Mrs. Simperkins, to Major Murray, and by him to the minister, and by the minister to Mrs. Boreman, the minister's wife, and by her to the fair and slender-waisted Lucinda, the minister's daughter. The minister invited the "divinity student" to sit with him, and assist in the exercises. He was astonished, and concluded at once that the essence of all the politeness in the world, as well as every other excellence, was concentrated in Wolfsden. But he declined the parson's invitation, on the ground that he had already engaged to sing with the choir. The parson's wife hoped he would make them an early visit, and the fair Lucinda looked a kind welcome; and Harry, always complying, promised to come. Uncle Lemuel and Aunt Nabby were a little surprised at this scene; but they were acquainted with Mrs. Simperkins' officiousness, and her presence explained it.

The parson had woven his dissertation upon the lost tribes into a long forenoon and afternoon sermon, for the new year. All the divine attributes were illustrated in a signal manner by his theory of their dispersion from their ancient inheritance on account of their transgressions; their banishment to the wild and benighted region of the western world; their long seclusion of three thousand years from the benefits of civilization; their judicial blindness and heathenism in consequence of their apostasy; their subjugation and extirpation; all which prove the justice and fearful vengeance of God descending on original offenders, and, through them, to their latest posterity.

In illustration and proof of the principle chiefly vindicated in this view, he cited the case of the children of Canaan, doomed to everlasting servitude for the transgression of Ham; assuming the Africans to be the Canaanites, and the slavery of the present age their appointed punishment. To this latter point he gave particular distinction and emphasis, considering it providential that he had put it into his sermon; for Mrs. Simperkins, in her hurried account of the divinity student, had mentioned his being the son of a southern planter, and he was willing that it should be understood in such high quarters that here in Wolfsden the scriptural supports and warrants of slavery were properly taught. Whatever may be thought of the philosophy and philanthropy of his sermon, its patriotism and conservatism were unquestionable.

There was but a short recess between sermons. The wind without was keen; but fuel, like everything else, was plenty in Wolfsden, and the meeting-house was warm within; and therefore many of the congregation, who came from a distance, remained and digested the sermon within the sacred walls. Not alone with spiritual food did they improve the hour. From many a capacious pocket came forth, in various packages, such samples of substantial fare as serious people may in good conscience enjoy. The more refined and fastidious were more reserved and private in their repast. The young women, and girls especially, munched their cake and cheese behind veils and kerchiefs, or with their faces turned devoutly to the wall, as though mindful of the proverb, "Bread eaten in secret is pleasant." Not so the children, who, each with a rosy-cheeked apple in one fist, and a huge doughnut, or turnover, in the other, ran about to the neighboring pews, as determined to investigate every other bill of fare before deciding upon the sufficiency of their own.

Meantime, Harry went to pay his dutiful respects to his grand-uncle, the captain. Alek accompanied him, and so did Uncle Lemuel and Aunt Nabby. The captain brought in the schoolmaster, in whom he found a former acquaintance. He also recognized and invited Hezekiah and Helen, so that a large circle assembled in his pleasant parlor. The old captain is genial — a genial old gentleman of the old school. To maintain this position is now his sole business, and he does it very well. In his well-provided and comfortable parlor the severe frosts of winter are tempered by the blaze and bright coals of the glowing hearth, and the frosts of age he tempers with timely supplies of toast and toddy; "And thus," says he, "I keep my outer and inner man in trim." By his outer man he means his skin, and by his inner man his stomach; and these, as he evidently conceives, make up his whole being. He is a regular attendant at Parson Boreman's meeting, and subscribes ten dollars a year to support the minister, and one dollar to convert the heathen. The old gentleman understands very well that a due regard for religion is essential to the perfection of gentlemanly character, and therefore he gives it his patronage.

The captain seldom discusses the doctrines taught from the pulpit; indeed, he generally nods in his pew, as one who is willing to trust his minister that he will go right without watching. But to-day he had gathered up some of the parson's remarks about the lost tribes, and rather dissented from that part of the sermon which identified them with the Indians. He had seen Jews and Indians enough in his day, and they were no more alike than a grenadier and a powder-monkey. The Jews wear long beards, and the Indians have no beards at all. The Jews deal in old clothes, and let money on pawn (here Harry winced a little); but the Indians have neither clothes to sell nor money to let. The Jews eat no pork; but the Indians eat hog, dog, and whatever else they can catch or steal. He, however, agreed with the parson that it was a good thing in God and our forefathers to kill them off, and put the country to a Christian use; and, if they were in reality the lost tribes, he thought it a pity the other two had not been lost with them.

Harry, who generally fell in with the prevailing tone of conversation, followed his uncle's lead in dissenting from the parson's expositions. He said that the offence which Ham gave to his drunken father, and the curse which the old toper gave to his grandchild in consequence, was rather a vague and unsatisfactory foundation for so extensive a superstructure of theory. If the curse had any effect on succeeding generations, it seems to have included the posterity of Shem and Japhet, as well as the dark descendants of Ham; for there certainly have been many more white slaves since that time than black ones; black slavery being of recent institution, while white slavery has prevailed extensively through all the nations of antiquity, and even at the present day, said he, there is a pretty free infusion of white blood among our slaves, often to such extent that it would puzzle Ham to pick out his posterity on some plantations.

The old captain presented a theory in explanation, by supposing that Canaan, when he heard his grandfather's curse, cursed the old man and all his boys back again; which would account, not only for the confusion of servile consequences following in after ages, but also for the habits of cursing which old men and boys are apt to fall into, where people are in the habit of getting drunk. Not, said he, that he would cast any disparaging reflections upon the venerable patriarch, whom he felt under particular obligation to reverence; and who, being a gentleman of the old school, might without censure be sometimes a little over-indulgent in wine, for which he had also an excuse of peculiar force, for he had certainly been over-dosed with water beyond any other mortal.

Hezekiah expressed his dissent from any defence of the extirpation of the Indians which might be derived from Scripture, as a perversion of the principles of the Good Book, of which the preceptive parts enjoin justice and mercy, and forbid cruelty and bloodshed, although the historical parts abound with examples of the latter, by no means recorded for imitation. He thought that our Pilgrim Fathers, though endowed with noble and manly virtues, were also fallible, like men of the present day; swayed by similar motives, and subject to similar self-delusions; often pursuing selfish ends, regardless of right, and afterward soothing their consciences by supposed warrant from Scripture.

The schoolmaster observed that the fate of the aboriginal inhabitants of this country must always present a gloomy page of history to the philanthropist; and, though the political economist might find ample equivalent in the vast increase of population and happiness resulting from their displacement, the Christian would still wish, with the apostolic Eliot, that the pilgrims "had converted some, before they killed so many." The character of the Indians has been drawn in too dark colors, in order to palliate the wrongs done them. The vices of ignorance and poverty must always be expected among the uncivilized; but, in making our estimate, we should take into account their capabilities, which, in such cases, should be judged of by favorable specimens. The history of Logan, of Pocahontas, of Tecumseh, of Red Jacket, and Osceola, prove the capability of the Indian race for whatever virtues have found praise among men; and in looking at their fate, and that of many like them, we must confess that the present good which we enjoy has grown out of much evil done to others. It will not do to shield ourselves from the reproach of wrong by pleading that the plans of Providence are thereby wrought out. The Indian race would undoubtedly have been extinguished or absorbed in the march of civilization, even if justice and kindness had kept pace with it. Perhaps they did not suffer more in the process of extirpation than other nations who have died by pestilence, famine, or inundations. The chief thing to be regretted, in all human suffering proceeding from human violence, is that *right* has been violated, and the moral sense of mankind corrupted, especially where the sanction of religion is sought and pressed into the defence of the act.

CHAPTER X.

We will do the parson a good turn by exciting public interest in his researches concerning the lost tribes, without so far satisfying curiosity as to spoil the sale of his dissertation. Therefore we omit the afternoon continuation of the subject; but must not omit to notify the reader of a meeting, this evening, of the Philharmonic Band, in Squire Noseby's hall. With what eager delight is the hour anticipated by the happy-hearted youths and maidens of Wolfsden, who, from far and near, gather in these weekly Sunday evening musical meetings, to do their part, either as zealous performers or admiring listeners. How full of music are their souls! With what alacrity they come from miles around, in sleighs so liberally loaded, through roads so recently broken, and still piled with many a half-subdued drift, the seat of many a funny disaster!

From far and near, from many a sequestered dwelling, in valley or on hill-side, from the wide circumference of happy homes, to the common centre of Noseby's hall, come the rustic youth, overflowing with energy and good-nature; prompt with politeness, uncultivated, yet true, because heart-inspired; officious with gallantry, awkward, yet welcome and well-appreciated. They come convoying many a fair freight of country maidens, whose shining cheeks glow in the healthy exercise with universal red, while their bright eyes sparkle with various hues.

To all these, however remote from fashion their abode, nature, ever the accomplished patron of the sex, has imparted the charms, the wiles, the graces, the all-prevailing power, which subdues generous and stout hearts, and vindicates the universal empire of love.

No neglected maiden pines at home for lack of a brother, or cousin, or lover, to escort her thither. A circuit of a dozen miles is a slight feat for the ambitious youth, whose partial pride exults in the fleetness of his steed, and the charms of his sweetheart. The heart-flowing sounds of merry voices, and glad, laughing shouts, mingle with the joy-jingling bells, and fling upon the echoing air a melody more cheering than the liveliest strains of even the Philharmonic Band.

Brief be our record of the brilliant company assembled. The fair Lucinda, of the many curls and slender waist, was there; by long prescription, the undisputed and unenvied belle of Wolfsden. Great was the sum of her attainments. She had explored the paths of philosophy, scanned the secrets of science, revelled in the regions of romance, and plumed the pinions of poetry. She had often kept the village school, and has been talked of as preceptress of an academy. Her presence was an honor and ornament to every assembly, and her fame belongs to Wolfsden.

Yet impartial fate scatters her favors with equal hand, and those to whom their own sex willingly award the palm of superior attractions seldom find their charms so effectually appreciated in the market of matrimony, as others, whom their fair sisters often spitefully disparage. So the fair Lucinda, sweet as the last rose of summer, still fluttered on the ancestral bush, while a hundred newer and humbler flowers flaunted in bridal bouquets.

Helen Arbor came. So seldom was her appearance where amusement is the chief attraction, that her presence was always noticed. It was noticed now more than ever; for a stranger accompanied her, one who evidently stood in some intimate relation to her. He was a dignified and remarkably good-looking gentleman. Curiosity was excited, for Helen had never before been seen so squired. What could it mean? Fortunately the Bowlers were present. Whispers were circulated, and the cat, so long confined in the traditionary bag, escaped once more, and roamed at will in the wonder-loving world. It was Helen's choice that the secret should come out all at once, rather than by the usual process of leakage; for, when everything is once known, gossip dies of a surfeit, and the world ceases to wonder.

Harry was there, of course. He was specially invited by the leader and chief singers of the choir; and, therefore, he came to please his new friends, — otherwise he would have come to please himself, for it is Harry's "genius" always to please somebody.

Margaret was there. If she were not, everybody would have regretted her absence. Margaret makes no pretensions on the score of music, — indeed, she never makes pretensions of any sort; there is no need; the diamond will sparkle, however unostentatiously it is placed. She commonly sits near the foot of the choir, with Hannah Bowler; but the chorister knows where the music comes from, and upon whom he may rely.

Margaret moved among the animated circle with a mild and retiring dignity, gentle and unassuming, but yet not self-forgetful. She felt her soul's superiority, and was not unaware of her personal attractions; but her sense was equal to the task of concealing her vanity, though she might not repress it. Hitherto she had thought little of her superior advantages, for she had no occasion to employ them,—no aim to win admiration or mortify rivalry, — so that her self-conscious worth rested as quietly in her thought as the conscience of a good man, giving solid but unseen enjoyment. But now that the calm current of her life had met a new and disturbing influence, her mind was excited to a closer self-examination, and it may reasonably be supposed that, in her close scrutiny of self, the fair exterior was not wholly forgotten. Yet who can explore, or, having explored, can describe, much less account for, the complicated emotions, motives, and methods, of the female heart?

Individuals blend in society, like tones in music, or colors in dress, sometimes with pleasing harmony and sometimes with disagreeable discord. Good taste will arrange each so as to produce the most pleasing effect. Margaret had the intuitive perception of good taste, and therefore she usually accompanied Hannah Bowler. Hannah was a little younger than Margaret, and only a little; not quite so elegantly formed, or so beautiful, but nearly so; a little less maturity of mind and sprightliness of wit, yet well gifted in both; a little less richness and fulness and compass of voice in music, but equally true and clear in tone; and in all respects adding a welcome charm to the society of her companion, and giving strength to her dominion, without dividing her empire. The alliance, though not concerted with that view, was mutually advantageous in its magnifying effect, as when a brilliant barrister forms a partnership with one less eminent, preserving, and perhaps increasing, his own importance, while he reflects the lustre of his fame upon his humbler brother.

The chorister knew well what voices would blend with best effect. A composition for two voices was included in the order of exercises. He requested Harry and Margaret to perform it. To refuse was impossible; yet how, with palpitating hearts and perhaps tremulous voices, could they sing? Each was unconscious of the emotion of the other, yet both were equally embarrassed. Harry had never before met an emergency to which he did not feel himself equal. Yet he had often declaimed before censorious judges, and wrangled with invidious rivals, and had sometimes been called to render account before grave and reverend professors; or, worse still, to meet a monstrous bill of irregular and disreputable expenses, with an exchequer already exhausted. With strong effort he concealed his emotion; or, if some few observed it, they readily imputed it to the natural diffidence of a young man among strangers. A fine notion, truly! Harry Boynton embarrassed by a Wolfsden audience! It was the audience alone which sustained him; otherwise, how could he proceed with the thrilling emotions which the unexpected proposition excited? Yet he did proceed in his best style; and, though Margaret's voice was thought to be a little less full and clear than usual, yet the marked and silent admiration of the audience, and the gratified expression of the chorister, showed that their performance was not a failure. At the request of Colonel Bowler, they again performed the duet; and this time Margaret's voice was full and firm, so that even Harry, who expected nothing less than perfection from such a source, felt his high estimate fully realized.

"That 's what I call singing," whispered Ike to Alek. Alek assented, with a delighted ear, but a heavy heart. It was to him sadly beautiful, like the requiem of departed joys and hopes.

The divinity student rode the topmost wave of popularity. A frank address and good voice were always a passport to the confidence and esteem of the villagers of Wolfsden. Cordial civilities and earnest invitations overwhelmed him. Squire Chinby, from the "North Neighborhood," was introduced, and earnestly invited him to visit that part of the town. The "North Meeting-house" was a sort of rival religious institution, built up by the union of several scattered fragments of different sects. It was four or five miles from the centre of the town, and was only casually supplied with a minister, being commonly a meeting of exhortation and miscellaneous exercises. Sometimes an itinerant preacher startles the echoing walls with a new voice, and perhaps new notions of divinity. The walls receive and echo back, with impartial assent, each varying form of doctrine. The more discriminating audience receive and respond with less unanimity. Yet each new preacher finds some to support and "bear testimony" to the truth of his teachings, while on every occasion dissent may be seen plainly marked on many faces; for none come to be convinced or to be swerved from their long-cherished faith, or from the doctrines to which they are committed, but all to hear their own opinions repeated, and their neighbors refuted. When a Calvinist comes, though he should say nothing of election and reprobation, Mr. Clack and his wife detect him, and look querulous and dissentient, but Mr. Click and his wife look pert and "edified." If a Freewill Baptist hold forth, Mr. Clack and wife listen with pleased eyes and ears, and nod assent to each other and their neighbors at each well-put period; while Mr. Click and wife, though listening earnestly to detect contradictions and unscripturalities, put on all the mask of indifference. When the Methodist, in turn, finds his way there, neither Clack and wife nor Click and wife find spiritual food in sermon or prayer; but Mr. Clock and wife are ecstatic with illumination. They mutter audible amens in sermon, and give groans of gratification in prayer. Mr. Cluck, the Universalist, helped build the meeting-house, and sometimes vindicates his right to be taught what he already pretends to know, and invites a stray Universalist preacher; and then all the other vowels look glum at what he calls the "glad news;" that is, the old vowels look glum; but there are graceless young Clacks, Clicks, and Clocks, as well as Clucks, who approve of Universalism out of spite, and, though they have no peculiar predilection for the tedious heaven, "where congregations ne'er break up, and Sabbaths never end," yet they choose to have the gates thereof kept open, as an alternative retreat from the fiery and unsavory opposite. Thus each is fed in turn with the food his sectarian palate affects; the sectarian spirit is kept sharp, and the "union meeting-house" is well filled.

Squire Chinby is recognized as the great man of the region, which is often called the "Chinby neighborhood." He is an independent farmer, — one of the selectmen, keeps the Chinby school in winter, and leads the singing in the union meeting-house. He pretends to no preference of sects, and sings dolorous reprobation or exulting universal salvation, in their appropriate tunes, with impartial execution. All the vowels say that he is a Gallio, "caring for none of these things;" yet his influence is decisive with them all. Such is the advantage of a non-committalism. They each hope yet to get him on their side, and therefore speak him fair.

Chinby has a large family, all good-looking; but his two blue-eyed daughters look best of all. They are the prettiest and best-dressed girls in the region. All Chinby's things look well; he takes pride in having everything, including himself, look well.

Chinby pressed the invitation to the "divinity student" to come to their meeting next Sunday. There was to be a celebrated minister there, — a heathen missionary; for so he, with malicious humor, designates the missionary to the heathen. The "divinity student," however, was not much attracted by the promised treat, and rather evaded the invitation, till Chinby introduced his blue-eyed daughters. Then he somewhat relented; observing that he was in his friend Alek's hands, but should come if possible. Alek, thus appealed to, readily promised to bring his friend; and thus Parson Boreman, who elaborated his sermon for the next Sunday with peculiar care, that the divinity student might know what it is to be a minister, lost his labor, so far as Harry was concerned.

Alek still held his resolve to be quiet. He determined that none should suspect his trouble. His unrequited love and wounded pride, already sore enough, shrunk from the blistering salve of sympathy, so generally applied in such cases. So he kept secret the disorder of his heart, and wore a brave face.

Wounded pride, though often the bitterest ingredient in the cup of disappointed love, added little, however, to Alek's grief. His self-estimate was based on such strong convictions of his capabilities, that he was not much humbled. He cast his mind forward to overlook the intervening space which separates present gloom from the possible brightness of the future; for his inquietude was that which inspires resolve and prompts effort, even in desperation. In the smooth current of reciprocated love his manly virtues would have been gently and surely developed, but his deeper and dormant energies might not have been awakened. The deep strife of his passion roused his soul to a new self-estimate, and new resolve. The day was to him an epoch. It finished the soft and pleasing dream of the past, and filled him with a sense of the faculties by which he must work out the untried duties and unknown destinies of the future. The hopes and remembrances so dear to him he would not regret nor cast away; but he determined to remain no longer in their view. He repeated his resolve of quiet — the quiet of firm resolve.

Harry was happy enough. It was his genius to be happy. The bright side of everything reflects its brightness upon him. When the resources of enjoyment are abundant, he revels in them; when they fail, he is none the less happy. Whatever is pleasant in his possession he enjoys. The pleasant possessions of others give him equal pleasure. As once a learned Bonze followed a rich and ostentatious Mandarin, repeatedly thanking him for his jewels, "Friend," said the Mandarin, "why thank me? I give thee none of my jewels." — "True," replied the Bonze; "but you permit me the pleasure of looking on them, which is all that even yourself can enjoy." So Harry enjoys every pleasant thing, regardless of possession.

The deep fountains of his feeling were opened, and the repose of his soul's quiet disturbed; yet the element of self-satisfaction still prevailed, and will still prevail, whatever results may follow.

He appeared more thoughtful, more earnest, more manly, than before, but not the less bright and joyous. He thought of Margaret as the knights thought of their lady-loves, invested with unapproachable grace, whom the privilege of sometimes seeing and always adoring was its own ample reward; and with whatever pangs strong emotion and uncertain hope pierced his heart, they still more endeared to him their object, as Tony's fair cousins loved best the books which made them cry the most.

Alek and Harry were fast friends. Though so different in their experiences, habits, and elements of character, their differences were such as combine in mutually agreeable and profitable companionship. Harry had looked abroad, and learned the knowledge and the ways of the world. Alek had looked within, and drawn knowledge from the heart. Each surprised and pleased the other with novel ideas. Each imparted, received, and shared with the other, in social feeling and generous confidence. Yet upon one subject both were instinctively silent; and that very silence suggested mutual inferences vague and erroneous in both. Each generously awarded the chief interest in Margaret to the other, and each with equal pangs of regret.

Next Sunday promised a nice day for enterprise. A week's fair weather had made the sleighing smooth, and Alek arranged a party to patronize the "heathen missionary.'

Margaret was invited, but declined. The Simperkins was not invited, but strongly inclined to go. Heathen missionaries are her delight. But remembrance of disasters past, and fear of like catastrophes to come, deterred her. She was also piqued at the neglect of the "divinity student," who had learned to whom he owed the reverence for clerical dignity which had so much annoyed him. It was not from delicacy of sentiment, but fear of some mad freak, by way of punishment, that she did not, in some of her irresistible ways, press her claims to make one of the devotional party to the North Meeting-house.

But the pung was well filled, nevertheless, and fleetly the spirited colts skimmed the road. But, swift as they went, Harry's fame had preceded him; and he was received by young and old with the reverence, and scanned with the criticism, due to a scion of divinity. He was half amused and half vexed, and meditated how he should shake off his unmerited and unwelcome honors. Fortunately the missionary soon arrived, and absorbed most of the reverence and criticism kept on hand for such occasions. Fortunately, also, the worshippers at the union meeting-house are careful not to commit themselves by too much cordiality, or too much criticism, till the sectarian character of the claimant shall be known. It was uncertain what wind of doctrine the young man might have brought with him; and Clack, Click, Clock, and Cluck, each devised their plans to sound him.

Meantime the missionary took his position. Harry recognized him, at once. It was Rev. Titus Twangson, one of the devoted and self-sacrificing band who sailed, some two years before, in his uncle's ship, the "Main Chance," from New York, bound for the Sandwich Islands. Harry was at that time a visitor at his uncle's; and, as the missionary ship was then a chief object of interest with the family, he frequently went on board, and became quite well acquainted with its arrangements, from the splendid cabin and saloon devoted to the missionaries and their wives, to the less inviting forecastle devoted to the sailors. The cargo of the Main Chance was made up partly of barrels of New England rum, with muskets, powder and ball, and boxes of hardware, some of which, marked "Hints for Brawlers," "Peace Persuaders," "Kentucky Codes," &c., excited his curiosity, till told they were daggers, bowie-knives, and other trinkets of commerce. Harry had previously, like many other thoughtless boys, felt a strong inclination for the excitement and adventure of a sailor's life; but the conversation at his uncle's concerning the great work of the missionaries, and the great rewards to follow, and especially a comparison of the cabin and saloon with the forecastle, gradually changed his views in favor of a missionary life; in preparation for which, he cultivated a sentimental acquaintance with Miss Neverspin, a young lady about his own age, and one of the missionary's daughters, who, with her parents, sojourned a few days at his uncle's while the ship was in preparation for departure. He also formed a particular acquaintance with Mr. Ramble, second mate on board the Main Chance, — a young man of superior education and congenial disposition, who promised to communicate to him whatever of interest he might find in the voyage. Harry witnessed the celebration of the departure of the missionaries, and helped sing the parting hymn.

> "I must leave you, I must leave you,
> Far in heathen lands to dwell."

But Mr. Twangson did not dwell long in heathen lands; for he had returned, some few months since, to recruit his health, and awaken missionary zeal at home, by telling his experiences among the heathen. Harry had already been informed, through Mr. Ramble, of a portion of his experiences, especially that he had entered into a matrimonial engagement with Miss Neverspin, which was to be fulfilled on his return. Harry, of course, hated the missionary who had thus supplanted him. Not that his heart was wounded by Miss Neverspin's inconstancy; for his own tender remembrance, as well as his missionary zeal, had faded away long ago. But it was provoking to have the tender reminiscences recalled by the presence of his successor. Therefore, though having no real cause of provocation, he felt a kind of good-natured malice against the missionary, as though he should like to see him "cornered," or upset in a snowdrift, or something of the sort, which might ruffle but not hurt him.

The missionary performed the services of the day with the grace and readiness which habit gives. He depicted in gloomy colors the degradation of savage life before the advent of the missionaries, and summed up the countless loss of souls through idolatry and want of Christian instruction. He spoke in general terms of the sacrifices and privations of the missionaries' life, separated from native land and cultivated society; but represented them as willing to do and suffer all, for the souls of the heathen, of whose worth he made a high estimate, and by a plain arithmetical process proved the profits of their redemption. He earnestly recommended the formation of a union missionary society, auxiliary to the American Board, to be aided by a sewing-circle of the ladies; and also the children should be permitted and encouraged tc help by the cent-a-week plan, upon which "infant offerings" he laid much stress; and, by his economical calculations and pathetic appeals, he persuaded many a tender mind to forego the customary stick of candy,— the cost of which might prove, in some future age of eternity, to have been the price of a soul, — and to put the money into the mission-box, and thus lay up treasures in heaven. By way of exciting emulation, he gave accounts of the zeal and liberality of other places, some of which had guaranteed a certain sum annually, and some had assumed the responsibility of educating and supporting a missionary in the field. He suggested several ingenious expedients for increasing the interest and swelling the contributions for the cause; and praised the memory of several pious benefactors, who had left liberal bequests in their wills, thus leaving a record which would not be forgotten at the judgment-day.

When he concluded, Mr. Click, wearing the well-pleased countenance of one whose doctrinal star is in the ascendant, partly to signalize his triumph, and partly to show his soundness of doctrine, made a speech in support of the views of the minister. The other vowels, partly to cover their retreat from the vanquished field, and partly to prove their independence, made commonplace, non-committal speeches. Mr. Click, wishing to pursue his victory, looked significantly towards Harry, and presuming, from the circumstance of his being a divinity student, and a visitor at Deacon Arbor's, that he would be a good ally, arose, and "hoped that the young brother from abroad, who had doubtless given the missionary subject his prayerful consideration, would favor them with his views."

Harry felt himself in "a tight place." Without fault of

his own he was in a wrong position. Half vexed and half amused at the absurdity of the blunder, he resolved to right himself in such a way as to throw the embarrassment of the mistake upon those who had made it. The meeting had already assumed something of a debating character, and therefore the way was open for him. He felt stimulated by various motives, principally mischievous, to take the negative, in opposition to the minister, who, he perceived, had not the general and zealous support of the majority.

He rose and expressed himself willing to give his opinion upon the subject, for he always felt liberal in the way of advice, however parsimonious he might be in other matters. The question, like all others of a moral or economical nature, had two sides, both of which should be fairly considered in making up judgment. Religion is an excellent thing, especially when it makes people better; it is good for something when it only makes them *appear* better,— for decent hypocrisy is not so bad as open profligacy. It is better that the outside of the cup and platter be clean than to be dirty on all sides; though it should be considered that this convenience may cost too dearly, as is often the case when things pass for what they are not, thereby shutting out the demand for the true article. "As," said he, "should the people generally become satisfied with a religion which dispenses with truth and honesty, and other essential items of morality, perhaps the world may be the loser upon the whole, however some parties might profit by the traffic." He presumed, however, it was the general intention to send the true article to the heathen, whatever might be kept for home use. Still he thought the expediency of the enterprise was an open question. The data relied upon to prove the economy of saving the heathen should be closely examined. Admitting their inestimable worth, two points remained to be proved: First, that their loss is certain without missionary aid, and second, that missionary aid could save them. Upon the first point he would not argue, as it involved theological questions, which he said emphatically never had been his study. He would only observe that a very numerous and respectable Christian sect believed that God would finally save all mankind, and supported their belief by Scripture (here Mr. Cluck, the Universalist, brightened up); perhaps he would save all who are worth saving, and it would be poor economy to go further than that. As God is to be the final judge, it is right to assume that he will be a good judge, and, if he had decreed the utter reprobation of some, they might depend that it was for good reasons (here Mr. Click, the Calvinist, looked approvingly); but he was of opinion that everybody would have a fair chance for a free choice, and would not be damned but by their own free will (here Mr. Clack, the Free-will Baptist, nodded assent), and there might be good hope of a good time coming, when all the world, and the isles of the sea, would land on Canaan's happy shore, and shout glory to God together. (Here Mr. Clock, the Methodist, fervently shouted, Amen.)

As to the other point, concerning the competency of the missionaries to save the heathen, something might be said. He had received some direct and reliable accounts from the Sandwich Islands, the most famous missionary ground, which showed that rather a low morality prevailed there, even among the most cherished converts. He proceeded to detail facts concerning the prevalence of polygamy, concubinage, drunkenness, theft, serfdom, compelled ignorance, degradation, and subjection of the masses to the irresponsible and abusive power of the chiefs, and the absence generally of all the principles which Christianity pretends to, and argued that the religion which did not show better fruits in this world afforded a poor promise for the next, and might be dear even at a cent a week. His sarcasms became so severe, that Mr. Twangson, who had for some time been uneasy, rose and observed that the friend's remarks did not appear wholly appropriate to the occasion, and that the time had arrived for concluding the meeting; but Mr. Cluck, the Universalist, interrupted him, saying that the brother had been invited to speak, and must be permitted to proceed, adding, with emphasis, that this was a free house for all sides. Mr. Twangson, seeing no remedy, yielded, and Harry proceeded.

He said that, even conceding the points just argued, the question remained whether a shorter and cheaper way of doing the work might not be adopted. Why spend so many years and so much money to teach missionaries Greek and Hebrew, to convert the heathen? Would not carpenters, and fishermen, and tent-makers, and farmers of the right sort, do as well now as in olden time? He considered it a poor preparation for missionary hardships, if such there were (though he had heard of some luxuries on missionary ground, and had seen something of missionary cabins and saloons, which gave him the suspicion that the missionary lot was as good as the average lot of life). Yet, allowing the hardships, he thought a college life a poor preparation for them, not only physically, but morally. He had seen enough to know that. If he had a genius for anything, it was for withstanding temptation; but he suspected that even himself was less qualified to teach things essential to make the right sort of men and Christians than his friend here (patting Alek on the shoulder), who had been brought up in the bush, innocent of a college, or than either of the brethren who had addressed them, *from the pews*, with so much sound doctrine.

The timely and graceful compliment to all the vowels with which Harry concluded his speech served to soften any dissatisfaction which he might have excited in some; and Harry, though the partisan of none, had succeeded in generally pleasing or conciliating an audience made up of adverse elements.

Mr. Twangson, after giving notice that he should preach upon the subject next Sunday in Rev. Mr. Boreman's meeting-house, and should remain in town during the week to coöperate with the friends of the cause, dismissed the meeting. Mr. Chinby urged Alek, with all his company, to go to his house for dinner, and remain to an evening concert. Alek declined, but suggested that his friend Harry might remain, and he would come for him, and be present at the concert. Harry consented to the arrangement, and presently was snugly stowed in Chinby's family sleigh, with half a dozen happy-looking Chinbys, including the blue-eyed daughters, as pretty and well-dressed as ever. Chinby's horse moved off with his load as though he liked it. The snow from his hoofs rattled against the fender, and flew over the sleigh. The keen air, as they glided rapidly along, congealed their breath in white frost upon hair and eyelashes, and gave a glowing red to cheeks and noses. None the less bright and happy-looking are the half-dozen Chinbys; not the less pretty, the blue-eyed daughters. It is but a mile in distance; and in a few minutes they were at Chinby's door. The very door-yard speaks the character of the man,—prompt, provident, neat, hospitable, and happy. The ample wood-pile rears itself a high barrier against the biting north. On the south, elevated on ambitious legs, the corn-house exhibits, through latticed crevices, its golden stores of shining ears. Upon the east a row of barns and sheds form a high enclosure open to the south, where, in the gathered sunshine, stately oxen, and quiet cows, and meek-looking sheep, and querulous geese, and cackling hens, make a miscellaneous assemblage, among which the self-inflated turkey-cock struts and ruffles his feathers with the well-grounded pride of some "Ancient and Honorable Artillery" officer.

The kitchen receives us with a cheerful welcome. It is the kitchen, yet, for pleasant and inviting aspect, it might vie with the proudest saloon of fashion, so clean, so light, so bright, so pure and fresh its atmosphere. From its wide fire-place the glowing heat radiates through the ample room, and is reflected from the white floor, and its long-worn but still substantial furniture. In his round old arm-chair, near the chimney-corner, sits the superannuated father and grandfather of the family; for Squire Chinby, though sixty years old, is but a younger son, and Grandfather Chinby verges upon his hundredth year. Grandfather is quiet, cheerful, and happy. He needs but little help, though everybody wants to help him; for everybody honors him. He moves about the house, and in pleasant weather visits the barn and the nearer fields. His son the squire, though, in fact, needing no advice, always asks his father about the more important farming operations; and the old man is as clear-headed as ever, and often gives really valuable hints. He says it is pretty late in the evening of life for him to be up; but soon it will be morning, and then he expects to be as bright and early as the best of them.

Mrs. Chinby, wife of the squire, and mother of the rest of the family, is of delicate appearance, and infirm health. She has long been unable to superintend her household affairs; but her blue-eyed daughters, scarcely sixteen, have for years kept things right. Look about you, and see if anything is wrong. Every room is as neat as this, and always so. And the daughters, do they not look equally agreeable? One would like to have such daughters of his own; or, at least, to live always with such as these.

A pleasant, mild-looking man, of intellectual countenance, and more delicate appearance than is common in the country, is introduced. He reaches out his hand, and welcomes you without rising. It is Charles, the squire's oldest son, deformed and unable to walk from infancy. His chair is so contrived that he can move about the room upon it; and he has another for locomotion out of doors. He is the schoolmaster, shoemaker, basket-maker, tailor, and universal genius of the family; and often repairs watches, clocks, and musical instruments, for others. He is always busy, and, as they say, always *just so;* meaning always pleasant and agreeable. He has the reputation of great learning; but his learning, like all his other attainments, is self-acquired. Converse with him, and your pity for his infirmity will be forgotten in respect for his knowledge and understanding. Of all the squire's family, none are more highly prized than Charles.

We give this exact description from real life, to show the position of an independent Maine farmer, of thrifty habits and respectable understanding, self-cultivated a little beyond the general average of his neighbors, but not more so than the best of them. Without further detail, we request the reader to imagine whatever of comfort, convenience, and luxury, may be enjoyed in that condition, under the best circumstances, and he will have a fair picture of constant every-day life at Chinby's. Wealth could reasonably desire nothing more. Wealth in cities could not buy so much; for its glow and freshness cannot be transferred thither, any more than the wild warblings of the birds, or first dewy fragrance of the flowers, or the racy flavor of its summer fruits.

Why should not a true history, like this, include an idea of the economy of country life. At the risk of tediousness, we give this plain account, believing it will be of interest, and perhaps of value, to some. Let us briefly finish it by summing up the cost.

Squire Chinby's farm, the only essential source of all his abundance, the ample and independent home of his family, yielding support, for successive generations, in sickness and health, is valued at no more than two thousand dollars. Surely it requires but little wealth, when well employed, to enable man to sustain the dignity, fulfil the duties, and enjoy the benefits of life. Let the anxiously-toiling and harassed sons of trade, and slaves of city life, think of this. Yet, should some city wight feel disposed to break his chain, and flee to the freedom of a farm, let him not deem himself at once endowed with the faculties of a Chinby. As the country boy makes many blunders and provokes much derision before he can learn to prosper in the ways of the city, so the cit upon a farm, though blessed with more self-conceit, is generally as unsuccessful in his early essays, and is sometimes the subject of similar though more courteously restrained ridicule.

CHAPTER XI.

Winter wanes from Wolfsden. The bland gales of the south dissolve his snowy mantle. The swollen streams burst his icy chains. The mayflower peeps from its leafy bed by the sunny margin of the forest, or on mossy banks, diffusing sweet odors. The frogs trill their evening concert, and the robin wakes the morning with a song. The forest unfolds and spreads abroad upon the fragrant air its dress of leafy green, while orchards and meadows bring out their vernal ornaments of bright blossoms. Nature calls her children forth to new pleasures and new duties. She spreads before the farmer his pleasing and well-rewarding work.

But the mind of youth is often thrown from its even and well-ordered balance. A single disappointment, like a stone thrown into the placid lake, breaks and distorts the fair vision on every side. Youth waits not its returning repose, but turns impatiently from the no longer lovely view; for experience has not yet taught the sad but salutary lesson of control, or given the habit of endurance.

Alek was no longer satisfied with the pleasures and duties, the realities and anticipations, of his rural life. He must see the world, must try its fortunes, and test his own powers. His best reasonings, drawn into the channel of his feelings, urged upon him a new line of action. He will not, like the unreasoning brute, suffer his course of life to be controlled by circumstance; for, even should it chance to be the best, the merit of choice will not be his. He will examine the ways of the world, and choose as his informed and ripened judgment shall decide; and then, should he find his present lot the best, it will be doubly so, for he will know how to value it.

He talked with his father, and his father, though wise in experience and observation, considered the immaturity of youth, and deemed content not too dearly purchased at the expense of hard experience. He had confidence in the discretion and principles of his son, and feared not to trust him abroad. He preferred, since some opportune advantages now offered, that he should go soon, trusting that, whether successful or not, he would the sooner return.

From his mother he feared the greatest objections to his enterprise; for, without her free consent, he would not go, and he knew the strength of her attachment. He told her his thoughts, his wishes, and plans, and she approved and encouraged them. He understood her; he knew the power of her self-sacrificing love, and he again resolved that her affection should ever find in him a worthy object and reward.

It was of a Sabbath evening, a few days before the arrangements of his departure were completed, that she talked with him at length, and alone. Let the holy words of a mother's counsel be recorded. They who are already wise enough may pass them by; to others, as to Alek, they may be words of salvation.

"My son," said the mother, "you are now going, without experience, into a world where the ways are dangerous, where nearly all suffer great losses, and many are wholly lost. I have no experience of the dangers you will meet; but I know that they are great, and that those most to be feared are those of which you little think. I have learned the means by which so many young men, who started in life with every hopeful promise, have been driven or deluded into ruin. My love for you, my oldest son, the joy of my early motherhood, and the hope of my declining years, has sharpened my reflections, and prepared me to say some things to you, which something higher than my own reason prompts, and tells me will be useful to you. I know that you, who have always shown your unbounded love for me, and respect for my sentiments, will give due weight to all I shall say; and that what you know to be right you will receive and cherish with still more care and fidelity because your mother enjoins it. But I do not wish for my influence to go beyond its proper limits. I only ask, as the extent of a mother's privilege, that what I say to you in accordance with what you feel to be right and proper in itself for you to observe, that you will esteem it still more sacred and binding because of your mother; so that, if your own good principles should ever be in danger of yielding in the hour of strong temptation, your mother's memory and love may come to their aid, and save you. Will you promise me this, my son?"

"My dearest mother," said Alek, much affected, "my whole soul tells you YES. I think I have better principles and more wisdom to direct me than most young men who go out into the world; and it is because I was so fortunate as to be born of you, and be educated by you; but I should lose all my self-respect, and all my pride of parentage, if I should find in myself a disposition to undervalue your instructions, now that my reflection enables me more than ever to see their pure worth, and now that I shall need them more than ever, when I am away from under your eye; though," continued he, playfully, "I can hardly think *that* can be the case at all; for I know by experience that your eye follows me wherever I go. And if I should be tempted to do a wrong thing a thousand miles off, I should feel as if you knew it."

"And be assured," said the mother, "I should know it,—at least, I should *feel* it. It would be like a sigh breathed into my spirit, or a drop of sadness falling into my heart. And by this I know that the consequences of any sinful act are eternal. The act may be repented of, and the wound of sin cured, but it can never be as if it had never been. The remembrance will always remain. How great is the cost of every sin for which sorrowful remembrances and regrets must be paid forever! O, how desirable to pass through this life so as to have no cause for regret in the life to come! Before your birth, how anxious I was that you should come into the world a fair and unblemished child; but how much more do I hope and pray that, when this mortal life is done, you may be born into the immortal world a pure and unblemished spirit! You have, thus far, fulfilled my hopes, and filled my heart with joy and pride; and I trust that in all the eternity, of which this life is to us the beginning, I shall forever rejoice in you."

"Dearest mother," said Alek, "if I should ever forget to value my eternal welfare for my own sake, I shall, at least, remember it, and strive for it, for yours. It would make even heaven uncomfortable to remember that I had slighted your admonitions, or failed to fulfil all you expect of me."

"I have," said the mother, "thought for a long while of

what I shall now say to you; for I have anticipated this hour of separation long before you thought of it. There is nothing marvellous in this. The mother's instinct, deepened by reflection, and elevated by prayer, is sufficient to account for what might seem prophetic foresight. I have long known, in my heart, that your path of life would lead you away from your mother's side, into scenes and circumstances different from anything we know of. The thought has lain heavily upon my heart when your heart was light; but I have felt sustained by an abiding confidence that the God of your father and mother, and of your blessed grandparents, will also be your God, and that you will not forsake him."

"Beloved mother," replied Alek, "if every other bond which binds me to God and my duty shall fail, my mother's memory, her prayers, and her love, shall still hold me from falling away. I hope that I may have grace to love and obey God from still higher principles; and till then I will love and obey him from love and obedience to you."

"My precepts," continued the mother, "will now be few, and chiefly on one point, of which mothers seldom speak to their sons, and too seldom even to their daughters. On other topics I have so carefully instructed you, that you know my whole mind, and have profited by it in forming yours. You have come to the age, and the maturity of thought and reflection, when boyish follies and indiscretions are no longer likely to degrade you. You have too much self-respect and nobleness of nature to allow anger, or envy, or mean ambitions, or jealousies, or fear of the censure or ridicule of others, to make you do a wrong act, nourish an unworthy feeling, or neglect a known duty. You know and I think coincide with my religious views, which partake largely of the sentiments of our Quaker ancestors. The Scriptures you will continue to study; for they teach of wonderful dealings of God with men, which cannot elsewhere be learned. You will ever reverence the teachings of Him who spake as never man spake, and fix them on your memory and heart, as the sure guide of life. But the most noble result of this study will be the nourishing in your heart of the *inward light*, superior to all other guides, and without which even the Scriptures are vain. That is the SPIRIT, which shall lead you into all truth. It is the voice of the Shepherd. If you watch, you will *know* his voice. Fear not to follow it. It is more certain even than the written word; for this may be misinterpreted, but the voice of God, speaking through a pure and cultivated conscience, kept awake by constant watchfulness and obedience to its teachings, will never permit you to be led astray. It is only by turning away from this light that you can fall.

"The danger which I fear for you is one into which many noble and gifted men have fallen; and their nobleness and their gifts have become degraded and lost. Even the best and most generous feelings of your nature, which would keep you from falling into other dangers, may, in some circumstances, be a snare to lead you into this.

"My son, *be pure*. Keep your soul free from the pollution of an unchaste emotion. Blessed are the pure in heart, for they shall see God. The pure in heart always see him. His light shines within and about them, and they walk with him. O, how noble and blessed they become who always walk with him! But, alas! how many and how alluring are the temptations which lead astray! They often seem innocent when most to be feared. The way seemeth right when the end thereof is death. Venture not near that dangerous boundary where virtue relaxes into the fashions of vice, and vice puts on the pretences of virtue. Enter into a holy covenant with your mother, and your own soul, and with God, that you will shun every path which leads into this temptation; that, as soon as you see the first approaches of that sin, you will turn from it. To your own soul, and your mother, and God, will you promise this?"

"I will," said Alek. His voice was deep; so was his resolve.

"And may God give you discernment and strength to truly keep this covenant!

"Your enlightened judgment and conscientious reflection will guide you to a right application of these principles. To the society of pure and elevated women, even the beautiful and accomplished, I would gladly commit, not only the forming of your manners, but also the cultivation of those qualities of mind which make men amiable, as well as good. The purest and most refining human influence comes from refined and virtuous women. The best men are far inferior in their goodness to the best women, and have far less power to influence others to goodness. I have sometimes thought that our Saviour took the form of a man, rather than woman, that he might show how grace can elevate that form of humanity which has the least of native goodness.

"Men naturally expect women to be more virtuous than themselves, and it therefore is that an indiscreet or wanton woman is so dangerous; for even men, who by themselves and others are accounted virtuous, seem to think woman alone the guardian of that purity for which both men and women are justly and equally responsible, and will therefore approach as near the boundary of vice as she will permit Let this base weakness never influence your conduct; and let this be your rule, the best that my inexperience in this matter can suggest: that you will never approach to a conduct, utter an expression, or even indulge a thought, which you would be unwilling to have your mother and sisters know; and that, if you shall find yourself in any society, however attractive, where you shall be in danger of violating this rule, you will give it up at once, and avoid it henceforth. In so doing," said the mother, "God will reward you. In due time you will be crowned with all the happiness he designs for our mortal estate. You will know what woman is worth when God shall lead you in the way of one whom you shall first understand, and then honor, and then esteem, and then love, and who will understand, and honor, and esteem, and love you. Love which is built on these foundations is durable and happy. Domestic life, which is bound up in such a love, is the highest of earthly happiness, and the most advantageous state of preparation for eternal happiness. I trust that you will so wisely and truly live as to secure both."

They sat in silence many minutes. At length the mother rose, and, placing her hands on Alek's head, and parting his hair, said: "My son, we have still some days to be together, but remember this as our parting interview, and let all that we have now said be treasured in your heart. Farewell, my son; may the blessing of the God of thy fathers be with thee, and bring thee again in peace!"

And, with a parting kiss, she went cheerfully from the room.

Harry had now left Wolfsden. His enforced indulgence of absence terminated several weeks since, and he returned to college life, but not to the college of frivolities and dissipation which he so unwillingly left. The professors and tutors were surprised at his thoughtful and earnest manner and manly bearing, and reflected with self-complacency upon the salutary effects of their admonition, and the benefit of their discipline. Could they know the source of his reform, they would say that a wilder folly, like a stronger evil spirit, had driven out the lesser demons, and taken sole possession.

Harry's elevated reputation, wherewith he was so gratuitously honored on his arrival in Wolfsden, was quite as unceremoniously shorn from him before his departure. The good name, which is better than precious ointment, is often a precarious possession among those good folks who have naught to do but mark and tell their neighbors' faults and folly. The voyager, who finds the sea always smooth and the winds always favorable, either sails in a very large ship, or steers a very crooked course. It was not Harry's genius to mind the winds and courses much. He took no pains to preserve his unexpected honors, and no wonder he lost them. His exposition of doctrines at Chinby's Meeting-house, though original and able, was not thought to be "to edification;" in short, it was unlucky. To expose the folly of the eminently good, is often to excite their animosity.

Mr. Twangson had good reasons, or, at least, strong motives, to rebuke the presumption of the young man who had so audaciously disputed the prerogative of infallibility which pertains to a missionary as surely as to the Pope. He soon learned Harry's history as understood in Wolfsden; and, by direct inquiry of Uncle Timothy, at Deacon Arbor's, he found out the cause of his absence from his class in college. He then expatiated with severity upon the depravity manifested, when a person in his position, under censure for bad conduct, assumes a religious chara‘ter for a cloak under which to attack the most sacred institutions.

Deacon Arbor and his family, who had now become well acquainted with Harry's frank and open disposition, and who knew all the circumstances of the debate at the North Meeting-house, could not fail to perceive that personal feelings entered somewhat into the missionary's maledictions, and therefore kept their own opinion; but with Parson Boreman, Deacon Murray, Mrs. Simperkins, and other elders, the missionary had it all his own way, and Harry was denounced and anathematized where he had been most zealously lauded and magnified. The parson, who remembered with angry mortification that he had taken special pains to propitiate him, besides having invited him to his pulpit, felt the holy horror and indignation of one who has taken a viper to his bosom unawares. Mrs. Simperkins said it was the weriest piece of himposition that hever come hunder er hobservation. Poor Mrs. Simperkins had many mortifying remembrances with which to nurse her wrath and keep it warm; and not even the remembrance of being honored with Harry's Latin and Greek could mollify her. She could not assert that he had claimed to be a divinity student, yet she insisted that he had assumed the character and conversation of one, on purpose to deceive her and others; and to this view the parson and major both assented, for why else had he not declared himself when invited to the pulpit? Deacon Arbor's good opinion of his guest was set down to his own faulty good-nature, which was always seeking excuses for everybody; and it was feared that the deacon, though sound, was not too well grounded in the doctrine of total depravity. The deacon was compelled to own that Harry had knelt on occasion of family prayer, which they considered tantamount in him to a hypocritical profession of religion, or a contemptuous mockery of it. Deacon Murray's deep and settled principles of doctrine and prejudice were as grappling-irons and cables, to hold Harry's soul in the predestined pit of perpetual perdition.

The busy world made its comments upon this repudiation by the church, according to the previous feelings of individuals. Some, who had envied Harry's honors, felt gratified at seeing his reputation so suddenly rent to rags, and the divinity student proved to be no better than themselves. Others, who really liked him, but supposed that he had intentionally put on the pretence of piety for the sake of mischief, laughed at the joke by which "the elect" had been quizzed; while others, of a higher character, who had an esteem for him, and knew not the facts, regretted the deceitful part they supposed him to have acted. Margaret, especially, was astonished at the development of the wolf from the garb of the lamb, as the missionary expressed it; and felt all the sincere regret of a delicate mind, on finding duplicity in one whom she had believed worthy of all confidence and honor.

But Harry did not remain long enough to observe the regretful or averted looks of former friends. In Deacon Arbor's family he was as well regarded as ever; and in a few days his pleasant visit at Wolfsden terminated. During this time, he had learned of Alek his determination to travel and seek his fortune; and had given him much wise advice, drawn from his own experience, and such as might formerly have been profitably adopted by himself, however little adapted to Alek's probable contingencies, — in addition to which, he gave him the more promising benefit of an earnest introduction to his uncle in New York, with whom, notwithstanding his irregularities, he still had some influence.

Dressed in a new and substantial suit of clothes, in which a city tailor might perhaps see something to remind him of the description of Yankee Doodle's dress, bating the striped trousers, with a bundle under his arm, and a stout staff in his hand, and a leathern pocket-book weighty with silver coin, tokens of love and resources in exigency, Alek departed from his home on foot and alone. He could have commanded an escort of friends and horses, but he determined to begin as he expected to go on. Adopting Harry's phrase, he said it was his genius to go away on foot; and if his genius should find horses and coaches for him, he would come back in different style; otherwise, his return, however humble, should not shame his departure. His friends were satisfied with his reasons and his resolution. He departed laden with blessings, prayers, and prophecies of good.

The freshness of early morning strengthened the elasticity of his vigorous frame and youthful spirits. His firm resolve fortified his heart against the weakness of regret. The many-linked chain of home affections and habitudes he might not break, but he was strong to drag its increasing length. The conscious heaviness upon his heart he would not throw off, if he could; for he felt that, like the dollars in his pocket, it was a salutary weight. His countenance was not the less bright nor his step less light.

Of the younger ones left behind, he foresaw the most troublesome parting with little Amy, for she would cling to his neck, and insist that he should not go; therefore he started the earlier, and passed Colonel Bowler's before the family had risen, and Amy only knew he was gone when Fanny came over, after breakfast, to give the present and the kiss he had left for her. Alek was already many miles away, for he walked like the man in Bunyan's Dream, who believed the avenger of blood to be pursuing him, or rather as one whose resolution is wound up so tightly that his body must go, perforce. His path first lay across the pasture and woods, by which he saved a long distance; after which, he pursued the crooked and irregular yet generally smooth and pleasant road, which follows the Saco's winding stream, along green banks or through dark woods, or often among abrupt and precipitous rocks, where a traveller is seldom seen. The robin welcomed him with her brisk and cheerful morning melody. The squirrel, perched on a projecting bough, chattered an angry remonstrance at his approach. The distant quail still at intervals recalled in mournful monotony the remembrance of Poor-Bob-White. Yet on moved Alek, unmindful of the morning melody, the angry clamor, or the mournful monotony. His soul was absorbed in contemplations too deep to be disturbed by external sights or sounds.

The sun rose high, and exhaled the dew. The road wound along a high embankment, which rose upon the right towards a precipitous hill of rifted granite, where the broken and cavernous sides sometimes gave root to a tall, waving pine, or a spreading beech, but where mostly the sharp rocks elevated their points above the scanty shrubs of dwarf oak and white birch. On the left, the river stretched its silvery line far away toward the south, often losing itself, and still returning to view, — now with gentle embrace surrounding little islands, and lingering lovingly among green meadows, and anon sweeping rapidly by the base of overshadowing hills, and leaping with foaming fury along its narrow and shelvy channel.

A rocky rivulet, dashing from among the cliffs upon the right, glided with a gentler but still rapid flow along its rough bed, and gave its slight but constant tribute to the sovereign stream. A shady nook, upon its margin invited repose. Exercise had sharpened appetite; and Alek sat down by the rivulet, beneath an overhanging beech, and spread out the plentiful and inviting repast provided by loving hands. He ate with a good will, and drank from the cool waters. He reclined upon the mossy margin, and indulged reveries of the home from which he was now a wanderer, and of joys and hopes now departed. He thought of the vicissitudes, the efforts, the possibilities and uncertainties, to come.

The soft murmur of the stream, the drowsy hum of busy insects, the hollow drum of the partridge far in the woods, the stillness of the air, the sultry heat of the sun, and the refreshing coolness of the shade, combined to prolong his rest. Sleep, of late defrauded of its due, now stole upon him unawares. The unguided current of his busy thought still moved on, and in fancy he still pursued his uncertain way. Difficulties and dangers obstructed him, but were magically surmounted and overborne. Bright visions of prosperity surrounded him. He found himself the favorite of fortune, and the companion of fortune's favorites. The latent feeling of doubt that there might be fallacy in what seemed so fair, gradually gave way to assurance and security. He congratulated himself upon the self-discerning merit which at length had raised him to his proper sphere.

Still there were incongruities in his position which per

plexed him. He wished to justify to himself and others his self-estimate and his fame by great deeds, but found not the opportunity. It was in the dim past that his claims of merit lay, or in some great thing which he was about to accomplish; yet he could not remember what it was that he had achieved, or was yet to achieve. He received praises and honors with pain, fearing that, after all, they might belong to another; and he dreaded the moment when the mistake should be discovered, but found no friend to aid him with explanation or advice. Like a monarch doubtful of the allegiance of his subjects, and distrusting most of all his obsequious servants and flatterers, he secretly regretted his miserable splendor.

A lovely female form, blending the fair proportions and dignified grace of Margaret with a softer beauty, and a strange and incomprehensible kindness and condescension, as if to atone for past coldness, hovered about him, ever displaying new fascinations. His mother's hallowed counsel girded him about with a panoply which no seductions could penetrate. Yet he felt ashamed of his reserve, lest it might be mistaken for clownishness, and timidly relaxed his rigor. He gave smile for smile, endearment for endearment, and caress for caress. Suddenly a strange sense of danger startled him. He turned and saw in the shadow of his fair companion the grim and fearful form of death, with upraised dart, in attitude to strike. He started with horror, and his dream was gone. His head reclined against the smooth rind of the overshadowing beech, but still the sense of danger thrilled his nerves. He turned his head and moved his hands, to assure himself of his position, for he was yet scarcely awake. Instantly a sharp and prolonged rattling noise, near his side, startled him. With instinctive horror, he threw himself, by a sudden impulse of his body, to a distance of several feet in the opposite direction, and was instantly erect and facing the deadly peril. It-was the fatal rattlesnake. With head raised above its coiled body, and with flashing eyes, he was in the instant preparation for the deadly spring. But Alek was now at a safe distance. By a hairbreadth of space, and a point of time, he had escaped a horrible death. His nerves were strung to the tension that comes only when men are surest of what they attempt. He seized a stone, and threw it with the force and precision of a rifle, and the reptile's head was dashed from its writhing body. He then looked cautiously about, but no mate of the hideous reptile was in sight. With fervent devotion, he knelt and thanked his Maker for his preservation, and prayed that the lesson of his dream and his danger, whatever it might be designed to teach, might not be lost upon him. He then hung up the lifeless reptile by the road-side, as a warning to other travellers not to rest in the dangerous place, and pursued his way.

CHAPTER XII.

THE reader, if a "friend of humanity," remembers the poor hut of Bang, and his deserted forge, and sorry cow, and discontented pig, upon whose forlorn lot we cast a passing glance, while buffeting the storm and breaking the road on the day before the new year. The only pleasant thing we saw about the cheerless dwelling was the brave face of the boy Ax, the youngest son of Bang, who, with stocking upon his head and new boots on his feet, reinforced our party. We have since met with Ax in the schoolmaster's story, but have hitherto necessarily delayed the history of the family, which, as an essential part of this impartial record, can no longer be neglected.

Twenty-five years ago, Mr. Benjamin Barker married Miss Susan Twist. So were the names spelt in the town-clerk's publishment; and so were they pronounced by the Rev. Mr. Boreman, who solemnized the bans; that is, who pronounced them man and wife, and, over a glass of toddy, wished them good luck. That was a jolly evening. The ceremony was performed at Colonel Bowler's, and young folks and old folks, parson and all, had a good time. To the principal parties the good time lasted some half a dozen years, with occasional interruptions, growing more frequent and serious, till at any time within twenty years the good time was all gone, and all times were bad at Bang's. For now everybody called him Bang, and he had come to call himself Bang.

In the first bright beginning of his career, he had procured a new sign, on which a rampant red horse was painted, with himself in the act of shoeing him; and underneath, in letters as large as the sign would hold, and bright as red ochre and oil could make, was painted, B. BARKER, BLACKSMITH. The sign did not overstate the owner's merits. He was a blacksmith, every inch, and his inches were many. From a jewsharp to a ploughshare, from a pegging-awl to a bear-trap, nothing was beyond his skill; but he prided himself most in his superior success in shoeing horses and oxen, and tempering axes. Custom came in plenty. His hammer's ring might ever be heard from dewy morn till dusky eve; and none made money faster than "B. Barker, Blacksmith." Mrs. Susan Barker, to use teamster's phrase, kept up her end of the yoke. She had been for several years the principal tailoress in town. Deacon Arbor has still a great-coat with two great capes, made by Susan, a little before she had taken upon herself the dignities of married life, unknowing what indignities were to follow. If activity in all domestic duties could make a good housewife, Susan was a pattern to housewives. Everybody said she was as "smart as a steel-trap," and was born to make her way in the world. The description of her qualities was true, but the prophecy of her success was a failure. Whether the milder and more endearing qualities of womanhood, if she had possessed them, would have improved her condition, may not be provable; but certainly there was an abundant lack in her dwelling of those gentle influences which make home the nursery of good habits. And yet there was no lack of religion among her elements. She had experienced religion when young, and joined Parson Boreman's church; and for many years before her marriage, and several years afterward, was prominent and zealous in all church matters, pushing forward all sorts of movements favored or tacitly allowed by the minister, — such as begging subscriptions for a bell; starting the Sunday-school, where little boys and girls recited whole chapters of the Bible, in competition for the picture-books which should reward the most successful, and excite the angry discontent of the unsuccessful competitors; settling the disturbances of the musical choir, self-styled the "Philharmonic Band," whose inharmonic bickerings were frequently felt, in dissonant undulations, from the centre to the furthest verge of the society.

Some movements in which her influence was not allowed its accustomed weight had long ago offended her, and she had withdrawn in dudgeon from active interference in church and parish affairs; not, however, till a little before the birth of her fourth son. To the preceding three she had given the evangelical names of Matthew, Mark, and Luke, and her fourth was in due time christened John. The joke then passed round, that the next one was predestined to the name of Acts.

In the interval between the birth of John and Ax an affair of great and tragic interest had occurred, which overthrew the already waning respectability of the Barker family, and fixed their position in the pariah caste, who still will have a place in every community. A brief account of this affair may properly be given here.

Susan Twist had an only brother, one year younger than herself. They were left orphans at an early age by a worthless pair, who died, or disappeared in some forgotten way. The boy and girl, whose education and whose inherited tendencies were of the most unfavorable kind, were then separated, and bound, or adopted, into respectable families. The girl was taken into Colonel Bowler's family, where she was properly employed and provided for till she came of age, when she chose a situation where she could learn the tailor's trade, in which she was very successful till her marriage, as already recorded. The brother Jotham proved less manageable, and, after a few years, in which he was at first the plague and afterwards the terror of his benefactors, he ran away. He was then but about a dozen years old, but of strength and activity extraordinary for his years, and with a temper and disposition which promised anything but good from his physical qualities. A daring act of insubordination in school, at the beginning of the winter term, had compelled the master to inflict chastisement. A violent conflict ensued, in which Jotham fought desperately, but was soundly beaten, and compelled to yield. Stung with mortification and rage, he determined on revenge; and at the recess he watched the opportunity, and while the master stood at the window within, he hurled a billet of wood from without with such force that it shivered the sash, prostrated the master, and scattered the glass throughout the school-house. This done, he took to his heels; and, though pursued by the whole school, with the master, who had quickly recovered himself, at their head, he made good his escape, and immediately absconded from Wolfsden, and nothing reliable was heard from him for twenty years. It was rumored that he had gone to sea, had become a pirate, had been caught and hung, had become a prize-fighter in New York, had beaten a dozen champions, and at length had met with more than his match, and after a desperate conflict had finally been killed outright; that he had entered the burglary and counterfeit money business, had been sentenced to state-prison for ninety-nine years; that he had gone to Texas and Mexico, had joined the Indians and been made a chief, and distinguished himself with the scalping-knife and tomahawk.

His real adventures were probably as various and desperate as the rumors, though not exactly coinciding with them; for it is certain that in little more than twenty years afterwards, when he had become pretty much forgotten, he reäppeared, looking much like any ordinary mortal, who had not been an executed pirate nor an Indian chief, though there were scars about his face which seemed to favor the prize-fighting report, to which also his swaggering air gave further confirmation. Indeed, his whole appearance, indicating strength, pugnacity, and recklessness, was such that none, even among the stout and hardy yeomen of Wolfsden, would willingly have disputed with him; and it was conceded that the wisest way was to give him few words and a wide berth, although a few resolute fellows had made the observation that he must keep his insolence within reasonable limits, unless he felt himself able to flog the whole town at once.

Circumstances soon led to a conflict, which, though less general and more equal than that which had been talked of as possible, was sufficiently tragical in its results. Jotham had naturally taken up his abode with his sister and brother-in-law, where he was received and entertained with the hospitality to which his relationship was a sufficient claim. For some time previous, the condition and respectability of the blacksmith had been declining. His wife, from being a thrifty manager, a busy neighbor, and a restless parish meddler, had gradually degenerated to a noisy, quarrelsome shrew. Her boys, like the tiger's whelps, so pretty before their claws are grown, had, notwithstanding their evangelical names, matured into very unevangelical characters, whom careful neighbors cautioned their children to avoid. His horse, and cow, and pigs, which generally ran in the road, showed their disposition and education to be no better than those of the children; for they broke into other people's enclosures, where, not content with satisfying their appetites, they wrought much wanton mischief and waste. Bang himself had also degenerated from a good blacksmith, a decent citizen, and a fair neighbor, into the opposite of all those characteristics. Home influences had doubtless done much of this; for it is to a great degree the wife who moulds the husband's character. No man is more than half developed till after marriage; and it generally depends upon the wife whether his possible good qualities shall grow and give color to his character as husband and head of the family, or whether these shall be repressed and choked by the harsher and less noble dispositions which have their elements in every human heart.

Here we might introduce a valuable dissertation upon family economics; the relative and reciprocal influences of husband and wife; the comparative importance of different domestic qualities in each; what are the incompatibilities and what the indispensable conditions of a congenial home; and how far outward circumstances, as wealth, poverty, refinement, simplicity, and other accidentals, enter into those conditions; and how qualities which, carried to a proper extent, are virtues, may, by their excess, produce the worst results of vice — unhappiness, discord, degradation. But, in the mean time, who shall help along our story, which, not lagging for the sake of philosophy, must carry its moral with it, or leave it to the reader's reflection? Besides, it is well known that those who most need maxims of wisdom for the guidance of domestic life are those whose unteachable tempers, perverse dispositions, and headstrong habits, disqualify them for profiting by counsel, whether preached from the pulpit or inculcated in history.

But there were bad things abroad with which the things at home were only subordinate helps to hasten the ruin of Bang and his family. Bragly's Corner was a little beyond Bang's shop. Bragly's store was on Bragly's Corner; Bragly kept groceries and other small notions, and especially rum, in all its vile varieties. Here the thriftless coopers and shingle-makers from Herring Cove brought their manufactures and exchanged them for rum, tobacco, and other domestic delicacies. Herring Cove is a poor neighborhood, behind Saddle-back Hill, and is so called in derision from the quantities of smoked and pickled herrings bought at Bragly's and consumed there. Here Chadbourn, the shiftless mason, spent for like luxuries the avails of occasional jobs; and here also his lean old crone brought skeins of flaxen thread, small baskets of eggs, an occasional pair of woollen socks, and such small ware, to exchange for tea and snuff. Here also congregated the idle and dissipated from various quarters, to spend rainy afternoons and winter evenings in maudlin mirth, drunken dispute, angry altercations, and sometimes bloody-nosed battles. While business was good, Bang seldom visited Bragly's; but either his visits became more frequent because his business became more dull, or his business became more dull because his visits became more frequent, or these two facts coöperated, till, after a time, it came to be understood generally that if Bang was not at his shop he might be found at Bragly's; and, after a still further time, that the first place to look for Bang was at Bragly's. Even when in his own shop, he was commonly saturated with Bragly's fluid, and surrounded with Bragly's atmosphere. Iron and coal were not more indispensable to his operations than his bottle. The consequences are already recorded. The profits of his industry were absorbed in the profits of Bragly's trade. Poverty, waste, discord, recklessness, and all the demons of ruin, printed their cloven hoofs and grinned with their ugly visages about the premises of Bang. Sullen discontent, rude taunts, and finally downright quarrels, made a part of the daily family life. Neighbors at first interfered, advised, took sides, and, as usual, made matters worse, and then discontinued the common civilities of reputable acquaintanceship, and left them to their inevitable infamy.

It was at about this stage of downward progress that Jotham returned to Wolfsden, and took up his residence at the house of his brother-in-law Bang. At first it seemed that his advent was salutary. For some time there was no noisy quarrel in the house, and there happening to be a good demand for work at that season, the shop presented a scene of unusual activity. Jotham gave good aid with the sledge-hammer, and Bang did a good business.

But the malign influences had too long established their sway to allow their permanent power to be doubted. Household quarrels became more violent than ever. Jotham naturally took his sister's side, and, thus backed, she became more violent in her temper and speech than ever, until, one day, Bang being half drunk and quite abusive, she proceeded, for the first time, to personal violence, and struck him over the head with a broom. Bang gave her a kick in return, which sent her prostrate across the room, and was in turn knocked down by Jotham. A regular fight commenced, in which, notwithstanding the great strength of Bang, he was severely beaten, without being able to inflict any serious injury upon Jotham, who, either from the advantage of what pugilists term "science," or by his greater activity, was able to parry the blows of Bang, and to "plant" his own with frightful effect.

Bang seemed to digest his beating well enough; for, though horribly disfigured about the face, and lamed in both arms, he kept at work, and associated with his brother-in-law as usual. Mrs. Barker, who was the beginner of the fray, was perhaps the greatest sufferer by it; for, besides being hurt by the kick, and frightened by the fury and blood of the combat, the like of which never had been witnessed in Wolfsden, she suffered still more in her property, the furniture and crockery of the room being generally smashed in the conflict, and little could she expect that her beaten husband or victorious brother would repair it.

Things went along without further disturbance for a week or two. Bang recovered from his bruises, and was less devoted to the bottle. Some said that since he got his "gruel" he had less appetite for his whiskey. Others thought he kept guarded, that, in case of another quarrel, he might not be taken at advantage; as he had intimated that his recent defeat was owing to his being drunk. It is not known how the second conflict occurred. One afternoon, the loungers at

Bragly's were suddenly summoned by the screams of a woman, soon recognized as Mrs. Barker, at the blacksmith-shop. Hastening hither, they found Jotham prostrate on the floor, with a frightful wound in his temple, through which blood and brains were oozing. An old axe lay on the other side of the shop, which had evidently been thrown with great violence, as it had made a deep indentation in a block by which it was lying. It was free from any stain of blood, and was supposed to have been hurled with such fury as to have accomplished its murderous mission in its passage without receiving a stain. The shape of the wound, which indicated that the instrument had glanced from it, together with the position of the body, favored this idea. Bang was not present, but soon came in with a pail of water, a part of which he threw in the face of the dying man, with the purpose of recovering him. No other remedy was attempted; and in a short time the broad chest of the victim ceased to heave, and he breathed his last.

Bang made no attempt at escape, and gave no explanation of the circumstances above described. There had evidently been a severe fight. Bang was bruised in his face and various parts of his body, though his brother-in-law seemed to have suffered no wound but that which terminated his life. It was supposed that Bang, being foiled in "planting" his blows by the superior "science" of Jotham, and being severely "punished," as his various bruises showed, had, in his exasperation, seized the axe, which he hurled with such fatal aim at his adversary's head. Bang's persevering silence on the subject, which was probably from sullen doggedness, or perhaps from confusion and inability to recall the incidents of the struggle, was, in his situation, the course which policy would have dictated, as thereby he avoided committing himself by contradictions or confessions. In the judicial investigation, which took place afterward, the whole affair was involved in so much doubt and obscurity, that the jury, after a long consultation, acquitted Bang, who went back to his family. Mrs. Bang's testimony, if it had been admissible, would probably have changed the verdict to manslaughter, or perhaps murder; yet, though it could not be doubted that Bang killed Jotham, few affected to view him as a murderer, and none regretted the fate of his victim.

From this time till about two years afterward, Bang continued his downward course of drunkenness, degradation, and ruin, with even accelerated speed, working only enough to get the means of filling his bottle at Bragly's, and bearing in sullen, sottish silence the eloquent exhortations and angry reproaches of his unhappy vixen partner. Meanwhile his boys of evangelical names and anti-evangelical dispositions had grown up to precocious manhood and precocious depravity. Home lessons had not been lost upon them. Kindred accomplishments, gained from other sources, or adopted from instinct, had supplied the deficiencies of home education, as their frequent depredations upon neighbors' gardens, orchards, hen-roosts, and other exposed property, plainly showed. Finally, they had successively run away, each one after having perpetrated some more than usually daring outrage, as if to prove the maturity of his attainments, and his fitness for a wider space of action. Another son had also been born some six months after the tragic event before recorded, whom the mother, in memory of her murdered brother, named Jotham, but, through the potency of persevering jest, he was now only known as Ax.

Some months after the last event, a better day dawned upon Bang. It dawned, but, alas! it did not brighten into perfect light. The temperance movement had already included Wolfsden in its sphere, and there was a numerous and popular society (composed chiefly of young ladies), pledged to total abstinence, which had its annual celebrations its occasional lectures, its Fourth of July picnics, and other social attractions. The chief object of this society was to preserve the virtue of temperance where it already existed, and it made no effort to reclaim those who had become drunkards, such being generally considered irreclaimable. Some philanthropists abroad, however, adopted a different view, and, under the able leadership of Mr. Hawkins, a man gifted with rare powers of persuasive eloquence, and himself a reformed drunkard, instituted most active and successful proceedings for the reformation of drunkards, even of the most abandoned class. This was called the "Washingtonian Movement," and the history of its labors and triumphs is well known. It is one of the brightest and most cheering pages of the book of humanity. The world owes a debt of gratitude to the devoted, laborious, and eloquent apostles of this mission of mercy, which it can never repay, and never will even appreciate, till truth and worth shall triumph over the falsehood and folly which have so long ruled mankind.

One of the earnest advocates of this reformation came to Wolfsden, and succeeded, by means of that peculiar art of persuasion, which only a good cause and sincere devotion to it can inspire, in making several converts among the worst inebriates. Several signal trophies of this remarkable reformation remain in Herring Cove and other parts of Wolfsden tc vindicate the divinity of the mission, and the claims of humanity, even in its lowest estate, to the respect, the pity, and the help, of the brotherhood of man.

It somehow happened that the church in Wolfsden did not favor this innovation. Deacon Murray replied to the zealous Washingtonian that his doctrine appeared unsound, in not sufficiently recognizing the total depravity of man and the sovereignty of God. Parson Boreman said the matter was not in his line. His duty was to preach the Gospel, which invites sinners to come, letting them hear or forbear, as they might choose. Deacon Arbor showed a disposition to help the Washingtonians, and made the agent welcome at his house while he remained; and Aunt Deborah, when she heard of the parson's answer, said that the MASTER came to seek and to save those who were lost, and did not wait for them to come to him.

Although many, perhaps most of the Washingtonian converts in Wolfsden, held fast their integrity, yet several, after running well for a time, fell away, and became sots as before. Among these was Bang. The wonder was not that he relapsed, but that he stood so long; for it was about a year before he returned to his old habits, and it may fairly be presumed that, but for the near vicinity of Bragly's and the many temptations to which his employment subjected him, and perhaps the want of that constant supervision of encouraging friends which was one of the chief reliances of the Washingtonian reform, but which, in sparsely-settled towns, is not always available, his reformation might have been permanent. Its good effects, while it lasted, were remarkable. Though far from possessing the energy of his youth, he was perseveringly industrious. His shop was frequented by good employers. His doors and windows were mended; his garden and wood-pile and other surroundings showed signs of thrift · and, what should have been taken as an omen and pledge of continued blessing, a daughter was added to the household, one which the better guidance of the mother, under these more favorable auspices, might have brought up to redeem the reputation of the blighted and doomed family. That the promise of better days might lack nothing of its fulfilment, Mrs. Bang seemed to have met with as favorable a change as her husband. Whether the tragical death of her brother, the trial and almost conviction of Bang, the profligacy and flight of her boys, and the continued and hopeless misery of her domestic life, had broken down her violent spirit, or whether the hopeful reformation of her husband, with the earnest exhortation and entreaty of the Washingtonian missionary that she would encourage his reformation by making his home congenial, added to the mollifying influence which maternity and infant dependence exercises in the female heart, or from whatever cause, Mrs. Bang became comparatively a mild and patient woman, fulfilling with fidelity the duties of mother and wife. There can be no doubt also that the frequent visits and encouraging words of Aunt Deborah and Helen, and other members both of Deacon Arbor's and Colonel Bowler's family, helped to prolong the improvement. Little Ax's disposition formed under the improved domestic examples which this reformation introduced; and especially the lovable and winning ways of the little daughter, as she grew, proved the reality and the value of the change. And though Bang afterwards fell into his old habits, yet Mrs. B. remained, in a great degree, improved. She could not become quite a lamb in her temper; nature and long habit could not be so entirely subdued. Yet she exercised a mother's powerful influence for the well-being and right guiding of her children. And though poverty and evil example hindered her, yet she managed to shield her little ones from their worst effects. Ax was equal in natural intelligence and principles to other boys; and little Susan — for she was named for her mother — was, notwithstanding her parentage, the favorite of the neighborhood.

I think it unfortunate that any occasion was given to the enemies of religion of accusing the church of being the cause of Bang's relapse. I think it would perhaps have been better, considering the results, that, since it had done nothing to prevent Bang's ruin, and nothing afterward to redeem him, if it had continued its forbearance till the experiment of his redemption by other hands had been fully carried out. It is proper, however, that the facts, as they actually were, should be recorded, for the light they may cast on future cases of the kind.

It was about a year after Bang's reformation, and when it came to be understood that he was a man to be depended upon, and was getting up in the world, that it was suggested in a church-meeting that some watch and care should be extended over Sister Barker and her family (for she still belonged to the church, though so long neglected and forgotten); and, since there appeared to be a prospect of their being respectable members of society, it would be as well to look after them, and bring them within the means of grace. This was assented to, and Deacon Arbor was named to manage the matter. The deacon declined the service, saying that he feared such efforts would be unavailing, as the course of the church had created some prejudice among the Washingtonians, which would be hard to overcome; and that, in his opinion, the time was past for attempting to bring them into the church.

Parson Boreman replied that "it was never too late to do good; that we must be instant in season and out of season; and while the lamp holds out to burn the vilest sinner may return," and much more of the same sort; and nominated Major Murray to the duty declined by the deacon. A worse choice could scarcely have been made. Major Murray was as upright and irreproachable in his life as a man made of cast-iron, but was also as stiff and unconciliating. A rigid Calvinist, and firm believer in the sanctity of the church and its ordinances, through which alone salvation could be obtained. his rule of Christian duty ran exactly in the groove of the Westminster Catechism, doing what might be done in that track, and running over or knocking aside whatever came not in that scope of action.

Major Murray called upon Mrs. Barker, the next day, and opened his embassy in a style worthy of Cotton Mather himself. He told her that the church had regarded with great grief her absence from its ordinances, and felt it their duty to admonish her, and that he trusted she would feel the importance of the stated means of grace, &c.; that the awful inflictions and warnings which she had experienced in her own family ought to humble her under a sense of divine displeasure. And then he compared her case with that of Abigail, who, though the wife of a churl, and a man of Belial, nevertheless found favor; and also that of Eli, whose two sons, Hophni and Phineas, were reprobates, and were destroyed, though he was saved; and also Jacob, who was chosen, though his brother Esau was rejected; and, with these precedents for her exclusive salvation, and the reprobation of her kindred, he told her that she should look only to God's glory, and put away the carnal affections. "For," said he, "in heaven we shall be so changed by grace that we shall rejoice in the vindication of his divine justice, through the torments of the lost, though they be our nearest kindred."

Poor Mrs. Barker, though generally so prompt in reply, was silent and submissive under this authoritative admonition. Having no doubt of the truth of those doctrines, she could not resist their application, and she shrunk back with instinctive terror from that fiery gulf of everlasting torment and despair to which all her kindred were so evidently predestined, but from which she had still a hope of escape through the *calling*, *election*, and *predestination*, fore-ordained and decreed before the world began, and which, though absolute and unchangeable, still involved a necessity of church ordinances, without which she could not be saved.*

In this terrified and unhappy mood, and thinking little of mere temporal matters, she neglected the household duties which she generally performed so well. Bang, who had seen the arrival and departure of the major, towards whom he felt strong dislike, was little disposed to overlook the uncomfortable results of his visit. He said that, as the church had never done them any good in their best days, and had kept out of the way in their worst days, he would thank them to

* Parson Boreman and his predestinarian teachings represent a class of ministers and ideas more common in past generations, and in remoter towns, than among us. Whether those doctrines were true or false, this, at least, may be said in their favor, — that under their prevalence the noblest traits of human character were developed and cultivated. The boasted triumph of what are termed more liberal views should not be too much magnified until their efficacy to produce equal or better results be proved.

keep away altogether; and when they came again he should have a word to say.

Accordingly, soon after, when the major had reported his proceedings to Parson Boreman, and the parson, feeling compelled to do something in the business which he had advocated, called upon Mrs. Barker, Bang bolted in, all begrimed and sweating from the forge, and, with a familiar swagger, welcomed the parson, shook hands, told him he was glad to see him looking so hearty, *after so long a time*, asked "how he left the old woman and Lucy, — that is, Lucinda, — a fine daughter that of yourn, Parson Boreman — not married yet, I s'pose — think she might have offers enough — a fine girl like her — and why don't she come round this way, and pay us a visit? Always liked Lucy; that is, Lucinda." And so he went on, with a pretended good-natured familiarity, more annoying and insulting than any other treatment, because so difficult to repel. At last he asked the minister if he would take something to "wet his whistle," adding, "We don't keep nothing on hand, now-a-days; but Bragly is as accommodating as ever." Parson Boreman, with offended dignity, replied that he did not choose to take anything, adding, in a censorious manner, that he should suppose he (Bang) had seen enough, and done enough, and suffered enough, by rum, to quit it altogether.

"So I have," says Bang, still more provoked by the minister's manner and allusions; "only when I see an old friend like you, been away so long, I like to treat him, for the sake of old lang syne. Here, Ax, take this pint bottle to Bragly's, and tell him to fill it. You and I have drank together, parson, and it 's about time we should again. You have n't signed the pledge, I understand; and, as for me, an old reprobate, bound to the devil's kingdom come, any way, it 's no matter what I do."

If Mr. Boreman had had the good sense to depart immediately, or the magnanimity and tact to conciliate Bang by acknowledging his fault in not supporting the temperance cause, as he should have done, and declared himself ready to sign the pledge, all would probably have been well, and he would have had the merit of having saved a soul from death. Instead of this, he angrily replied that he disapproved of strong drink; that he seldom took any, and only when he required it; and that he trusted he was man enough to guard himself from excess in eating or drinking, without any pledge.

By this time, Ax, who little knew how fatal was the errand upon which he was sent, had returned, and Bang, pouring out drams in a couple of glasses, set one before the minister, saying: "Come, parson, drink to our good luck, as you did the evening you married us. Here 's to you and your old woman, and Lucy,—that is, Lucinda. May she soon get a good husband, and have as good luck as we 've had!" Bang probably did not mean to drink when he sent for the rum; but he was now excited by passion and swelling with bravado, and as he took in the fumes of the tempting glass, forgetting his pledge, he raised it to his lips, and drained it to the bottom. The minister, seeing no chance of introducing the business upon which he came, took his leave, well aware that he had done no good, and perhaps half aware that he had done harm.

Dreadful and fatal was the harm of which his visit had been the occasion, if not the cause. The pledge was violated. The charm was broken. Bang had once more tasted the soul-poisoning cup, and all his furious appetites, so long nourished and so long enchained, rose to complete mastery over his better resolutions. He emptied the glass which the minister had refused to touch. He emptied the bottle. It was again filled, and Bang was again a drunkard. "Behold the end of unsanctified reform," said Parson Boreman to Major Murray; "the dog has returned," &c. "Behold the end of sanctified meddlesomeness," said Aunt Deborah, when she heard of the parson's remark.

Since Bang's relapse he had become rather the passive and resigned slave of rum, than the brawling and turbulent drunkard. None of the active energies of either the human or brutal kind prevailed; and nothing but the low, grovelling appetite of selfish gratification remained. He would perform any service for rum, but make no exertion for any solid advantages. He would bear the grossest insult, and make up the bitterest quarrel, for rum. He would lie, steal, or fight, for rum; and would swallow the most nauseous compound, of which rum was an ingredient. Without any actual vice, except the absence of every virtue or redeeming quality, he was a most revolting example of entire subjection to base appetite. No doubt the soul within him had struggled severely before it yielded to this degradation; and even now it writhed in its place of torment, and gave utterance, through the drunkard's lips, to self-execrations and blasphemies, superstitious fear, and heaven-defying despair.

It will be remembered that on our first glance at Bang's dwelling we noticed some small signs of improvement, in reference to which some significant gestures passed between Alek and Isaac, upon which we will here throw light.

The universal custom of distributing gifts and good wishes on Christmas and New Year's Day is by no means neglected in Wolfsden; and among the young hearts made glad by pretty presents the families of the deserving poor are not forgotten. Some savory cheer in the shape of mince-pies and other culinary compounds, with a fat chicken, a spare-rib of pork, some comfortable articles of dress, &c., had already found their way to Mrs. Barker's chest, when, on Christmas eve, a knock was heard at the door, and a figure of strange attire and unwieldly dimensions, enveloped in a shaggy bear-skin, a high raccoon cap, and what seemed a beard of monstrous growth, entered the kitchen. The action of the intruder was as strange as his figure. Thrusting one hand into a bag hanging to his side, he drew forth a substantial pair of boys' boots, which he tossed upon the floor, and growled, in a gruff voice, "Ax." Thrusting the other hand into the opposite side, he drew out a pair of girls' boots, and, throwing them with the others, he growled "Sue." Detaching two bundles which hung round his neck, he tossed one towards Mrs. B., with the uncomplimentary grunt of "Old Woman," and threw the other with some force towards Bang, and then, turning round, took his departure. An immediate examination of the presents so strangely brought was quite satisfactory. The boots for Ax and Sue were found to be crammed with woolen yarn, and two or three sets of knitting-pins; and the other bundles contained, one, a pair of second-hand trousers for Bang, the condition of whose unmentionables had evidently prompted the charity, and the other, sundry tokens of good-will to Mrs. B.

The children were delighted, and, believing it a veritable visit from Santa Claus, insisted upon taking their presents to bed with them. Bang received his in sullen apathy. There were in him no emotions of gratitude, surprise, or shame which any event could excite. His ever-craving appetite for rum, which had been for several days ungratified, was now raging within him. Waiting till the children were asleep, he groped to their bed, and, securing the boots of Susan, and providing himself with a jug, he went to Bragly's store. It was growing late, Bragly's customers had retired, and he was about to shut up. Throwing the boots on the counter, and exhibiting the jug, Bang called for a gallon of rum. Boots were current barter with Bragly, and the rum was furnished, and a paper of tobacco to make up the balance, with which Bang proceeded home. Mrs. B. had not attempted to prevent the act, knowing that it would be of no use. Bang proceeded, as usual, to get drunk. His wife went to bed, as usual, with a sad heart; and Bragly probably retired with a comfortable consciousness of having finished up a good day's business with a good additional profit.

Poor little Susan's disappointment, the next morning, may be imagined; but retribution, though often slow, is sometimes sudden. A neighbor, calling at Bang's that day, found out the facts, and in the evening a big figure, in a bear-skin, entered Bragly's store, and, seizing a pair of girl's boots which hung upon a string for sale, thrust them into his pocket, growling " Sue's boots," and departed, Bragly not deeming it prudent to intercept his progress. Entering Bang's house as unceremoniously as before, he threw down the boots, and, proceeding to a corner where Bang sat half drunk, he seized the jug by the handle, and Bang by the nose, and with a backward step retreated toward the door. Bang roared with pain. His nose was swollen and tender with carbuncles, and his outcry showed plainly that he had still one susceptible spot. The strange figure maintained his grip till he had dragged Bang across the floor, and then, with a parting wring, gruffly muttered, "Beware of Santa Claus!" and departed, taking the jug, which was found next morning, emptied of its contents, and standing on a log near the door. A neighbor, who called the next day, found little Susan rejoicing in her restored boots, and Bang with a bandage about his face, busy in mending the chinks of his dwelling. Nobody knows who personated Santa Claus; but it was remarked by Ike to Alek, with a wink, which was answered by a nod, that Bragly would probably decline any future dealings with Bang in the boot line.

CHAPTER XIII.

He said, "This will I do. I will pull down my barns, and build greater, and will say to my soul, Eat, drink, and be merry." But God said, "THOU FOOL."

SULTRY summer pours down intolerable day in Wolfsden. It is the hottest season of many years. Corn-leaves curl and shrink; unmown grass turns to premature hay; idle, dainty cows, and luxurious swine, seek cool shelter in shady pools. Sheep stretch themselves upon the sod behind stone walls, and beneath wind-fallen trees. Restless children escape from the hot school-room with pretence of replenishing the water-pail from the distant spring, and loiter long in the grassy meadow. Their fingers are stained with ripe strawberries, betraying their truancy. The schoolmistress winks sleepily at the transgression. There, in the green meadow, gay grasshoppers sing away their sunny life, forgetful of the fabled counsel of the frugal ant, who still toils on, laying up stores for future want. In vain the tantalizing almanac predicts "sharp — lightning — and heavy showers — about — this time." The prediction is spread, like a long net, through the calendar page, but catches not a clap of thunder, nor a drop of rain, to save its credit. All signs fail.

Parson Boreman moves in the matter. He cites Scripture

proofs of like cases, and preaches a sermon upon the drouth of Elijah the Tishbite, in the days of Ahab, showing there were dry times in old times as in modern times, and from the same cause, namely, want of rain. And when Elijah prophesied rain, the drouth ended; but not till Ahab had sent seven times did a cloud like a man's hand appear, and then there was an abundance of rain. Therefore Parson Boreman predicts rain when the drouth shall be ended, and fortifies his position by the words of Ahab. To hasten this consummation, he mentions the subject in his forenoon and afternoon prayer. Yet the heavens relent not. Prediction and prayer must wait this fulfilment.*

Business is dull at Bragly's. Loafers lag at home. Empty bottles remain unfilled. The gill-cup intermits its retail measure of cumulative misery. The grinders cease, or slowly move, and tobacco remains unchewed. Trade is flat, and Bragly is uneasy. One gets tired in a long time of doing nothing, and thinking nothing, and being nothing.

Bragly is prosperous in his vocation, yet his ambition is not fully satisfied. Tedious leisure nourishes his discontent. His position is not prominent enough. His merits are not duly appreciated in Wolfsden. Sixty years of shrewd and saving thrift have gained him wealth, and why not honor and office?

* It was on this occasion that George Bowler wrote with his pencil, on the partition of the singers' seats, the following epigram, which, I am sorry to confess, was remembered in Wolfsden longer than the sermon which occasioned it:

> "Our parson makes his doctrine plain —
> Dry *seasons* come from lack of rain.
> Proceed, good parson, let us know
> The source whence drouthy *sermons* flow."

He has often contrived to be nominated ; but, though shrewdly arranging to have all his partisans at the polls whom liberal drams and vague promises would purchase, he has always been defeated. In his younger days he was elected ensign of the Wolfsden Light Infantry, but, being twice superseded, he resigned without getting a title. Once, in a thin town-meeting, by rallying his force unexpectedly, he was nearly chosen representative. Since that time, he has waited in vain. He now meditates the policy of a more ostentatious style of living. A fine house, with corresponding surroundings, will show that self-appreciation which challenges and commands the consideration of others. Great men dwell in large houses, and this is not only the sign, but often the source, of their greatness. Bragly will have a great house. Such things are quickly done in Wolfsden, as elsewhere in Maine, by those who have the ambition. A pine frame of two stories, covered with boards and shingles and white paint, with plenty of windows and green blinds, makes an imposing outside, which is for the public. The inside belongs to the owner, and may be as unfinished and unfurnished as his head.

He reviewed the selected site, and drove stakes at the corners. Their regular appearance confirmed his choice. He proceeded to count the cost, and chuckled in the prospect of cheap magnificence. Poor men, of whose farms he has mortgages, must sell him timber at a low price. Thriftless but strong men will dig and lay the foundations for little besides rum and tobacco, and that little he will pay in refuse goods. Meanwhile, he must board them ; but for this he has a stock of poor salt beef and pickled fish. Drunken laborers are not difficult to feed nor to pay, and will be quick customers for his garbage. Bragly understands business ; his talents lie in that line. Sometimes he philosophizes, but always in a vein corresponding to his vocation. Mankind, says he, are divided into two classes. The upper class, who cheat; and the lower, who are cheated. He plumes himself upon belonging to the upper class. Bragly is aristocratic.

In his mind's eye he sees his shingle palace already built. He sees himself its proud proprietor. He looks upon himself with new respect. He will make himself better known. He possesses wealth, and wealth will secure dignity. At least, he can be justice of the peace — Solomon Bragly, Esq. It shall go hard, but he will yet be representative. Bragly is ambitious.

But business must be minded; even genius must have tools. Bragly proceeds to count up and catalogue the tools he can command.

Bang was the nearest and first on the list. He had grown very seedy and shaky. He was evidently on his last legs; but, with proper nursing, might last through this service. Bragly's nursing always answers the purpose; that is, his own purpose. He knows, by long experience, how to deal out his drams so as to get the greatest possible amount of work. He calculated that this job would just about use up Bang, and the contemplated result was not an unpleasant item. Besides the natural antipathy which the rum-seller, like the cat, feels towards his victim, Bragly had an old grudge against Bang. Many years ago, he had refused to vote for him, and had uttered some contemptuous remark; and also, at the time of his brief reformation, he had indulged in some severe reflections upon him. Bragly never forgot nor forgave things of that sort. He has long been revenging himself. He will now finish up his revenge, and finish off Bang.

Herring Cove would furnish its quota of material to be used up in the enterprise. There was a numerous shoal of the Herring tribe, whom Bragly had for many years fed with vile bait, and dried and smoked with poisonous tobacco, and pickled with fiery N. E. rum. These, by long possession, belonged to Bragly. He had caught them in his net, and brought them up in his school. Scaly fish, at best, but Bragly could use them with profit.

Chadbourn, the shiftless mason, he safely reckoned upon; also some others, yet hesitating in the road to ruin, but who he shrewdly guessed would come along with the crowd. King Solomon, with all his wealth and wisdom, had no surer resources for his temple than Bragly for his shingle palace.

Bragly proceeded with fervor in his enterprise. Besides the cellar, a well was necessary; for the old well always failed in a dry time, just when water was most needed. Bang once said that Bragly had exhausted it in watering his rum. Now he should pay for the sarcasm by digging a new one. A dry time is a good time to dig a well, for water then obtained will hold out.

And so he summoned Bang and Chadbourn to dig his well. Chadbourn was sometimes called the sexton's clerk, for the sexton usually employed him to assist in digging graves. Being the most reliable of the two, he was appointed master-workman; and, beginning on one side of the well, placed Bang on the other, and they proceeded to dig. Chadbourn's excavation, from his habit of grave-digging, took the form of a parallelogram. Under the influence of his morning dram, he worked fast and dug deep. Bang copied the example of his leader, and dug a hole of like dimensions and depth; and when Bragly, after an hour or two, came out with some visitors to see the progress of the work, they were struck at seeing two deep graves in near proximity. Bragly shuddered, but the feeling soon passed away. Thoughts of the grave seldom disturbed Bragly, though he had led so many miserable victims thither.

The well progressed. The two parallelograms were merged in the wider circle, which sunk deeper and deeper. Platforms were placed within the sides, and the earth was tediously thrown out by progressive steps. Yet the work went on; the well still deepened, and the diggers descended.

Bragly's ambition sought for yet other developments. He meditated the chance of elevating his position by a matrimonial alliance. His "old woman went off," for so he spoke of his wife's death, a dozen years since, and left no incumbrance but a boy, begotten in the likeness of Bragly, whom he had educated in his petty arts, and sent into the world. So the old man was free to begin the world again. His matrimonial experiences were not such as to stimulate him to a new venture, for the sake of domestic bliss; but policy prompted a thought of other advantages to be gained in that way.

Lucinda Boreman, the minister's daughter, she of the slender waist and long curls, the long-established belle of Wolfsden, was still in the market, — a precious commodity, but with no customer. The thought was aspiring, but Bragly, who saw himself the proud proprietor of his imaginary palace, and the justice of peace, and representative yet to be, encouraged aspiring thoughts. It would be a fine speculation, if a possible one. Lucinda would be an heiress when the parson and wife should die, for Lucinda, who had lived so long without growing old, would outlive everybody; and this, also, was Bragly's own plan of life. He was not sixty, and when put in trim by the tailor was young again, — so he judged, and with some reason. His still, sly, spider life had not worn him much. Such folks live long.

By soft approaches Bragly resolved to win his way. In such affairs nature and love teach the young, — policy and craft, the old. Nature and love are the best teachers, but policy and craft are often unexpectedly successful. Bragly's expectations were preposterous; but expectations equally preposterous have been realized.

Religion would serve as a stepping-stone to his ambition. He thought it was often so employed. Bragly reflected upon the different sorts, that he might select that most easily put on, and best adapted to his purposes. A genteel, aristocratic religion would suit him best. Bragly had hitherto been non-committal on religion, but might easily step on that side of the fence. A life of utter depravity and vileness is thought to be fair preparation for conversion; whereas the practice of morality and virtue generally hardens the impenitent in unbelief.

Bragly became serious. He attended church regularly, in white cravat and kid gloves. His little cunning eye, and puckered contriving mouth, practised solemn grimaces. He laid in a stock of Bibles, and "Calls to the Unconverted," and urged them upon his customers. He mentioned to the tract distributor his willingness to take charge of a few, and circulate them. His devotional deportment attracted attention. Deacon Murray called, and bought a pound of tea;

Bragly (by mistake, of course) handed back too much change, and, when called to rectify it, remarked upon his habit of this sort of blunder. All this was set down to concern of mind, which Bragly was striving to conceal and quench. The deacon watched the progress of Bragly's case closely, and mentioned it to the parson. Bragly's tactics thus far succeed.

The work of the well goes on. Deep in the earth the diggers delve. Three, four, five successive platforms descend the subterranean profound, and are manned by gaunt and grim wretches, whose muscles, stimulated by infernal potions, labor incessantly, tossing the mud and stones from the cold, wet bottom, to the hot, dry surface. At length another contrivance is adopted. The platforms are removed, and a huge windlass, with long projecting arms, is erected across the yawning depth, by which empty buckets descend, to return laden with heavy freight. Far down in the dark abyss, the bulky bodies of Bang and Chadbourn seem like pigmies, compared with the gaunt laborers who sweat at the windlass above.

It is a fearful thing to look down from the dizzy brink into the profound depth. What if the solid wall of earth should suddenly bury the diggers alive,—perhaps in a living grave! Such things have been. Or, if the brink should fall from beneath the beholders' feet, precipitating their bodies, a mangled mass, upon the devoted wretches beneath! Let long timbers and strong planks be laid around, to prevent the catastrophe; and let the diggers hasten their work, that the danger may be sooner past. Alas! their danger, and ruin, and death, may not be so escaped; for, though the earth remain innocent of their blood, yet their souls' life is buried and suffocated in a lingering death in the living tomb of their besotted and beastly bodies. Bragly's tools perish, but his tactics succeed.

He made an incidental call on Parson Boreman, and suggested the idea of a tract depository at his store, and offered to take upon himself the trouble of distribution. He was happy to hear that the missionary had been so successful, in spite of the evil-minded opposition he had met (referring to Harry), and regretted that he had neglected handing in his mite, which he would thank the parson to receive; and, taking out a well-filled pocket-book, he presented a five-dollar bill. He would also be pleased to subscribe for a missionary paper. The parson, though partly prepared for the miracle by Deacon Murray's communication, was astonished at such liberality from such a source. He had evidently overlooked and under-estimated one of the treasures of his parish. He atoned by unaccustomed affability for past neglect. He invited Bragly to remain for tea. The ever-charming Lucinda was present, and bestowed her ever-ready and practised smiles. The parson was plainly pleased with the convert. Perhaps Lucinda might not disdain the conquest. Bragly's tactics are wonderful.

His well, like his profound calculations, grows deeper and deeper. Forty feet have the diggers descended, and yet deeper must they delve; for Bragly says, with authority, that he will have no half-way work. Let him hasten, for his tools begin to fail. Bang digs, and totters; yet still he digs, for Bragly's potions still stimulate nature's expiring energies to extremest efforts. Chadbourn is pale. His eyes are red, his lips are blue, his visage is haggard,— yet he and the other wretches labor on. Bragly will have no half-way work,— his work and his tools will soon be finished.

Materials were wanted, as well as tools, and Bragly had a fine lot of timber in his eye. It was on Dick Freeport's farm. Dick's farm was just beyond the school-house, before referred to. His father gave it to him several years before, and he settled with a good wife and good prospects, for his farm was an excellent tract of good soil, besides the valuable lot of timber; and, his father dying shortly after, he received a portion of the remaining property, with the charge of his mother, whose discreet and careful aid was a valuable acquisition, for, besides other treasures, Dick's children multiplied amazingly. But his chance of prosperity and happiness was soon clouded, for he gradually fell into Bragly's hands. Bragly's store was nearer than any other, and Dick could not withstand the temptation of unlimited credit. Drunkenness was not his vice,— at least, not at first; but he would drink a sociable glass, and then he would buy whatever Bragly recommended,— for Bragly was ostentatious of his accommodating disposition and liberal credit. Dick bought largely, scarcely asking prices; and gave notes on interest for large balances, at each quarterly settlement.

Accumulated notes, with interest, had long ago placed him in Bragly's power, and now was his time to take advantage of it. He knew the value of the timber-lot,— it would of itself be a moderate independence to a judicious manager,— but Bragly resolved to have it at his own price. He understood business, and had his victim in his power. With this acquisition he could build a very large house.

He proposed the matter to Freeport, who, in spite of his

thriftlessness, was much disconcerted. He had long been troubled with a consciousness of accumulating debts, but soothed himself with the promise of paying off with a portion of his timber. Bragly now proposed to take the whole at a price which would but half satisfy his claim, leaving him still hopelessly in debt; and the ruinous proposition could not be refused, for Bragly spoke peremptorily, as Freeport had not heard him speak before. He saw that Bragly had a rough side, as well as a smooth one. He stammered some plea of temporary delay, and wisely, or luckily, went home and laid the whole case before his mother. She was astonished at his large indebtedness to Bragly, and distressed at the sacrifice proposed. She sent him immediately to consult Squire Chinby, the old friend of the family, who had advised settling Richard on this farm, and had himself drawn the writings. Richard repaired at once to Squire Chinby, and stated the whole case, —his manner of dealing with Bragly, his large indebtedness, and Bragly's imperative and ruinous proposition. Chinby's deep black eyes were filled with calm indignation. He saw through the matter in a moment; and showed Richard his folly, and Bragly's knavery, by producing his own domestic accounts, which fell far short of Richard's, though his family was larger, and more abundantly supplied. Richard asked, despondingly, what he should do about it.

"Do!" said Chinby; "why, let Bragly eat you up, since he has got you in his jaws! It is such as you that he lives upon, and the sooner he disposes of his fodder the better; for it may diminish the breed of fools."

Chinby sometimes spoke roughly; but Richard was toc much depressed to be angry, and, besides, he had a strong impression, from old experience, that his help, if anywhere, was in Chinby.

Chinby proceeded with his reproaches and assurances of irremediable ruin, and pictured the coming misery of his family, till poor Richard was in despair. "But," said he, "it may as well be so now as at another time. If you were free from his clutches to-day, he, or some one like him, would grasp you to-morrow." Richard caught at the implied suggestion of freedom to-day, and solemnly protested that, if he could be put in a way of relief, he would pay for his folly by future self-denial and hard work, till the debt should be cancelled, and would never be such a fool again. Chinby heard him through, and told him that he would go with him to Bragly, and see what could be done about it.

It was not easy for a rogue to maintain his position when brought to account by Chinby. Duplicity shrunk before his unquestionable truth and uprightness, and conscious villany saw itself thoroughly exposed in view of his keen eye and clear understanding.

Besides, Chinby had the reputation of legal knowledge, which had been, in several cases, of signal service to justice. Bragly knew, and was as well prepared for all this, as a mean, prevaricating knave can ever be prepared for the ordeal of stern, scrutinizing justice. He had managed his affairs with sufficient skill to defy, or at least evade, legal inquiry; and, divining Chinby's purpose, he resolved to vindicate his own position in the upper class of mankind, by opposing bold effrontery to Chinby's interference.

In this he was moderately successful. His brassy resolution was not quite sufficient, but he took refuge in stolid doggedness, as impenetrable as the hide of the rhinoceros. He refused to exhibit his accounts, saying they were settled, and that his only claim on Freeport consisted of promissory notes. Chinby was compelled to admit Bragly's boast that he understood business. The utmost he could do was to induce him to give twice what he had proposed for the timber; which sum, being still less than half its value, but just covered Richard's notes. Having obtained this concession, Chinby proposed that the business should be finished immediately. Richard would have delayed, in hopes of better terms; but Chinby now took Bragly's side, and insisted upon a prompt settlement. He would not be a party to any trifling. Richard reluctantly consented. The papers were soon drawn and duly authenticated, by which, "for value received and acknowledged, said Freeport conveyed to said Bragly, his heirs and assigns forever, all his right, title, and interest, in the timber on said lot, situated as aforesaid," &c. &c.

The document was drawn with lawyer-like circumlocution, verbosity, and tautology, and exchanged for Richard's notes, and a receipt in full of all demands, with impressive ceremony. Chinby was grave and decisive as a judge, Freeport as spiritless and passive as a convict, and Bragly as business-like and blandly ferocious as an executioner. Chinby bade Bragly good-evening, and retired with Freeport. "Now," said he, "we will go and see your mother, and while on the way please to lay up my counsel. You are now clear of Bragly,—keep clear of him, and keep clear of debt. It is the only safe and pleasant way of life. Debt is the destroyer of more happiness than all other causes combined. It rides like a nightmare on the necks of thousands, who all their life long are struggling to hold their heads up, in spite of the depressing weight. If you break every other commandment, keep this, '*Owe no man anything.*'

"Say nothing about this transaction, and you will save your timber. When Bragly proceeds to meddle with it, your mother will send him a note which I will prepare for her, and which will stop his proceedings. You may pay the amount of whatever real value you have received to other families whom he has defrauded and ruined, for otherwise your hands cannot be clean. It is bad to be in Bragly's debt, but worse to adopt his principles."

Richard's mother was gratified with the arrival of her old friend and adviser. She was for the first time made acquainted with the fact that she, as residuary legatee, was the real proprietor of the timber, Richard's "right, title, and interest," being nothing at all; for Chinby, who drew the deed of gift, and knew Richard's simplicity, which might make him the prey of sharpers, had, with the father's approbation, inserted a clause reserving the timber. Richard knew nothing of it, and never could have been injured by it; for his right as heir would be good on the death of his mother, and she, even if she knew her right, would not interfere in any fair transaction of her son. Bragly's tactics were defeated; but as yet he knew it not. Why should he be told till it should become necessary? Troublesome tidings are best delayed. Who can say, amid the casualties of life and death, that they need ever be known?

Bragly's well is sunk to a fearful depth. So are his tools, the diggers. But the work is not yet done. The well must be walled with stone. It is necessary to keep the power of work in his human machines till their work is done.

The drouth is ended. Parson Boreman's prediction is accomplished. A chill wind comes from the east; leaves flutter and rustle; swallows fly low; swine gather up sticks and straws and carry them to their beds; geese and ducks smooth and oil their plumage; sheep and horses ranging in distant pastures draw nearer home; signs multiply; the night is dark, and there is a sound of abundance of rain.

In Bang's dwelling a severer storm rages. Sounds of violence, of raving fury, of supplicating terror, of fierce execration, howlings as of madness, wailings as of anguish, frantic yells and sobbings of despair. Such scenes have often been there, but now the dire furies rage more fiercely than ever. The livelong night the terrible tumult prevails.

Delirium tremens, the most horrible precursor of the horrible death of the drunkard, is upon Bang. His maniac eyes glare upon imaginary monsters. Huge, crawling serpents surround and encircle him. Demons guard every door, and grin with ghastly malignity at every window. A fearful shape, meditating some dire purpose, sits in the chimney-corner. It has the burly body and sits in the sullen posture of the long-murdered and long-remembered Jotham. The head is swollen with horrid deformity, and ever and anon shakes as with some settled purpose of revenge. Bang shakes with terror and raves with alternate defiance. His eyes turn restlessly in every direction upon horrible enemies. He seeks to shun the monsters, and rushes violently in various directions for escape. He foams with fury, he yells with terror, he groans with anguish. The rain pours down in torrents without, but not enough to drown the terrible storm within.

In vain the terrified wife seeks to soothe him with entreaties and cries. The fearful children hide in remote closets, and tremble and moan piteously. The live-long night doles out its successive hours of misery.

When the morning comes, the fit has somewhat subsided, and Bang lies in the sleep of exhaustion; yet his convulsed and starting nerves show the agony that racks his frame. The fires of hell, self-kindled, as ever, torture and consume him.

Bragly has not passed a pleasant night. Something has murdered sleep. His thoughts have taken an uncomfortable turn. Conscience troubles him, or rather that feeling which is the poor substitute for conscience in base minds,— the conscience which never suggests moral dissuasives from evil, but often darkly hints terrors of retribution. He revolves the unwelcome thought that he is near sixty. How short seems the last ten years! He will soon be seventy, soon eighty, soon be dead!

A strange impression that this inevitable destiny may come, without even this reprieve, haunted him. It had unaccountably done so at other times of late. Remembered omens and superstitious forerunners thickly forced themselves upon him. The two deep graves with which his well was begun,— strange circumstance! He had heard it remarked that when old men build houses, and lay new plans of life, they soon die. His thoughts came unbidden, and obstinately remained. He could not rest. He rose and lighted a candle, and proceeded to inspect his accounts. His eye fell upon Freeport's conveyance. Even the thought of this gainful transaction failed to cheer him. He opened and examined the paper more attentively. It had many useless words, but lacked some which would make it more satisfactory. It did not even claim or represent the timber, of which it conveyed Freeport's "right, title, and interest," to be his property, nor did it guarantee against other claims. Why did he not notice this at the time? A self-abasing acknowledgment of his awe of Chinby was his only excuse. He could not satisfy himself, and laid aside the document, and vainly tried to dismiss the discontent. But even this discontent relieved him, by taking place of the worse bugbears of his grovelling conscience.

The rain poured down upon the roof. The winds whistled dismally about his dwelling. Sharp sounds, like yells and shrieks, mingled with the storm. He looked from the window in the direction of Bang's house, and divined the cause. Some obscure gleams of light shone through the broken panes and chinks, showing unrest within. The distinct clamor showed the usual cause. Bragly muttered about the annoyance of such neighbors so near. His new mansion should not be disgraced by such surroundings. Bang and his family should go to Herring Cove, and his unsightly hovels be demolished. He resolved with the undebating decision of a Russian despot, for he relied upon his power. He returned to his bed and slept, but disquietly, and rose in the early morning in morose mood.

He heard knockings, and, on opening his door, three drenched and shivering wretches appeared. A woman, haggard and bruised, the revolting image of wretchedness, leading in each hand a younger heir of misery. It was Susan, the wife of Bang. Such was her extremity that now she came even to Bragly, the instrument of all her desolation, for present help, — a little help, shelter, warmth, and food, till Bang would let them go home, and seek other help.

The Russian despot, in his angry pride, might have been

as auspiciously approached by the meanest and most despised of his serfs. The application brought no relief to Susan, but it relieved Bragly, for it gave opportunity of exploding his pent-up discontent.

"What are you here for? You 're a pretty object to come draggling in the mud with your brats! D' ye think I 'll have such critters in my premises? *Freezing*, do you say? — A likely story, in dog-days! *Wet and cold?* — Well, go home and dry yourselves! *Afraid of Bang?*—You look more like frightening him! *No wood nor vittels?* — The more shame for you! Go to the town, — I owe you nothing!"

"O, Mr. Bragly!" implored Susan, "do not drive us off so, or a terrible judgment will come on you! I know it! The Lord tells me so. You have worked Bang for weeks, and given his family nothing. It is your rum that has done it all! Now, if you will help me and the children a little, to keep us from dying, I will forgive you. If you don't, we shall die, and God will punish you!"

Susan had a little, though but a little, of her old spirit left. Bragly quailed a little, only a little, under it. He belonged to the upper class; it is the prerogative of aristocracy to be unmoved by the complaints and appeals of the poor.

But Bragly saw, in the hazy distance, some one approaching. He wished to be rid of the dismal group before him, and told Susan to be off, to go home, and he would send some wood and some victuals; and with this promise, which, if he meant to redeem it at all, would tax him but with the smallest and meanest portion, he shut the door in Susan's face, and peeped from the window to see that she departed. Susan evidently was not encouraged by his surly promise. She lingered a moment, but her shivering and moaning children urged the mother's instincts to her extremest efforts. If she could only hold out to get to Colonel Bowler's, she could get relief. It was more than a mile through the muddy road of the woods, and the wind and rain beat pitilessly upon her exhausted frame, and upon her cold and hungry children. But there was no other resource; and Bragly saw her trailing slowly off-home, as he supposed, and he felt a pleasure in the success of his tactics.

The approaching figure was Chadbourn's; not a much more creditable visitor than those just departed. But Bragly could dispose of him more conveniently; and, besides, he had still a use for him. So he supplied him with the soul-expelling liquid, and seated him in his shop.

Suddenly the storm lulled; the wind abated; the clouds parted. It looked light, — almost sunshine. Bragly threw open his shop door, and walked out into his front yard, debating of the weather, and the expediency of sending for his workmen to draw the stone and wall up his well. Bang just then made his appearance out of doors, looking about as usual, and Bragly resolved to send nothing to Susan, who had evidently told too big a story. As Bang approached, he appeared to step more briskly, and his countenance was more animated than usual. His blood-shot eyes did not hang heavily, but gleamed with sharp brightness. Bragly supposed him just stimulated with a strong morning dram, and rejoiced that there was still so much material in him to be used up; for his plans were expanding, and he needed more tools.

Bang approaches, and beckons as though he has something to tell. Bragly has heard Susan's story, and would like to hear Bang's, and therefore meets him half way. Bang familiarly lays his hand on Bragly's shoulder, and begins to talk incoherently of Jotham.

"'T was I killed him, ten years ago! I killed him dead, dead, dead! But he came again last night! He brought ten thousand devils with him! He sat in the corner all night, and the devils kept round the doors and windows; — but I have just killed him again, and drove them all off! They have carried off the old woman and children with 'em; but will be glad to let 'em go again, — ha! ha! ha! — hurrah for Bang!"

Insanity is in his eye. His familiar grasp tightens upon Bragly's shoulder, who tries to shake him off. But the effort only excites Bang, who grasps like his own iron vice. The returning fit comes more violently upon him. He glances wildly about; and Bragly, alarmed, in vain endeavors to free himself.

"There they come!" exclaims the frenzied Bang. "Jotham and his devils! Ho! keep 'em off, off, off!" and he whirled Bragly about, so as to interpose his body between himself and the visionary objects of his terror. His maniac strength is that of a giant. Bragly's struggles are impotent in his grasp, as he whirls him about to keep off the demon crew. They are not far from the well, and in their struggles upon the slippery ground are approaching nearer to it; but the demons are in the other direction, and Bang sees not the danger of the well.

With increasing terror, Bragly tries to draw Bang another way; but his struggling efforts and loud appeals are lost in the stronger power and louder howls and shouts of Bang, while each moment brings them nearer to the dreadful abyss.

Bragly screams to Chadbourn for help; and he comes to the door, in maudlin drunkenness, incapable of giving aid, or even understanding the danger.

"I say-er," he drawls, "wot you-er doin', wrastlin'there for? Goit, oldBang! Goit, busters! Wot makes yer holler-so? Come, takeadrink! Goit, — hic!"

The struggle ceases not. The sweat of deadly terror drips from Bragly's pallid face and quivering limbs. They are upon the slippery margin of the well. The agonizing screams of Bragly mingle with the maniac howls of Bang, and are answered from the echoing woods.

Susan hears, and hurries on, for she fears the pursuit of Bang. But the dreadful screams and yells have suddenly ceased. Only the driving rain and moaning winds disturb nature's silence.

Pale, drenched, shivering, exhausted, staggering, Susan reached Colonel Bowler's, with her wretched children, and briefly told her story. Pitying eyes and ready hands received the sufferers. Susan was quickly placed in bed, and her trembling limbs chafed and warmed; and she was refreshed with nourishment, as fast as safety allowed. The children required less cautious treatment, and in an hour were bright and active as ever.

Ike started off to see about Bang, — chiefly that Susan might be satisfied. Arriving at the miserable dwelling, a scene of wild disorder was shown. All doors were open, all windows broken. Crockery, clothing, furniture, and rubbish, were mingled and hurled in every direction. The chimney-corner, where Bang saw the spectral Jotham, was filled and battered with various heavy missiles. But no living being remained in the house. Looking in the direction of Bragly's,

Ike saw Chadbourn near the well, in loud consultation with the deaf old housekeeper in the door, each shouting question and reply, but neither understanding the other, while Chadbourn pointed to the well with earnest gesticulations. With some misgivings of what may have happened, Ike approached Chadbourn, who, still drunk, pointed to the well, and exclaimed,

"Theretheybe, goners,—gone-downers! Tumbledin, all of-'m, wrastlin'! Bangandallof'em, wrastlin'! Old Bragly-andallof'em, wrastlin'!"

Ike placed a plank and looked over the edge. Down fifty feet in the murky depth, the straining eye indistinctly saw two bodies lying across, and partly covered with mud and water. The dreadful truth of Chadbourn's incoherent explanation was apparent. People were summoned, and the lifeless bodies of Bang and Bragly, the mutual destroyers and avengers, the aristocrat and plebeian, the tactician and the man of muscle, each bereft of their power and levelled now, were drawn up and laid side by side.

There was a great concourse of people at the funeral;—curiosity attracts more strongly than sympathy. Parson Boreman preached with his usual eloquence, from the text, "Man goeth to his long home, and the mourners go about the streets." He proved at length, from Scripture and nature, that all men must die, sooner or later; that no man knoweth the time or manner of his death, or who among us shall follow next, &c. &c. The widowed Susan being not yet enough recovered to attend the funeral, Bang's present condition was pretty plainly assumed as anything but enviable, and his eternal ruin plainly shown to be from his habitual neglect of Sabbath ordinances; and not, as some may have supposed, from neglect of week-day duties, and indulgence of every-day drunkenness.

Bragly's state of mind not being fully known to the minister, his fate was left somewhat dubious; though the fact of his recently awakened interest in missionary and tract operations gave consoling grounds of hope. From which it may be inferred that the aristocrat yet maintains his ascendency, in spite of the leveller Death! Bragly's five dollars to the missionary fund was a lucky investment. His tactics are an example.

Not having room for a synopsis of the sermon, we can only hope that the parson may be persuaded to gratify the public, and console perambulating mourners, by publishing it, either separately, or as an appendix to the treatise of the lost tribes.

CHAPTER XIV.

We left Alek on the road by the banks of the Saco. If the reader expects to find him there still, then we have failed properly to represent his onward energy. Alek is in New York. He has been there three months. He knows things not understood in Wolfsden. His eyes are wider awake, his step brisker, his attitude bolder and more self-confident.

He does not slouch along the sidewalks jostling the passengers, nor stand in the gutters to give them room. He does not pause to read the Valentines, or gaze at the caricatures in the shop-windows. He does not follow the strutting military feathered bipeds, whom Plato excluded from his definition of man; nor loiter near the organ-grinder, nor mingle with the simpletons about the mock-auction stands. The Jews of Chatham-street do not pull him in at their doors to buy second-hand finery and gilded jewelry; nor the Bowery boys familiarly address him with schemes of raffling and lottery speculations; nor the frail women accost him with their enticements. When he moves, it is with the manner of one who has business to do; and when he stops, it is because he has arrived at the place to do it.

Alek found business. Prompt men can always find something to do in New York. Those of small ambition may enter menial employments. Those who have a knack at shrewd tricks can live by their wits. Men of higher capacities, and better energies, can quickly find or make a way to respectable employments. Alek was not avaricious nor sensual; his motive was not to hoard money, nor to spend it in vulgar gratifications. To learn men, manners, business, and the philosophy of life, he counted the best present use of the new school to which he came. A moderate salary satisfied him, and with it he gained a character for energy and reliability which would be a sufficient stepping-stone to another position when he should choose.

Alek's access to employment was, however, made more easy and speedy by Harry's introductory letter to his uncle, the merchant.

Mr. Samuel Boynton was a merchant of the old-fashioned sort, high-minded, methodical, somewhat formal and self-opinionated, and having faith in the old institutions and doctrines in which he was moulded. He believed in Fast-day sermons and Fourth-of-July orations, in the piety of his church and the patriotism of his party. He was nobly educated for times long since gone by, and he still nourished and brooded old notions, as the careful hen broods her eggs, after they are long addled. But his practices, prompted by the instincts of a benevolent heart, were often at variance with the policy and feeling of the society and party to which he was allied, and in whose support he was compelled to suppress many misgivings. He was life-member of the A. B. C. F. M., and yet contributed to the Union Missionary Society, which condemns the A. B. C. F. M. At his table sound doctors of divinity sometimes met radical reformers, and would find the *Boston Liberator* side by side with the *New York*

Observer. His toleration satisfied neither party. Conservatives saw that his influence encouraged disorganizing principles, and radicals complained that conservatives were able to claim so liberal a man as one of their party. Yet neither ventured to remonstrate; for Mr. B. was not a man to bear dictation.

Alek chanced to arrive in New York during the "anniversary week," celebrated by religious and other associations; and, accepting Mr. Boynton's cordial invitation, found himself, at the dinner-hour, seated at a more sumptuous table, with a finer and better-dressed company, than he had before seen; for those who attend the anniversaries are generally the most respectable of their respective societies, and of those some of the most distinguished were always allotted to Mr. Boynton's hospitality; such matters being mostly arranged by private understanding of the leaders, though the entertainer is also entitled to invite whom he chooses. This privilege Mr. Boynton had exercised by inviting not only Alek, but also another person, more prominent, though much less congenial to the general taste and feelings of the guests. This was no other than the noted Mr. Paradox, the incendiary leader and agitating apostle of one of the most radical, subversive, and formidable associations of the time.

No other person had so early in life engaged so large a share of public attention, or been the object of so earnest and opposite feelings. Scarcely a paper in the United States was issued without an article or paragraph relating to him, of which a large proportion expressed the severest condemnation and abhorrence; the soundest and most patriotic of the political and religious papers being most frequent and earnest in their anathemas, which, indeed, was the surest proof of their soundness and patriotism.

Mr. Paradox well deserved all the abuse he received; for he had done more to overthrow and destroy the deference and veneration attached to the time-hallowed institutions which divines and patriots support, and by which they profit, than any man or demon since the days of Dr. Faustus; having, besides his individual influence, opened sluices of public thought and feeling, through which an increasing current of opinion still rushes, endangering the sacred foundations of church and state.

By the side of Mr. Paradox sat no less a personage than the Rev. Dr. Paragon, so celebrated for his learning, his piety, and his position, being the acknowledged head of the only true and infallible religious sect in the land, all the other ninety-nine being clearly gone astray, and corrupted with the most palpable and damning errors.

Thus, by chance or contrivance, were these champions of their respective fields placed in proximity, and compelled to the interchange of courteous salutations. Dr. Paragon being much the oldest man, and also an official dignitary, the option of debate properly belonged to him; and therefore Mr. Paradox, who is always the most civil when he meditates most mischief, abstained from provocation, and joined blandly in general remarks. But, under the circumstances, collision was unavoidable; for the reverend doctor was surrounded by friends, who expected the onset, which his position would not allow him to decline, and, therefore, gathering up his learning, dignity, and eloquence, he proceeded to an overpowering onslaught upon his adversary.

He began by showing the disorganizing character of all

radical movements, which, originating outside of the church are unauthorized by Scripture, and necessarily hostile to divine authority. He instanced the dangerous character of abolitionism, which he pronounced false in its principles and fatal in its tendencies. He proved from Moses and St. Paul the scriptural sanction of slavery, as an institution appointed by God and approved by his apostles; and testified to the general piety of the slaveholders, which he favorably contrasted with the want of reverence for the Scripture, the Sabbath, and the church, shown by leading abolitionists, some of whose attacks he specified and repelled; and also showed that his own sect were faithful to their duty in preaching the Gospel, in whose light slavery, and all other evils, would finally be overcome. He also claimed for himself and brethren, north and south, that they were the only true abolitionists, inasmuch as they sincerely mourned and prayed over the evil, and patiently waited God's time for its removal; which might, perhaps, have already been accomplished, but for the mischievous agitation of professed abolitionists.

The dignified company were pleased with the ability and approved the severity of their champion's discourse; and even Mr. Paradox, by the respectful attention he gave, showed that he appreciated the honor of being demolished by so distinguished a divine. Yet, true to his name and nature, he must needs reply, and that, too, in a manner both perplexing and provoking.

He said that he would not dispute with so learned a critic upon interpretations of Scripture, but thought that, if its mission in the world was to establish slavery, mankind might have managed to get along without its light, since many heathen nations, unaided by revelation, had adopted the institution. He apprehended that, with such interpretations, the Bible would lose its authority, in reflecting minds. "As," said he, "it seems already to be disregarded by yourself and brethren, since you 'mourn and pray for the removal' of an 'institution which it sanctions, as appointed by God himself, and approved by his apostles.'" Upon the doctor's claim for himself and friends to be the only true abolitionists, he expressed pleasure in hearing of the progress of truth in such quarters; and, as to the imputation of having put back God's time for doing the work, he replied by a modest doubt of his ability to control the purposes of Omnipotence, even if he had the wish to do so.

Notwithstanding the conciliatory manner of the reply, the reverend doctor was not mollified, and answered, quickly, "Sir, you misrepresent my views. I was discussing the *abstract* question concerning the fundamental principles of the relation, whether it be necessarily such a *malum in se* as may not exist *salva fide et salva ecclesia.*"

"Sir," replied Mr. Paradox, "as to misrepresenting your views, I cannot do that knowingly, for they are to me incomprehensible; but, as it seems they relate only to abstractions, they do not concern me, for my business is with realities."

Such was the irreverence with which Mr. Paradox sometimes replied to the most revered dignitaries. Alek, who had been but a few hours in New York, and whose rustic reason was as yet unused to the refined light in which matters are judged in the city, supposed the reverend doctor vanquished in the debate; but the evident disapprobation with which the remarks of Mr. Paradox were received by the clerical company, and the deference and admiration with which the doctor was listened to, showed that an opposite opinion prevailed. The matter was soon set right before the public by the following paragraph in a popular daily paper:

"The Rev. Doctor Paragon, while dining with a company of distinguished divines, was bitterly assailed and denounced by the notorious Mr. Paradox, who had, by some means, obtained admission. The venerable divine, in the most gentlemanly and Christian manner, rebuked the incendiary fanatic, and, with the ready eloquence which marks his private conversation, no less than his public performances, vindicated Christianity and the church from his imputations, and exposed the reckless folly and impiety of the fanatic crew who are endeavoring to excite the public mind, and disturb the peace of society. If these proceedings are persisted in, it may become a duty to arrest them by summary process. Let the outraged public see that order and decency are preserved in their meeting at the Tabernacle this evening."

Alek, to whom such views of life were new, resolved to attend the meeting at the Tabernacle, where, notwithstanding the suggested summary process, a very large audience assembled. As the addresses proceeded, it soon became evident, by the increasing uproar, which, commencing with hisses and stamping, soon grew to shouts and yells, that many had come, according to the suggestion of the papers, to preserve order and decency. But, notwithstanding their efforts, the most violent disorder soon manifested itself, until, at length, a gallant and distinguished captain (whose patriotism has since been politically rewarded) sprang upon the platform occupied by the speakers, and, brandishing a formidable weapon, solemnly swore, by the powers celestial and infernal, that the speeches should be stopped; and, being backed by a band of choice spirits, soon caused the dispersion of the assembly.

Among the speakers was a lady, who, in the mildest manner and most impressive language, insisted that manly honor, equally with Christian duty, required of men to protect the humble and proscribed; and that to uphold the oppression of the poor — for thus she designated slavery — was unmanly as well as unchristian, and, when done by those who themselves belonged to the industrious class, and were therefore bound by policy to preserve the rights and dignity of labor, was inexpressibly mean, and was sure to incur the contempt of honorable men, even among slaveholders themselves, as well as to provoke the vengeance of God. These and the like obnoxious sentiments were promptly hissed, and stamped with the disapprobation of the orderly and decent portion of the audience.

Alek, who occupied a remote part of the gallery, was not an indifferent spectator; and we are compelled to confess that his rustic sympathies were not on the side of the preservers of order and decency, but rather with the fanatics on the platform; so that, when several brave fellows about him proposed to second the laudable exploits of the valiant captain, by mobbing the ladies as they emerged from the door, he grasped his cudgel tightly, with an impulse to remonstrate. He, however, said nothing, but kept with those about him, who supposed him to be of the same mind; and they, observing his stalwart and vigorous frame, proposed putting him forward as leader, — which honor he declined, as being a stranger. This position was voluntarily assumed by an able-bodied patriot, named Bludgeon.

Although Alek declined leadership, he kept in front of the enterprising squad; and, as they neared the female group, and Mr. B., supported by those behind him, rushed forward to execute the "summary process" by seizing the female orator, Alek, with a powerful and dextrous blow upon the head, doubled him up, there not being room to fall prostrate, and then, thrusting the end of his cudgel furiously into the faces of his supporters, to the irreparable damage of eyes, noses, and teeth, so discouraged them that they desisted from their purpose, and the fanatics passed unharmed, while Alek mingled with the crowd, and left the ground. Full details of this affair may be found in the secular and religious papers of the time, under the head of "*Abolition Riots*," recorded with that admirable regard for candor and truth which has always characterized their representations of such affairs.

CHAPTER XV.

In recording Alek's adventures, exploits, mistakes, and mischances, we do not pretend to portray a perfect character, such as a mere novelist might invent, but only to tell things as they took place, without embellishment or concealment. But, in our comments, modes of expression, and moral reflections, now that we have introduced our hero to the arena of city life, we shall carefully conform to the fashionable tone. Far be it from us to violate the proprieties of the press, by giving utterance to unpopular sentiments, or disturbing the placid stream of public opinion, upon whose unruffled surface we hope to sail. The polite reader may, therefore, confidently expect to be gratified with refinement of expression and sentiment, and perfect conformity of taste and principle with prevailing modes; and, if any unfashionable sentiment should unawares appear, the reader is begged to consider it a mistake, and to cancel it accordingly. With this definition of our position and plan, which the last few pages illustrate, we proceed in the same spirit to this new chapter.—*Vive la bagatelle!*

We have already announced that Alek had obtained employment. It was with Messrs. Greening and Russet, and through the introduction of Mr. Boynton. Mr. Greening was partner and chief business agent of a manufactory where many strange and uncouth instruments are made of wood and iron, for the convenience of a rustic and semi-civilized people, who occupy remote regions of considerable extent, and find in rude occupations some solace for the deprivations of their condition. Adapted to their simple tastes is a beam of strong wood, to the centre of which projecting portions of iron, crooked and clumsy in form, are attached, while one end of the beam is ornamented with handles, bent like the ivory end of a parasol, but much larger, and very strong. This preposterous and absurd instrument they call a "plough," and count it of more use and advantage than piano or harpsichord, which they even affect to disdain. Huge iron spikes, driven through a strong wooden frame, with the points left projecting on one side, make what they call a harrow, with which they are much pleased. A flat plate of iron or steel attached to a wooden handle is also in request among them, and is called, according to its size and form, "spade," "shovel," or "hoe" (the term "spade" is most absurdly applied, as the instrument has no use analogous to the suit of cards of that name). It should be observed that when the plate of iron which forms the termination of this toy is divided into separate prongs, as the web-foot of a duck may be divided by removing the filmy skin which unites the toes, the mutilated instrument is then called a pitchfork, — the use, however, differing from the pitchfork of musicians. Long, curved knives are also fastened to handles, sometimes long and sometimes short, and called sickles, or scythes; and these are used to cut down the vegetation, which, growing up to two or three feet in a season, would otherwise, by the accumulated growth of a few years, render the region impassable, pavements and sidewalks being there unknown.

The reader would perhaps be pleased with a personal description of Mr. Greening, the manager of this manufactory. Mr. Greening is a pleasant elderly gentleman, — elderly in years, but juvenile in appearance, being fat, round, ruddy, and agile. Good nature, good living, and good luck, have kept him fat, round, and ruddy, and much business has kept him agile. He does not look like a man of much calculation ; yet his face is mathematical, or, at least, geometrical, for it is formed of circles — wheels within wheels. Its outline is a circle, bounding the front disk of a spherical head. The tip of the nose is its exact centre. Between this and the upper segment two circular blue eyes expand their orbits, and on either side the ruddy cheeks repeat the orbic order. In the lower segment the smooth-shaven lips enclose a circular puckered mouth — puckered, but yet smooth. A hemispheric chin, like half an orange, with a central dimple, completes the physiognomy. The whole is not badly represented by the moon on the old-fashioned clock-face. People, at first look, might not think him profound; but in his business he is prompt, shrewd, and successful.

No man is more than half known till you know his wife, and therefore Mrs. Greening must be introduced.

Mr. Greening must have been led to his wife by that mysterious affinity which disposes so many to choose, as the complement of their sphere, partners as opposite as possible, not only in sex, but also in all physical and mental characteristics. Thus men short and fat look for ladies long and lean. Black eyes look lovingly upon blue. Pretty faces wed with plain; the philosopher fancies a fool; and the strong-minded woman is willingly wooed and won by a simpleton. The man of stalwart stature is entangled and captured in the net of some tiny sylph; while an ample and robust virago seizes a dapper dandy in her Amazonian embrace, and bears him in triumph to the matrimonial altar.

In one respect Mr. and Mrs. Greening come under the same description; for she is also formed geometrically, — not of circles, but of angles. Her body is almost linear, for it has extension without much breadth or thickness. Her head is a polyhedron; her face, a trapezium; her chin, a truncated pyramid. Though not a projector, she is full of projections; she is not a speculator, but is always cornered.

Not that Mrs. Greening is ugly; her sharp black eyes, and delicate complexion, and lady-like expression, and judicious arrangement of curls and ribbons and muslin, rounding the corners and filling up the crannies about the boundaries of her countenance, redeem her from that imputation. The remainder of her frame the dress-maker covers and finishes to a charm; in fact, to many charms, demonstrating the triumphs of padding, buckram, whalebone, cord, and all the materiel of female architecture.

Mrs. Greening is a pensive lady, serious, devout, and valetudinarian. She never visits the theatre, and she disapproves of dancing; yet she has resources of enjoyment exquisite and unfailing. They come in packages, in powders, in boxes, and bottles. Brandreth, Moffat, Old Dr. Jacob Townsend and young Dr. Townsend (rivals, whose mutual vilifications she discredits, but whose self-boastings she has full faith in), Swaim, Jayne, and the immortal inventor of Russia Salve, and a hundred other empirics — these be her gods. Their oracles she studies, and their nectar she sips.

Her medical researches, if not profound, are extensive, experimental, and persevering. She has been steamed by Thomson, and soused by Noggs; braced by Consumption Fitch, and manipulated by Dislocation Hewett, and every bone, spine, corn, and other deformity doctor.

Blessed be the man who first invented patent medicines, and thus opened regions of delight unknown before! A luxurious Cæsar, in degenerate days, offered rewards to him who would invent a new pleasure; but Nature had not yet perfected the brains that could devise luxuries like these for the delectation of half mankind.

Why sing of the "good time coming"? O, that the poet of quackery would arise, and sing the advent of these auspicious days — of the good time already come! Why do not a grateful people bestow rewards, and decree triumphs, and build monuments, to these joy-producing benefactors?

Shall it be replied that the injury they do exceeds their benefit? — that they poison constitutions, weaken and destroy the sanative functions of nature, shorten lives, rob the foolish and ignorant of money on false pretences of cure, and fill the papers with lying advertisements, supported by forged and fraudulent certificates? Of what account is all this? Perish the paltry objections! What is life without luxury? What is the use of money but to purchase pleasure? Of what use is the press but to circulate mingled falsehood and truth, that people may select as fancy wills? Shall we forego the subtle virtues of essences, elixirs, anodynes, panaceas, balsams, and balms distilled from a thousand flowers; got from mountain tops and valleys deep, and subterranean caves; from islands of antipodal oceans, and barbarous lands beyond Japan; handed down from seventh son to seventh son, through countless generations; obtained from Indians of undiscovered shores; revealed by miraculous accident; set forth in luminous literature; attested by victims reprieved from predestined death, whose souls still linger on this stormy side of Styx, to give supernatural testimony to supernatural cures? If it be shown that wedlock and motherhood impair health and shorten life, who for that would forego the dearest delights of life, to extend the joyless days and nights of cold celibacy?

Uncork your bottles, unseal your boxes, mingle your powders, sip your drops, swallow your pills, and spread your salves, ye daughters of delicate complaints; so shall you sweetly live and softly die!

CHAPTER XVI.

ALEK soon stood high with his employer. His business related to the selection and adaptation of the materials for the fanciful trinkets manufactured at Greening & Russet's establishment, as already described, the uses and proper qualities of which Alek understood long ago. He possessed rare judgment and faithfulness, as his employers speedily ascertained. Mr. Greening shrewdly foresaw prosperity in Alek's path. His inquiries confirmed his good opinion of Alek and of his family, and he cogitated secret thoughts.

Mr. Greening had a daughter whom he doted upon, and with good reason; at least, such good reason as fond parents usually have for their partiality. Sophia was blue-eyed, like her father, and moulded after the same order, but much beautified. His circularity was in her abated to a graceful roundness and lovableness, such as the eyes willingly linger upon. Sophia was her father's favorite, as her brother Augustus was the mother's. Augustus resembled his mother in her style of structure, but was built with more symmetry. It is perhaps for this mutual softening of opposite qualities in the race that nature contrives, by instinctive choice, to bring together parents so dissimilar.

Son and daughter were educated as those who have much wealth, much fondness, and not too much severe philosophy, educate offspring whose natural perfections need little training. The best-endowed mind cannot arrive at a right education but by a tedious road through an uninviting region. Augustus never travelled much, except in pleasant paths ; yet he became very accomplished. In his mother's eyes he possessed but one fault — he hated medicine.

Sophia was all perfection. So her father had always decided, and freely expressed. So also Edward Clevis, who had long been in her father's employ, and had attained to a distant and tremulous acquaintance with the daughter, thought. But Edward sighed in secret, and said nothing. She was a bright, unapproachable star, moving in regions of wealth and fashion which he could not hope to attain. Such are the distinctions which wealth makes among mortals, and which Edward, spite of his romance, was compelled to feel. He therefore sighed in secret, and said nothing; but Edward found or fancied some little ground of hope, upon which to build airy castles. When did ever romantic love fail to find ground for hope?

Troublesome fears and anxieties pervaded Mr. Greening's mind. Parents, who desire peace of mind and tranquillity in age, should not pray for the gift of beautiful daughters. A vision of a fashionable, dashing, daring, dangerous young man came unpleasantly across his parental views and hopes. He had met the original a few times; at first with an unpleasant impression, which soon deepened into dislike and dread. Mr. Mercutio Fitz-Faun was the heir of a family old, rich, and renowned. He was introduced to Mr. Greening's house by Augustus, who had a predilection for dashing acquaintances, which the father had not. Mrs. Greening and Sophia saw nothing objectionable in the young man. The devil, for his own purposes, often gives his worst imps a pleasant aspect in ladies' eyes; and ladies in such cases always persist in judging with their own eyes, in spite of judicious husband or father. By the father's eyes the devil-look of Fitz-Faun was plainly seen. He expressed disapprobation of the acquaintance to his wife and daughter. Fitz-Faun already instinctively understood it, and avoided the old gentleman's sight. He had experience of vigilant fathers. He cultivated the friendship of Augustus, and made brief calls at safe hours, offering delicate attentions, such as could hardly be refused without rudeness; but, if they were declined, Mr. Fitz-Faun never was offended. To Mrs. Greening he was all deference and gentleness. He showed regard for religion and for medicine; recommending Pollok's Course of Time for her reading, and Darby's Carminative for her complaints. To Sophia his admiration was half expressed, by looks and words that venture not too far, but yet prepare the way for further venture.

Sophia thought sometimes of his words and looks, and how odd it would be if he should fall in love with her, and make her the subject of a romance; and then she thought of Fitz-James and the Lady of the Lake. How odd the coincidence of names — Fitz-James, Fitz-Faun! Then she reflected upon the sorrows of Werter and the fair Charlotte, and looked in the glass to see if her own fair features resembled those of Charlotte. She judged, and very justly, that they were as beautiful; only she had never seen Charlotte, nor even her picture. Then she reflected upon Conrad the Corsair, and Medora, and Don Juan, with the fair Haidée. She had seen a print of Haidée, with which her own features compared favorably. Then she meditated upon Moore's Melodies, and Willis' Sonnets, and various heroes and heroines of the Lady's Magazine, and other classic creations of lady-like literature, till the music-master came to dispel idle thoughts by laborious lessons.

Mr. Mercutio Fitz-Faun assiduously cultivated the society of Augustus Greening. In company with him, and sometimes without him, he frequently met the ladies in their walks and resorts, in public places and at social parties; for he had boldness, skill, and facilities to obtain introduction in most places, when he had a motive to come. Augustus was unconsciously his instrument, and he had other instruments. His advances to Sophia were cautious, without the appearance of caution; covert, but with seeming frankness; artfully contrived, yet apparently accidental; designing, but innocent-looking. He sometimes seemed absent-minded, but never forgot his purpose. He often spoke of personal matters, in which he incidentally betrayed some romantically-generous act of his own; then suddenly recalled to himself the impropriety of egotism, and made interesting confessions, lamenting his impulsive disposition, and the difficulty of seeing suffering or wrong without interfering to relieve it; but she is a friend, and will excuse his unguardedness. He could not avoid confession to one so good and beautiful. And then he quoted some pretty sentiment. Thus he gained a step in her confidence, and made himself the subject of her thoughts. Transparent artifices are these; yet they serve to beguile confiding maidens.

Mr. Greening had no distinct and obvious cause for anxiety, and yet he was anxious. He knew nothing sufficient to justify his forbidding the acquaintance, which, considering the circle in which the young man moved, would cause some inconvenience. He explained his anxiety to his wife, and she gave him assurances which did not assure him.

His confidence in Alek's personal worth and future prosperity was fully established. He looked upon him as endowed with the very virtues which he gave himself credit for possessing, and by which he had arrived at his present prosperity,—integrity, firmness, good judgment, quick discernment of the character of others, energy, perseverance and due caution in business, and the manly bearing which inspires general respect.

He felt himself like a vigorous tree, firmly rooted and flourishing; but reflected that years must bring decay, and he considered the advantage of having a thrifty sapling growing beside him, upon whose firm trunk his own might lean, when age should bend it down with the heavy weight of years and cares. His natural partiality for his own son did not blind his eyes, and he never thought of leaning upon Augustus.

He conversed freely with Alek upon every topic of business, and even upon personal matters, and gave particular proofs of confidence and respect. He invited him to his house frequently, and requested him to come familiarly, as among intimate friends. Mrs. Greening was gracious and conversational; Augustus, spirited and social; and Sophia, lovely and condescending. Alek found it very pleasant to come, and was made to feel himself always welcome. Mr. Greening's family never failed to manifest full welcome to all whom he inclined to favor; besides which, Alek proved himself no unpleasant guest. He had not remitted in his endeavors to learn men, manners, and the philosophy of life;

and he rapidly added to his attainment of what is solid and important the propriety and polish which most adorns the sound understanding.

He appreciated elevation and refinement of sentiment as readily in the diffident and unpretending as elsewhere. Among those whom business led in his way, he was attracted to Edward Clevis, before mentioned, in whom he found qualities worthy of regard; and he often conversed with him. Edward quickly considered him in the light of a judicious friend, and, being himself of a frank and confiding nature, it was impossible that the chief burthen of his thoughts should escape Alek's penetration. But Alek was delicate, and said nothing; and, though unlucky himself, generously wished good luck to Edward, whom he believed to merit it. It did not even occur to him that the beautiful Sophia might be made to fill the place in his own heart, so long occupied, and so recently vacated, by one who had left it desolate and aching; and, therefore, no feeling of rivalry interfered with his sympathy.

Alek found his new privileges pleasant enough, and still the more agreeable to him for the opportunities of improvement afforded by introduction to cultivated society; and, therefore, he was careful to be always accessible, and ready to accept such invitations and intimations of welcome as might be given, so that he became the most frequent companion and protector of the beautiful Sophia. He considered this a trust from his employer, and kept the same vigilant eye upon his duty as in other trusts, and with no more thought of turning it to his own advantage. He had received an intimation from Mr. Greening of his distrust of Mr. Fitz-Faun, and therefore honored that gentleman with a little closer observation than he gave to others. It was not marked, yet Fitz-Faun suspected it, and also observed closely. He concluded that Alek, encouraged by the family, aspired to the beautiful Sophia, and fiercely determined to frustrate him and revenge himself. He was aware that the enterprise might be difficult; but the more difficult the more glorious its achievement, for of such achievements he was emulous, not only for private benefit, but for glorious boasts among his compeers, and to sustain the ancient renown of the Fitz-Fauns.

Mr. Mercutio Fitz-Faun had a somewhat narrow range of ideas and aspirations, but within that range his enterprise, perseverance, and success, were wonderful. Of the profound maxims and established rules of life and conduct, founded on morals or policy, he had small store; yet there was one which he constantly quoted and applied. "All stratagems are lawful in love," was his axiom. By "love" he meant whatever the low, base, and sensual, imply in that term; and by stratagem, whatever fraud, falsehood, treachery, violence, and villany, might be effectual to his purposes.

He fancied that he ran a brilliant career. He plumed himself upon his genius and his good fortune. He affected to be styled the Napoleon of gallantry, and named his victories Austerlitz, Lutzen, Marengo, Borodino, and the like. He trusted not alone to chance and the inspiration of the hour, but proceeded by system, with appropriate aids, resources, and instruments, in all emergencies.

He prided himself especially upon what he called his *diplomacy*. By diplomacy he had often made persons of honorable intentions the unconscious instruments of his plots for the ruin of their nearest and dearest connections. By diplomacy he managed Augustus, evaded the father, blinded the mother and hoped to baffle and circumvent Alek, and add another victory to his list of Lodis, Lutzens, and Jenas.

Of the allies and aids of this Napoleon of gallantry, Count Flummery was the chief, and was supported by a regular gradation of Talleyrands, Metternichs, Grouchys, Soults, and subalterns, in the character of procurers, bullies, bribed coachmen, and courtesans.

By the arts of diplomacy Fitz-Faun decided to commence the campaign against Alek, holding other resources in reserve. Augustus served to introduce him, and he opened his battery of smooth pretences and artifices. He professed particular pleasure in gaining the acquaintance of a friend of Harry Boynton, for whom he avowed much respect, though he had seen him but a few times. He made many remarks meant to be agreeable, and offered his services and good offices on all occasions; particularly proposing to introduce Alek to some of his own friends, who he judged might be agreeable, and perhaps serviceable.

Alek did not decline the civilities. He thought that perhaps they might be sincere, or, if otherwise, he considered himself competent to detect and baffle treachery, when already put upon his guard. He desired, also, to ascertain how far Mr. Greening's ill opinion was well grounded; and, perhaps, liked the chance of testing his own diplomacy. Alek's self-estimate had not declined. In that respect he was not much behind Mr. Mercutio Fitz-Faun.

Two days afterward, Mr. Fitz-Faun called upon Alek with a card of invitation from Count Flummery, whom he described as an English nobleman, of generous spirit, who had lately set up his establishment in New York, temporarily, and in a private way, for the sake of familiar acquaintance with the social and political institutions of the American people.

"By great good fortune," said he, "I was introduced to him when abroad; and he honors me with his friendship, and gives carte blanche for my friends. My introductions have been few and select; and I am particularly glad that I mentioned you, for I think you will be pleased with each other. The count can read men as other men read books; and he does justice to merit, of whatever kind. The countess is a fine woman, and the young ladies, her daughters, have taken a fancy for, and formed an intimate friendship with my cousins, the Miss Dryades,—Erycina, and her elder sister, Messalina, — who will also be there, with others of the best society. The Miss Dryades are superb, spite of their cousinship."

Alek expressed a proper sense of the honor, and engaged himself for the occasion; and Fitz-Faun kindly offered to call for him at the proper hour.

CHAPTER XVII.

Quips, and Cranks, and wanton Wiles ;
Nods, and Becks, and wreathed Smiles. — L'ALLEGRO.

IT was an epoch of great interest in Alek's history. He was about to appear a guest in the very central circle of fashion, where modes and ceremonies to him unknown have the force of inexorable laws ; before the brilliant and polite, where dulness is disgrace, and awkwardness is crime ; before a count and countess, who read men as men read books, and decide their worth as a money-changer tells the value of coin ; among the most select of the crowd of wealth and fashion, the most educated and elegant among men, and the most beautiful and accomplished among women ; where, perhaps, his principles may prevent the graceful compliance which fashion requires, or where his ignorance of ceremony may expose him to juster ridicule ; and where, perhaps (for his distrust of Fitz-Faun was not diminished), the purpose of his introduction may be unfriendly and dangerous.

Alek, however, accepted the invitation, not capriciously, but in accordance with views of his own, and determined to abide the result as bravely and warily as his abilities might permit. He was not altogether unprepared. He had now been in the school of general society for several months, and had been an attentive student. At Mr. Greening's suggestion, he had provided a proper dress, and had the tailor's authority, as well as his own opinion, for his outside appearance. He had also received some instruction in ceremony and deportment from Mons. Legerité (maitre de danse), who pronounced him "accompli," "un homme d'esprit, qui fait des choses galamment," "un homme bien fait pour le monde." These compliments Alek, spite of his self-complacency, thought too unqualified; yet he allowed himself to be not altogether a clown; he knew where to put his hands and feet, and that it is better to say nothing than to stammer. To these attainments he added his stock of mother-wit, brought from Wolfsden, and improved by use, — and trusted that he should find himself competent to the crisis.

Having dressed, and perfected his outward appearance, he thus apostrophized himself in the glass:

"Now, Alek Arbor, son of Deacon Arbor, of Wolfsden, you are about to step into a new position. Keep your wits awake. Be not betrayed by negligence, or forgetfulness, or irresolution. If possible, secure the good-will and respect of others, by due observance of what belongs to them; but, at all events, preserve your self-respect, by firmness of principle. Be not suspicious, but have perfect presence of mind to detect, if cause for suspicion shall arise. Conduct yourself so that on your return you shall not be ashamed to look yourself in the face."

At the appointed hour, a coach containing a gentleman and two ladies called for Alek. The gentleman was Fitz-Faun, and the ladies were his Cousins Dryades, Miss Erycina and Miss Messalina. Alek was introduced by his friend

Fitz-Faun, and graciously received. Their dazzling and overpowering beauty was such as he had never before encountered. Well did they deserve Fitz-Faun's eulogium, — they were "superb, spite of their cousinship."

A place was reserved for Alek beside the splendid Erycina. Fitz-Faun sat by his superb cousin Messalina, and the coach drove to the count's. The ride was a long one, but the ladies were full of spirits, and their lively chat and familiar gayety made the way seem short.

Arrived at the elegant house of the count, Fitz-Faun and Messalina preceded Alek and Erycina up the magnificent marble entrance. Lackeys in white kid gloves obsequiously received them; and soon Alek was introduced to a scene of splendor and luxury before inconceivable.

Spacious parlors, their sliding doors thrown back, were magnified and multiplied by the reflection of large mirrors, advantageously arranged, so that their extent seemed interminable. The lofty ceiling was adorned with the most elaborate ornament in stucco and gilding. The walls were bordered and festooned with fanciful tracery in blue and gold, and hung with paintings and engravings of the rarest kind. Carpets of the softest texture and most brilliant colors covered the floors. Sofas and lounges invited luxurious repose. Sideboards glittering with vessels of crystal and silver, filled with the choicest fruits, confections, and sparkling liquors, tempted the palate. A grand piano, of splendid workmanship, occupied one end of a room, and a harp of still more imposing appearance occupied a corner at the other end of the double parlors. The space between and around was variously supplied with marble tables, velvet chairs, glittering screens, tasselled ottomans, costly vases, many curious and rare productions of oriental taste.

The company was as various and splendid as the furniture. There were many beautiful ladies, and all appeared in the youth or the prime of their charms. Of the men, some were evidently past their middle age, yet full of the spirit and versatility of youth. Some were remarkably young, yet with the assurance and forwardness of premature ripeness. All appeared on equal terms; and there was somewhat less of the polite deference of youth to maturer dignity, of manhood to beauty, and of all toward each other, than Alek expected in society so refined and elevated.

Count Flummery, to whom Alek was immediately presented by his friend Fitz-Faun, seemed, however, to fulfil Alek's idea of the exterior, at least, of a perfect gentleman. He was about forty years of age, of good person and elegant dress. His hands were taper and slender, as though his fingers might be nimble in any dextrous art (piano-playing, for instance); his eyes were deep and penetrating, — so much so, that Alek at first thought they indicated apprehension or suspicion, but, upon reflection, concluded that there must necessarily be something peculiar in the glance of one who could read men as men read books.

The countess appeared young, and as gay as her daughters; for Alek, without any further information than Fitz-Faun's first description, counted several of the youngest of the ladies present as the daughters of the countess, who, in their sweet superabundance of sentiment, had attached themselves to the superb Dryades, spite of their cousinship to Fitz-Faun.

The company was dispersed in various conversational groups. Here and there a congenial pair sat tête-à-tête.

Some solitary amateurs studied the paintings and engravings on the walls, or turned over the collections of a gold embossed and clasped portfolio. A few sauntered about, as if undecided, among the various attractions; and others still, as caring little for any of them. Some, both in male and female attire, might appear to the attentive observer as practising attitudes, and choosing positions for effect; and others, as trying to conceal weariness and discontent. And Alek could not help reflecting, that, though he had never seen so many aids and means to enjoyment, he had never been in a social company of so few happy faces.

Alek was introduced to a few of the groups about him, but their conversation was confined to local and personal matters, which he knew nothing of, and regarded as unimportant. He therefore returned to the splendid Erycina, who, besides the personal charms which render even dulness tolerable, had much vivacity, and an infinite fund of personal gossip. Through her he was able to learn something of the company around him, including herself.

"See," said she, "that tall fellow, with a hanging underjaw, and lank gray earlocks. His clothes hang about him like drapery about a skeleton. It is not the tailor's fault, — his clothes are well cut, but he is not well made. Take his clothes off, and he 'd look worse than now. Nothing could be made to fit him, except by the rope-maker, who might adjust a very suitable cravat to his scraggy neck. He saunters about and attitudinizes, as if to bring draperied skeletons into fashion. Strutting and attitudinizing, sometimes sober, and oftener drunk, has been the only respectable business of his life. He has been trying to learn the trade of a swindler, but can't get the hang of it, — the sheriff should give him the hang of it. He belongs to one of our first families, but they have turned him off with a monthly pension, which he spends in debauchery, or something less respectable, and sponges his board out of credulous landladies. But you need no further description. He is edging this way; he always edges,—he can't do otherwise, go which way he will, for every side is an edge. He means to make your acquaintance to-night, that he may borrow a 'V' of you to-morrow.

"See that red-faced, snub-nosed, over-dressed, and over-fed gentleman. He began life a butcher, and got to be a pork merchant. He aspires still higher, and sets up for a debauchee. He has a wife and family at home, who are probably learning the same lessons. He spends fifty dollars a night, and makes a poor speculation of it. He does n't understand the business. He had better stick to his pork.

"See that heavy-browed, dark-whiskered Hercules of a fellow, with so many gold chains and jewels, who sits shuffling a pack of cards, to attract a party at whist or loo. He means to pluck a pigeon or two to-night; there are several here, and he will do it. He never fails. The count,—but I must n't blab; it 's a secret; and, besides, nobody can prove it; so promise to say nothing about it, 'pon honor."

Alek gave her the required assurance as gravely as if he understood the whole matter, and she went on:

"He is always here, and is thick with the count. He is no doubt a great gentleman in his way. He understands all the tricks of the cards, and all other games. He is a great character, and knows how to have things his own way. He has been in the ring, and they say tapped Yankee Sullivan's claret. How queer they talk. His name is Sir Mark Barsheer, — so they call him. I will get you his card from the case. You see how it is spelt, '*Sir Marc Barchier, K. B.*' I don't know," continued Erycina, "why they call him *Sir*. I am sure nobody would take him for a *madam*. But he is an Englishman, and the '*Sir*' is some sort of a title; — and then the K. B., — what does that mean? If it were S. B., I should suppose he meant to announce his claim to be Some-Body; but K. B. comes nearer to Know-Body, and I dare say he is ignorant enough to spell nobody with a K."

Alek examined the card. He had been for some time scrutinizing this same Sir Marc. A dim impression of something familiar in his features fixed his attention; but he could not trace it to a distinct recollection. Neither Erycina's account, nor the name and title, furnished any clue at the moment; and he noted the features and expression, for after study.

The promiscuous assembly, moved by the impulse of various motives, affinities, and tastes, formed various circles of amusement. Sir Marc gathered at a table a company mixed according to his views, — the calculating and the reckless, the designing and the deluded. A group of the more vivacious and conversational amused themselves with small-talk, lively repartee, sallies of wit, and laughter. Others sentimentalized, and talked poetry, literature, and scandal. The count told a story of himself, the Prince of Wales, and Charles Fox; and the countess related her parting interview with Queen Charlotte and the Duchess of Kent, and exhibited a bracelet given her by the queen for a keepsake. It was of unique workmanship, and studded with the richest gems. Its central lustre is a star, of which the disc is a diamond of great value;

and the five points are composed each of a different gem, and pointed with diamonds.

Alek, who, with the splendid Erycina hanging upon his arm, had drawn near to hear the count's story, listened with peculiar interest to that of the countess, especially to the account and description of the jewel, and he endeavored to get as near a view of it as possible, without attracting attention. The recollection of Mrs. Simperkins' story, and her description of her lost "hunique," struck him as a strange coincidence. He impressed upon his memory the features of the count, the countess, and the jewel, and reserved this subject also for after study.

Music was proposed. A lady took her place at the grand piano, and commenced a lively waltz. Quickly a dozen couples were whirling, in rapid yet harmonious motion, through the spacious rooms. The splendid Erycina passed her lovely arm, as if unconsciously, about the waist of Alek, and tapped the time with her taper foot. Alek, already excited by the soul-stirring music, could not resist the mute invitation. He joined hands, and clasped the lovely form, and whirled with his beautiful partner in the rounds of the glittering group. His pulse beat time with the enchanting music. He breathed an atmosphere of luxury and sweet abandonment. His eyes were dazzled; his soul was filled with the spendor of soft, inviting beauty. His arm was about a form moulded in graceful loveliness, — the perfection of nature and art. His hand clasped a hand through whose delicate fingers the electric fire thrilled along his nerves. Emotions uncontrollable fired his soul. He pressed closer the lovely and yielding form at his side, and bounded in maddening ecstasy through the voluptuous dance.

Soon the lively group exhausted their superabundant spirit, and sunk on the soft sofas, or retired for refreshment. The splendid Erycina led her partner to a corner retired and unobservable, and seated herself by his side. A gorgeous Indian screen hid them from view. It seemed a place for whispering lovers made. Love's mighty influence ruled the hour. Yet Alek resisted the mighty impulse, though with wavering resolution. His firm self-control faltered with each new onset.

Though hidden from view, an officious waiter found them out, and proffered cake and wine in silver baskets and crystal cups; but Alek refused all refreshment, except iced water. His wisdom had not wholly deserted him. His blood needed the ice, not the wine.

The dance ceased, and songs were solicited. The voluptuous melodies of Moore were breathed from enchanting lips, accompanied by piano and harp. Sweet sensations of mingled sentiment and passion overwhelmed the soul. Love's mighty influence ruled the hour.

At length the magnificent Messalina was urged, and took her place at the harp. Her skill surpassed others; and her song was such as the occasion and the ruling spirit of the hour demanded. With attentive ear all drank the melody, and applauded the sentiment.

MESSALINA'S SONG.

'T is the hour of gentle feeling,
   Tender thoughts and speaking sighs;
All the soul of love revealing,
   Panting hearts and sparkling eyes.
Not the gairish day's effulgence
   Suits the reign of soft delight;
Warmest wishes wait indulgence
   Till the genial shades of night.

Let the hero and the miser
  Toil by day for gold or fame;
We, all happier and wiser,
  Wait the night's propitious reign.
Hail the hour with joy o'erflowing,
  Social mirth and soft delight;
Love-enkindling, bliss-bestowing,
  Secret-keeping, favoring night!

Alek sits softly on the luxurious sofa, and the splendid Erycina sits closely by his side. An hour's acquaintance has brought them intimately near. Mutual attractions draw them closer, with resistless force. Tender sympathies unite them in sweet embrace. She reclines her lovely form upon his beating breast. Her bright blue eyes look tenderly in his, and then turn timidly away. He sighs in a transport of overpowering emotion. She lays her delicate hand in his open palm. His closing hand clasps hers with expressive tenderness. She turns upwards her blushing face with fond consenting look. He presses her yielding form to his breast, and devours her lips with burning kisses. Love's mighty influence rules the hour.

Is it love? O, power of supernal source! celestial bond of virtuous union! everlasting chain, let down from the throne of heaven, and embracing in its links the children and heirs of holy life! Eternal power! forgive the profanation of thy sacred name. Teach us, that we may not disguise the cup of hell with the perfume of heaven.

Away, Alek, away! The soul-debasing fire of sensualism rages in your veins. The siren charmer drags you beneath the waves of perdition. The angel fellow-voyagers are leaving your heart, and bearing away contentment, peace, and hope. Remorse, degrading self-contempt, and base remembrances, hasten to take their place, and be your future companions.

O, self-degrading soul! being of promised immortality, turning downward in thy course! O, mortal with heavenly gifts, betraying thy trust! heir of blessed life, forfeiting thy crown! Awake! resist! flee!

Thus shouted the angel of rescue to the yet unpolluted heart, yielding — blindly, madly, but not wilfully yielding to overpowering temptation. The warning voice thrilled in the inmost sanctuary of the troubled soul. The startled victim awoke in the moment of his extremest danger. He glanced at an opposite mirror, and saw himself bound in an ignoble snare. He remembered the vision, the danger, and the escape, when he slept by the rivulet, beneath the overhanging beech, on the day of his departure. In strong imagination, he almost saw his mother again, with terrified look, pointing at the fearful form of death, standing with upraised dart in act to strike. The strong reäction of his mother's remembrance, of the blessed teachings of his youth, of the moral training of his life, of the pure affections of home, of high resolves and holy aspirations, drove back the demon of sensual temptation. Not daring to trust himself with further delay, he hastened to the presence of the count, and explained that imperative necessity required his immediate departure. The count looked inquiringly, and, as Alek thought, hesitatingly and suspiciously; but Alek paused not for further ceremony. He passed to the outer door. The servant in attendance was slow in opening it; but he thrust him aside, turned the bolts, and in a moment was in the street.

He hastened along the deserted and silent pavement, and did not pause till he had reached his solitary room. From his open window he looked forth upon the gloomy expanse. How gloomy, contrasted with the bright scenes so lately left, whose splendor still filled and dazzled his brain! Obscuring clouds covered the sky, but they were driven by a viewless force, and soon broke and fled into the depths of night. The fair moon and silvery stars shone forth with accustomed brightness. The cool air fanned his flushed and fevered brow. The sublime majesty of the universe, whose silence is eloquent beyond speech, inspired and elevated his soul. He felt that he was not alone. HE who has filled the material world with life has not left the brighter and purer regions of space a void. Intelligences, far higher and nobler than those which grovel on earth, people all the ethereal regions with myriad angel forms. They surround us. They understand us. They see our inferiority, and yet they do not despise us; they know our baseness, yet they do not scorn us, for these emotions dwell not in angelic minds, who have cast off their lower nature, and expanded into perfect being. They see us on a lower step of the ladder of progression, where they once stood, and whence we, like them, shall rise to better life.

Thus mused Alek, and sought to soothe his self-accusing spirit. He was troubled, abashed, humbled. His self-confidence was abated; he had not stood firmly. His self-boasting was not justified; though he had not fallen, he had stumbled; for, though a timely flight from temptation is victory, yet his flight had been delayed too long — almost fatally. His victory was but an escape. He had partially yielded, and thus had forfeited the honors of triumph.

Upon further reflection, he doubted if he had not been the dupe of conspiracy. The questionable character of Fitz-

Faun, the worse than questionable character of others of the gay company, as described by the splendid Erycina, and even her own too facile charms, though in keeping with the sentiment and spirit of the assembly, all indicated the possibility that the society to which he had been so ostentatiously introduced belonged to a lower order than its pretensions claimed. His suspicions, once started, ranged through all the labyrinths of possibility, wherever circumstances threw light. He even conceived that the count and his friends might all be impostors, — perhaps a gang of swindlers, prostitutes, and dupes. At the head of the first order, in this imaginary classification, he placed his friend Fitz-Faun; and at the foot of the latter class, himself. With sarcastic bitterness, he looked in the glass, to learn the lineaments which characterize a dupe. He saw the lines of folly very plain, and wondered that he had not marked them before. No wonder that Fitz-Faun read him at a glance, and set him down as a fit subject for cheap experiment. He stared himself in the face, to see how a fool stares. He assumed an air of sagacity, to see how the grimace of wisdom sits on the face of folly. He looked complacently, to see how a foolish face looks when taking the bait of flattery. Having completed his self-examination, he thus again apostrophized himself:

"And so you, Alek, idiot son of Deacon Arbor, of Wolfsden, are the nice young man who judged yourself capable of detecting treachery, and protecting yourself! You are the sagacious genius, who was to behave so warily and circumspectly as not to be ashamed to look yourself in the face! How do you look now? Could you look your dog Lion in the face, if he were here? Do you think you could find your way back to Wolfsden, and re-learn the knack of raising turnips, and pumpkins, and calves? Perhaps you might in time get cunning enough to palm off your own head for a turnip or pumpkin, or yourself for a calf, upon some customer about as wise as yourself."

Having thus vented his self-reproach, he seated himself by the window, and again reviewed the affair. He was more and more convinced of the imposture of the pretended count and his high society. A hundred recollected circumstances confirmed his suspicion.

The dim though fixed impression of having before seen the pompous personage styled Sir Marc puzzled him. He almost fancied it must have been in some previous state of existence that he knew him. He explored his memory for some clue, and recalled the expression of his features, to compare them with all whom he had seen abroad; for it did not occur to him that such a magnificent "swell" could ever have been seen in Wolfsden. At length he recurred to the remembrances of childhood, and soon hit upon a strange coincidence of form, features, expression, and even name. Sir Marc certainly belonged to the breed of Bang, the blacksmith. Is it possible that he should be no other than the reprobate Mark Barker, who absconded fifteen years ago, after robbing widow Bowler's turkey-pen? Alek remembered the looks of the boy, but he identified the man chiefly by the resemblance to Bang. He felt strongly persuaded of the truth of his conjecture, and determined to verify it.

The affair of the remarkable and valuable jewel displayed by the countess as the gift of a queen, and its exact resemblance to that described by Mrs. Simperkins as stolen from her by Count Flipperton and his lady, employed his reflections. Wonderful, if the jewels should prove to be identical and Count Flummery the very Count Flipperton! Here was matter to be explored, a riddle to be solved. Alek debated whether his own abilities were equal to the occasion. He had just now berated himself as a dupe and a fool, by no means the fit agent to explore mysteries and solve riddles; but perhaps his self-judgment might be revised, now that his self-indignation had subsided. Upon a calm review of facts, he gave himself credit for having acted with some little common sense. He had not been entirely duped. He had escaped the snare at the last moment, even when escape was most difficult. It was his first venture into the enchanted den; and he had baffled the enchanter, and had also gained the experience which would make him wiser upon a like occasion. He had now more of the sagacity of self-distrust, and, therefore, of self-watchfulness. He now knew something of the smooth tactics of the enemy, and the necessity of instant and constant vigilance.

Upon the whole, he determined to give himself further trial. This might have been but the preliminary skirmish to a coming campaign, which should test his generalship. His self-confidence, so lately humbled, again inspired him, and he summoned his energies for the strife.

He impressed upon his mind that of all perils the most dangerous is self-betrayal. So long as he should be vigilantly true to himself, he could not suffer serious injury. A divine power aids and guards those who faithfully endeavor to pursue the path of duty. He recalled the timely warning of the dream which saved his life when he slept under the beechen tree by the rivulet, and the mysterious impression which so lately startled him from the more dangerous trance of voluptuous temptation. His relation to the unseen power so repeatedly manifested for his preservation, filled him with wonder and awe, and he bowed his head and his spirit in grateful adoration and fervent prayer. His soul was purified and strengthened for duty and for danger; and he felt reënlisted for the battle of life.

CHAPTER XVIII.

The moment Alek left the count, after taking so abrupt a leave, that high personage immediately found Fitz-Faun, and told him of the flight, as he termed it; and such was Fitz-Faun's patronizing zeal, that he instantly rushed to the door to intercept his friend's departure, but, finding himself too late, in consequence of Alek's impetuosity in thrusting aside the dilatory porter and opening the door for himself, he hastened back to a private room, and, sending for the noble count and the splendid Erycina, demanded of them an account of his friend, and the reason of his flight. The noble count protested that he had acted in every point exactly according to directions; and the splendid Erycina declared that she had not been wanting in politeness, and could give no reason for his abrupt departure. "He started," she said, "not like a person angry, but suddenly frightened, as though he saw a ghost." She feared he was insane, or eccentric, or something of the kind; which she protested was a pity, for he was certainly a most interesting character, and quite an original.

Fitz-Faun was disconcerted, and hesitated not to let his anger manifest itself in expressions which, considering the elevated society present, were, to say the least, anything but gracious. The count, with remarkable humility, repeated his excuses, and deprecated the anger of his guest, while Erycina sat mute. Perhaps she was terrified at his reproaches. Perhaps she was indignant. Perhaps her thoughts were turned in another direction, and cannot now be fathomed. Fitz-Faun intimated to her that her presence might be spared. As she retired, Sir Marc was sent for, to whom Fitz-Faun announced that the bird had flown, for so he facetiously communicated the news of his friend's abrupt departure.

"How 's that?" said Sir Marc. When the circumstances of the event were told, the valiant knight, — for such, we presume from his card of address, is his proper title, — the valiant K. B. took a knightly attitude, and stood erect just two minutes. He looked considerate and contemplative for a minute and a quarter. He then looked sagacious and self-possessed for half a minute. For the remaining fifteen seconds he looked determined and unrelenting, and then took a seat.

"This is what I call a clumsy piece of business," said the K. B.

"The question is not what to call it, but how to remedy it," said Fitz-Faun.

"Do you give him up on this tack?" said the K. B.

"I rather think he suspects this game," replied Fitz-Faun.

"Is he worth your while to turn over to me?" inquired the K. B.

"I 'd give a cool five hundred, to fix him," said Fitz-Faun.

The K. B. walked softly to the door, which he suddenly opened and looked about, and then, as if reässured, returned to his seat. (A gliding apparition without had suddenly disappeared as the door-handle turned, but now resumed its position at the key-hole.)

"I think," said the K. B., after a moment's consideration, "I 'm your man for that craft; that is, if *crippling* is all you are after. If you go in for *scuttling*, that 's another affair."

"What I want of that craft," said Fitz-Faun, adopting the knight's nautical phrase, "is to get it out of my way. I want a clear coast just at present. I don't care whether it 's for a few weeks, or a few months, or forever. I don't want a vessel of his class convoying sails that I have a mind to overhaul. I don't owe the fellow a grudge, — he 's acting under orders, and also keeps an eye to windward for his own sake. I should prefer to out-manœuvre him, or decoy him on this Circean quicksand, to founder of his own accord. But, if he won't be diplomatized, he must be driven. I 'll see him and sound him once more, and, if I find him incorrigible, I 'll turn him over to you. If finesse fails, force must do, and we 'll 'conquer a peace.'" With these words, this Napoleon of gallantry broke up the council.

Pursuant to his plan, Fitz-Faun, the next day, found Alek and sounded him. Alek was prepared for the process. He had all the advantage over Fitz-Faun which plain, uncompromising integrity ever has over dissimulation. Alek was not deceived by Fitz-Faun; for falsehood when once suspected loses its power to deceive. But Fitz-Faun was puzzled with Alek; for nothing is so impossible to be comprehended by cunning knavery, as the plain maxims and motives of common sense and honesty.

"You took French leave, last evening," said Fitz-Faun.

"Not exactly," replied Alek. "I paid my parting respects

to the count, and requested him to excuse me to his friends, which is all, I believe, that etiquette requires."

"But why did you come away so abruptly?" said Fitz-Faun.

"My duties require that I should keep early hours," said Alek; "and I think it easier to practise self-denial by beginning with the first temptation, than after having formed a habit of indulgence."

"Speaking of temptation," said Fitz-Faun, "I suppose you refer to my fair cousin Erycina. I knew you would be smitten with her. Is n't she splendid?"

"She is splendid," replied Alek, "and fascinating. But I would not be understood as referring to a lady when speaking of temptation, which would hardly be compatible with proper delicacy and respect. I referred to the temptation of late hours, for the sake of any agreeable company."

"Then you confess she was agreeable company, and somewhat tempting? I thought as much from your intimacy. Upon the whole, I think you went about far enough, upon first acquaintance. I presume you will call this evening to inquire her health, as you are an observer of *etiquette*. I have brought you her card — No. 16 Cytheria-street. But, by the way, don't encumber yourself with too strict notions of 'proper delicacy and respect,' as you term it. That is n't etiquette in New York, — nor anywhere else, I suspect, where the ladies fashion the laws of society. The only way to win the ladies' regard is at first to go so far with them as to offend them, — or so far that they ought to be offended, — and the next time to go further still. That 's my rule, and it never fails!"

"Then I may presume that you are quite successful in winning the respect of the ladies," said Alek.

Fitz-Faun started. He thought he perceived the slightest tone of contempt in the reply, and the slightest shade of emphasis on the word *ladies*, as though he had no title to the respect of men. He was already somewhat disconcerted with the easy indifference, and, as he sometimes fancied, the air of superiority, which Alek maintained. But his scheme required affability and conciliation, and he therefore smothered his resentment; and, being resolved to press the conversation to some development, he replied that he made no boasts of his own successes, and no interference with the pursuits of others. Though," continued he, "I half envy the favor you seem to have gained with our fair friend Erycina. I rallied her upon your exclusive attentions, and could see that she was pleased. I ought not to betray her secret, but I know she likes you. It is n't her way generally, for she is thought to be hard to please; so you should value your victory the more highly."

"Well," said Alek, "I will be careful to preserve her regard, by doing nothing to offend her, and nothing that ought to offend her, notwithstanding your infallible rule; for I mean to deserve her respect, and, if I cannot retain it in that way, I shall at least preserve my own."

"I see you mean to keep your own counsel," persisted Fitz-Faun; "yet I suspect you understand the epicurean philosophy of enjoying life while it lasts, as well as myself; for I am frank to avow *that* as my philosophy, and have no doubt that cousin Erycina will find it to be yours. What is life without love, as the song says?"

"Life without love," replied Alek, "would be but an abject

affair; but what you term love would debase it still lower. Your mistaking such a passion for love is even a greater error than that of supposing me capable of trifling with the affections of a virtuous woman, or seeking the society of a wanton one. But you have made one correct supposition, — for I do mean to enjoy life while it lasts, though not according to your views."

Fitz-Faun, still more disconcerted and embarrassed by the direct and earnest manner of Alek, wished to continue the conversation only till he might effect a retreat; and he asked, with a bantering tone, if Alek would favor him with *his* views of enjoying life, and also inform him where he got such a stock of fine sentiments.

"My sentiments," said Alek, "I learned of my mother, from whom I also learned not to despise, but only to pity, those who are incapable of appreciating them. My views of enjoying life I am happy to explain, for I acquired them from the same source, and my first lesson was received very early. I was about three years old, and dressed in my first frock and trousers, when I strayed into the field a little way from the house, and found a small tortoise. I raised my stick to strike it, when something within me seemed to say *No!* Perhaps it was the echo of something that my mother had inculcated in my infant ear. I held the stick still uplifted until the animal had crawled away out of sight, and then went into the house and asked my mother what it was that said *no*, when I wanted to strike the tortoise. She took me in her arms, and taught me that it was something within me, which people call *conscience*, and which the Bible calls the *good spirit*, or the *still small voice;* and she told me that if I would always listen to that voice, it would always teach me, and keep me from doing wrong, and would guide me in the way of happiness. From that time, her precepts have always inculcated the love of what is right, and instilled the true principle, that the highest happiness of which we are capable depends upon the culture of the moral powers. To dwarf and corrupt those by sensual indulgence, is to abuse and destroy all the sources of true enjoyment which make life worth having. My observations and reflections, since I have become capable of observing and reflecting for myself, confirm the incalculable value of this truth; so that I look with the utmost pity upon those who are incapable of understanding it, however they may be favored by fortune in every other respect."

Alek looked firmly but mildly upon Fitz-Faun while speaking, and that epicurean philosopher fancied that he saw a gleam of pity in his look, for which he was not particularly grateful. He affected to yawn, and drawlingly replied,

"Please give my respects to your good mother, and also to Miss Erycina, to whom I suspect, in spite of all your fine sentiments, you will pay your first visit."

As Fitz-Faun departed, he muttered, "The fellow is incorrigible; I shall hand him over to Sir Marc, and I hope he 'll *scuttle* him, as he says. Impudent dog!—pity *me!* He little knows that I hold the thread of his fate in my hands, to snap when I choose." And Fitz-Faun snapped his fingers by way of illustration.

This conference took place in an office of the agricultural ware-rooms, from which it was separated by only a glass partition. Various customers were examining the crooked and uncouth articles exhibited for sale outside, while quizzing clerks commended their finish and beauty. After Fitz-Faun had gone, a countryman, who had observed him through the glass, came in and asked Alek if he was acquainted with the Mr. Smith who had just left him.

"His name is not Smith, but Fitz-Faun," said Alek.

"Fitz-Forn!" said the countryman; "strange! — but do you know his wife?"

"He is not married," said Alek.

"Fitz-Forn! — not married! — strange!" muttered the countryman.

Alek asked no explanation; but when the countryman had made his purchases, he took note of his name and residence. It was George Washington Bowpin, of Furrowdale.

CHAPTER XIX.

> What should she do? Attempt once more
> To gain the late deserted shore?—FEMALE SEDUCERS.

NOTHING could be further from Alek's intention than to renew his acquaintance with the splendid Erycina; yet it happened that Fitz-Faun's prediction, that his first visit would be paid to her, was verified. Scarcely had that epicurean departed, when a prompt young man brought a billet to Alek, informing him that a person wished to meet him on important business, at the Astor House, in private parlor No. 12, at seven o'clock, P. M. Alek accepted the appointment, and in due season repaired thither; and, being shown into the dimly-lighted parlor, was welcomed by a very young gentleman, very elegantly dressed, and very handsome. When their eyes met, Alek started with surprise; and Erycina, seeing herself recognized, blushed, but commanded herself sufficiently to commence the conversation.

"I wish," said she, "first, to inquire the reason of your abrupt departure."

"Because," said Alek, "I felt that my only safety was in flight. I would not be guilty of trifling with your feelings, nor of proceeding in a course incompatible with your honor and my own. To be perfectly frank with you,—for my conduct demands, at least, this reparation, — it was the sudden recollection of my mother, so strongly impressed that I seemed to see her face, filled with solicitude and warning, and bidding me to flee. I regret that I have ever for a moment disregarded her pure instruction; but I rejoice, for both of us, that she was not quite forgotten."

"I understand you," said Erycina; "I had already begun to understand you, but I wished to hear your explanation, for I doubted whether men were ever conscientiously pure. You would not wonder at my doubt, if I should tell you what I have seen. I am glad to change my opinion; and I will not again be tempted to believe that all virtue is pretence.

"I presume that you wonder at my expressing a regard for virtue; for, notwithstanding your reference to my honor, no doubt you understand my position as one whose honor is lost. I am, indeed, one of that unfortunate class whom the world so regards. But I do not love dishonor. O, how I hate it! My soul longs to fly back over the impassable gulf to purity and self-respect. O, MY mother! Yes, Mr. Arbor, I too had a mother! If her departed spirit still feels interest in her lost daughter, there must be sorrow even in heaven! Excuse my emotion. I know not why I am led to speak of myself!

"I sought this interview to bid you beware of Fitz-Faun. He is your enemy, and will spare no pains to injure or destroy you; and he is more to be feared than you suppose. He has wealth and cunning, and the resolution that hesitates at nothing to effect his purpose. If you had tasted the wine offered you last evening, his purpose would have been accomplished; for it was prepared especially for you, as I have since had reason to believe, and would have put you entirely in his power, so that not even your mother's call would have saved you. It was your voluntary self-ruin, the ruin of your character and reputation, that he aimed at then. Being foiled in that, he will not hesitate at treachery and violence. He has his tools. Sir Marc is one of them, and they have already conferred with regard to you.

"I do not know the cause of his malice, but suppose, from expressions I overheard, that he looks upon you as a rival, or as preventing his designs — probably *criminal* designs — elsewhere. Perhaps this hint may enable you to understand his motives, which I do not. Now my errand is done, I will not detain you longer."

"I thank you much," said Alek, "for this information. If I can be of any real service to you, you may command me. I judge, from your expressions, that you are not satisfied with your present position. Why not leave it, while it is still possible, before your mind shall become corrupted?"

"I *have* left it," said she, with earnestness; "and I will die before I will return to it. To regain an honorable position as a woman, is impossible; but I will not lead a life of self-loathing infamy. This disguise will serve me among strangers, where, as a man, I can gain honorable employment without reference for my character, which would be required of a woman; for, though every stranger, if a man, is presumed to be respectable, every woman whose history is unknown is suspected and condemned. Such is man's justice to woman!

"I have skill to earn a support by teaching music. In a few hours I shall be in a distant city. I have money to last till I can obtain employment; and I shall be happy when I can again live by my own exertions, — and perhaps recompense my angel mother with the joy which the angels have over repentant sinners.

"I thank you for your kind wishes. But you owe me no gratitude, for I was bound to atone for the intended evil, of which I was made the instrument, though not the accomplice, for I was not then aware of his malignant and treacherous intentions. I was then the slave of the wicked Fitz-Faun. He would make my ruin of soul and body complete; and through me he sought to ruin you. Your mother's image saved you, — the memory of mine shall redeem me. It is but a few months since I was led away. Few know me, and none of those, not even yourself, do I wish to see again. When I shall be among those who know nothing of my shame, I shall have the luxury of an untarnished name, and can the better deserve it."

"I am glad to hear your resolution," said Alek; "but your plan, though better than none, is not the best. Your best chance of usefulness and happiness requires that you should regain your proper position as a woman; and this, though perhaps not so speedily attained, is not difficult. Tò conceal your sex long is entirely out of the question. But in your own attire the few who know you would not be likely to meet and recognize you in a distant town, and in the plain dress and respectable employment of a music-teacher. In many places sufficiently remote, yet sufficiently populous, may be found discreet women, whose protection would be a sufficient passport to respect, and who would have the delicacy to understand and appreciate your object, without requiring an account of the past, for the instincts of benevolence in women are disposed to search out only what is good and hopeful.

"If you will allow me to advise you, and will give me so much of your history (since I already know the worst of it) as shall enable me to judge how best to aid you, you may rely upon my zeal, and you still will be at liberty to follow your own counsel."

"I need counsel wiser than my own," said Erycina; "and my history is a brief one.

"I lost my parents in early life, and was brought up by an uncle and aunt, who gave me all the advantages of the village where they resided. My natural talent for music was particularly cultivated, with the view of my becoming a teacher, and I had commenced giving lessons when my good uncle died. My aunt, with whom I continued to reside, was a woman of most amiable disposition, but too unacquainted with the world, and too deficient in prudence and precaution, for our safety. My skill in music gained for me attention and employment, and my aunt was gratified with the praises bestowed on me.

"In one of the few wealthy families where I gave lessons I first met Fitz-Faun. He was the most accomplished person I had ever seen, and all his accomplishments were from that moment devoted to my ruin. Nothing could be more delicate and refined than his first advances. My aunt, with whom he immediately made acquaintance, believed him a paragon of every excellence, and particularly praised his candor and sincerity. He can counterfeit every virtue with such perfect seeming, that, on finding out his true character, one is tempted to believe all seeming virtue but counterfeit. His hypocrisy is the most complete of all his accomplishments, and he possesses every accomplishment consistent with utter depravity.

"My heart was full of confidence and love, ready to be bestowed on the first congenial object, and I thought him worthy of it all. I gave him my whole heart. I would have died for him; but he required more than that, — even to the utter extinction of my moral being, — the death of my soul.

"He managed to deceive me by a mock marriage, while on a pleasure excursion, and we lived several months in a beautiful retreat near the city. His real character soon became apparent; but so entire was my devotion to him, and so impossible was it for me to harbor a thought of censure, that I lowered my standard of morality, and strove to think villany excusable; and when my moral sense was most outraged by his avowal of the worst sentiments, I only regretted that I had formed such ideas of goodness that the idol of my love held them in contempt. I began to believe that all proper and virtuous sentiment among men is but fashionable pretence; and only lost my respect for my betrayer, by learning to despise all mankind.

"Of course I could not be happy while thus parting with all that is elevated and beautiful in existence, and dragging my soul to be fit companion to a depraved sensualist. I felt myself a wreck upon a dark ocean, without a guide or even an object to strive for. Though it had been but a few months since I left my happy and innocent home, I knew that, sooner or later, I should be cast aside a worthless thing, and I firmly resolved that when that moment should come I would cease to live. But the dread of the death I determined on kept me still more subservient to my tyrant's will. I feared to provoke him to discard me, and thus hasten my fate. I hoped that death might reach me in some other way, and save me the horror of suicide. I welcomed the news of pestilence; and when I heard of a shipwreck, how I envied the victims! Yet I was forced to appear gay, and to study the arts of fascination, that I might protract my wretched life!

"It was but recently that I revolved thoughts of escaping from my condition. I began to reflect, that since men are privileged to act either wickedly or virtuously, without forfeiting the respect of society, I might assume the dress of a man, and, by concealing my sex, hide my reproach, and be permitted to live without purchasing existence by shame. Yet these vague thoughts might not have ripened to resolution, but for the events of last evening. I saw you, and by some strange influence my former ideas of the reality of manly virtue revived, and I looked upon you as their embodiment. Your behavior during the evening weakened the impression, and gave new attractions to evil. But when you broke from me and fled, I was not surprised. I understood you, and was glad that you had not fallen. Fitz-Faun reproached me for your escape, and for the first time used language of insult and threatening. I did not reply, but I *resolved*, and you see that I have *acted*."

"Who is Messalina?" said Alek.

"I know not. I never saw her till yesterday, when I was required to appear as her sister. She is probably another victim of Fitz-Faun's, as wretched, and, perhaps, as unhappy as myself. If she is less unhappy, she is more wretched; for, if her mind is reconciled to infamy, there is no hope of her escape."

"How much do you know of Sir Marc?"

"But little. I know nothing of his history. He is as bad

as he is capable of being. How great his abilities are, I cannot tell. He is illiterate, though he has generally the tact to conceal it. But his knowledge of the world, especially the bad world, is complete. He is a tool of Fitz-Faun; which proves that he has abilities for evil, for Fitz-Faun employs none but capable tools. He is doubtless employed chiefly for desperate enterprises, where fraud will not prevail, and where force and courage are required."

"And what of the count?"

"He is a pretender, an impostor, a tenant and tool of Fitz-Faun. You see that he is polished. He is an imported article. Fitz-Faun prides himself on the perfection of his tools."

"I see," said Alek, "that he is a systematic villain. I am fully convinced of your sincerity, and will assist you to place yourself beyond his power, and to recover a proper position in life. I have relatives in Saco who will receive you, and their reception will enable you to renew your vocation as a teacher. They would receive and aid you still more zealously, if they knew your history; but there is no necessity for your suffering that humiliation. Let the past be buried in forgetfulness. I will simply write to my aunt that a young woman, dependent upon her own industry, wishes employment as a teacher of music. She will probably invite you to come, and offer to receive you temporarily into her own family; after which, your destiny will be what you may make it."

Alek looked and spoke with the decision and gravity of his father. The spirit of his mother prompted his action. The impulsive and passion-driven youth of the preceding evening was merged in the considerate and virtue-guided man. The generous warmth of sympathy prompted him, but he reflected before he acted. He considered that there would be some inconvenience, and perhaps risk, in what he proposed, but that the promise of good overbalanced both. He would not be governed by prudence alone, but employed it to direct his benevolence.

The result was, that the fallen Erycina rose again, and there was joy in heaven over the returned sinner. Uncle Lemuel Hobart and good Aunt Nabby received the plainly-dressed and modest music-teacher, Miss Meekly,—for such was her proper name, which she now resumed. The grace and beauty of her person became, under the good influences which now surrounded her, the fit adornments of a heart and life equally graceful and beautiful. Her talents as a music-teacher commanded patronage, and she again knew the luxury of virtuous independence.

CHAPTER XX.

Mr. Samuel Boynton, the uncle to whom Alek took Harry's letter of introduction, and through whose recommendation he obtained his present situation, continued to treat him with kind notice; and as he observed the young rustic's improved manner and deportment, and received from Mr. Greening the most satisfactory reports of his ability and reliability, he treated him with still more consideration, — and especially after he had received particularly gratifying accounts of Harry's reformation and honorable career. Harry frequently wrote to his uncle, and his letters bore the evidence of a newly-awakened dignity of character; — he constantly referred to Deacon Arbor's family, and especially Alek, as having developed "his better genius."

A better genius had certainly been developed in Harry. His aroused emotions seemed to have called up other and nobler faculties, hitherto dormant. With the opened fountain of his love had been unsealed deeper fountains of thought. He pondered upon the endowments, the capabilities, the responsibilities, of life. He reflected that each day's history might be pregnant with an endless series of consequences, and that even now his character might be taking its bent for eternity. The solemn thought matured in his mind to conviction. It was not difficult to discard his frivolities. They had lost their power to please. He had become a man, and his manly spirit rejected childish things.

His keen intellect, no longer obstructed by folly, was more than equal to the assigned studies of his class. He reviewed and accomplished the tasks formerly slighted or evaded, and though he had been once "degraded" and twice "rusticated," he now, at the close of the term, graduated with the highest honors.

He immediately repaired to New York, on his way homeward. His uncle received him with gratified pride. Harry was his favorite nephew; and having once predicted his future success, his pride of opinion had ever since led him to look upon the best side of his character, and now his regard for Harry, and his regard for his own discernment, were equally gratified. He gave a "soiree" in honor of his nephew's honors; and Harry carried his uncle's card of invitation to his friend Alek.

The two friends were delighted with each other's improvement. Alek saw in his fashionable friend the elevation of those solid elements upon which full reliance and lasting esteem can be based; and Harry saw with surprise how quickly the rustic had acquired a becoming address. In their intimacy he alluded to this improvement, and Alek playfully rejoined, in Harry's old phrase, "O, if I 've a genius for anything, it 's for gentility."

Harry inquired about Wolfsden, and Alek gave him the latest advices, and asked how soon he intended to again explore that remote region, and look after his conquests. Harry replied that he had found the natives too refractory, and had abandoned the province to his rival, the heathen missionary.

"I doubt," said he, "if I have any adherents there, except my good allies the Arbors and Bowlers; and, unless they have revolted, the Chinbys."

"You do not forget the Murrays, — at least, my fair cousin Margaret?" said Alek; for, though he still felt sore upon the subject, he determined to break that icy barrier to perfect confidence.

"Certainly, *I do not forget*," said Harry, with more of feeling in his tone than he meant to betray; and then, to correct himself, added, with a forced and unhappy smile, "I shall not forget any who are dear to you."

Alek immediately apprehended his friend's mistake, more from his manner than his words, and hastened to set him right.

"But Mrs. Simperkins," said Harry, "told me positively that you were engaged."

"Mrs. Simperkins is not reliable authority," said Alek. "She told Cousin Margaret that you was a student of divinity. I think you had better hasten to Wolfsden, and 'define your position,' as the politicians say."

"I 'll go and disclaim the divinity, at any rate," said Harry, "even if I have to 'stump the district,' as the politicians also say."

He said it with a forced and very solemn gayety. The impassable wall which had so long shut up the way of his heart's longing desire was now thrown down, and hope, new-born and doubtful, allured him in the path of promise, whose end was hidden in the mists of uncertainty. But hope soon grows confident when mated with earnest resolve.

"I will go to Wolfsden," soliloquized Harry, "if but to discard the divinity. Provoking Simperkins!"

In every heart there is a cell formed by nature for connubial love. In generous hearts it is a large cell, and takes up much room, and its walls are expansive, and extend indefinitely to receive and cherish the progeny of tender responsibilities which follow in the train of connubial love. In niggard hearts the cell is small, and its walls are rigid and unyielding; connubial love is cramped for lack of room, and chilled by want of warmth; if love's fond pledglings peer about, they find no entrance, and soon the cell is tenantless, collapsed, obliterated. But whether hearts be generous or niggard, and the connubial cell little or big, it is fitted for but one tenant, and, however other cells may be filled, this still waits impatient for its proper guest.

Harry's heart is large. It has many cells, richly stored. In one there only hangs an idolized image upon its spacious walls. The image may be worshipped in the silence of deep love, but its original is beyond his reach. Suddenly hope points a way of access. He is no longer satisfied with the image. He aspires for the substantial bliss.

"I will go to Wolfsden," said Harry, "if but to disclaim the divinity."

"To *claim* the divinity, I guess," replied Alek.

Harry's soiree at his uncle's was elegant and delightful. He named such guests as he chose, and others were invited with reference to his preferences. Mr. Greening, senior, and lady, came together in the same coach, notwithstanding Harry's opinion that he came round and she cornerwise. Mr. Augustus Greening and his sister Sophia came with them. Mr. Greening, with partial pride, handed out his lovely daughter, and Augustus dutifully assisted his doting mother. With Alek came Mr. Edward Clevis. Great was that young man's surprise at receiving a card to a soiree at the rich Mr Boynton's. Alek treated it as a matter of course, but Mr. Clevis justly suspected by whose interest he had received it. He was exceedingly and nervously gratified with the honor. He could see and perhaps speak with the beautiful Sophia, whose idolized image adorned the connubial cell of his expansible heart. It gave him self-confidence to hope for more substantial possibilities. Mr. Greening, his employer, father to the adorable Sophia, would see that others thought him not unworthy of such honor; and perhaps this step would lead to further advantage, and so on to the summit of his hopes. On how slight a foundation will hopeful youth erect a superstructure of happiness! Yet Edward Clevis, though possessing the self-respect which conscious rectitude inspires, was one of the least presumptuous of young men.

Mr. Mercutio Fitz-Faun was not there. Alek's suggestion to his friend had erased the distinguished name of Fitz-Faun from the list of invitations, and substituted the humble one of Edward Clevis. Fitz-Faun well knew to whom he owed this exclusion, but he cared little for it. It would not facilitate his plans to meet Sophia in company with her father. He held the final issue of the campaign in his own hands, and only waited his own time to give the decisive blow. Like Napoleon, he scorned the feeble machinations of other powers, and revolved in his breast the mighty scheme which should assert and signalize his star-led destiny. "Yet," said he, "this Alek shall none the less be punished. Sir Marc shall — throttle? — no, '*scuttle*' him."

Harry was not one to do good offices by halves. Having

introduced Mr. Clevis to the soiree, he took care by his own considerate attention to put him at ease, and in a favorable position with the company; and, divining the state of affairs, either by a hint from Alek or by his own observation, he contrived to obtain for the young man the hand of the lovely Sophia in a dance, which opened the way for his presenting refreshments and partaking them with her. His tremulous happiness was too apparent to the amused Sophia; yet she could not be offended with the unspoken sentiments of one who worshipped her beauty, and whose deportment was so respectful, and even reverential.

"In his proper sphere," said Sophia, "he would be a charming lover."

Proud Sophia! she considered not that her honored father had once been a humble apprentice. The only elevated sphere is that to which virtuous industry can surely, sooner or later, attain.

Proud Sophia! Weigh in equal scales your sincere and respectful lover with the heartless and malignant Fitz-Faun. The one rich in the solid endowment of purposes and resolves for earnest life; the other possessing the specious blandishments of fashionable vice. The one would sacrifice his life to guard your honor; the other seeks to sacrifice you to his idle caprice. The one sees and magnifies your merits, and would devote his dearest interests to your happiness; the other counts upon your weakness and frailty, as the means for your ruin. Yet the vain Sophia receives with pride the false homage of Fitz-Faun, and would be embarrassed if he should see her receive the attention of Edward Clevis.

O, that man and woman might have power to read the

hearts of those who seek their love! — that some unerring test were given to detect the false, and prove the true! O, for the life of that higher sphere, where congenial souls are attracted by mutual faith, and where falsehood dares not approach the clear-seeing eye of truth!

CHAPTER XXI.

AUTUMNAL breezes fan and loosen the matured foliage of the forest trees. It is pleasant in childhood to be let loose in the wild garden of nature; to range at will over the uneven ground, slippery with polished leaves, and spread with rich abundance of scattered nuts. To see the nimble squirrel leap among the lofty boughs, or dart under the leaves and fill his cheeks with supplies for his winter hoard. His provident economy is his pastime; were there no winter to come, still he would gather nuts for sport. The red-tufted woodpecker flies swiftly among the branches, and, lighting upon the smooth trunk, stands, regardless of the laws of gravitation, and hammers his rapid tattoo above the insects' hidden nests. From the depth of the wood the drum of the partridge is heard, beginning in slow and measured beats, but rapidly increasing in velocity, till the ear can no longer distinguish the intervals. In each open glade or bushy dell the clustering blackberries tempt the eager grasp, but the briery bushes often revenge the rifled fruit.

Let merry childhood range the uplands, and gather the scattered nuts, and chase the nimble squirrels, and admire the gay plumage of the autumn birds, and listen to the mysterious drum of the distant partridge, and leave fluttering trophies of torn garments upon the briery shrubs. The pure air and active pastime shall strengthen the sinews for future usefulness, while expanding minds mature to deeper and higher pursuits.

But let the thoughtful wanderer range along the river's level bank, where the tall maples, and the spreading beeches, and the giant oaks, scatter from their waving arms the silent falling leaves, glowing with every varying shade of nature's autumn hues. The dark rippling water is decked with myriad trophies of the forest. Its shadowy surface reflects inverted banks and trees. Its tranquil depths teem with quick though silent life. The perch, mailed in scaly armor, lurks in the deep eddies and quiet pools, well known to the truant school-boy. The pickerel, tyrant of ponds and streams, waits in patient stillness among the tall grasses and floating leaves near the river's border, whence he darts upon the venturous frog or excursive minnow. The trout, speckled with vermilion, silver, and gold, frequents where cold springs abound; the chub, or cheven, loves the quick water rippling among the rocks; and the silvery-gliding eel winds among the aquatic plants in still waters. The angler knows the favorite haunts of all his finny prey, and often fills his basket with the struggling victims of his fraudful skill.

Far from my delight be the cruel pastime to bait the barbed hook with the pierced insect or the writhing worm! Disport yourselves securely, ye scaly inhabitants of the deep pools and swift waters! Often I visit your silent haunts to bathe in your cool element, but not to prey upon your harmless race. Man's sustenance and enjoyment require not the pain and death of inferior creatures, for nature's guiltless bounties are spread on every side.

Let us walk upon the soft turf in the shady orchard, and pause under the trees laden with mellow fruit. How pleasant, how nourishing, how abundant! The neatly-cultivated garden invites our notice. Here is rich supply for present and future luxury. Dinners of many autumn days yet to come shall owe their abundant variety to these fruitful beds of beets and parsnips and onions, and those long rows of cabbages and beans; to that patch of turnips and corner of celery, and those spreading vines of squashes. Green peas and ripe currants and cherries have had their day; but the purple plums, and the yellow pears, and luscious melons, take their place in the list of luxuries. The garden is the delight of flowery spring, the storehouse of summer and autumn, and the bountiful source of the winter cellar's ample supply.

Already are the fields of grain gathered into the barn, but the corn-fields still wait the harvest. The heavy ears rustle among their white husks above the huge yellow pumpkins which strew the soil. There will be merry evening huskings when the crop shall be piled into the barn, and all the family with social neighbor friends shall gather around the heap, with laugh, and song, and merry joke, and brisk reply, and vaunting boasts, and trials of expertness, while successive baskets are heaped with golden ears, and borne on broad and willing shoulders to the granary.

Heap high your granaries, ye young men of broad shoulders, and strong backs, and willing minds! How may your cheerful hearts expand with all the genial virtues, — your cheerful hearts, never fated to know the fear of soul-contracting want!

And you, above all, fair daughters of rural abodes, pure

as your mountain air, sweet as the wild-flowers of your fields, bright as your sunny hills, gay as your warbling birds, generous as the soul of all-bestowing nature! Ye have nurtured my childhood, and rejoiced my youth, and blessed my manhood. My love shall repay your care, and reward your tenderness to the advancing infirmities of age.

Churn the yellow butter; press the white curd; pick and prepare the sweet preserves and the sharp pickles; stir the bubbling pudding; knead the white bread, and mix the brown; roll the cream-shortened pastry, and overspread the broad platters and the deep pans; pare and slice the crispy apples; stew the ponderous pumpkins; beat the new-laid eggs, and fill the expectant crust; with watchful eye explore the glowing oven, and when the rightly-tempered heat shall serve, commit your labors to its perfecting power. Now spread the table, draw the tea, and blow the horn. Soon shall my willing feet obey the welcome. Sweet shall be my repast, prepared by your neat hands, and partaken in your cheerful company. Though my hands be hardened with labor, and my face be embrowned by exposure, and my clothes lack the dainty gloss and my tongue the smooth polish of city refinement, yet have I the wisdom to understand your worth, and the heart to reciprocate your faithful care.

When dainty-fingered foppery, from Fashion's beaten walks, shall come to court your partial favor, let not your eyes be dazzled nor your judgment be deluded by the unaccustomed outside show. Weigh with double scrutiny the worth set off by double pretence. But, if your heart incline to yield, let some faithful friend inquire what impartial fame reports. Poor is the hope from the plighted love of the inconstant, the selfish, the vain, the idle, the imprudent, the improvident.

Above all, as you would shun a life of mortifying humiliation or disgraceful strife, reject the imperious, the exacting, the jealous, the envious, the easily offended and quick to retaliate! Better beneath the paternal roof to keep your unwasted freshness till a worthier destiny shall offer, or till Time's finger shall write the lines of ancient maidenhood upon your peaceful brow.

New England homes, New England comforts and enjoyments, New England intellect and beauty, New England domestic and social life, — here abound the solid virtues, and all that is of permanent value in elegant refinement. In her healthy clime the human germ expands in its highest perfection. Domestic duties direct and nurture its early strength. Its common-school system calls forth, by skilful instruction and worthy emulation, its native powers. All become informed, and some in every town rise to eminence. These supply the learned professions, the places of public life, and the remunerative pursuits and enterprises of manufactures and commerce, while many, discarding ambition, remain to adorn and elevate society at home. Females seldom permanently leave the vicinity of their native place, and therefore New England country society has a still larger portion of intellectual women, whose fame, though confined to their own circle, no less effectually serves the higher purposes of humanity.

Wolfsden has sent forth its proportion of enterprising men, and retains the material of many more. That group of younglings issuing from yon red schoolhouse, with glowing cheeks and wide-awake eyes, though rough and rude in manner now, are in good hands, and will fulfil good hopes. Careful mothers gently bend the pliant shoots of manhood, and shower good influences upon susceptible hearts, which shall mature into right thoughts and firm principles. Gentle sisters and cousins, and favorite female companions, shall soften and polish their manners, and excite the desire of being loved. Life's opening prospects and responsibilities shall awaken serious resolves and efforts, till the wild, thoughtless fry shall be transformed into men, ready to take manhood's stations and duties.

Those little bashful girls, who hide at the stranger's approach, shall soon enough learn the powers and privileges of their sex. They will put on airs, they will coquet, they will tease, they will affect disdain, they will jilt, they will play unnumbered mad pranks; and then, like the unbroken colt, which has spurned its pursuer, and proved its ability to maintain its freedom, they will relent, and receive the matrimonial curb with docile grace, and at once step into the sedate ranks of young wives and mothers, to lead another generation by the same devious paths to the same fair destiny.

But some will decline the matrimonial bond, and prefer their maiden freedom. Not less happy are they in their contented singleness. It is not determined celibacy, but prolonged girlhood. They contemplate matrimony, but place it in the uncertain future. They are in no haste to give up the privileges of maiden life — of attracting and rejecting, of plotting, expecting, debating, delaying, denying, disappointing and being disappointed, and then, like Penelope with her web, again renewing the interminable task.

Happy maidens! Still weave and unravel your unprogressing web, while impatient lovers wait around. Life has various delights and destinies. Yours is not less bright and worthy than others.

Fair Lucinda — she of the slender waist and many curls —

still helps her mother in the mysteries of the kitchen. Yet she is ever ready for the parlor. Her hair is glossy. Her ringlets know and keep their place. Her dress receives no smutch nor unseemly rumple. When a stranger knocks, she lays aside her apron, and is at once the fine lady of the parlor, netting the everlasting purse, and endowed with all the graces which shall bewitch the new comer. So her reverend father, his books of divinity laid carefully open, and his study-chair ready for his reception, comes in by a back way from inspecting his cattle, or conducting his farm, and receives his guests in clerical state.

Let not the parson be blamed for whatever of *sham* may be implied in these dexterous arts. They are required by his position. It is tacitly understood by his parish that he shall not impair the dignity of his office as minister of Wolfsden, by doing anything or knowing anything that is unministerial, or that is useful. A neighboring minister lost his parish in consequence of putting on working-day clothes and holding his plough a day or two in public view, and refusing to promise better *fashions*. He replied that his Master was a carpenter, and his most eminent predecessors in office fishermen and tent-makers, and he therefore felt it a duty to do with all his might whatever his *hands* might find to do, since he did not neglect his parish duties. Some thought his plea reasonable, especially as his salary was small, and his talents and zeal above the common order; but the malcontents prevailed, and Parson Probe left Noodleville to a softer-handed successor.

Parson Boreman, therefore, though he indulges in the luxury of out-door labor, preserves the meritorious pretence of being always in his study. To be sure, everybody knows the facts of the case, in his private capacity, for everybody knows everything about everybody in Wolfsden; but everybody in his public capacity knows nothing about it, but assumes exactly the contrary, and therefore no principle is violated, nor dignity impaired.

Parsons have hearts and consciences even as others. Parson Boreman has probably reflected that old Bang's fatal relapse and tragic end might have been avoided but for his unlucky visit. Whatever the motive, — and we will not harbor the suspicion that it was but to strengthen his influence in Deacon Arbor's neighborhood, where it was rather declining, — he was very kind to poor Susan and her son Ax. To the latter he offered a home and a good common-school education, if he would remain in his service till of age. The Bowler family, where Susan and her boy remained, would like to keep them both, but advise that Ax should accept the parson's offer, as affording better prospects. Ax, who remembered his first benefactor, the schoolmaster, with gratitude and admiration, had ambition also to become a schoolmaster, and stipulated accordingly. The parson promised to aid him with extra instruction to that extent, if he should prove capable and worthy of it, which Ax considered a fair condition, and the bargain was made, with the consent of all concerned. So Ax served the parson. He proved a trustworthy lad, ready and pleasant, and became a favorite in the house. His ambition for learning was commended by the old lady, and applauded by Lucinda, who offered to hear the lessons he might find time to get. Ax was thankful for the favor. He found a good deal of time; he was up early, and found time where most people do not think of looking for it. He found time in the evening, when others might be too drowsy to notice it. He got his "stent," and made time out of that. All he gained was diligently employed with his book, that he might be a schoolmaster. Such is the power of a particular object in stimulating youthful ambition to its best efforts. The general principle that "learning is better than houses and lands," though eloquently urged by official school-visitors, and written in every copy-book, fails of the effect so easily produced by the promise of some particular reward for diligence. Ax learned fast. What he learned he remembered. His look of cheerful intelligence won him favor. Lucinda was proud of her pupil. Like Desdemona, she wished Heaven had sent her such a — boy. Be patient, fair Lucinda! Heaven is all bounteous!

CHAPTER XXII.

Where the road lies along the side of yonder hill, which, as you pass by, towers on the right away up into the sky, and on the left slants away down into a dark valley, — so far down that its tall trees look like bushes, — along that quiet road, looking like a green-bordered ribbon bound on the mountain's forehead, let us loiter, and pick ripe blackberries by the way. How high up in the world, and yet how solitary! Nature's softened voices float in the stilly air, — the busy insect hum, the murmur of the far-off falls, the barking of the distant fox, the screaming eagle, the clamorous crow, the drumming partridge, and often the muttering thunder heard afar in a cloudless sky.

As we look downward far behind us, the fair home and extensive fields of Deacon Arbor look like a little green nook in the midst of a vast surrounding forest. Beyond that, another green spot, reclaimed from Nature's wild domain, marks where the Bowlers live. Beyond that, other patches of green, with houses and barns which look so small that pigmies and mice would seem their appropriate inhabitants, stretch away, growing smaller and smaller to the sight, till lost among the dark, forest-clad mountains. The road upon which we now linger winds along among them, and links them together, as children string green leaves upon a slender thread, and form a waving garland.

As we pass onward and leave the view behind, the road declines and is lost in a woody valley; but it reäppears on hills and mountain sides beyond, still strung with green patches like a waving garland, and pigmy houses like little pictures on the stringed leaves.

On our right, a little further on, before we descend far, is a pleasant-looking house on a pleasant spot, where the early morning sunshine comes, and the last rays of sunset linger. The house looks old, but cheerful in its old age; it is innocent of paint, or other needless ornament. An ample orchard overlooks it from the rear, and in its turn it overlooks an ample garden in front. Fields and pastures, dotted with various cattle, extend on every side. It is evidently a home where peace and plenty abound. It is Major Murray's. Let us enter.

A cheerful matron, whom the suns of sixty summers have matured to a becoming ripeness, welcomes us. She is busy in various matters between the kitchen fire and kitchen table, transferring white things from the table to the fire, and brown things from the fire to the table, still entertaining us with pleasant inquiries and remarks. Her active industry is her life. Like Milton's Hobson, her destiny is that she shall never rot, while she can still jog on and keep her trot. Remove from her the cares and labors which employ each cheerful day, and her earnest spirit, now rejoicing in its active sphere, would pine and perish in discontent. Should some imp of evil offer to aid her labors, and demand employment, as once the devil did of the wizard Michael Scott, she would seat him at her table, and stuff him with good things till his evil should become good. A hungry vagabond is a godsend, before whom she delights to spread a bountiful supply, that he may eat till he can eat no more, and store the residue in his empty sack for future use. Give her some pretence for ostentatious display, and with what bustling pride will she show you the treasures of her well-ordered house, — her dairy, with its stores of sweet yellow butter and savory cheese; her chests and dressers filled with bleached linen and fleecy blankets, all the products of her busy wheel and loom; and the patchwork quilts and lamb's-wool stockings which have employed her leisure hours. Such ever be New England mothers and aunts!

Enter her choicely-kept parlor, whose polished floor, consecrated to neatness, is seldom trod by sacrilegious feet. See the upright shining chairs, and round table made to move on hidden hinges from its horizontal plane to a vertical position, by the side of its tripod pedestal; and the looking-glass of curious frame, surmounted with peacock's plumage; and the fire-set of well-polished brass. All have served their stately use for two generations, and still are in their fashion's prime. Look with reverence upon those oak-framed pictures of hallowed scenes, where Abraham lifts the sacrificial knife; where Lot leaves the doomed city, and his saline spouse; where Samson, with asinine weapon, smites the Philistines hip and thigh; and where Saul evokes the hoary witch of Endor. By the side of these triumphs of xylographic art hangs the genealogical tree of golden fruit, inscribed with the sum of all human history — births, marriages, deaths.

Up the narrow and angular flight of stairs, protected by curiously turned and twisted balustrades, we may pass to a dainty chamber on either hand. That one is the spare chamber, kept for choice occasions, and guests of note. Its high, smooth bed of gay patchwork and diamond quilting, and all its prim furniture, proclaim the matron's care, and justify her decent pride. Let us award the praises due, and linger no longer.

The opposite door opens upon a view where we might love to linger long. The chamber is smaller. Its two windows open, one toward the east, upon a far-extended view of green fields, and pleasant valleys, and winding waters, and distant farms, and an interminable forest beyond. The other looks towards the north, upon hills surmounted by mountains, rising higher and higher still, in gloomy grandeur, to the clouds.

The neat and tasteful arrangement of the room shows it to be the favorite resort of a female occupant. A few unframed paintings in water-colors, and drawings in crayon, showing taste and nicety in their execution, are pinned against the walls. Upon the mantel-piece is ranged a compact tier of books, embracing all science, abridged or in full, from a, b, c, to algebra; and all religion, from the "New England Primer" to the "Whole Duty of Man;" and all literature, from the "Ladies' Looking-glass" to the Lost Paradise of Milton; and all romance, from Bunyan's Pilgrim to "Thaddeus of Warsaw." But why detain the reader with description of these? Because the heedless reader will not note them, when once admitted to behold the fair occupant of this favored room.

The pen of history holds a magic power. At its "open sesame" the secret chambers are disclosed. Softly let us enter, lest we disturb the genius of the quiet place.

She sits at her table absorbed in thought. Her light basket, filled with various implements and patterns of female industry, is laid aside. The fair hand rests upon the snowy page, where she traces lines so delicate that they scarce soil its whiteness. The face is eloquent with thought, more beautiful than words. Are you a phrenologist? Admire that head! How the delighted fingers measure those organs replete with everything that is witty, and delicate, and wise, and benevolent, and reverential, and self-reliant, and just, and kind, and true! Fowler might here afford, without price, the flattering "chart" which he sells to others for money; for its truthfulness would soothe his too often tried conscience. Are you *no* phrenologist? Then look upon her face, and let your eyes read with rapture that heaven-impressed page of virgin beauty, love, and truth. She seems absorbed in thought. Poetic images crowd upon her active brain. Slowly she ranges them in order, and marshals them in verses, pensive, plaintive, even mournful, yet, like herself, sweet in their sadness.

"I'm weary of this weary world, I'm weary of its grief;
My sickened spirit turns away, and vainly seeks relief;
In vain, in vain I seek for peace, in vain I pray to know
If pure, unsullied happiness dwells in this vale of woe;
My wounded soul can find no joy, no healing balm, to stay
The deep and fearful gush of griefs that on my spirit weigh.
On through the dim, dark dreariness of coming shadowy years,
My fancy roves, and meets a waste — a wilderness of fears;
So dark, so drear, that death's dread vale to me would be more sweet,
And all the terrors of the tomb I would not fear to meet.

"One voice is wanting to my ear, — one deep, low, silvery voice,
To breathe its tones of music out, and bid my heart rejoice;
One glance forth from that flashing eye, to chase away my night,
One glance of love; O, would it not o'erwhelm me in its light!
To hear love's own sweet language fall from his dear lips on me!
Peace, peace, my fondly-picturing heart! — it is but mockery.
It may not be, it cannot be, for '*woman's lot*' is thine;
Concealment shall feed on thy cheek, and thou in sorrow pine.

"Cannot I bid my heart be free? Will not my woman's pride
Come now, in its o'ermastering strength, my wasted love to hide?
Shall all the gushing tenderness which others sought to wake
Come rushing from unfathomed depths, with its own weight to break?
I will not yield me up to dreams; my spirit shall not bow
In tame submission to a spell *his* heart can never know.
I will awake my slumbering soul; I will again be free,
And change into forgetfulness all my idolatry;
No flush shall deepen on my brow, no trembling seize my frame,
When from the gay and heartless throng I hear his own loved name.

"'T is vain! I wreathe my face in joy, and teach my lip to smile,
But, O! my saddened, aching heart seems bursting all the while;
For sorrow's wasting blight has found its way into my heart,
And now hope's budding visions fade, youth's morning dreams depart;
And the bright, sunny smile of joy, that on my cheek should bloom,
Has given place to sorrow's sigh, the gushing tear of gloom;
And joyous glances of the eye, that once could flash with mirth,
Have gone, and tell in quenchéd beams how fade the joys of earth.

"They tell me I am beautiful, and speak to me of love;
But life too early lost its charm — *their* praises cannot move;
I listen to the honeyed words they breathe into my ear, —
They fall like Afric's parchéd sands on the wild desert drear.
I listen, and I smile, perchance, or wipe a tear away;
O, might the hope of that blest world, unsullied by decay,
Buoy my sad soul above this gloom, above this earthly strife,
And bid me plume my fainting wings for realms of endless life!"

CHAPTER XXIII.

Thus the fair Margaret, in life's bright morning, meditated and mournfully mused. And thus, full often, the sensitive soul, as yet knowing nothing of the hard ways and heavy burthens of earnest life, faints ere the early dew is dried from its morning path of flowers. Soothe your sorrows, ye sensitive souls! Your appointed duties and destinies may not thus be evaded, nor can you as yet "plume your fainting wings for realms of endless life." You must learn to bear bravely, and strongly strive. Your strength and faith must be increased by patient use, till your power shall be greater than your burthens, and you shall walk in your appointed way without weariness, and run with unfainting speed. So shall you fairly aspire to nobler destinies, and plume your stronger wings for realms of endless life.

The fair Margaret sat and meditated, and mournfully mused. A slight knock, and her lovely cousin Frances entered. Her cheeks glowed with exercise, and her eyes shone with intelligence. The fair friends embraced, and kissed. Thus with sweet affection do angels meet.

"Come," said Fanny, "I have come for you to take tea with us. A friend has come. I was forbidden to tell whom, but you are wanted to make us all perfectly happy. Don't ask who; it will be a pleasant surprise, and, besides, it is so agreeably provoking not to know, and to guess wrong, and to anticipate and be disappointed! But it is somebody who will be delighted to see you, and whom you will be delighted to see, unless you are more unlike me and every other girl than I guess. So make haste, there 's a good cousin! And put on your prettiest things; but not too particular, — look *pretty*, but not *grand*."

Margaret soon started off with her lively and lovely cousin. She seemed not at all "weary of this weary world." How poets deal in fiction! Her step was light and elastic, and her countenance rivalled her cousin's in radiant and joyful beauty.

"There they are, coming to meet us!" said Fanny, while yet half their way was before them.

Surely enough, they were coming. Billy and Tommy, escorting somebody. Who could it be? It was not Alek, — not so tall and not so stout, but more graceful. Who could be that somebody?

Billy and Tommy seemed quite at home with *somebody*. *Somebody* seemed giving lessons in oratory to Billy and Tommy; for Tommy would mount upon a bank, and stretch forth his hand and put forward his foot, apparently in the exordium of a speech; and then *somebody* would seem to correct him, and show how to do it better, by advancing his foot not quite so far, and stretching forth his hand more moderately. And then Tommy would begin again upon the improved model; and then Billy would mount, and show how he could do it. They were evidently practising oratory, — perhaps for the coming occasion. Who was *somebody?*

Margaret looked earnestly at *somebody*, and then inquiringly at Fanny, — but Fanny was dummy.

And so they loitered and lingered lovingly along. Margaret seemed now the tired one, — at least, so Fanny thought. She seemed to hesitate about proceeding at all. She seemed even to meditate turning back. But she did not turn back; only she turned aside and plucked fern twigs, and wild briers, and seemed discomposed, and did not look at Fanny while speaking; and Fanny asked her if she was well. Margaret answered yes, and came and gave her hand to Fanny. Her hand was cold, and her clasp tighter than usual, as if nerved by resolute effort; and they went on to meet the boys and — somebody.

As they approached, Tommy and Billy, earnest with tidings, like Cushi and Amihaaz the son of Zadok, outran each other to announce the already very obvious fact that

"Harry Boynton has come, and we are having a famous time!"

"My name is Norval on the Grampian hills!" shouted Tommy, hurriedly, that he might be the first to show his improved oratory. But Billy interrupted him.

"No, that 's not right. Look!" and, placing himself oratorically, he spoke on the improved model:

"*My* name is *Norval!* on the Grampian hills" —

By this time their oratorical oracle, Harry Boynton, had come up. The onset of the boys had broken the ice of formality and the spell of embarrassment, and Margaret gave her hand to Harry, and welcomed him with self-possessed grace. But she saw in a moment, for she read it in his sparkling eyes, and deep voice, and tremulous lips, that he loved her—(let woman alone for that!)—and she knew that he had come to tell her of his love ; and she cast down her eyes, that no one should see the joy which gladdened them ; and she looked and spoke *at* the boys, that no one should see how the red suffused her cheeks.

"But," said she, "he shall not know that I love him, nor think me too easily won." And so she schooled herself to cool dignity and formal decorum, and wondered how he would proceed, and *when* he would propose.

Fanny suspected something of the truth. There is a sympathy of intelligence between hearts entwined in sisterly love, and each shares the other's secret thoughts. Besides, Harry, who arrived the previous evening, had that morning a long and private conversation with Helen, who, shortly afterward, requested her to invite Margaret, and cautioned her not to tell who was the visitor. And so Fanny's curiosity stimulated her sagacity to suspect something.

There was in Wolfsden at that time what is there called a *reformation*. In other places the like is called a *revival*. We cannot give a perfect account of Wolfsden without including its "reformations." They occur sometimes twice or thrice in a year, and sometimes but once in two or three years. Generally they are local, — in the east or west or north or south part of the town,—but sometimes they spread, or occur in different quarters simultaneously, so as to include the whole town. The philosophy of these movements is not settled. Like other phenomena of society, they are the result of general laws, whose operations may be traced in all nations and ages. The solemn feasts and jubilees of the Jews ; the idolatrous festivals and processions of Egypt ; the eleusinian mysteries of Greece ; the pagan saturnalia and Catholic carnivals of Rome ; the Mahometan pilgrimages ; the frenzies of oriental devotees, and the superstitious juggleries of heathen tribes, all are manifestations of the soul's spiritual affinities, struggling for higher associations. Among the most ignorant and debased the only result is wild disorder, folly, and cruelty; among the enlightened, a true and fervid piety is sometimes unduly stimulated and misled by emotional excitement, and the religion which should be as a river of life, nourishing and beautifying its borders, with equal flow, is a tide of uncertain motions, now inundating its shores, and now leaving bare its barren sands. Instead of being, like Christian's roll, a support and guide on hills of difficulty, and over the enchanted grounds of temptation, and through the valley of the shadow of death, it tempts to by-paths and short passages, which look toward the celestial city, but lead to the dark mountains of stumbling.

The periodical religious excitements, or "reformations," of Wolfsden, often produced good fruit, — twenty, sixty, and some an hundred fold; but many of the converts relapsed, so that, though one fifth or sixth of the population was converted annually, yet each successive reformation found as much to do as the preceding. Yet, except so far as they might prevent something better, they were not unprofitable efforts. It is better that men should be awakened to their immortal interests, though ever so rudely, than that they should still sleep in the stupor of sin; for of the many awakened a few are saved.

One of the series of meetings was to be held this evening at the school-house before referred to, in Deacon Arbor's district. Elder Kraken, a great reformation minister, was expected to preach. Apart from the attractions of a famous minister, it was the *duty* of the people of the district to assemble and fill the house. This, and another good motive, led Helen to encourage the proposition to attend the meeting; and, therefore, after tea, she and Margaret, and Fanny, and Harry, and the boys, went over to the school-house.

The services began at early candle-lighting, and they arrived as the people were collecting. Elder Kraken soon made his appearance. He was a man advanced in years, yet still in the full vigor of his powers. His head was a little bald, and well constructed for his calling. The organs of benevolence, firmness, reverence, self-esteem, ideality, and combativeness, were well developed, giving that combination which is favorable to fervent devotion and fearless zeal, and to which his vigorous bodily powers gave full effect. His preaching was earnest, and in its way eloquent, though rather dogmatical in tenets, and very barbarous in style, — being full of the idioms, technical terms, uncouth words, figurative phrases, and peculiar expressions, which make up the dialect that many persons think necessary for the expression of religious sentiments.

So remarkably was his preaching moulded in that style, that Harry was often puzzled to translate his meaning, and was amused when he should have been impressed. Yet he listened with becoming seriousness, which was the more favorably interpreted by the observing minister, as he had by accident taken one of the seats appropriated to the converts, and those "under conviction."

After the sermon and other exercises, the meeting took the form of an "inquiry meeting," in which the minister separately addressed those upon the seats where Harry sat, calling upon some whom he knew personally to "speak in the name of the Lord," and addressing exhortations and questions to others. Harry, who observed the style of answer, evidently expected and duly repeated, was tolerably well prepared for the examination when his turn came; for the minister naturally took him for one of the converts.

"Well, my young brother," said the minister, "how is the state of your mind, — has the Lord dealt bountifully with you?"

Harry. Yes, the Lord has been very good to me.

Minister. Blessed be the Lord! And you feel that the filthy rags of your own righteousness are taken away? You are washed and made clean?

Harry. Yes, I have been washed and made clean.

Minister. Glory to God! And you are sure that you have a comfortable and well-grounded hope?

Harry (thinking of Margaret). The hope which I have is very comfortable; but I have some doubts.

Minister. Praise the Lord! Your doubts will soon be swallowed up in faith. You mean to seek and strive till you obtain the promise?

Harry (still thinking of Margaret). Yes; that is what I came for.

Minister. Amen, brother! Be of good courage, and you will get the reward; for you have put on the wedding garment, and put off the old man with his deeds.

Harry (thinking of the minister, and very willing to put him off). I hope so.

After the examination was over, the minister requested all about him to kneel, which Harry, with the rest, complied with; and after a fervent prayer, he shook hands with all, giving them encouragement and exhortation, and, especially addressing Harry, to whose good looks he took a liking, he bade him strive to make his calling and election sure, and to contend earnestly for the prize, and the Lord would prosper him.

Harry was much vexed to be again made so conspicuous an object of ministerial misunderstanding, which he could not well correct without embarrassing the important objects of the meeting; and, as they returned homeward, he observed to Helen that the people of Wolfsden seemed resolved to make him a saint in spite of himself.

"I suppose," said he, "they consider it a duty to sinners 'to *compel* them to come in.'"

"The minister took you for one of the converts," said Helen, "because you took the convert's seat."

"Then," said Harry, "I had better have sat in the seat of the scornful. However, I am in the descending scale, and shall soon find my proper level, for they made me a divinity student, or perhaps a doctor of divinity, formerly. Probably they mean to let me down by degrees."

"O, you have been ranked a reprobate since that time," said Fanny. "Mr. Twangson, the heathen missionary, excommunicated you to save himself, some folks say."

"And I have understood," said Harry, "that he represented me as a deceiver and mocker, which was untrue, for I was innocent of their blunder. I think," continued he, "that I must take some opportunity to vindicate myself in this matter publicly; for, apart from other considerations, it does not suit my pride to be ranked with hypocrites or scoffers."

"I think you may properly explain the facts in some conference meeting," said Helen; "and, if you do it without reflecting severely upon others, it will be well received."

She then informed him how he had, through not knowing the usages of the place, confirmed the report of his religious character; so that Harry was able in a future "conference meeting" to explain how certain mistakes arose without his fault, and to rectify his position. This he did in so proper and conciliating a manner that Elder Kraken accepted the explanation, and only "regretted that so talented a young man was not yet quite ready to come up to the help of the Lord against the mighty."

Harry and Margaret parted from the rest of the company when they arrived at Deacon Arbor's, for Helen had told Margaret that Harry wished to walk home with her, and, therefore, she would not invite her to stop at her house. And so Harry walked with Margaret alone.

It was a beautiful autumnal evening. The moon played bo-peep between the fleeting silvery clouds. A gentle breeze fanned the air. The whip-poor-will from the near grove chanted his oft-repeated counsel. The cricket chirruped in the wall, and the fox barked at intervals in the distant forest.

The writer of this history regrets being compelled to substitute these commonplace circumstances for the story which the reader justly expects to be told; but, being uncompromisingly opposed to the license, too often indulged, of inventing imaginary incidents and sentiments, when what really transpired is unknown, he must confess his ignorance of Harry's and Margaret's conversation after they left their friends at Deacon Arbor's, or how they beguiled their homeward way. It may, however, be observed that Margaret, though she afterwards indited many a sonnet in her solitude, wrote nothing more about being "weary of this weary world." And as for Harry, it is enough to say at present, that he did not hang himself, — being reserved for another destiny.

CHAPTER XXIV.

Sir Marc Barchier, K.B., sat in the splendid saloon of "Professor Pericrania," proprietor of the "Emporium of Fashion," in Broadway. The long row of stately chairs was filled with incumbents, upon whom the expert assistants and students of the presiding professor demonstrated their tonsorial talents.

"Turn!" said the professor, solemnly, as one of the finished specimens of his skill left the chair of state.

Sir Marc removed his glossy cravat, turned down his shining collar, and surrendered himself to the operator, who, with the sure and dextrous skill which genius, aided by philosophy and cultivated by patient practice, can attain unto, with the aid of saponaceous cream, smooth-gliding razor, clicking scissors, caloric curling-tongs, fragrant oils, and magic evolutions of brush and comb, at last put the finishing touch upon the noblest part of the knight's noble structure.

Along Broadway, after due acknowledgment of the professor's aid, the knight proceeded. As he walked leisurely and dignifiedly adown that fashionable avenue, sometimes glancing superciliously upon the humble crowd of plodders in life's lowly vale, or nodding graciously upon the aristocratic occupants of proudly-passing coaches, what friend of humanity, observing the vast disparity between mortals of one common mould, but would sigh that fortune should make such wide distinctions among men, endowing some from birth with the golden spoon of pride and luxury, and others with the wooden ladle of poverty and debasement?

His hair, perfumed and shining, was surmounted by a hat of Genin's latest style. His glossy whiskers and mustaches curled and shone with redundant oil. His shirt of resplendent whiteness was adorned with diamond studs. A magnificent breast-pin glittered upon his bosom. The tie of his cravat would have won an approving nod from Brummel. His vest of richest fabric was hung with burnished chains of gold, giving security to his sumptuous watch and richly-mounted eye-glass. His coat was cut by Swell, and his pantaloons by Strutt. His French boots were imported by Crimpp, and his kids supplied by Fripp. His ebony cane was the present of a duke, and his rings the gifts of duchesses, countesses, and ladies fair of high degree. His stature was massive and imposing. His eyebrows were bushy, and if his nose was somewhat snub, his prominent cheeks made full amends. Unassuming men turned aside to give him room. Languishing ladies looked up with pleased approval; and saucy news-boys vulgarly shouted, "*There goes a swell!*"

He moved along the thronged way, as some proud bark laden with the costly tribute of foreign climes is borne majestically, with full-spread sails and pennons flying, through fleets of petty fishermen and other ignominious craft that infest the ocean.

Arrived at the Astor House, he stood a while beneath its massive portico, among others of like lofty bearing, and leisurely scanned the passers-by; sometimes tapping his polished snuff-box, or twirling the pendent seals of his watch.

Soon a well-known person ascended the steps, and, with a significant look, entered the hotel. The gallant knight followed him. They ascended different flights of stairs, and with a turn of a key entered a private and well-furnished chamber. The well-known person threw himself upon the sofa, and motioned the knight to a chair.

The well-known person was Fitz-Faun. He had decided Alek to be incorrigible, and had therefore resolved to turn him over to Sir Marc; and he now dictated his instructions to that chivalrous knight, with Napoleonic terseness.

"Anything," said he, "to put him out of my way for a few weeks. Scuttling or stranding, or whatever your sailor lingo likes, so it be effectual. Some splintered ribs, or a broken nose, or an eye spoiled, or any other decided disfigurement or disablement, that will keep him in limbo long enough, will do. But manage it so as to swear the blame on him. I should like to throw him out of old Greening's confidence. If you can get him to take a glass of wine with a few drops of this flavoring in it (handing a vial), you can then manage him as you like. He shirked it the other evening, or he would have been in the watch-house before morning, and in the Tombs before getting sober. But I put him into your mess; you must have wit enough among you to manage him. But, mind, I am not to be mixed up with it. You take the management and risk for the pay."

Sir Marc undertook the service with alacrity, being stimulated by the five hundred dollars, — half in advance. Less sums have purchased baser services in later times.

He was well aware of the principle involved in Mrs. Glass' famous receipt for cooking a hare, which makes it requisite first to catch a hare. The same prerequisite is indispensable to the success of any plan for "scuttling" young men. Sir Marc planned his enterprise with due regard to first principles.

He requested Fitz-Faun to write to Mr. Arbor, in his name, a card of invitation to his rooms in the Howard House, that afternoon at six o'clock, observing that his own hand was a little cramped.

Fitz-Faun, with a contemptuous look, took paper and wrote:

"*Sir Marc Barchier, K.B., snob by profession, blackleg and cut-throat by practice, invites A. Arbor to his rooms at Howard House, this evening at six o'clock, having a design to scuttle him.*"

"Will this answer?" said Fitz-Faun, handing him the note.

Sir Marc, whom nature had not gifted with the art of reading, but who made it a point not to acknowledge the deficiency, took the paper, and, glancing over it, approved it, and requested Fitz-Faun to direct it. Fitz-Faun laughed at this detection of the knight's ignorance; and, tearing up the note, wrote another to the effect that "Sir Marc Barchier, K.B., would be happy to receive A. Arbor, Esq., at his rooms in Howard House, this evening at six o'clock; or, if the appointment should interfere with other engagements, at such other time as Mr. Arbor might appoint." Calling a rvant, he sent the letter, directing the messenger to wait or an answer.

In due time the messenger returned with a note to the

effect that Mr. Arbor would wait upon Sir Marc at the hour appointed.

It should be explained that Sir Marc (whom the reader already recognizes as the reprobate son of old Bang) knew Alek very well; at first from his name, and afterward more certainly by ascertaining from whence he came. But he supposed his own disguise too perfect for detection by one whom he remembered but as a mere child at the time of his own flight from Wolfsden.

Fitz-Faun, after reading Alek's note to Sir Marc, told him that, now he had put the game in his hands, he would dismiss him with the exhortation not to let the pigeon again escape.

Sir Marc returned to his room to prepare for the expected pigeon. At the appointed hour Alek appeared, accompanied by Mr. Edward Clevis, and they were shown to Sir Marc's room. Sir Marc was unpleasantly surprised to see two gentlemen, when he expected but one; and still more, as they looked rather too self-possessed and business-like for his purpose, and too little like pigeons come to be plucked.

Sir Marc, however, welcomed them with extreme cordiality, and invited them to seats; which, to his further surprise, they declined.

"We have come," said Alek, looking Sir Marc in the face, and speaking deliberately, "not to accept your hospitality, but because we have business with you. My name is Alexander Arbor, commonly called Alek. *Wolfsden is my nation, and New York is my station, and you know my occupation.** *Your* name is Mark Barker, of Wolfsden, aforesaid,

* Alek partly quotes from a rustic rhyme, well known in Wolfsden and elsewhere in New England.

and your occupation is also perfectly well known to me. I have come to let you know that I am not the man you want. If I prove to be the man you don't want, it will be your own fault. I shall not go out of my way to trouble an old townsman, but I am prepared for emergencies. I shall not expose myself unguardedly; and if, unawares, any accident should befall me from an unknown source, you will be held accountable, for I have already given your history and my suspicions to one or two prompt friends, and to one of the police. I will only add that in my opinion this city will not henceforth be the safest sphere of your operations; and with this hint I bid you a very good-night."

With these words and a ceremonious bow, the friends departed. Sir Marc attempted no reply, nor even moved his position till the echo of their footsteps had ceased. He then went to the window, threw open the sash, and gazed out as if consulting the aspects of the stars, or the state of the weather. Then he took a glass of brandy and water, as an aid to reflection, — and reflected.

"This is what I call a clumsy piece of business," soliloquized he, repeating the words in which he expressed his opinion on the former occasion of Alek's escape. "A darned clumsy piece of business! — '*Not the man I want!*' Pretty true that. '*Thinks I had better be off*,' eh? Not a bad notion. I 'll be hanged if I don't think so myself. Things look squally. We must stand out for sea-room.

"But, then, we must look this matter on all sides. First, there 's Fitz-Faun. I 've got his check for two hundred and fifty dollars, and want the balance. If I had the knack of the pen, I 'd alter the check and make it look a little more generous, if only for the sake of upholding Fitz-Faun's liberality. The schoolmaster told me I should some-day regret neglecting my learning, and I feel the truth of his remark when I get a bit of paper like this, that needs doctoring and I can't doctor it. However, Fitz-Faun shall do it for me. I 'll get up some pretence. If I can't pluck a pigeon, I 'll pluck a hawk.

"And then there 's my Messalina. How she 'll take on when I take myself off! But I must leave her, for I can't afford to take her. She 's too expensive, and needs too much watching. Besides, if I don't jilt her, she 'll jilt me the first opportunity; and I 'll save her the trouble by doing it myself.

"Then there 's some other little affairs. Money and trinkets to borrow, tailor's and jeweller's bills to run up, and other little speculations that I have deferred, to save my reputation, for bigger hauls. But, if I must be off, I 'll use up my credit before I go. It 's an extravagance I can t afford, to leave a good name behind, when I may as well dispose of it and pocket the proceeds.

"But where shall I go? — Into the smuggling business again, or back to Carolina and into the nigger speculation, as Bob Cantwell proposed? Cute dog, that Cantwell! He 'd steal a nigger or eat one for ten dollars, but I 've a little too much conscience for that. I got sick of the business when I sailed from Boston in that ship. To see the poor nigger whimpering and pining all the way, and then the cutting up they gave him when they got him to Charleston. It rather stuck in my crop. But I think I am not so soft-hearted now, since I 've heard Scripture for it. 'T is n't so bad, after all, sending off a darned nigger, as if 't were one's own mother. That I would n't do. As for sons and brothers, they sell them off every day at the south, and I s'pose I might get used to it. I hope I 'm not such a reprobate as not to profit by the good preaching I 've been hearing."

Fitz-Faun met Sir Marc the next day.

"All right!" said Sir Marc. "This Alek is a jollier fellow than we took him for. We took wine together, but left out the flavoring. I was not quite ready for operations. I want to get his full confidence. I understood you to prefer that he should ruin himself, if he would do it effectually. I prefer it also, for it involves no risk; and now that I have sounded him, I know how to do it. He let me into a little secret last night. He has got a mistress for the first time in his life, and wants money. By the way, you must come down a little more liberally, if it 's only by way of loan. I want to let him accidentally see me overhauling a few large bank-notes, just to convince him of my ability to put him in a way of doing the like. I 've a scheme, — the same that did young Clodpole; — this fellow is greener than Clodpole, and, besides, he 's in for it a considerable already."

Fitz-Faun, who had full confidence in Sir Marc's ability in the line of his profession, and who had his own reasons, since the flight of Erycina, for crediting the report of Alek's having an expensive mistress, was deceived by Sir Marc's plausibility, and gave him a new check for five hundred dollars, which the knight took care to get cashed as soon as possible. And, having finished sundry other little speculations, by way of turning his credit into cash, he informed his landlord that he might not return till next week, and so took his departure for parts unknown.

When Fitz-Faun, after some days' delay, became aware of the knight's delinquency, he was shocked at the baseness and depravity of mankind, which, in his first indignation, he pronounced without parallel ; but, afterward reflecting upon Erycina's flight, he matched it with the falsity and treachery of *womankind*, and, like Byron, sighed that his own true heart so ill deserved the fate it found.

"Strange," said he, "that the two trusted friends whom I relied upon to serve me in this matter have successively betrayed my confidence!"

Like Napoleon, his great archetype, when informed of his favorite Moreau's defection, he was more pained by the per fidy than disheartened by the loss.

He now resolved to bring his own invincible genius to the task, and, having maturely reflected upon the hidden springs of human action, he concluded that Alek probably had not involved himself with Erycina, but was playing for a more profitable prize. He again gave to the ambitious Yankee the credit of being a shrewd, circumspect, designing fellow, who would do his best to obtain the beautiful Sophia, and thus secure to himself present enjoyment and future solid advantages, — a scheme which his evident good standing with the old gentleman made very possible. If he himself, therefore, could by any means get possession of that young lady, he would thus thwart and punish Alek (whose presumption in pitying him and out-generaling him deserved punishment), and would gratify his own wishes at the same time.

To this end he devoted his talents; and, after several weeks' assiduity, Fortune, the patroness of the persevering brave, gave him a golden opportunity, which, with praiseworthy promptitude, he instantly seized. It happened that he met the fair Sophia unattended, as she was returning from a short walk, and, joining her, he pleaded his own cause so successfully, that the generous-hearted and somewhat sentimental young lady agreed to come out alone the next day, and meet him at a fashionable place of resort.

Sophia, observant of the promise exacted from her, made no report of her interview with Fitz-Faun, and went out to meet him the next day without giving notice of her departure, fully intending to return in an hour at farthest. She met Fitz-Faun, and he told her all the cherished hopes and wishes of his true heart, and vowed eternal constancy. He lamented that the unfounded prejudices of her father, whom he highly honored, should preclude the hope of getting his immediate consent; but, if she would give him any hope, however distant, it should be the leading star of his life, and prompt him to every effort for conciliating the father's favor, and ultimately gaining his consent.

His honeyed phrases fell sweetly on the believing maiden's ear. She knew Fitz-Faun to belong to the highest circles of fashion, with riches, elegance, accomplishments, and every outward advantage to support his pretensions; and he assured and convinced her that the reports which had prejudiced her father were groundless, fabricated by his enemies, or imagined by others on no better grounds than the innocent gayety which sometimes disregards grave conventionalities. He acknowledged his former indiscreetness in trifles, but averred that since he had become older he had learned to place a proper value upon outside appearances, as well as inward virtue. "He had never gone about to vindicate his character; he would not condescend do so, except to her, whose esteem was dearer to him than life. As for others his friends knew him; and even his enemies would, in time, forget their animosity, and do him justice."

Nothing more effectually wins woman's sympathy than the complaints of injured innocence. Sophia pitied Fitz-Faun, and pity is a long step toward love. She hoped her father would learn to look upon him favorably. He might count upon her friendship; more than that she hoped he would not require her to say at present.

This was, in fact, enough for the present (this opinion is expressed for the benefit of others in like cases); but Fitz-Faun fancied that her eyes and cheeks said even more. At any rate, he meant they should.

Just then, by chance, the Miss Dryades came by, Messalina with another Dryad who had taken the place of Erycina. Fitz-Faun rejoiced to meet his superb cousins, and introduced Sophia. The young ladies were full of good spirits and good feeling, and immediately adopted Sophia as one of their dearest friends. At another time she might have detected something equivocal in their appearance; but her own thoughts were now preöccupied by an all-absorbing theme, and her instincts directed more to the concealment of her own emotions than to the scrutiny of others.

The young ladies explained that they had come out in the coach with their mother, who desired to call upon Bishop Onadonky's lady, and while the mother was making her call the daughters had driven round the square, and were now about returning. As Sophia was also about to return home, they insisted upon setting her down, before returning for their mother. Sophia consented, and Fitz-Faun, "wishing to improve the opportunity of a longer chat with his cousins," whom he protested he had not seen for an age, also entered the coach, and they drove rapidly away.

They drove a long time. Sophia would have wondered that they drove so far, but her attention was engaged with the brisk conversation of the Miss Dryades, and she forgot to think of anything else. At length the coach stopped, and before a stately mansion. Messalina, looking out, exclaimed,

"Why, sister, here we are at Bishop Onadonky's; — the coachman has made a mistake. Why, John," continued she, as the coachman opened the door, "why did n't you drive round to Mr. Greening's?"

The coachman pleaded that he had received no orders.

"I declare!" said Fitz-Faun, "I must take the blame myself, or rather throw it upon the ladies, who were the cause of my forgetfulness. But never mind, — John can drive us back in a few minutes, and we can have the longer chat."

"Wait a while," said Messalina, "till I run and tell mother."

The sprightly young lady skipped up the marble steps of the stately mansion of Bishop Onadonky, and soon returned, saying that mother must have the coach a few minutes to be set down in the next square, and that they would all alight and wait its return. So they all alighted, and Sophia was in a moment safely housed, — safely, as she supposed, in the stately mansion of Bishop Onadonky; but really in the house to which Alek was formerly introduced as Count Flummery's.

Sophia was introduced to a splendid drawing-room, and presented to the supposed lady of Bishop Onadonky. All were excessively delighted with Sophia, and profuse in attentions. Cake and wine were presented, and the bishop's lady insisted upon her taking a little of her own favorite cordial. Sophia had been educated by her medicinal mother in the duty of taking whatever remedies, preventatives, and strengtheners, might be prescribed; and, though she would rather not, she took the cordial. It was finely *flavored.* In a few minutes she was as lively as the best of them. Her eyes sparkled with animation. Her cheeks glowed with excitement. Her gayety became excessive. She talked, and laughed, and sang, and heard Messalina sing, and laughed at her song. She waltzed about the parlor with her and with Fitz-Faun. She ran up stairs with the charming counterfeit daughters of the Onadonky. Fitz-Faun was already there. * * * * * * Alas! deceived, betrayed, lost Sophia!

It was immediately after dinner when Sophia left her father's house. It was tea-time before her absence was known to her mother, who was during the intermediate time in her own private room, studying some descriptions and certificates of a new medicine to purify the humors of the blood, ventilate the vapors of the brain, and fortify female weaknesses. When she found, upon inquiry, that none of the domestics had seen Sophia during the afternoon, she became alarmed. Mr. Greening, soon coming in, soothed her with the suggestion that she had probably gone out with Augustus, and would soon return. They sat down to tea, expecting every moment the return of their children. Soon Augustus came. He had not seen his sister since dinner, but laughed at the idea of alarm; and they took their tea, but not with accustomed pleasure, for she who shed light and beauty upon the repast was absent. After tea Mr. Greening proposed to walk to a neighbor's, where Sophia had probably called, and wait upon her home. It is needless to say that his inquiries there and elsewhere were fruitless. The evening wore on, and the anxiety of all increased. Some accident had doubtless befallen their beloved child. At a late hour application was made to the police, and every possible means of discovery employed.

Anxiously wore away the night. In the morning, more extensive inquiries were instituted. Messengers were despatched to every place where she was known, and the day was spent in searching wrong places, investigating false rumors, and pursuing wrong directions. In the afternoon, it was believed that her retreat was discovered; but, after the loss of several hours, this discovery was also proved false.

In the first moment of real alarm, Mr. Greening suspected Fitz-Faun, and went to that gentleman's residence; but was there informed that he had been absent from the city for several days, and, on pressing his inquiries, was shown a letter received from him the day before, dated and postmarked several hundred miles away, stating that business having detained him some days longer than he expected, he should not return till the ensuing week. Mr. Greening, therefore, dismissed his suspicion of Fitz-Faun.

Mr. Greening had made known his daughter's absence, and his own apprehensions, as little as possible, consistent with active inquiry; for he wished to prevent injurious suspicions and ill-natured gossip, to the injury of her reputation. When, however, the second morning arrived bringing no resource, he sent for Alek, and told him of the dreadful bereavement, and all the circumstances of his fruitless inquiries, and asked if he could suggest any plan of discovery.

"Yes," said Alek. "We must trace her through Fitz-Faun. We must search all his premises, and examine all his associates and servants."

"But I have told you," said the father, "that Fitz-Faun has long been away from the city. I saw the letter in his own hand, dated and postmarked hundreds of miles away."

"That is what confirms my suspicion," replied Alek. "Himself or his agents have accomplished this villany, either by force or treachery. Will you give me authority to act?"

"Yes," said the father. "Here, take money—spare nothing. O, God! what would I give to save my child?"

Alek paused not to hear the agonized expressions of the despairing parents. His resolution was taken. Count Flummery's establishment must be searched; but perhaps a shorter way of discovery might first be tried. Hastening to the coach-stand near the City Hall, he singled out the carriage in which he had been driven with Fitz-Faun and the Miss Dryades. The driver was lolling idly upon his box. Alek, who wished to be out of hearing of others, sprang up and sat by his side.

"Tell me," said he, "where you took the young lady, the day before yesterday, by Mr. Fitz-Faun's order."

"Fitz-Faun, Fitz-Faun!" said the faithful John; "I am not certain as I know him. Where does he live?"

"Come, come," said Alek, "this is no trifling matter. Tell me where the young lady is, and you will save yourself trouble. I know who took her away, and now the question is, where to find her. Let me know where she is at once, and it will be fifty dollars in your pocket, and nothing said. Look at this" (and he exhibited a well-filled pocket-book); "now look at me, — are we friends, or not?"

"Well," said faithful John, "I 'd help you fifty dollars' worth, if I could do it, and nothing said. I don't pretend to know anything, but you may have my opinion, if that 's worth fifty dollars."

"Then," said Alek, "let me have your opinion, and if it proves true the fifty dollars is yours. I 'm in Greening's employ, and, if my promise needs backing, just drive me to his house in two minutes."

"I 'd rather trust you," said cautious John, "than to be seen in the affair. But I 'll give you my opinion, and if it comes true you may give me the fifty dollars. But you must take another coach. I don't want to get mixed up in anything against my customers."

Alek agreed to the terms, and John, with a meaning wink, whispered,

"You know Count Flummery's."—Alek assented.—"Well, *that 's my opinion.*"

"It 's mine, too," said Alek. And, taking the next coach, he drove immediately for Edward Clevis, and, telling the young man to enter without delay, they proceeded to the police station, and obtained an ample force, with which they proceeded to Count Flummery's, whose residence Alek had taken care to remember.

Alek explained the matter to Edward, while on their way to the police station; and nothing could exceed the interest and zeal of the young man. He warmly expressed his thanks to Alek for calling upon him to aid in the search. It was not only because Alek knew the deep interest his friend would feel in the affair, but also because he had observed his shrewdness and capacity in other matters, which made him, as it soon proved, a very fit person to select for the occasion.

Count Flummery was no way disconcerted or offended at the visit of the police. He was "very glad," he said, "since there was suspicion, that there should be an examination, by which the suspicions would be removed. Besides, his purpose in residing for a short time in this country was to examine its institutions; and he was pleased with this visit, as it would give him an opportunity, which might otherwise have been wanting, of observing the police system, which he "doubted not that he should approve, as he did other features of our institutions." He invited the gentlemen to take wine; and, in short, presented in his own person a most favorable specimen of foreign manners.

The policemen, however, to whom Alek had given his opinion of the count's real character, and who had perhaps some knowledge, or suspicions, concerning it, performed their duty faithfully. Every room was searched, every door opened, and every possible place of concealment explored. At length they all returned to the parlor, convinced that, whatever might have been the fact previously, the object of their search was not now concealed in the house.

They remained in the parlor a few minutes, exchanging civilities with the count, expressing regret at the intrusion which their official duty required, and their satisfaction at the honorable result, which indeed his eminent position and character made obvious from the first. They were the more earnest in their civil expressions, because they still suspected him to be cognizant of the affair, and purposed to watch him secretly.

They were about to depart, when Edward Clevis, who had all the time been musing apart, expressed a wish again to examine the rooms of the fourth story; and immediately proceeded thither, accompanied by Alek and one of the police. On entering one of the rooms before searched, he remarked that he had observed it to be narrower than the room below it, although it extended further toward the staircase, making the entry narrower; and, therefore, it could not occupy the whole width of the house on the side opposite the entrance; and he asked the others how to account for the diminished size of the room, since there was apparently no other beside it. The truth and importance of the suggestion was at once perceived by the others, and they proceeded to examine the wall for a concealed opening, but without success, — only they observed that, on striking the wall, it was evidently not of masonry, like the outside wall, but of carpenter's work.

They then examined the room in the rear and adjoining. It was of the same width with the last, and, like it, elegantly furnished. Against the wall which contracted the width of the room was a beautiful wardrobe, movable upon castors. Slipping it on one side, a door was brought to view, which, on opening it, disclosed a large wardrobe closet, hung thickly on every side with various garments.

"It is evident," said Clevis, "that there must be another room cut off from the front room, and the access to it may be through this closet."

The reasonableness of this supposition was clear, and they proceeded to remove the clothing and other furniture from the closet; and Edward examined the end of the closet toward the front room. The closet had little light, but the policeman remedied the deficiency by producing a dark-lantern. By close observation, it was found that the wall was a movable one. Edward found that one of the pegs on which clothing had been hung was loose, and in endeavoring to remove it he turned it round, and heard a click, like the pushing back of a bolt. With a slight effort, he then slid the whole wall, which moved in a groove to one side, and discovered an additional wardrobe, with a door opposite. Opening the door, he saw the object of his search.

Sophia was sitting in an arm-chair, enveloped in a loose dress of rich fabric, but carelessly adjusted. Her face was pale. Her eyes were inflamed, as if with weeping. Her hair was disordered, and her whole appearance that of affliction and fear. A young girl attended her.

The room, though small, was splendidly furnished. A couch of the richest drapery occupied one end. The walls were covered with costly mirrors and beautiful paintings. Nothing which luxury could devise and adapt to the room was wanting. A soft and beautiful light was diffused from the ceiling, which seemed composed of a single plate of glass, tinted and traced in the most beautiful colors, and with the most exquisite taste.

Upon seeing Edward enter, Sophia started with alarm, but as he approached her, saying, "Dear lady, your mother has sent for you," she sprang toward him, exclaiming, "O, take me to my mother!" and, reeling, she would have fallen, but Edward caught her in his arms, and placed her upon the couch, as Alek and the policeman advanced to give their aid. Alek, telling them to await his return, ran down stairs and reported the discovery, requesting one of the police to go immediately in the coach for the parents, and the others to secure and detain the count and all other inmates of the house. His directions were obeyed, and scarcely an hour had elapsed since Alek had first been consulted, before the daughter was enfolded in her parents' embrace.

When the parents returned home with their daughter, they found Augustus just returned from a search in a different direction, whither he had been sent by false information, and which had consumed several hours. He was extremely affected by his sister's sorrowful appearance. He embraced her affectionately, and conjured her to tell him all the truth.

"O, my brother!" said she, "I am not guilty, but I am ruined! The wicked Fitz-Faun deceived and lured me in his power, and I could not escape! They gave me drink which took away my senses. If he had murdered me, it would not have been so cruel! But he has left me alive to be a shame and reproach to you and our dear parents."

"Dearest sister," said Augustus, "do not speak so! You are our joy and pride. Do not think we can value you the less because you have suffered wrong and violence. But your wrong shall be avenged. Fitz-Faun shall pay dearly for this. My sister, you shall see, and others shall see, that you have a brother to protect you, or at least to punish those who dare to injure you!"

"Dear brother!" said the agitated girl, "do not attempt it! Do not take any steps that may involve our parents in deeper distress, or make this dreadful affair any more widely known. O, what distress has my indiscretion brought upon you all! But wait, at least, if anything must be done, till there is time for thought. Do not attempt anything rashly. O, brother! promise me this favor, for our dear parents' sake, as well as your own, — and mine, if you can still love me!"

"Sister, I will do as you say. I will do nothing without due deliberation. It will take time to decide how to act. Be quiet, now, upon that point, and reässure yourself every way. You are my own dear sister, and our parents' love and mine should console and comfort you. Compose yourself to sleep, while I watch by you, for you look weary."

Augustus assumed calmness to quiet his sister's apprehension, but a settled purpose of vengeance upon her betrayer had taken possession of his heart. His sister composed herself at his request, and he took a book and sat by her, that his moderation might give her assurance of his purpose to obey her wishes.

However faulty Augustus might be in other respects, he was by no means wanting in the impulsive virtues of what is generally called a "high-spirited fellow." He was generous in any direction where his feelings or fancy might lead, and brave to repel or avenge insult. If his principles were not always strict to observe the respect due to another man's or woman's honor, at least his pride was sufficiently sensitive to what might wound his sister's or his own.

His energies were of that kind which, if not the most durable, is nevertheless capable of being wound up to the highest pitch of immediate action. Nothing was wanting in the present case to inspire the most desperate resolution. His sister's injury, his own insulted honor, the vengeance due to violated friendship and hospitality, the sting of scorn which tameness would provoke, these were more than enough to fix his fiercest determination.

He continued to look over the pages of the book for some time after his mother had entered the room. He then went carelessly out, as if for an ordinary purpose. Once out of hearing, he hastened to his chamber, and examined the pistols which he had used in the shooting gallery. They were in excellent order, and he loaded and capped them in the most careful manner. He then cloaked and capped himself with equal care, and in a few moments gained the street without exciting observation.

He repaired hastily to a public house which commanded a view of Fitz-Faun's residence. His faculties were sharpened by the emergency, and he sagaciously reflected that the surest way to effect his purpose was to await Fitz-Faun's appearance in the street, as he was probably guarded against attack in his own house. His vengeance was impatient, but he resolved not to frustrate it by want of due caution. He therefore waited in the window where he was seated till Fitz-Faun should appear, or till he could devise a sure means of access to him. As destiny would have it, he did not wait long. Fitz-Faun had been informed of the discovery of Sophia, and resolved to leave the city till the affair should be blown over. He probably thought that, as Napoleon had sometimes retreated when he could do no better, it would be no impeachment to his own generalship to retreat upon like occasion. He therefore had already made preparations for departure, and ordered his carriage. It was soon at the door. He entered it just as Augustus, who had advanced as rapidly as possible without exciting observation, had reached it; but the coachman at that instant snapped his whip, and the horses started rapidly away. Augustus, nerved to desperation, followed with equal rapidity, resolved that his prey should not escape him. The direction of the carriage made it necessary to cross Broadway, which was then thronged with carriages, so that Fitz-Faun's carriage was for a moment stopped. That moment sufficed for Augustus to gain the carriage window. He saw Fitz-Faun reclining in the back part of the carriage, his face mostly concealed by a travelling-cap. Augustus, throwing off his cloak, broke in the window with the butt of his pistol. Fitz-Faun looked up. Their eyes met, and in that moment he received the contents of the pistol in his throat.

The ball cut its way through his cravat, his windpipe, tore the carotid artery, and, passing through the neck, lodged in the cushioned side of the carriage.

Fitz-Faun, in the agonies of death, dashed through the opposite window, and fell heavily upon the muddy pavement. He sprang, in his death struggle, again upon his feet. The blood foamed from his mouth and nostrils, and his eyes protruded with suffocation. He faltered a few steps, and fell headlong. The horrified spectators attempted to raise him. His struggles became less violent, and shortly ceased. They placed him in his own carriage, which returned immediately to his house.

When Augustus discharged his pistol, his excitement had risen to the pitch of frenzy. His cloak and cap had fallen in the street, and he sprang around the carriage to the side whence Fitz-Faun emerged, with his remaining pistol prepared for action. Facing Fitz-Faun as he rose, he would have again fired, but the bloody and ghastly spectacle deterred him. But he shouted, in the madness of ungovernable rage,

"Die, wretch! — die, dog! Do you know me? I'm your old friend, Augustus Greening. Yes, gentlemen," said he, looking round on the gathering crowd, "I'm the man that killed that dog! He was the Napoleon, but I'm the Wellington. Yes, sir (to a policeman who advanced to him), I'm your man!"

Alek had remained at the count's till Sophia departed with her parents; then, leaving the count and his household in charge of the officers, he hastened to the court of police, and entered a complaint against the count, and also stated his belief concerning the bracelet in possession of the countess. An examination of those eminent persons was ordered; and it appearing, among more important matters, that the object of the count's brief residence in this country was chiefly to examine into American institutions, the judge very graciously awarded to him an apartment peculiarly favorable to his studies, in an edifice of Egyptian architecture, sometimes styled "The Tombs."

An examination of his effects proved that the count had a decided talent for choice collections; and a list of articles being taken and exhibited for the benefit of the curious in such matters, a number of gentlemen, tradesmen and others, formerly patronized by the count, appeared and identified many choice articles, to which they laid claim, forgetful of the delicate feelings of their noble friend, who had privately appropriated these trifles as keepsakes and memorials of friendship, as was afterward proved by his own declaration in his defence. The countess objected to the indignity of being searched, as the operation seemed to imply suspicions derogatory to her honor and rank; but, being told that the ceremony was indispensable, she finally submitted; and the bracelet, the gift of a queen, with many other costly trinkets, doubtless presented by duchesses, peeresses, marchionesses, and other high pomposities, were all carefully collected, catalogued, and safely kept, as was her ladyship, for further consideration.

Alek had scarcely returned to his place of business, when a farmer-looking man, attended by a young man who was his son, came hastily in, and inquired for Mr. Greening. Alek recognized him as Mr. George Washington Bowpin, of Furrowdale, the same person who had formerly inquired of him concerning Fitz-Faun, whose name Mr. Bowpin supposed to be Smith. Mr. Bowpin had witnessed the death of Fitz-Faun, and, hearing the homicide declare himself as Augustus Greening, he had come to announce the fact to the father.

Alek heard his story, and, requesting him to await his return, ran to his employer's house, and, calling him in privately, communicated the intelligence in the terms the least likely to agitate a father in such a case. They at once proceeded to Augustus' place of confinement; Alek, in the mean time, suggesting to the father the justice and expediency of withholding all censure, and vindicating his son's act as the necessary result of virtuous and honorable impulses.

"For," said Alek, "the law is now his accuser, and both nature and justice require of you to be his advocate until acquitted by the law, and then you may properly judge him as a parent. Mr. Greening took the same view, and in his interviews and consultations with his son, then and afterward, gave no hint of disapprobation, but supported him with unqualified tenderness and encouragement.

To avoid the necessity of recurring to this affair again, it may as well be here stated that the trial took place shortly afterwards, and Augustus was honorably acquitted, on the ground of temporary insanity. His frantic gestures and exclamations at the time of the murder, as sworn to by Mr. George Washington Bowpin and his son, and other spectators, gave a sufficient pretence for acquittal in this case, though it would hardly have availed in case of a murder committed with less provocation. The verdict was received with a burst of applause by the spectators which the court reproved with unusual mildness.

CHAPTER XXV.

WHEN Alek returned to the office, after communicating the manner of Fitz-Faun's death to Mr. Greening, and accompanying him to his son's place of imprisonment, he inquired of Mr. Bowpin more particularly about the circumstances of the tragedy; and also the meaning of his expressions of surprise on a former occasion, when told the real name of Fitz-Faun. Mr. Bowpin replied that, some few months ago, that person had brought to his house in Furrowdale a lady whom he introduced as his wife, and with whom he took a room, which they occupied several weeks. The gentleman gave his name as Smith. He was absent most of the day, sometimes leaving the lady, but often he took her with him. The lady was very beautiful, and seemed much attached to him, but appeared not perfectly happy, especially when he was absent. He was liberal in his expenses, but by no means communicative, and appeared to avoid observation.

Mr. Bowpin was certain that Fitz-Faun was the person; and the son, who recognized him as he sprang from the carriage after receiving the fatal wound, was equally certain of his identity. Their description of the lady answered to the appearance of Erycina; and Mr. Bowpin expressed the opinion that she was innocent of any intentional deception. Both the Bowpins said that they should know the lady again under any circumstances.

Alek took a note of these statements, and told the Bowpins that there might be occasion to verify the facts by their testimony, for the purpose of maintaining the lady's right of dower as Fitz-Faun's widow, and they agreed to be ready when called for.

It had occurred to Alek, that if Miss Meekly's statements could be proved, namely, that Fitz-Faun had lived with her, or represented her as his wife, she might perhaps have a legal claim to be so considered; and, since he had deceived her by means of a marriage ceremony, nothing could be more just than that the marriage should thus be legalized.

The opportune discovery of the Bowpins seemed to supply an important part of the needed evidence; and he immediately consulted counsellor Grappler, who, like faithful John the coachman, was ready to dispose of his opinion, which Alek found sufficiently favorable to encourage him to proceed — as is generally the case when litigants ask legal advice.

Alek had lately received a letter from his Aunt Hobart, which gave so favorable a view of Miss Meekly's character and disposition, that he was the more earnest to obtain for her the just redress which her case claimed. The letter was as follows:

"My dear Nephew: Miss Meekly requests you to send the enclosed twenty dollars to her aunt, Mrs. Sarah Meadows, whose place of residence she says you are informed of. She speaks of her aunt as being in circumstances which may make the money needful to her; but wishes her not to know where it comes from, for reasons which she thinks you will understand.

"The young woman is much approved here, being discreet and well-favored. It is very good of her to bestow her earnings to help her aunt; and it is hopeful that she will not lose her reward.

"I am glad to hear good accounts of you, and hope that you will always remember to wait upon the Lord, and not let your heart be puffed up by prosperity; for the Lord hateth the proud, but giveth grace unto the humble.

"Your cousin Hezekiah sends his kind regards. He is to visit Wolfsden next Thanksgiving; and I trust that we shall have Helen with us the coming winter.

"Your affectionate aunt,

"ABIGAIL HOBART."

Having received counsellor Grappler's advice, Alek wrote to Miss Meekly, informing her of Fitz-Faun's death, and stating in detail the discovery and the importance of her legal rights as his wife and widow, to vindicate which required her immediate return to New York. He enclosed the letter in one to his aunt, in which he stated more briefly that Miss Meekly's rights in the property of a person lately deceased required her presence. He also wrote to Mrs. Simperkins, detailing the developments concerning Count Flummery, and his probable identity with her former friend, Count Flipperton, especially as a bracelet displayed by the countess answered her description of the one formerly belonging to herself. He advised her, that she might probably recover it by early application.

In due season the winning old lady came, and made such excellent impression upon the chief of police, by her appearance and her story (which Alek confirmed as being her old story), and also by other proofs (the strongest of which was her instantly identifying the count among a crowd of prisoners), that the bracelet was restored to her; perhaps partly through virtue of an ancient precedent established by a famous judge, "Lest by her continual coming she weary me."

Mrs. Simperkins, having regained her long-lost bracelet and having duly considered the fleeting nature of such ornaments, and having, perhaps, some vague impression that the period of youthful vanities was passing away, and that the solid charms of a well-lined purse might better become her maturer years, took the advice of Alek, and, applying to a jeweller in Broadway, whom she convinced that the ornament, or at least herself, was "ha hunique," she received the cash value of her treasure, which paid her expenses and carried her home with a heavier purse than she had ever before possessed; and also with a heart from which all traces of resentment toward Alek, for her long-remembered shipwreck in the snow-drift, were forever obliterated.

CHAPTER XXVI.

Miss Meekly, upon her arrival in New York, being advised by Mr. Grappler (whose activity in behalf of his fair client, aided by the zeal of Alek and the recollections of the Bowpins, had already accumulated an amount of evidence sufficient for present purposes), took the name of Fitz-Faun, and immediately proceeded to his late residence, accompanied by that eminent counsellor. At the house they found the elder Fitz-Faun, father of the deceased, under whose orders some of the furniture was being removed. Mr. Grappler, in behalf of his client, commanded a stay of proceedings, and introduced the lady to Mr. Fitz-Faun, senior, as the widow of his son, who had come to claim her dower and take possession of the house and personal effects of the deceased, by virtue of her legal right. The old gentleman was astonished at the announcement; but the highly respectable character of Mr. Grappler, who briefly told the fact of the private marriage of his son, and that it could be substantiated by the acknowledgment of the deceased, and other sufficient proof, prevented resistance, and the old man left the house in possession of the new claimant and her adviser, and proceeded to the office of his legal counsellor, the equally eminent Mr. Grinder; between whom and Mr. Grappler the business was settled to the advantage of all parties, Grappler and Grinder included. A compromise was effected, by which Mrs. Fitz-Faun yielded all interest in the estate of the deceased, and received ten thousand dollars, and a proper acknowledgment of the legality of her marriage.

Alek had in the first place stated her case to Mr. Greening (omitting the circumstances of his first acquaintance with her), and it was by his advice that Mr. Grappler was retained in her behalf. When her claims were adjusted, Mr. Greening desired to see her; and, on being introduced, after some conversation, he inquired the place of her early residence.

"Cedar Grove," she replied.

"Cedar Grove! — why, my daughter spent several weeks there, two years ago."

"Your daughter? — is her name Sophia Greening?"

"The same."

"Why, she is my dearest friend. Can I see her?"

Mr. Greening explained his daughter's misfortune, and added, "If you can still condescend to claim her as your friend, I will take you to her at once."

"Condescend!" exclaimed she. "Why do you speak so? — as though she were degraded by the villany and violence of another. To admit such an idea is to degrade me also! Let me see her as soon as possible. She is an angel of purity and goodness."

The gratified father led the fair Fitz-Faun to his daughter. As soon as they met, Sophia sprung to her arms, exclaiming, "My dear Emily Meekly!"

Fondly sweet was their sisterly embrace. Emily remained and comforted Sophia. They confided to each other all their history. Together they visited the imprisoned brother, whose acquittal, or pardon, Mr. Grappler assured them might be relied on. Together they attended the trial, where Sophia was compelled, as a witness, to tell her story; which she did with such simplicity and clearness, as aided not a little her brother's cause, and together they rejoiced at his acquittal.

The heart of Augustus was touched with the sympathy and the charms of Emily; and after his release he proved his unabated love to his sister, by falling in love with her friend.

That this episode may not hang upon our hands, we will add, that Augustus became sobered down to a rational being by the late tragic events. He concluded to exchange his chivalrous notions and high-life pretensions for a common-sense character, as more useful and respectable; and he resolved upon matrimony, as the first decided step in his new career. Parents approved. Sophia solicited. Emily hesitated, and insisted upon a year's probation; but finally compromised for six months, a part of which time she spent with her aunt, Mrs. Sarah Meadows, at Cedar Grove, to whom, with the approval of Augustus and his father, she secured an independent support during life, by the purchase of an annuity. In due time Mrs. Fitz-Faun became Mrs. Augusta Greening (adopting the feminine of her husband's name). It is now some years since, and they all profess never to have regretted the transaction.

CHAPTER XXVII.

A DAY or two after the acquittal of young Greening, the father called Alek into his private counting-room, and thus addressed him :

"My young friend, your faithfulness and ability have been of the utmost service to me and my family, — more than I can express. It is to your efficient aid that I owe my daughter's restoration. It is impossible that I should fully repay you; and it is not in your disposition to expect it; indeed, no person of right disposition desires to be fully repaid for the benefits which his abilities may enable him to confer upon others. We are bound to help each other according to our several needs and opportunities, and God has appointed a sufficient recompense for every good deed. I wish, however, to show you that I appreciate your services, and am grateful for them. I have made an entry on my journal which doubles your salary for the present year, and it shall be proportionately increased beyond our first agreement for the time that you shall remain in my employ. I intend in a reasonable time to make you an advantageous offer of a partnership in the business, which, whether you accept it or not, will show my perfect confidence in your ability and zeal. In the mean time, consider me a friend and adviser, more than an employer; and when you have need of my influence or resources, they are yours. I need not say that your company is always particularly welcome at my house, since I am commissioned by the unanimous request of my family to invite you to take residence with us, if agreeable to yourself, as soon as convenient."

"Your kindness to me," replied Alek, "is more than anything I have done deserves, but I will make every effort to deserve it, as I have opportunity. You are, however, under a misapprehension as to the person chiefly instrumental in rescuing your daughter, and I should be guilty in receiving the praise belonging to another. It was Edward Clevis who liberated her, by insisting on a second search, when we were on the point of leaving the house, supposing that we had examined every possible place of concealment."

Alek then gave an account of all the particulars of the search, and placed his friend's promptitude and sagacity in the fairest light, and added, "I think it proper, since you have admitted me as a friend, who may allude to your domestic affairs, to give you information that may enable you to act understandingly in whatever marks of favor you may be disposed to show him. Mr. Clevis has long been deeply impressed with the merits of your daughter, and probably might have the presumption to make his partiality manifest, if admitted to a position giving him encouragement. He never has spoken to me of his attachment, nor probably to any one else; but I am positive in my opinion, and I have so good an impression of his personal merits, that I wish his situation in life were equal to his good taste and ambition."

"You mean that you would like to speak a good word for

him," said Mr. Greening, goodnaturedly. "Your honorable conduct, in explaining his share in the important service rendered me, is worthy of you. It does not lessen my obligation to you, though it admits him to an equal claim. The young man has always stood well in my opinion, though I have not had occasion to employ him in any service requiring more than ordinary ability. Your opinion of his merits weighs much with me, and I shall give him opportunity to prove them. By 'his situation in life,' I suppose you refer to his not possessing property; but if he possesses talent, it is an equivalent. Both you and he are richer than myself, taking the difference of years into account, provided you have proper business ability; for the thirty years which you have in prospect before attaining my present age will, if employed in making money, as I have, perhaps too assiduously, employed my years, will make either of you richer than I am, for you have a much better beginning than I had at your age; as I had neither instruction in business, nor available friends, and you have both. You may bring your friend to my house, and I doubt not that his discretion will be equal to his other good qualities."

Alek rightly understood this last remark as an intimation to check any undue forwardness in his friend, but not to forbid his hopes, and he therefore modified the invitation to Edward accordingly. Edward visited his patron's house with his friend, and made himself agreeable by his unassuming manner, and soon became on familiar terms with the family. It has already been told how Sophia perceived his partiality on the occasion of their first interview at Mr. Boynton's soiree, and was not unfavorably impressed by it.

Her deep humiliation and sorrow since that time had disposed her still more favorably to appreciate the regard of a sincere and honorable heart; and it may be inferred that Edward, who had much love, had also some ground of hope.

CHAPTER XXVIII.

O, FAIR flowers of life's dewy morning! O, breezes redolent of youth's balmy breath! O, gleams of early brightness still gilding the fading horizon! O, memories still fresh and fragrant, — ye choice treasures of the secret heart, no longer open to gather joys from without! Let your influence exhale from the recording pen, and crystallize upon the descriptive page. So, though the dust of present neglect should settle here, yet some future explorer of ancient lore shall find the long-forgotten tome, and, scanning its pages, say, "These are the traces of a faithful pen."

Harry and Margaret sit together upon the shelvy rock in the mellow autumn evening, and watch where the rays of the yet unrisen moon silver the tops of northern mountains. His arm encircles her graceful form. Her clasped hands rest upon his shoulder. His fond eyes are fixed upon her radiant face. The evening breeze fans her waving ringlets till they touch his inclining cheek. They speak to each other in sweet tones, the ever new language of a thousand years, — of unknown ages, of unnumbered worlds, — the speech of the soul, the language of love. The silence of nature's solitude suits their listening ears. Her soft murmur, blended from a thousand distant sounds, borne upon the breeze, disturbs not their thoughts. There is a universal harmony of peace and love.

She tells him of the thoughts of her young days; of her aspirations for the beautiful, the spiritual, the elevated, the refined. How, though inward purity and goodness commanded her esteem and reverence, yet, wanting in outward grace and elegance, they could not touch her heart. How, though she dared not hope to possess, she had sighed at least to see the perfection which her fancy pictured; a diamond sparkling with wrought and polished lustre, a soul of inward worth and outward adornment.

"God is good to me," she said. "He has given me my soul's desire. I feel your purity and truth; they are the deep foundations of my reverence and esteem. I am charmed with the outward grace which sets forth the inward worth. This is the superstructure within which my heart of love delights to dwell."

Thus the love of pure minds exalts its object, shedding thereon the light of its own brightness. It also elevates and refines that upon which its light is thrown. The generous soul, which finds itself prized above its deserts, will strive for the excellence which shall make it worthy of all the praise it receives.

Thus Harry Boynton resolved to strive and attain the exalted sphere of purity and goodness, where the love of Margaret placed him. His conscious faults he would amend; his hidden evil he would detect and subdue; he would strengthen his reverence for goodness, purity, and all that elevates the soul. He would be worthy of Margaret's priceless love.

He told her of the larger experience of his life; how he

had dwelt among the high-wrought scenes of artificial society; how his fancy was fascinated by the grace and elegance with which polished culture gilds outward forms, though moulded of mean material; how pretty lips are taught to counterfeit the language of the soul, or speak the senseless babble of fashion in such enchanting tones as charm away the soul's discrimination; how he scanned their affectation, and thought he scanned the female heart; how he discarded serious thought, and laughed, and sported, and sung the songs and danced in the idle rounds of frivolity, and said that all life was but an empty show, for man's illusion given, — being as yet unaware of its deep meaning and high destiny. How, as a dreamer long entranced in gay delusions, half conscious of their unreality, is wakened by the rising sun to worthy duties and delights, so the light from a true soul had beamed through her dear eyes into his welcoming heart, and wakened it to a glorious life.

Thus does love exaggerate its history, and exalt its votary and its object above the mortal sphere, perhaps above mortal comprehension.

The risen moon ascended in serene majesty among the twinkling stars. Nature listened in silence to their sweet accents of love, or responded in softened echoes of distant sounds. With encircling arms or clasping hands they slowly wind along the rustic pathway, — by gray lichened rocks; by hillocks of green tufted moss; by young birchen trees that greeted them with the gentle murmur of waving leaves; by scattered ferns that offered the incense of their sweet fragrance; through the broken wall which bounds the orchard, beneath the apple-trees whose yellow or ruddy fruit bestrewed the soft turf; by the well, where the old oaken bucket swung idly from the sweep; through the deserted porch where milk pails and pans were piled for morning use; through the spacious kitchen, swept and silent, save the cricket chirruping in the hearth; whence, lingeringly separating, they sought their several rooms, and adored the Power who formed the soul for love.

Much was little Amy vexed when Fanny told her, as a great secret, that Margaret was to marry Harry. She said that "It was a shame for Margaret to do so, when everybody said that she was to be Alek's wife, and she had got the promise to go and live with them when they should be married; and now there is nobody left good enough to be Alek's wife only you, and you can't be his wife because you are his sister; and, besides, you are only a little girl, and I am only a little girl; and, besides, I am to be his daughter, and so I can't be his wife,—and I wish Harry had got somebody else. He might have had Sister Ann, only Josiah Brown wants her; but he might have had Sister Hannah, only mother can't spare her and Ann and me too. But now Uncle Alek will never be married when he comes back, and I never can live with him." Thus little Amy mourned, but Fanny soothed her, saying,

"Alek will have a nice wife, one of these days; for mother says there is a sweet girl growing up for him, and what mother says always comes true. So I think you will have a chance to live with him, and we shall have nice times, after all."

Then Amy wondered who the sweet girl could be, and if she should love her as well as Margaret; and she resolved to ask Aunt Deborah about it. But Aunt Deborah told her it was a great secret yet; and Amy puzzled herself to think who it could be.

All over town they talked of Harry and Margaret's engagement, — they always do so in Wolfsden. The girls who judged themselves handsome thought, if Harry looked for beauty, he was not the best judge in the world. Those who prided themselves upon their skill in housewifery reckoned Harry would be disappointed when he found what sort of a housekeeper she would be. Those who counted themselves among the aristocracy of Wolfsden thought Margaret a proud minx, — "just as if nobody in Wolfsden was good enough for her." Those who were become sensible of the full maturity of their own virginhood thought Margaret a forward miss, to be engaged before she was out of her teens. And so they all envied her, and congratulated her, and told her they were glad to hear it.

The young men "thought it a good joke that Alek should be jilted, when he counted his game so sure. Would n't he swear when he heard of it? True, his mother had taught him not to swear, but they should like to be there and see. But it was not a handsome thing in Harry to cut out his old friend and crony. That 's the way of those city chaps; give 'em a spoon, and you may as well give up the whole platter, — they 'll take it, anyhow. Harry 's got his eye-teeth cut. He thinks the major may die and leave 'em the farm. May get cheated, after all, — some old folks never die. However, Harry 's a generous fellow, and we 'll hope for the best; — he must stand a treat, anyhow."

And so they envied Harry, and censured him, and prophesied ill luck, but greeted him with double complaisance; "For," said they, "we now look upon you as a Wolfsdenner."

The mothers of fair daughters "wondered what Mr. Boynton saw in Margaret so much better than anybody else, and hoped it might all come out well in the end; but they had known things which did not come out so well in the end, after all," and they shook their heads negatively. But they told their daughters that they might invite the young couple to tea, some afternoon; they wanted to be neighborly.

The brethren of the church thought Major Murray would do well to look to the ways of his household. They should feel it a duty not to let a daughter of theirs marry an unconverted person, especially one brought up among the Episcopalians, who read their prayers and sing the Scriptures, and all that heathenish sort of thing. But it would be of no use to interfere. The major was a set man in his way. And so when they met the major they shook hands with double vigor, to atone for uncharitable thoughts.

Thus the people of Wolfsden endured what could not be cured. Harry and Margaret were allowed to have it all their own way, and their own way was to be married next Thanksgiving; and in the mean time Harry would go to his home in Carolina, and make preparation.

CHAPTER XXIX.

Harry's father, Mr. Pelham Boynton, was declining in health, and glad to have his son return; and glad when he asked permission to bring a Yankee girl to share his paternal benediction. Since his strength and ability to look after his own affairs was abated, his estate had become ill-managed and unprofitable, and his neighbors predatory, thievish, and insolent, as they generally are toward those who lack strength or spirit to make themselves feared; so that his life was an uncomfortable monotony of petty miseries.

His only daughter Angelina was his chief society. She was some years older than Harry, and in merits and attractions quite above the average of Carolina home-raised ladies. For her superiority she was partly indebted to nature, having been born a good-looking and promising baby; partly it was in her blood, for she was a Boynton; something she had gained by reading, for her father had a small library, — a rare possession on a plantation; somewhat her father's society had done for her, for he was originally a man of good mind, though rusted by long residence in Carolina. Her brother's suggestions and example had helped her much, so that, though raised in Carolina, she had through these extra aids attained to more than Carolina cultivation.

The mother's lingering and fatal sickness had prevented her being sent away for education while young; and when her mother died, she was too tall and plain for promising experiments, and her father too lonely to spare her. So he gave double advantages to the brilliant son, and kept the plain daughter to soothe his solitude.

But neither the brilliant son nor the plain daughter demurred at their parent's economy. They were both of amiable and yielding dispositions, and loved each other spite of all disparity of years and habits. Harry saw few faults in his sister, and these were more than atoned for by her affection; and Angelina thought her brother faultless.

Their plantation home was in Beaufort County, North Carolina. Judging from its name, we might suppose it a very pretty place. A brief description will enable readers to appreciate the appropriateness of its pretty name.

Beaufort County lies around the head of Pamlico Sound, and is traversed by Pamlico river. Pamlico Sound is an extensive sheet of half-stagnant water. It is a thin sheet, and a very dirty one. Navigators, laboriously paddling their cypress canoes two or three miles distant from the shore, drag their keel through the sludge, and leave a muddy wake behind. Huge snakes and lizard-like reptiles abound in the rank, unsightly vegetation which surrounds and covers the flat islands that in many places elevate themselves a few inches above the water's surface, to an extent sometimes of several acres, though generally of but a few rods. Slimy crabs, and testaceous reptiles, and sluggish, unwholesome fish, swim or crawl where the water is deep enough. Black cypress swamps mostly bound the view, except toward the sea, which cannot be seen, for long reaches of dry sand-banks intervene. This is Pamlico Sound.

The dry sand-banks, and the cypress swamps, and creeks, called "branches," bordered with extensive marsh, covered with tall, coarse, useless grass, and the pine barrens beyond, make up the territory about Pamlico Sound; and this is the lower part of the county called Beaufort.

Pamlico river runs, or rather creeps, into the upper end of Pamlico Sound. It intersects the upper part of Beaufort County, which answers nearly to the description of the lower part; only the water of the river is somewhat less stagnant than that of the sound, and the land is more embellished with pine barrens, and less adorned with cypress swamps, "branches," and marshes. Sometimes a ridge of oak-land is seen, or a mixed and tangled wood of hard pine, loblolly, gum-tree, &c., thick with rank mildewy vines and parasitic plants. But the prevailing feature is a sandy plain, sometimes warted with sandy hillocks, and furrowed by deep gulleys, but mostly of an irregular monotonous level, covered with shrubs and coarse grass, and scattered pitch-pines, dwarfish, scarred, hacked, denuded of their bark for many feet from the ground, and covered with dripping turpentine "scrape." This beautiful region is the upper and remaining part of the County of Beaufort.

At the upper end of Beaufort County, at the head of the shallow navigation of Pamlico river, is a town, equal in extent (but not in neatness, convenience, taste, or wealth) to an average New England village; and it is dignified with the title of "city," — WASHINGTON CITY. The population numbers a little more than two thousand, of all shades of color, from dingy white to decided black; and equal variety of moral and intellectual complexion, beginning not too high in the scale, and ranging downward indefinitely. Such is the circle of society in the North Carolina Washington City.

In little shops are displayed coarse miscellaneous goods,— sometimes a horse-load, and sometimes a pedler's pack full; and the sallow, cadaverous possessor lies at length upon the counter, saturated with whiskey, shaking with fever and ague, and smoking a pipe or cigar. And this is a North Carolina city merchant.

Ranged along the foot pathway (which serves also as gutter) are little stalls, or booths, where superannuated slaves, worn out with labor and the lash, tempt passengers with ginger-pop, sweet cakes, and like luxuries, whereby they earn a few dimes weekly, to pay their magnanimous masters for the rent of their own out-worn bodies.

Sometimes sweet, molasses-looking damsels, dressed in cheap finery, parade in frequented places, and with winning smiles and siren songs entice the sentimental swain to the soft delights of southern life; and these blissful belles also pay so much per week to their noble-minded masters, and delicate mistresses for the rent of their own bodies — and souls.

Sometimes a sentimental journeyer (not a STERNE, for he hated slavery), seeing those petty traders and these contented-looking courtesans, with their flaunting dresses and enticing looks, and, though perhaps a divine, not divining the meaning of all he sees, even though enforced by "rhetorical liftings of the leg,"* is "deeply affected with patriotic feeling;" and ere he lays him down to sleep, and prays the Lord his soul to

* See Rev. Dr. Nehemiah Adams' "*South Side View of Slavery.*"

keep, he writes another chapter in his book, which he fondly hopes "may quiet northern sentiment."

Paltry scenes tire the beholder, and we will not further describe the city but by comparison. It is better than Timbuctoo or Booriboola-gha. It is worse than Paris, or Pekin, or St. Petersburg. The travelled reader may, from these data, classify the city of Washington in North Carolina.

The reader will be glad to escape from this same city. He may do so (if white). There are various directions of egress. He may take a canoe and paddle down the Pamlico; or he may take a plank and pole up the Tar river; or he may take stage and go north or south. Let us take stage and go north, by all means.

Wearily borne along in a vehicle that creaks, and flaps, and jerks violently, though it scarcely moves ahead; that jolts, and pitches, though there are no obstructing stones or solid soil; buried beneath its felloes in yielding sand; buried all over in a cloud of dust just large enough to envelop and suffocate us; dragged slowly along, with writhing, wriggling progress, by skeletons of hungry horses, driven by a dirty, drunken, pipe-smoking coachman, — still it is something to be going, or at least heading, north. The slow tortoise won the race at last, and the history of his travels may console us. At any rate, we are now at the bottom of fortune's wheel, and, though it turn but as slowly as the creaking four which bear us, it may bring us upward at last.

Looking from either crisped, torn leather window, the same sandy, scathed, pitch-pine, scrub-oak monotony prevails. We have travelled half a day at a rate somewhere between that of a snail and a streak of lightning, and find ourselves almost in sight of something. By and by we see it. It is a plantation. It is an oasis in a sandy waste, — not exactly an Eden, but pretty fair by contrast.

There is a two-story whited house, surrounded by a piazza, and shaded by various shrubbery. Apple-trees, and fig-trees, and peach-trees, that should bear and will not bear, and persimmon-trees, that should not bear and will bear, and some climbing scentless roses, and briers that are not sweet, comprise a scanty paradise. The negro "quarters," some twenty rods distant, complete the view of the two extremes of southern life, — scarcely tolerable luxury here, scarcely endurable wretchedness there.

At the entrance of the carriage-way to the lordly mansion stand two painted gate-posts with a high cross-beam. The gate is broken; but we will pause by the gate-posts, for on them our present history hinges.

Some forty years ago a traveller from the north came in view of this gate, then newly erected. He drove his own high-spirited horse, and rode in his own elegant sulky, and he was a high-spirited and elegant young man. He drove leisurely, for his object was pleasure and observation. His horse saw the gate too, and pricked up his ears. It was worth his while. A dozen children, of various complexions, were playing about the gate, climbing the posts, and venturing with fearful steps across upon the overarching beam.

Among them was one so far superior to the rest as to seem like a being of another sphere. She was a vision of all-surpassing loveliness. Her head was adorned with a slight wreath of flowers, which the children in their gay mood had woven. Her rich golden hair fell in profuse and golden curls upon her neck and shoulders, of faultless form and grace. Her deep blue eyes were fraught with beauty, gentleness, and intelligence. Her transparent, pure-veined complexion, heightened by sportive exercise, excelled the artist's highest skill. Her form was a model of symmetry and active elegance. Her movements were spirited, yet graceful; youthful, yet dignified. She was twelve or thirteen years old; just budding from lovely childhood into lovelier maidenhood. Her companions were as the dusky attendants of some peerless Circassian queen.

The traveller — we may as well tell his name — was Mr. Pelham Boynton, then of New York, — all unconscious of the years and cares which have since whitened his head, and furrowed his cheek, and weighed down his heart. He was fresh and buoyant with youth, and health, and hope. He had taste to appreciate and a heart to love the beautiful. He was educated a gentleman, and had the address by which even a stranger may make himself acceptable. Leisure and observation were his objects. He came near the merry-hearted group before he was seen by them, so intent were they on their play.

He bowed, and addressed the beauty, who received his courtesy gracefully, and invited him to alight and see her father. Relying upon the famed hospitality of the planter (a hospitality which the want of society will stimulate in the most churlish hearts, especially as it costs little and has seldom occasion for exercise), he accepted the invitation, and was introduced to the father, General Bateman.

General Bateman was really a hospitable and generous-hearted man. He was pleased with the traveller, and, learning his objects, invited him to pass some days, or weeks, at his plantation, — the name of which was Oak-ridge.

This was the commencement of an acquaintance which ripened into the warmest friendship and closest connection. Mr. Boynton became deeply in love with the beautiful daughter,—it could not be otherwise. Their love was mutual. The generous father was happy to promote the happiness of his daughter and his friend; and he joined them in marriage, stipulating that they should reside on the plantation, at least for the present. Their blissful honey-moon lasted many months, many years. Her name was Angelina. She became the mother of the present Angelina and of Harry.

Meanwhile the old general became infirm. His estate had long been embarrassed, and himself harassed with mortgages. Mr. Boynton, when he found out his situation, relieved him; and at length the planter proposed to sell to his son-in-law his plantation, with its slaves and other property. Mr. Boynton bought the estate, and thus became a Carolina planter. The general lived as before, only more happily. When he died, he left his remaining property to Mr. Boynton.

The reader now sees how our history, so far at least as Harry is concerned, hinges upon the gate-posts aforesaid. Had they not been erected, the children would not have played about them; Mr. Boynton would not have seen Angelina, but would have passed on his way; and there would have been no Harry Boynton, and no history of him.

Thus far this retrospect, though brief, is pleasant. But there is a sad side to it. The beautiful, the angelic Angelina, was, by Carolina law, a slave. Her mother, fair and beautiful as herself, was descended from some great-great-grandmother, kidnapped from some unhappy mother, African, American, European, or Indian (for all races are made to contribute to the stock of slavery).

General Bateman had married Angelina's mother, but that fact did not change her legal relation as his slave. He would have given her a deed of emancipation, for he loved and prized her above every other possession; but he was procrastinating, and hated to recur to the fact that his beloved wife was legally a slave. Also he supposed himself beyond the reach of adversity, and thought not of what might happen after his death; and so the good and beautiful wife of General Bateman, and his fair, angelic daughter Angelina, who of course followed her mother's condition, were, and remained slaves.

When General Bateman gave the beautiful Angelina in marriage to Mr. Boynton, he did not think it necessary to tell the fact of her legal condition. He expected to continue to live; perhaps thought of no other alternative. He could not become bankrupt, and so it was needless to mention the disagreeable subject, since Angelina must of course be safe while he lived; and even if he died, the heir was not likely to claim Angelina as a slave, and would naturally suppose that he had emancipated her mother, and thus made them both free. To guard against contingency, so far as the estate was concerned, he made the arrangement by which the plantation and other property became Mr. Boynton's by purchase, leaving only his most precious possession, his beloved wife, at the mercy of chance and Carolina slave-law.

When General Bateman died, his daughter, the wife of Mr. Boynton, and her children, Harry and Angelina, became the "property" of Timothy Bateman, legal heir of General Bateman; but Timothy was a half-brother, and something of a man, and therefore he did not interfere to claim his property, by which forbearance Mrs. Boynton lived and died in ignorance of her legal condition and danger. Timothy Bateman lived till about the time when Harry came home from Wolfsden to make preparation for his future bride. When Tim Bateman died, his estate fell into possession of a mean, miserable, miserly fellow, named Marshy, who lived near Pamlico river. Marshy had married Tim's only daughter, and had a minor son; therefore Marshy came into possession of the estate as guardian of his son.

Tim Bateman's daughter would never have stooped to marry Marshy, but for having already stooped to an unlawful intimacy with one of her father's servants, whereby her reputation was smutched. It made no difference with Marshy. Her father was wealthy, and willing to give a good sum of money and a plantation on Pamlico river, to get his daughter off his hands, even to Marshy; and finally, as we have seen, the whole estate of Tim Bateman, including Mr. Pelham Boynton's children (for his wife was now dead), fell by law into the possession of Marshy.

This monstrous and horrible fact, the legitimate result of slave-law, should be stated more emphatically. Harry Boynton, the noble-hearted, highly-accomplished gentleman, and his sister Angelina, were legally slaves of the mean-souled, miserly, and ignorant Marshy!

But the principal parties knew not of this fact, and were therefore unlikely to be affected by it. Harry never suspected that his honored mother was in law a slave; nor had Tim Bateman ever told Marshy, or any others of his family, of the fact. It belonged to a Yankee lawyer, belonging by birth to the noblest country under heaven, member of a profession founded on the noblest uses of man's highest powers, to a Yankee lawyer, or rather pettifogger, to ferret out this opportunity of perpetrating villany in the name of law.

The name of this vampyre was Buzzard, of a breed prominent in the annals of infamy. He came from Massachusetts, and settled in the Washington City, North Carolina, already described. Would that all of his race were there! He came of various stock, but all of like character. Kidnappers, slave-hunters, and other traitors to humanity, were his chief progenitors. They are a well-known ancestry, of different grades of society, but of one original stock. By the operation of some hidden laws of generation, he inherited the vilest qualities of them all.

This fellow, a fit agent and tool of Carolina law, began his crooked career by looking up and encouraging litigation among those who had more money than good sense or good nature, and by finding out loopholes and evasions for rumsellers and other petty violators of law. He tried the trade of politics, and figured successively as an abolitionist, an anti-mason, and a democrat, offering himself to all bidders, and gaining the sobriquet of "the soldier of fortune;" and now he speculated in slave-hunting, kidnapping, hunting up flaws in titles to estates and titles to freedom, so that by these ingenious enterprises he turned many a pretty penny.

In the assiduous pursuit of his vocation, he had ferreted out the legal relations of the Batemans and Boyntons, and after the death of General Bateman he offered his services to Timothy Bateman, the uncle, to reduce the young Boyntons to slavery, or compel their father to pay a high price for their freedom. Tim declined his offer, and so Buzzard filed away the papers, and waited for Tim's death. When that took place, and Marshy became, in effect, his heir, he posted to Marshy with the same offer. Marshy was ready to turn a penny, honest or otherwise, provided no risk was incurred; and Buzzard concluded a bargain with him, by which Marshy should have half the profits, but be subject to no costs in case of failure.

At the present period of this history, Buzzard was engaged in looking up and linking together his evidence, so as to strike sure. Much caution was required, lest his object should get wind. He must find or feign other business, and make acquaintance in different families, and introduce his subject indirectly; and, after finding out who knew exactly what he wanted to prove, he must then carefully sound the temper, sentiment, simplicity, or shrewdness, of the individual, and work upon his or her weakness, avarice, envy, self-conceit, or other folly, to secure and make available what might serve his purpose. All this mining, and burrowing, and tampering, takes time, so that many months transpired before his web of evidence was complete, and he thought safe to try its strength.

Meantime Harry was forming plans of a happy and noble life. Whatever a magnanimous mind can conceive, the ardor of youth and conscious genius counts as practicable. Since his nobler faculties had become awakened, he had reflected upon the value of life as a means of advancing noble principles, of promoting noble purposes, and accomplishing noble ends. "The elevation of humanity," said he, "is the noblest work of life. Whoever employs his talents in this direction advances toward a higher sphere; and whether he raises others or not, he at least elevates himself. His efforts may not seem fruitful of immediate results, but, if man is immortal, it will be his great reward to contemplate the progress of the good which he began, and to see it go on increasing forever."

His destined position as a slaveholder engaged his earnest thought. While a student in Harvard University, some sparks from Channing's mind had electrified his understanding, and left an ineffaceable impression of the wrong of holding human beings in slavery. Recollecting that such sentiments might become inconvenient to the son and heir of a slaveholder, he attended other churches in Boston, to get the impressions rubbed out; but the imbecile and canting defences and apologies which he heard only provoked his contempt.

"Surely," said he, "if slavery requires such prevarication of truth, such perversion of religion, such prostitution of principle, and stultifying of common sense, in its behalf, there must be something wrong in it." And so he set his genius to devise a way to correct the wrong without attacking the institution, — to prune the upas-tree without destroying it.

"I will educate my slaves," said he; "the laws forbid it, but, since the laws to prevent excessive cruelty to slaves are violated with impunity, I may with equal impunity disregard those which are made to degrade them. Such as show a capacity for freedom I will encourage to purchase their freedom, and aid them to settle where they can do well. I will promote the comfort and good morals of my slaves, and rule them by good will, and not by fear. I will make myself their guardian and benefactor, more than their master."

It may seem strange that the son of a slaveholder, reared among the practical workings of slavery, should suppose it possible to effect any real good for slaves without first emancipating them, and removing them from the region of its influence. But he had not spent many of his maturer years at home, and had not reflected upon the inevitable operations of arbitrary power; and if he foresaw difficulties, he trusted to overcome them. He talked over his prospects and his plans with Margaret, and she shared his enthusiasm, — and they perhaps already fancied themselves the patriarch and patriarchess of an Abrahamic household.

CHAPTER XXX.

So they were married, and there were present the Picninnies, and the Joblillies, and the great Panjandrum himself, with the little round button on the top. — FOOTE.

THERE are joys which we most enjoy when the world witnesses the enjoyment. There are pains that please, because they impart fame.

Romancing fledglings of youth most delight in dazzling delights, and spurn the dull happiness which challenges no admiration. Why do lovers roll the eyes in ecstasy, or clasp the heaving breast in anguish, and call upon the winds to waft their sighs and the briny waves to receive their tears? It is that the admiring world may write their names on the sentimental page, and that the muse may chant their plaintive story.

But the sober, solid joy of maturer manhood asks no applause of others. The possessor is content to possess, and cares not to awaken the astonishment or envy of the world. In his own heart he rejoices unboastingly. He displays no ecstatic raptures. He locks his sterling gold in strong though homely coffers, and sobers his brows to unpretending content.

But the muse of history lags. No entrancing scenes, no thrilling hopes and fears, point the recording pen. The world will not admire what was only made for use, and a useful life is of all lives the most useless to fancy's page.

Thus by marriage, as surely as by death, the admired actors slip from the stage, and are seen no more. When people are married, their story is told. What more can be said of them? Shall we surfeit fancy's guests with home-brewed beer? Shall we stuff the muses with plain beef and pudding? Shall we write a chapter, in a history like this, upon the subjects of common life? Let us put them in skeleton order. See the synopsis:

"Married in Wolfsden, Thanksgiving day, by Rev. Parson Boreman, Mr. Hezekiah Hobart, of Saco, to Miss Helen Arbor." — "Honey-moon — Settled down — Humdrum — Contented lot — Every-day life — Washing-day life — Ironing-day life — Sunday life — Jog trot — Petty cares — Dull visitors come — Go to see dull company — Linen to make up — Doctor — Cradle — Plot thickens — Culminating point — *Baby* — Grandmother comes — 'As well as could be expected' — Wonderful child — Teething — Rattle — Cries for moon — Baby talk — Measles — Rocking-horse — Bread and butter — Whooping-cough — A B C — Sled — Satchel — Quarterly bills — Economy — Small leaks — Schemes to get and save — Daughters' portions — Sons' settlements."

Behold the materials of the matrimonial chapter. Let some aspiring child of genius try his teeth upon the dry crusts, but let no dull descriptions compel my courteous reader to doze over the drowsy page.

CHAPTER XXXI.

Love makes strange metamorphoses. It converts a clown into a gentleman, a plodding mechanic into an airy spark; or, reversing its operations, it puts a distaff into the hands of a hero, and presents a spade and hoe to the delicate palm of the dainty-bred scholar.

Harry, the gay, generous, enthusiastic, sentimental lover, became a practical, energetic, efficient husbandman. He planned improvements, and calculated their advantages. He inspected the fields; inquired the history of their cultivation, their productiveness, the adaptation of different soils and different modes of culture to various products, and the profit of each; and estimated to what extent animal labor might be substituted for that of men, and what new implements might profitably be introduced.

At Alek's suggestion, he had brought various tools from New York, of a construction and quality very different from Carolina tools. There were ploughs, and yokes, and harrows, and hoes, and twenty other things, to take the place of the clumsy, inefficient contrivances with which the plantation had been worked. To one of his most intelligent slaves he endeavored to impart the teamster's art, as he had seen it practised in Wolfsden; and, notwithstanding his own small experience, and the awkwardness of the slave and the oxen, he soon showed them that two teamsters, at most, were sufficient to manage one pair of cattle, and that the plough had capabilities beyond the mere scratching of the surface of the soil.

He examined the negro quarters, and, though they were more comfortable than on most plantations in North Carolina, where they are generally better than further south, still he found much to mend, about which he gave directions, and also gave the occupants the time and materials necessary for the improvements, and although he soon found that enslaved human nature is little capable of enterprise, trustworthiness, sincerity, economy, or any of the virtues of self-respecting manhood, and that whatever may be done to ameliorate the slave's wretchedness serves chiefly to awaken hopes and stimulate desires incompatible with his condition, yet he persevered, and in improving their outward comforts and decencies hoped that he had already done something toward their real elevation.

It cannot be known what might have been the final result of his progress, after coming into possession of the estate; for while his father lived he would not presume upon any radical measures, and after his father's death his own course was suddenly arrested in a way which the reader may have already foreseen. It is probable that his growing convictions of duty, and his experience of the futility of half-way reform, would finally have led him to emancipate his slaves from servitude, and himself from the responsibility of managing human beings by any means, however mild, which denies the exercise of man's noblest birthright — the free exercise of his will. Perhaps his gradually advancing soul might have risen in the scale of justice and magnanimity, till his tongue would have been compelled to utter the thrilling words, "Be free! O man, be free!"

At first, his plans of improvement could not be expected to flow wholly in this channel. His approaching happiness, the preparation of his home for his coming bride, and all bright visions of the fancied future, filled his soul.

"I will give to my home," said he, "all the outward perfections and beauty it is capable of, till she, the soul of beauty and perfection, shall come to give it life. When it is made worthy to receive her, it will need no other adornment but her presence. It will then be an Eden of happy joys, and hopes, and attainments, that shall ripen unto immortality."

The home wherein Harry promised himself so much happiness certainly seemed to possess great capabilities. Bating the climate, which, even with the best circumstances, slackens and unstrings the firm fibres of the human frame, on which life's vigorous use and enjoyments, both bodily and mental, depend; and bating the deteriorating effect of isolation from cultivated society, by which alone the human faculties can be stimulated and balanced to produce their best results; and bating the restriction upon free thought and free action, except in accordance with institutions and usages hostile to generous thoughts and just acts; and making some other necessary deductions from what a New Englander includes in the idea of independence, and comfort, and home, Oakridge was a delightful place, — something dilapidated, but so much the better for one bent on improvement.

The house stood upon an eminence, which declined thence toward the road and toward the south, but gradually ascended toward the north and west, in which direction were many scattering oaks, irregularly but pleasantly grouped, and growing more thickly as the distance increased, till at length they formed a majestic grove, mostly excluding the sun, yet protecting a mingled grassy and leafy lawn, where it was pleasant to wander, and imagine how sweet would be such a solitude with a loved companion to whom one could say, "How sweet is solitude!"

On the southern slope were scattered various ornamental trees; two or three magnolias, many china-trees, and beyond them a mixed plantation of wild orange, persimmon, pomegranate, and wild cherry. Smaller fruit and ornamental trees and shrubs adorned the front view, among which were the fig, the peach, and the crab-apple, with rose-bushes, syringas, altheas, anemones, &c. An arched way, covered with climbing roses and ivy, led to an embowered summer-house; both of which, however, through neglect and decay, with the encroachment of weeds and mould, presented an appearance of doubtful ornament. Over the court separating the house from the kitchen an enormous grape-vine, supported by a rude trellis, spread its extensive branches, yielding abundant clusters of the rich and delicious "scuppernong" grape.

By Harry's energy and taste, all these decayed beauties and capabilities were restored and improved. The arched bower and summer-house were newly trimmed and opened to healthy and inviting light and air, and adorned with plants of choice beauty; camellias, japonicas, geraniums, and whatever nature makes beautiful, or rarity makes desirable. Trees and vines were pruned and cultivated to invite their appropriate fruit. The gate was newly hinged, and the house repaired and embellished.

Upon one room, whose windows opened toward the setting

sun through embowering rose-bushes, and jessamines, and honeysuckles, Harry expended his best resources and best skill, taxing his own ingenuity and his sister's taste to arrange and adapt the beautiful furniture and choice books he had provided, so as to combine the attractions and elegances of a library and a lady's boudoir. "For," said Harry, "our hearts and minds will take some influence from the things about us, and will tend more to refinement and beauty where all else is refined and beautiful."

CHAPTER XXXII.

MEANTIME many notes of preparation were heard in Wolfsden. Margaret threw aside her sketch-book and other idle amusements, and took to the spinning-wheel and other thrifty implements of female industry. It were vain to recount the webs of linen, coarse and fine; of flannel, thick and thin; of check for aprons, and stripe for skirts; of stockings, and yarns, and threads of every color, for knitting, and darning, and sewing; of quiltings, and counterpanes, and comforters, and curtains, which comprise the fitting out of a Yankee bride. Aunt Dolly, the bounteous mother, was determined that her one daughter should not go slenderly furnished. And Margaret, prompted by many admonitions and stories of her mother's experience, and also by her own activity, carded and spun and wove, and sewed and knit and quilted, colored and bleached, till those who had depreciated her housewifely qualities were compelled to acknowledge that she might be good for something, after all.

More than twenty maidens, mindful of customs which might some day bring them equal advantages, brought their marriage presents; so that when the wedding day came, a pile of chests, and bales, and bundles, of things home-made or bought, or given, were accumulated, which would have astonished the pilgrims of the Mayflower.

Some articles of doubtful utility were presented. Little Amy brought a basketful of little stockings and mittens of her own knitting, requesting that they should be given to the little slave-girls of Carolina, of whom she had heard that they had no stockings and mittens; and the adjutant brought a hand-sled and a pair of bantams for the slave-boys. Billy and Tommy brought a pair of pintadids, or Guinea-hens (most pugnacious of all gallinaceous fowl); "These," said they, "will drive away the hawks." The blue-eyed Chinby daughters sent some pretty night-caps, and also knit hoods and buskins, to keep out the Carolina snow-storms. Lucinda Boreman sent pincushions and fancy-worked moccasins; and Ax, who, since his prospect of becoming a schoolmaster, had put away childish things, sent his skates, to be kept for Margaret's oldest boy.

The wedding-day came as appointed. We will not describe it. All readers have had, or hope to have, a wedding-day of their own, compared with which all other wedding-days are but as fast days. Major Murray would have made a solemn affair of it, but the overflowing good-humor of the guests, and the fun of the boys and girls, were too much for his solemnity to repress; and, recollecting that he had no more daughters to marry, he let things go as they would, and all had a happy time. Parson Boreman performed the ceremony, and, while thinking all the time of the old mistake about the divinity student, tried to look as if he had entirely forgotten it. Harry, to please the parson and his new father-in-law by not appearing too happy, put on an edifying gravity, which made

Fanny ask Margaret, in a whisper, if he really meant to be a doctor of divinity.

All this was on Thanksgiving day. The happy couple soon departed for North Carolina, and passed the winter on their plantation; and when the reader is informed that they passed it happily, he must conclude that they carried a large stock of happiness with them, to outlast the drizzly, dirty dreariness of a Carolina winter.

CHAPTER XXXIII.

SPRING, which chases dulness and dreariness from its strongest holds, came to Oakridge, bringing bland gales, and green, flowering turf, and opening buds and leaves, and sweet fragrance, and sportive butterflies, and humming bees, and the welcome warbling of many birds.

But sadness came with the spring to Oakridge. The beloved father, who, for many months, had been declining, but who promised to himself and children that the spring would restore his health, found instead that his life was passing away.

He was prepared to die; for he was a Christian. To those who have hearts to understand (for it requires hearts even more than heads to understand) the wrongs of slavery, this may seem impossible. But a right judgment, formed from a just estimate of all the circumstances, will not make the slaveholders chiefly responsible for the guilt. Compared with northern abettors and apologists, and especially with those who press the Bible into its support, thus corrupting the very fountain of morals and religion, their sin is small. And there are some among them who sincerely strive to keep their hearts and consciences free from guiltiness toward their brethren in bonds, by doing all they think practicable to lighten and loosen the yoke, and whom a little instruction and aid would lead to break the yoke and let the oppressed go free.

Mr. Boynton was one of the best of this not too numerous class. His eyes were not opened to see the radical and inherent wrong of slavery. Perhaps the Bible arguments in its favor, emanating from northern theological schools, had convinced him that slavery was a divine institution, since no answering arguments are allowed to circulate in the south. Yet, though his religious light might thus be turned into darkness, his native benevolence and sense of right made him a kind master, even to the extent of offending the proprietors of neighboring plantations, who complained that the notions Boynton encouraged among his slaves would ruin not only himself, but, if allowed, would overthrow the whole system of slavery in his section.

And, indeed, there seemed good reason for their animadversions; for it was very clear that if Mr. Boynton had possessed no other resources than those derived from the plantation, he must long ago have become bankrupt. Such is the natural and necessary waste of slavery, that nothing short of severe and grinding oppression will make it profitable. Planters in the older states, who have not the perseverance or the heart to exact all possible labor from their slaves, and to watch and guard that they eat no more than barely sufficient to sustain life and labor, are frequently obliged, in their own phrase, to "eat a nigger," namely, to balance accounts by the sale of a babe, or a mother, or a maiden, or a "boy."

But Mr. Boynton was free both from the grinding oppression and the cannibalism; and though, perhaps, not a perfect Christian, was probably at least as good as many made by the missionaries at the Fejee or Sandwich islands, or on Greenland's icy mountains, or India's coral strand.

We have alluded to the church relations of the family as Episcopalian. Mr. Boynton was a faithful churchman. He had regularly read prayers to his slaves on Sundays, and Angelina constantly instructed them in the catechism. Often he had addressed them individually and collectively on religion, assuring them of their immortality, and teaching them the conditions of salvation.

When he now found that his life was drawing to a close, he called them together, and, addressing them with great solemnity, told them of his approaching death, and his hope to meet them in heaven, where there would be no masters nor servants, but where all would be brethren. He then read to them, from the burial service, the authoritative argument of St. Paul, proving the immortality of the soul.

1 Cor. 15 : 20. — "Now is Christ risen from the dead, and become the first fruits of them that slept. For since by man came death, by man came also the resurrection of the dead. For as in Adam all die, even so in Christ shall all be made alive. * * Behold, I show you a mystery: We shall not all sleep, but we shall all be changed, in a moment, in the twinkling of an eye, at the last trump. For the trumpet shall sound, and the dead shall be raised incorruptible, and we shall be changed. For this corruptible must put on incorruption, and this mortal must put on immortality. So when this corruptible shall have put on incorruption, and this mortal shall have put on immortality, then shall be brought to pass the saying that is written, Death is swallowed up in victory. O Death, where is thy sting? O Grave, where is thy victory? The sting of death is sin

and the strength of sin is the law. But thanks be to God, who giveth us the victory, through our Lord Jesus Christ. Therefore, my beloved brethren, be ye steadfast, unmovable, always abounding in the work of the Lord; forasmuch as ye know that your labor is not in vain in the Lord."

Thus, with religious rites and instructions, and many parting blessings, and tokens of remembrance, the good old man dismissed his slaves, who lingered and wept as they took their last earthly leave of one who was indeed their friend, and with a little better knowledge of duty would have been their benefactor.

To his children, Harry, and Margaret, and Angelina, he gave many salutary counsels and consolations. "I am going," said he, "to join your angel mother. Weep not for me, for I go in peace and joy, trusting to meet you again where we shall part no more."

As his children knelt by his side, he placed his hands on their heads, and gave them his benediction; and, having thus set his house in order, he gradually sunk to repose.

His body rests beneath the bay-tree which spreads its branches above yonder grassy knoll, and by the side of his once beautiful bride — the lovely Angelina.

How short the time since he first saw her playing by the gate of her father's dwelling, as he was journeying to the south, when her beauty had power to arrest his journey, and to bind him forever to her side in the strong bonds of undying love!

Clothed in celestial bodies, they now rejoice in a higher sphere. The once fair forms of mortal mould have served their purpose, and now and evermore they rest beneath the bay-tree, emblem of everlasting peace.

CHAPTER XXXIV.

HARRY and Margaret sat in their favorite room, whose windows opened to the setting sun. The spring was far advanced, and the summer approaching, yet the prolific rose-bushes still put forth and spread their swelling buds, which the slight breeze made to wave against the windows, as if seeking admission to the paradise of love, while the full-blossomed honeysuckle diffused sweet odors around.

Margaret had been sewing on some delicate fabric, of a form not as yet exactly defined, though, perhaps, a practised eye might detect its design. Harry had been reading to her the plaintive ballad of "The Somnambulist," from Wordsworth.

"Sir Eglamore and Emma loved as we love," said Harry, laying down the book, and lifting the fair hand of his lovely wife to his lips. "They loved as we love, though their fate was not so happy as ours."

"I was strongly impressed," replied Margaret, "by the saying of the wise Greek whom you read about the other day; that no man could be accounted happy till the day of his death, for there is no happiness in life so secure that a moment may not destroy it."

"The Greek's wisdom was not worth much," said Harry

"if it teaches us to undervalue present happiness, because we may at some time lose it. If I have a genius for anything it is for making the most of happiness, not only by taking all possible precautions to secure it, but also by appreciating it while in possession, even as now;" and the kiss before bestowed upon the fair hand was now impressed upon the lovelier lips.

"My kind husband," said Margaret, "your genius is worth all the wisdom of all the Greeks put together. Your never-failing cheerfulness is like the sunshine which makes everything pleasant; otherwise I fear that, with all my happiness in your love, I should be sometimes sad."

"Dearest wife," said Harry, "I shall tax my genius to chase away all your sadness. Perhaps what you told me of yesterday, and which makes me happier than ever, gives a temporary depression to your spirits. But you must be kept cheerful now, for your health's sake, and for the sake of our happy hopes."

Margaret hid her face in her husband's bosom, and replied, "Dearest, I am perfectly happy, even when I may appear sad. Do you not know," said she, again looking up, "that the best happiness does not always show outwardly, just as people may be very mirthful with no happiness at all? How merry the slaves often appear, though we know that their lot is not only wretched, but that they feel it to be so."

"How I wish," said Harry, "that I could make everybody happy! Do you think our servants would have a better chance of happiness if we should send them into the free states?"

"I know that they think so," said Margaret, — "those of them who think at all, — and indeed I think so. I know that the kindness they receive from you is everything it can be, short of freedom; and I suppose their inexperience would, if free, lead them into many hardships. But you know that much of our happiness comes from surmounting hardships; and, at any rate, the best chance of happiness to their posterity would be in freedom.

"And I have some thoughts," replied Harry, "that the best chance for our posterity would be in freedom — the freedom of the free states, which is the only freedom in the land. There all men may elevate themselves, and others, according to their abilities, and look with hope instead of fear upon the advancement of just principles, and the approach of the good time coming."

"My dear husband," said Margaret, "how perfectly united are our thoughts! If we have children, it is my most earnest prayer that they may have the advantages of the free states, and, if possible, that their home may be there. I wish for nothing to be done contrary to your judgment; but I am prepared for any sacrifice of position or property for this object, when you are ready."

"We will consider of this," said Harry, taking her hand and leading her to the window, where they looked upon the sunny landscape.

Many humming-birds darted and poised their tiny forms of green and gold among the festoons of lithe branches and sweet flowers which hung against the windows, and mingled their shadows with the rays of the declining sun.

The orioles sang at intervals their sweetly-wild and careless notes, as they wove their pendent nest to the end of a waving branch of a tall and slender persimmon-tree.

A pair of turtle doves mingled the varied notes of their

plaintive melody, sadly seeming, yet truly joyful in fond and faithful love, as they peered among the branches of the far-spreading grape-vine, now clothed in its young leaves, and putting forth its clustered blossoms.

Two Carolina mocking-birds, most wonderful warblers of all the feathered tribes, perched among the branches of a pomegranate, poured forth their inexhaustibly various songs, now of surpassing and original beauty, now plagiarizing and parodying the productions of every rival warbler.

Many robins hopped about the green lawn, and pecked the scattered seeds and crumbs, or gathered little filaments or feathers to line their connubial nests, and ever and anon peered around and above, that no treacherous beast or bird of prey should take them unawares.

A peacock, proudest and most splendid of all plumed birds, strutted in sight of his admiring harem, and spread his gorgeous train, reflecting the sun's rays in forms and hues of indescribable splendor and beauty, while with hollow, murmuring voice he expressed his amorous desires.

A flock of field-sparrows rose like a cloud from the twigs and garden stubble, and wheeled about in close phalanx, often and again opening and reclosing their ranks, till they settled where they rose, and vanished from view, as did Clan Alpine's warriors true on Benledi's side, at sign from Roderick Dhu.

Thus nature's broad bright page spread forth its lessons of love and joy, teaching how abundant is the benevolence of that Power who framed the universe on a plan of universal, all-embracing love.

But lessons of caution, of danger, and defence, need also to be taught. And while they looked, a sudden shadow flapped

35

by the window and darkened the sunshine. It was a monstrous turkey-buzzard, most obscene and hateful of all the vulture race. The merry mocking-birds, and golden orioles, and busy robins, and murmuring turtle doves, and bright humming-birds, and myriad field-sparrows, all disappeared — hidden in the branches, or fled far away.

The unwieldy and foul bird had alighted on a fence, and looked audaciously and securely around, like the horrid harpies whom Æneas encountered on dire Strophadean shores, — audaciously and securely, for it, too, like human harpies, is protected in its rapacity and obscenity by Carolina law.*

But, lo! a lesson of courage also, and defence. The two pintadids, presented by Tommy and Billy, set up a scream of defiance, and flew fiercely at their menacing foe; and, as the cock threatened him in front, the hen darted a stunning blow upon the back of the buzzard's head, which tumbled him from his perch. The clumsy creature, cowardly as voracious, spread his huge wings and flew skulkingly away, pursued and insulted by the screaming and triumphant pintadids. "Hurra for the Wolfsdenners!" exclaimed Harry.

These lessons of love, of danger, and defence, were seasonably given. Whoever watches the indications of nature and Providence will find counsel for every emergency.

At that moment the door opened, and a little woolly-headed house-servant announced that "a gemman wanted to see mas'r."

Harry stepped into the parlor, and was agreeably surprised to find an old college acquaintance and friend, whom he had

* It is unlawful to kill the turkey-buzzard and black vulture in Carolina.

not seen for two or three years, — Dr. Drinkmore, formerly for a brief space a tutor in Harvard University.

Dr. Drinkmore was a citizen of the world; one of its best-natured, but not best-respected citizens. He was one, like Hamlet's friend Horatio, whose revenue was his good spirits, and who took fortune's buffets and favors with equal thanks; that is, he abused the favors, and fought manfully against the buffets. He was an Englishman and a scholar, educated at Oxford. His besetting sin was conviviality, generally degenerating into drunkenness. He had reformed twenty times, and as often relapsed; and had out-worn the philanthropy of fifty friends, who had again and again reformed and re-reformed him. His learning and talents were eminent, and his manners so pleasant that he always found some patron to help and set him in the right way. Harry was one of those who had done him that service. He was grateful for such kindness. But, however he fortified himself by good resolutions and pledges, he would sooner or later relapse, though he sometimes persevered for one or two years at a time. When he had forfeited his position in England, he came to Boston, and, his abilities being discovered, he was employed as tutor at Cambridge, whence, but for a relapse to dissipation, he might have risen to a professorship.

Since about that time Harry had lost sight of him, and was now exceedingly pleased to see him, especially as his appearance indicated health and prosperity, and still more when informed, in a subsequent conversation, that he was a temperance man of "fourteen years' standing."

After a brief enjoyment of the hospitalities of the house Dr. Drinkmore requested of Harry to show him the plantation. When they had proceeded so far as to be out of hearing, the doctor told him the object of his visit.

"I have come," said he, "to warn you of a terrible danger. I knew of it but this morning, and have averted it for a single day, which I employ to warn you against to-morrow.

"I am nominally a law-student at Squire Buzzard's, in Washington. I am writing a book which requires me to know something of manners in the south, and also something of your rascally laws; so I avail myself of a lawyer's office, which serves both purposes, and, by entering myself as student, I avoid troublesome inquiries. In this situation, besides seeing many villanies which I have not interfered with, since I could not prevent them, I became cognizant of a plot to reduce a gentleman and a lady, his sister, to slavery. I was this morning invited by Buzzard to be one of a chivalrous party, armed with pistols and like persuasives, to accomplish that object, and was about declining, with proper thanks for the honor, when the name of the gentleman for whom the favor was intended happened to be mentioned. The name was HARRY BOYNTON! Upon inquiry, I found that it was doubtless my old college friend and benefactor; and I at once accepted the invitation, stipulating that the excursion should be put off till to-morrow. The time thus gained I have employed to learn the facts, or pretences, on which this procedure is based, and to give you warning."

Dr. Drinkmore then informed Harry of what he had found, by examining the papers in the office, relating to his descent from a slave-mother, and his consequent defencelessness by Carolina law, of which the reader is already informed. He added that Buzzard and Marshy, with several assistants, were coming, on the following day, to seize both him and his sister.

"It is their plan, however," said he, "not to use force, if they can prevail by stratagem. They will probably make some pretence of business requiring your attendance at Washington, where resistance would be out of the question. They will, however, come prepared to use force if fraud shall fail. Their object is doubtless to extort money from your family for your ransom; for I heard Buzzard say the prize was worth at least ten thousand dollars, which, I believe, is above the market price for mere human blood, and sinews, and souls, in this beautiful country. But, whatever their object, I am ready to help defeat it, and will give my services in any way you will command them — only the more fight the better."

Harry's countenance showed every variety of indignant emotion while the doctor told his story. At its conclusion he replied:

"My dear friend, you have rendered me a most important service. I know the character of that Buzzard, and I now recall that I have been informed of some inquiries of his in relation to my affairs, which seemed strange and impertinent, but not of enough importance to be noticed, though they now serve to confirm your account. It has been many months since, and he has doubtless thoroughly matured his plan; for he would not venture upon such an outrage except upon safe legal ground. My position requires decided, and perhaps desperate action. I think I am equal to it. My grandfather and my brave grand-uncle, still living in Wolfsden, fought for freedom, when their case was not so imminent as mine; and I feel some of their blood tingling in my veins just now. But I must not involve you in the affair. You have done a friend's duty, for which I am grateful. Now leave the affair to me, and I will fight or fly, as seems safest on reflection."

"My brave friend," said Drinkmore, "I see you mean to fight, which is also to my taste at present; so that you must receive me as a volunteer, or I will fight on my own hook. I shall not suffer you to be engaged against such odds without sharing your danger; and, let me tell you, I am no mean ally. Would you like to see me snuff a candle at twenty paces? I have brought my pistols on purpose to show you the experiment, and also for more important services. You will disoblige me if you refuse my assistance."

"I shall not disoblige you, then, but receive your aid thankfully. At what time to-morrow will they arrive?"

"At ten or eleven, at latest; perhaps earlier," said the doctor.

"Then let us plan the campaign at once," said Harry.

They did so; and, without detailing their conversation, we will briefly state their resources and plan of defence.

Harry's slaves were about fifty in number, of whom some fifteen were able-bodied men. They were all well attached to him; but their ability as soldiers had not been tried, and the present crisis was too important to be trusted to raw troops. There was one among them, however, called Ben Blacksmith, so named from his trade, being the Vulcan of the plantation, a fellow of herculean strength and dauntless courage, whom Harry counted as a match for a dozen common men without fire-arms.

"But, as they will come armed," said Harry, "we will combine our stratagem with his strength, and it shall go hard but we three can take care of at least a dozen such as you have described."

It was planned to take the assailing party prisoners, and thus prevent their seeking reinforcements, while Harry should have time to take other measures of safety. Angelina was already safe from present danger; for she had accepted an invitation from her uncle in New York, and was now there on a visit, a fact which, from the carelessness of their spy, had escaped the vigilance of Buzzard and Marshy. Harry was, therefore, the only person liable to be seized; and he might have arranged for his wife's protection, and sought his own safety in flight, but he chose to face the danger; "for," said he, "I, too, am a Wolfsdenner."

There was under a part of the house a wine-cellar, deep and securely built, where many barrels of the rich juice of the scuppernong grape had matured, especially in the old proprietor's day; and even now, though seldom visited, it was not destitute of the delicious beverage.

"It will be a very convenient prison for our invaders," said Harry, "if we can but persuade them to enter it."

"I will undertake that business," said the doctor, "'if I have a genius for anything,' as a certain college pupil of mine used to say, it is for leading and being led into wine-cellars; only you provide the force to keep them from coming out."

"That I will," said Harry; and, calling a velvet urchin playing near, he sent for Ben Blacksmith. Ben soon appeared, and, with hat in hand, bowed to the gentlemen, and drew himself up, as waiting orders. He was more than six feet high, and built on the most approved model of strength and activity; besides which, there was a look of intelligence and determination in him, which would have made him in the eyes of most planters what is termed a "dangerous fellow," —not the kind most coveted by buyers; but, having been raised on the plantation, and always treated with consideration, he was a willing and faithful servant. He stood before them grim and stalwart, as stood the genie of the lamp before Aladdin, ready to do his bidding, but conscious of his own power.

Ben was not a man of many words, often substituting a language of gestures and figures of action more expressive than words.

"Ben," said Harry, "can you fight?"

Ben closed his brawny hands and brilliant teeth, and, looking down upon his strong legs and arms, he inspected them separately, as a general inspects his troops before action, and, being satisfied that all was right, he gave an affirmative nod.

"Well, Ben, there 's a fight ahead. You know Marshy?"

Ben knew Marshy, and, sharing the general sentiment of contempt for him, he replied affirmatively by a disparaging snap of his fingers.

"Well," said Harry, "that Marshy and Squire Buzzard, and a dozen more such fellows, are coming to-morrow to make slaves of us. What shall we do with them?"

Ben looked about for an illustration. A huge spider was crawling upon the ground near by. Ben pointed at it with the toe of his brogan, and then, with a rhetorical lifting of the leg, he set his heel emphatically upon the ugly insect.

"That 's what you would do about it, eh?" said Harry. "Well, Ben, that 's my mind."

Harry then gave Ben particular information and instructions concerning the service required, and what subsequent proceedings would be necessary, as will hereafter be developed. Having dismissed him, and fully arranged the order of proceedings with Drinkmore, the doctor departed for Washington, to return on the morning with the marauding party, according to agreement.

Harry returned to his wife, and gave a full account of all that had passed. Margaret's confidence in her husband's ability and courage to meet this strange emergency was equal to her love. Like a sensible woman, she strengthened her husband's hands by approbation of his resolution, and proffered assistance. She expressed no fears for the result, and declared her readiness to take any part in the battle for freedom which might become a lady Wolfsdenner and the wife of a Boynton.

Thus sustained, Harry completed his preparations, not only to foil his foes, but for a final departure from the plantation. He knew that the estate, including the slaves, must fall to his uncle as collateral heir, if his own slave-descent and consequent incapacity to inherit under Carolina law should be proved; and therefore the property was safe from Marshy. He wrote immediately to Mr. Brooks, a respectable lawyer in Washington, stating the proceedings, and requesting him to act as attorney and agent for himself and his uncle, until one of them should appear. He then packed up his valuables and sent them with a wagon and team of mules to Plymouth, a port on Albemarle Sound, with orders of shipment to New York. The family carriage and horses were put in order for travelling; and, having prepared his pistols for action, he waited events.

It was nearly eleven o'clock the next day, when the boy whom Harry had ordered to watch for company announced that a " smart chance of gemmen and 'osses were coming up de lane."

" How many ? " said his master.

" May be twenty or forty," said the dark curly-pate, whose notions of numbers were not very definite.

Harry looked ; there were, as he expected, about a dozen. There was one carriage occupied by four persons, and doubtless intended for his own conveyance back.

Buzzard, and Marshy, and Dr. Drinkmore, were of the party. The others were also partly known to Harry, particularly a Mr. Sycophant Curtis, whom Harry counted the most despicable of the whole crew, inasmuch as the others were prompted by hope of gain or other common temptations to their base work, and showed some tokens of shame and repugnance, while Curtis acted only from inherent baseness, in which he felt no degradation.

Besides this cheesy, passionless-looking fellow, there were several of lower degree ; Butmans, Byrneses, &c., too insignificant even to be inscribed on the rolls of infamy.

Only four entered the house — Buzzard, Marshy, Curtis, and Dr. Drinkmore. The doctor appeared as a stranger. Buzzard put on a pompous business air, as usual, though evidently flustered and confused. Marshy skulked behind, like a cur who doubts his company, and keeps an eye on the door of retreat. But Curtis, who saw nothing in the business out of the common course, appeared as usual, bland and imperturbable.

Harry received the company with composed dignity. A servant handed chairs. Buzzard opened the business with a well-conned lie, saying that a measure of great importance to the public, especially to planters and men of property, required the presence and deliberation of freeholders and men of influence in Washington, and they had come to escort him thither.

Harry replied that he was very sensible of the honor they were doing him, and would readily reciprocate their kindness. Turning to a servant, he sent orders that dinner should be served up with despatch, and that the gentlemen's horses should be cared for. The outsiders were invited in, and a brief general conversation of news, weather, &c., followed, and Harry soon asked if they would like to look over his plantation while dinner was in preparation. Dr. Drinkmore assented, remarking that he felt somewhat thirsty.

"Then, we'll first visit the wine-cellar, and take your opinions of my wine," said Harry. And, ordering lights, he led the whole company down a labyrinthine flight of passages to a deep cellar, in which there was a long row of barrels on one side, and shelves filled with bottles on the other. There was a table on which were also bottles with glasses and cork-screws, and a huge covered basket. About the table were two or three chairs and a rude bench. Harry asked the company to be seated; and then, ringing a small bell, he stepped back to the door, and was immediately joined by Ben Blacksmith, with a heavy sledge-hammer in his hand.

Harry, standing in the doorway by the side of Ben, and exhibiting a pair of pistols, requested Dr. Drinkmore to pass out from the cellar, with which request he immediately complied. The astonished and alarmed company would have been glad to follow, but there was something in Harry's eye and attitude, in connection with his weapons and the giant Vulcan by his side, which held them motionless. Ben, perhaps, thought he saw a desperate purpose to force the passage; for he set his teeth with peculiar ferocity, and gave a flourish of his ponderous hammer, wielding it as lightly as the fencing-master flourishes his foils, and struck the granite wall with a force which scattered splinters over the cellar. The demonstration was sufficient.

Harry, looking at Ben, said, "These are the fellows I told you of; what would you do with them?"

Ben thrust his hand into a pocket, and, taking thence a handful of hazel-nuts, he threw them into his capacious mouth, and, shutting his strong jaws with an emphatic gesture, he ground them as a horse grinds oats.

"That is," said Harry, "you would chaw 'em up!"

The black nodded approvingly, as if to say that he could not himself have expressed it better.

"They deserve it," said Harry; "but they shall first have a fair trial. Buzzard," continued he, addressing that individual, "I hear that you have been making some inquiries concerning my family. I presume that bundle of papers in your pocket may relate to the subject. Toss them this way."

Buzzard saw that resistance was hopeless, and gave up the papers.

"Now, villains," said Harry, "I shall leave you here till I resolve upon your fate. You will find water in those bottles. The wine is removed, not being proper for persons in your condition. There is corn-bread and bacon in that basket,—lawful provision for a week; at the expiration of that time, more will be supplied. I leave you candles and a Bible and prayer-book, and advise you to spend your remaining days, or hours, in penitence."

Harry's calm and deliberate look and speech struck more

terror into the hearts of his captives than any demonstration of anger could have done. Buzzard, a poltroon in danger as a tyrant when in power, began to beg for freedom, and offered, in behalf of himself and Marshy, to cancel all claims against his person, and give legal papers of freedom, with whatever damages he might require; and Marshy offered to sign any papers and make any atonement in his power. But Harry knew, even if he had been disposed to compromise, that agreements made under such circumstances would not be legally binding, and that therefore no reliance could be put on their engagements. Poor Butman was still more humbled. With blanched face and chattering teeth, he begged piteously for liberation. He called heaven to witness that he intended no harm; that he did not come to kidnap, and never would do so again. He would be Harry's obedient servant and friend forever, if set free; and said that nothing but his poverty had induced him to join Buzzard. As Harry looked upon that abject wretch, and then upon the brave Ben Blacksmith by his side, he mentally said, "And that is one of the Anglo-Saxon race, who pride themselves upon their vast superiority over such as this African!"

Harry commanded them all to be silent; and, closing and double-locking the massive door, left them to their reflections. He did not intend to keep them imprisoned longer than necessary for his own safety, but meant thoroughly to frighten them.

The papers taken from Buzzard proved to be what Harry expected. Besides Buzzard's agreement with Marshy to do the business on shares, there was a complete history of the Bateman and Boynton family, with dates of marriages, births, deaths, connections, &c.; a schedule of slaves and other possessions, and a list of witnesses and particulars proving the fact of Harry and his sister's descent from a slave-mother, the property of General Bateman, whose children, not being included in the sale to Harry's father, were therefore the property of the heirs.

The evident accuracy and authenticity of the information, so far as Harry knew the various circumstances enumerated, left no doubt that Buzzard had made out a clear case according to Carolina law, and that there was no hope for safety but in flight.

As his indignant soul revolved the atrocity of the scheme devised against him, and of the laws which justified it; and as he reflected that the wretches who had come to reduce himself and sister to a state of unutterable wretchedness were now in his power, and that the papers containing the facts upon which they relied were in his possession, and that probably no other persons knew or would search out the facts, and therefore, if these persons and papers were destroyed, the conspiracy against him would be ended; and as he considered, further, that, since the laws of his country gave him no protection, he owed them no obedience, and he was therefore morally free to use his natural rights of self-protection, he felt a tide of unaccustomed emotions fill and agitate his heart.

Phrenologists say that when the organs of combativeness and destructiveness are strongly excited, they force the whole moral energies into their own channel. It was so with Harry. The protection of his own rights demanded retributive vengeance on his foes. He meditated on his position, — an outlaw, though innocent of wrong, and beset by ruffians protected by law. He walked the floor with accelerated steps. His hands were unconsciously clenched, and his teeth firmly set. The muscles of his face, formed to express good will, were now contracted into the lineaments of resolute wrath. His eyes glared with a terrible fire. His chest heaved with quick, panting rage. His breath came frequent and hot. He was ripe for a desperate deed.

Ready means for safe and speedy execution were not wanting. His friend Drinkmore would doubtless depart for the north immediately, if requested. Ben would do his bidding to any extremity. There was plenty of charcoal at the forge, and straw and sulphur were in abundance. In a few moments the villanous crew might all be suffocated in their dungeon, as other vermin are suffocated in their dens.

It is thus that emotions turned in one direction, impelled by an ardent temperament and driven by surrounding circumstances, soon gain an ungovernable fury. The soul, intent upon one point, ceases to survey the whole field of moral vision, and rushes onward with irresistible rage.

An angel intervened, or a deed of death had been done. The whole detail was already wrought in Harry's mind. He was in the act of departing to put it in execution, when a door opened, and Margaret entered. She saw and comprehended her husband's unwonted mood.

"Retire!" said he, with a sternness never used before. "Retire, and do not interrupt me!"

She suspected the terrible purpose he intended, and, with a pleading look, threw her arms about his neck.

"My husband," said she, "vengeance belongs to God. Let us do nothing to offend him. He is now on our side, and will protect us. Let us leave our cause with him, and escape from this evil land. We can now go harmless, and with no wrong on our souls."

"It is no wrong thing, but a *just* and *right* thing, which I mean to do," said Harry.

"O, it is wrong — wrong to *yourself*," replied the wife. "You are not called upon to punish wickedness, but to preserve your own goodness. Treat them not according to their deserts, but according to your own generous and noble heart. You have called me your angel; let me now be your good angel, and save you in this hour of angry temptation. It is your loving wife, and another still dearer to us, though yet unborn, who plead to you — *husband* and *father!*"

The tender embrace, the pleading voice, the magic words *wife, husband, father*, penetrated through the fierce passions which had fortified Harry's heart. The current of his emotions was checked. They turned to their accustomed channel of generous and loving purposes. He embraced his wife, and exclaimed: "You are, indeed, my good angel. You once saved me from sinking in the quicksands of dissipated folly, and now you have saved me from the whirlpool of ungovernable rage. We will fly from the evil intended by others, and from the temptation to revenge it."

In a few moments horses were put to the carriage, and, in an hour from the arrival of the hostile and treacherous crew, Harry and his wife, accompanied by Dr. Drinkmore, and driven by Ben, were on their way to Portsmouth, in Virginia, whence they would proceed by steamboat through Chesapeake Bay to Baltimore, on the way to New York. The keys of the house were given to a trusty servant, with orders to let no one enter till Mr. Brooks, or some one bringing a specified token from him, should come; and the necessity of keeping the prisoners safe till Mr. Brooks should come was particularly enforced.

The horses soon traversed the more than one hundred miles to Portsmouth, from whence, leaving the carriage, the whole party, including Ben, took passage for Baltimore; where Harry mailed his letter to Brooks, having first added a postscript, stating the imprisonment of Buzzard and his crew, and authorizing their liberation.

When they arrived in New York, Harry took carriage and drove to his uncle's, where, learning that his uncle was at his counting-room, he left his party, and proceeded thither without entering the house.

Great was the surprise of the old merchant at the entrance of his nephew. Still greater grew his surprise at the account which his nephew gave of himself. He was a fugitive from Carolina law, and had come to seek his uncle's protection for himself and family.

"Of what can you have been guilty?" exclaimed the uncle.

"Not guilty at all, dear uncle," said the nephew, "except of the sin of running away from slavery, which is crime only against slave-law and slaveholding divinity,—both of which I repudiate."

Harry then gave a full account of facts, and exhibited the papers taken from Buzzard, including the agreement with Marshy to do the work of kidnapping at halves. The merchant was astonished at the baseness of the wretch Buzzard, whom he knew, and who had once, in the character of an antimason and patriot, claimed the merchant's aid and hospitality. "But I never thoroughly trusted him," said Mr. Boynton; "there was something in his countenance which forbade that, though I did not think him capable of such villany."

Harry remarked that the climate of Carolina was favorable to the development of villany in such as have a natural inclination that way, which is the case with a large proportion of the Yankees who go there. "And, indeed," continued he, "I had pretty nearly determined not to trust myself there much longer before I found the necessity of immediate departure."

"Well," replied the uncle, facetiously, "I think I shall not send you back; for I have not yet 'conquered my prejudices,' and do not recognize any law or divinity which requires me to do it. Even Dr. Dewey's divinity does not apply here; for, though he spoke of sending back his mother, son, or brother, he said nothing of sending his nephew; and as for the example of St. Paul and Onesimus, I think you could scarcely be trusted with a letter to Marshy requesting him to receive you as a 'dearly-beloved brother.'"

"I think," said Harry, "I should rather be his slave than his brother."

"Well, my boy, we must not waste time. There is more to be done than you know of. Your sister Angelina is now on her way to Carolina. I must follow her, or rather 'head her off' by the first conveyance, lest she should fall into the hands of Marshy."

Great was Harry's surprise and alarm at this information. He was told that Angelina, having accepted her uncle's advice to remain in New York for a greater length of time than at first proposed, had thought desirable first to return and spend a week or two of preparation in Carolina. The sailing of a fine new schooner belonging to her uncle, and which, in compliment to her, he had named "Angelina," and which was bound for Newbern, N. C., whence the conveyance to Oakridge was easy, offered a pleasant opportunity, especially as some friends, desirous to try a sea-voyage, would sail in the same vessel.

The schooner had already been at sea one or two days, and might be expected in Newbern in two or three more; and there was, therefore, no time to be lost, as it was desirable to intercept the lady on the arrival of the vessel.

Mr. Boynton had conceived a high idea of Alek's sagacity and promptitude in cases of difficulty, as in the rescue of Sophia Greening, and one or two other incidents within his knowledge; and, thinking it possible that he might require such aid, he applied to Mr. Greening, who willingly consented to Alek's accompanying him, and Alek was gratified with the confidence and the excursion. In a few hours they departed, and in two days arrived in Newbern.

A severe storm had commenced soon after their departure, which increased to a hurricane by the time they had arrived in Newbern. Trees, fences, and buildings, were prostrated. Torrents of rain, driven by the fierce winds, flooded and gulleyed the roads. The Neuse river, swollen by the deluge, and driven back by the tide, overflowed the banks, destroying dwellings, and driving the vessels moored at the wharves and in the stream high on unnavigable sands. Disaster, discomfort, danger, and dismay, prevailed.

The storm lasted several days, which in such a place as Newbern must necessarily be tedious days, even without a storm. There was reason to fear great disasters and shipwrecks on the coast; but news in Carolina, like everything else, travels with a tardy pace, and several more days must elapse before definite knowledge would arrive. When a week had passed away the schooner Angelina had not arrived, but a most unpleasant visitor had come. It was Marshy. Being liberated from the cellar, and recovered from his terror, he had come prepared to assert his claim upon Angelina. It happened that she had, on the eve of departure from New York, sent a letter to inform her brother. The letter had fallen into Marshy's hands. He had quarrelled with Buzzard, to whom he attributed the disaster of his confinement and suffering in the cellar, and he was now resolved to seize Angelina, and save all the profits to himself.

He had come directly to the tavern where Mr. Boynton and Alek tarried, and soon the parties became aware of each other's presence and object.

It was unpleasant to Mr. Boynton to make any advances to such a grovelling wretch; but necessity required it, and he therefore sent for him to his room, and opened the business at once by asking what ransom he demanded for his claim. Marshy, who knew something of Mr. Boynton's wealth, and rightly presumed that he would ransom his niece at any price, grasped at the highest sum he could muster courage to name, which was ten thousand dollars. Mr. Boynton, to be free of the hateful business, would probably have acceded to the demand; but Alek, who had stipulated with his employer for liberty of interference according to his discretion, and who had all the time been scanning Marshy's countenance with a curious and puzzled interest, now took up the work, and replied, peremptorily, "We shall not give it. You must name reasonable terms, or we shall not negotiate." The effect of this prompt reply upon Marshy showed that he was not exactly sure of his ground, or at least had not the resolution to maintain it. It was well that Buzzard had not come with him.

Alek reminded Marshy that, as the vessel now so long due had not arrived, perhaps she might not arrive. She might have foundered in the storm, or been driven back to New York, or into some port whence Angelina would return thither. He hinted, also, that the Boynton family had many friends in Carolina, whom a much less sum than ten thousand dollars would stimulate to vindicate their cause, in spite of law; and that, for the sake of his own safety and that of his property, he had better be reasonable. In short, he so worked upon the cautious and cowardly nature of the avaricious knave that he at last consented to sell Harry and Angelina to their uncle for two thousand dollars, and the deed and payment were made accordingly.

Mr. Boynton, having thus secured the essential object of his journey, waited with patience the arrival of his vessel. Shortly she came, in gallant trim; for the captain, skilful and fortunate, had gained a safe haven and outridden the storm. The uncle and niece commenced their homeward journey through Washington; where Alek had already gone, and was spending a few days — not idly, as we shall see by and by.

In Washington Mr. Boynton saw Mr. Brooks, who had taken possession of the estate at Oakridge in behalf of his client, though uncertain whether the client was Harry or his uncle. Mr. Boynton requested him to hold the estate subject to Harry's control, who would soon dispose of it; and in the mean time to place on it some trusty white person, who might protect and employ the slaves for wages, but not coërce them.

Mr. Boynton also saw Buzzard. The fellow looked crestfallen, and would have avoided recognition; but, finding that impossible, he assumed a confident brazen-facedness, and offered to shake hands. Mr. Boynton only looked upon him with the steady scrutiny of one who studies a rare reptile, with mingled curiosity and disgust, till the fellow skulked confusedly away.

Mr. Boynton, with his niece, visited Oakridge, where each looked with tears of affectionate grief upon the graves of those so dear to them both. It is human weakness that sheds the tears. Had we angel natures we should rejoice with songs of triumph for those who have finished earth's pilgrimage and passed to a higher sphere.

CHAPTER XXXV.

ALEK'S investigations in Washington gave him a knowledge, general and particular, concerning the people and their institutions, which proved useful as well as curious. Among other particulars, he ascertained something of Marshy's previous history, which helped to confirm certain suspicions relating to his identity. He also learned that Marshy's wife resided much of the time in that uncelestial city, preferring its society to the solitariness of the plantation. She was not reported to possess much gentleness, or refinement, or other amiabilities, even according to the Carolina standard; but, as an offset, she was loud and bold, and had a just contempt for her husband. Marshy was, as he deserved to be, little better than her slave; but it was considered that by selling himself for the price of a plantation he had got his full value.

On the other hand, Mrs. Marshy was about as badly used by her son, little Bob Marshy, a snub-nosed, wide-mouthed, lop-eared boy of ten or eleven years, precociously profligate, and uniting the sly, sneaking, selfish nature of his father with the swinish coarseness of his mother.

She passed much of her time in coaxing, threatening, abusing, and bribing her whelp, who, as relentless as an old slave-driver in his tyranny, used all his perverse powers to plague and tease her. He had already the advantage in his own hands; for his mother, in her fits of fondness, and to inspire him with a proper contempt for his father, represented Marshy to him as a nobody, and himself as the important personage who inherited the estate from his grandfather, which Marshy could control only till the heir should be grown up; so that Bob even now despised "old Sneaky," as he called him, as much as the lady herself. But, as Marshy was not a man of much perception concerning the fitness of filial and paternal relations, nor of any delicacy of feelings, he probably suffered no regrets, but was in reality that which seems monstrous in imagination — a contented slave.

Alek, having stored his memory with these and all other historical and local facts concerning the paltry place bearing the august name of Washington, rejoined his friends at Oakridge, whence they all soon departed, and in due season arrived in New York.

Shortly after their return, Mr. Boynton sent for Alek to his counting-room, and presented him with a bank check for five hundred dollars. "Your prompt and able services," said he, "have saved me much more than that sum, and whenever you engage in any enterprise requiring assistance count me as one of your friends."

"I accept the money," said Alek, "only with permission to act in your service a little longer, and in a way for which the money will be necessary. My object is to make Marshy restore the two thousand dollars of which he plundered you; and, if you approve the object, and will allow me to proceed in my own way, without implicating you, I think I can convince the pirate of the propriety of his restoring the plunder."

"If you can do that," said Mr. Boynton, "you shall have the whole sum, and my thanks. My chief regret at losing it was that it went to reward a villain deserving the hangman's rope. But," continued he, "I give no consent to any plan which shall require you to return to Carolina, or incur any danger."

"No," said Alek, "I shall not leave New York. There is a *genie* who will do the business for me without risk, and you have furnished me the talisman (referring to the bank check) which will command him."

That evening Alek wrote a letter to his old friend Ike Bowler, of Wolfsden.

"DEAR IKE: You are wanted here for a particular occasion. Nobody but a Wolfsdenner will do, and of all Wolfsdenners you are the one. It is inexpedient to explain particulars till we meet. You will find them satisfactory. You remember that Santa Claus went to old Bang's with boots for Sue, and afterwards to Bragly's to recover them for her. That was a good thing. This is a good thing. Enclosed are fifty dollars to start with. Please to start suddenly, and be here before a week, if possible. With love to your folks, and especially my sweet daughter Amy,

"Yours, ALEK ARBOR."

Ike was punctual to the summons. He had never before left Wolfsden, but would have gone to China if invoked by Alek. Particulars were explained, and proved satisfactory, and Ike, with a new outfit, and three or four hundred dollars in his pocket, left New York as suddenly as he entered it. Few knew whither he went; but it was not in the direction of Wolfsden.

CHAPTER XXXVI.

About this time appeared a wonder in Washington. A stout, swaggering, odd-looking individual, with long hair hanging over his shoulders, and other peculiarities enough to make folks stare who have nothing else to do, as is universally the case in Washington, came suddenly into that once obscure, but henceforth famous city.

The odd-looking individual announced himself as Dr. Pollywog. He professed to cure all diseases by the application of cold water, and announced lectures to maintain his doctrine. The idea was very novel in that place, where whiskey is the general remedy. Everybody turned out to hear Dr. Pollywog. Though ignorant, as far as appeared by his lectures, of everything pertaining to diseases or remedies, or any other science, he managed, by his assurance, and volubility, and jocularity, and incomprehensibility, to make a wonderful impression. His audience were more ignorant than he. Ignorant people always take the side of ignorant doctors, and a lecturer who can make them laugh is more acceptable than one who requires them to think. The natives thronged to Dr. Pollywog to be cured of all manner of diseases; and he soused them, and packed them in wet sheets, and made them swallow quarts of hateful water, till they were glad to confess themselves cured. So Dr. Pollywog got much notoriety, and many dollars.

Besides his droll dress, his slouching hat and gait, and hanging hair, and flapping ruffles, and big bright buttons, and scarlet vest, and boots outside his trousers, he drove a stout, parti-colored horse, of extra spirit and speed, and a light, gay gig, in which he would every day whisk through the town in a manner that would have reminded the natives of "Tam o' Shanter" and his mare "Meg," only the natives never read Burns — nor anything else, except their paltry newspapers.

Among other oddities, Dr. Pollywog affected a great fancy for the company of vagrant boys (all white boys there are vagrant); and with them he would go on fishing and shooting excursions, supplying them with abundance of candy, cakes, whiskey, tobacco, cigars, and other luxuries congenial to Carolina juveniles, whom their wise parents are careful to bring up in the way they choose to go. Often he would take one or two of the rowdy young hopefuls and give them a rapid airing in his gig. The snub-nosed, wide-mouthed, lop-eared Bob Marshy, as being one of the rascaliest of the crew, was his particular favorite. Not even the mother's partiality for her pig-headed progeny exceeded that of Dr. Pollywog.

The doctor had patients in Newbern, a few hours' ride from Washington, and would often take one of the vagrant boys with him, who, on his return, would exaggerate the jolly times enjoyed, setting other boys agog for like delectations. The doctor invited Bob Marshy to go; and, though his mother objected to trusting him so long out of her sight, yet, as Bob swore he would go, the mother yielded the point, perhaps to prevent his perjuring himself, only exacting of the doctor a promise to be particularly careful of her darling. After he had gone once or twice and returned safely, the mother's confidence was fully established, and the doctor and Bob were absent sometimes one or two days at a time.

Pollywog told Bob all about the great cities, and the lots of fun going on there; the military companies, with swords and epaulets, and colors and feathers, and also the music-grinders and the monkeys, and all such wonders. Bob swore he'd go in for it, the first chance, and cut Sneaky and the old woman, — by which filial terms he designated his honored parents.

Dr. Pollywog and Bob started for Newbern one bright morning. They did not return that day. They did not return the next day. Madam felt a little fidgety. Dr. Pollywog had told her when she felt fidgety to cool off in a wet sheet; but she neglected his prescription, and therefore grew more fidgety. The next day they did not come, and she fumed and fretted furiously. The fourth day she sent Marshy in pursuit, but no Pollywog nor Bob had been seen in Newbern. They had not been there. Nobody had seen them anywhere.

There was a buzzing in the wasps' nest. The road to Newbern continues on south, and travellers may pursue it and avoid Newbern; therefore the fugitives had doubtless gone south. There was indeed an obscure road, which turns off and by a circuitous route leads north; but nobody would be likely to take it, and therefore their pursuers and advertisements were sent south.

They went a good ways, and inquired of many persons, but got no news of Bob. How could they? Bob was by this time in New York, enjoying lots of fun, and following the military companies, with their swords and guns, and epaulets and feathers, and the organ-grinders and monkeys, and other worthy curiosities.

In a fortnight Mrs. Marshy was frantic with all the strong emotions of her strong temperament. She did not "sulk," as her slave Lotty did, when Marshy, at his wife's instigation, sold off her little boy to a trader. Lotty "sulked," and Mrs. Marshy tried the whip, and then Marshy himself tried it, but all did no good. Lotty shammed sick, and Mrs. Marshy beat her till she was tired of it; and then, when she found, as she said, that the jilt would die, she sold her to a trader at half price. The trader would not have given half price for a sick nigger, but Mrs. Marshy told him Lotty was getting well; and, by telling Lotty that she should be sent to find her boy, which brightened up the wench wonderfully, she made the trader think so; but the trader lost money by the speculation, for Lotty died on his hands. This is Mrs. Marshy's own account of the affair.

Mrs. Marshy did not sulk, — not she. Hers was the feminine fury which a she-bear manifests when robbed of her whelps. Marshy himself was wonderfully stirred up. Something besides parental feeling was involved; for, Bob being the heir of his grandfather, by his guardianship a large property was held and enjoyed by the parents, and the possession of the property was identified with the safety of the boy. Other heirs, by will or otherwise, stood ready to claim possession if he should be put out of the way; and perhaps this was a scheme to put him out of the way. The Marshys had sufficient motive of apprehension.

But partial relief came in shape of a letter from New York, thus:

"MISTER MARSHY: You can have your boy by coming to New York and paying three thousand dollars. I could make more of him, but I only want what 's right. So, if you want him, come on with the cash. It's no use to come without it, for I shan't take off a cent. We shall sail in a week, if we don't get the money. Mr. Arbor, at Greening & Russett's agricultural store, will tell you where to find us. And so no more from your humble servant to command till death,

"WIDEAWAKE WOLFSDENNER."

This was not exactly the way to please Marshy and lady. *He* would have paid with his soul, or *she* with her good name, supposing them to have been possessed of such commodities, rather than with three thousand dollars. But there was a necessity to get back the boy even at that price; for, setting aside parental prejudices, several times the sum depended upon him as heir to his grandfather. So, as the letter was peremptory, they raised the sum and departed.

Alek Arbor had just closed his books and locked them in the iron safe, and was about closing the office, when a man and woman entered. It was Marshy and his wife, or rather Mrs. Marshy and her husband; for she entered first, bold, earnest, and business-looking, while he lagged behind, skulking, furtive, and suspicious-looking.

It was scarcely two months since she had seen him near her own home, and she claimed acquaintance. "I have come," said she, "to get my boy; can you tell me where to find Wideawake Wolfsdenner?"

"You may find a Wideawake Wolfsdenner without going far," replied Alek; "but have you brought the three thousand dollars, for without that I shall not introduce you to him."

"Surely you will not keep a mother from getting her own boy!" said Mrs. Marshy, suppressing for the moment her natural spirit, and putting on the pathetic.

"No, madam," said Alek, "I shall not interfere with your efforts. But, by the way, what became of Lotty and *her* boy?"

"You don't mean to throw that nigger in my teeth!" said Mrs. Marshy, laying aside the pathetic, and resuming her natural spirit. "She was my nigger, and so was her boy. I had a right to sell 'em."

"Well, madam," said Alek, looking at his watch, "I have no time to argue the matter. It is tea-time."

"O, Mr. Arbor," said she, again putting on the pathetic, "do let me have my boy, and I'll pay you anything you ask."

"Produce the three thousand dollars, then," said Alek, "and I'll do my part."

"Don't tell me about three thousand dollars!" said the virago, resuming her natural spirit, and dropping the pathetic. "Do you think to swindle me out of three thousand dollars? I tell you, young man," said she, marching up to him with a threatening look, "that you've got to give up my boy, or," continued she, abating a little her threatening look, on seeing that Alek did not quail before it, "or, if there's law in the United States, I'll have it!"

Alek pulled a bell, and a boy answered the summons. "Madam and sir," said he, addressing his company, "you may leave the office immediately, or I shall send for a police-officer to take charge of you."

"O, Mr. Arbor," exclaimed she, relapsing to the pathetic, 'don't do so, — don't treat a lady so! Come, now, say the best you will do. You know Mr. Marshy asked you only two thousand dollars for the Boyntons."

"Yes, he asked ten thousand dollars, and would have got it if you had been there to back him. But the case is different. He had not got the game quite in his hands, and was afraid of losing the whole. We have the game in our hands, and are sure of the whole; and, besides, you began the battle, and have no right to complain that we fight harder than you expected."

"But you mean to go according to law, I suppose," said Marshy, for the first time interposing a word.

"I have not decided upon that, sir," said Alek, fixing his eye full upon him. "I shall see how this matter ends before I decide upon the next business, sir. Do you know anything of Wolfsden, sir, — and of Bragly, the grocer, sir, — and of Simon Bragly, sir? We shall see about law, as soon as we get through the present business, — or before, unless it ends soon, sir."

Marshy quailed, and said no more; but ever and anon he stole a glance at Alek, as at a wizard beneath whose power resistance was vain.

The lady could not comprehend it, but, knowing her husband's character, and that he had before been in New York, she suspected that some former villany of his was detected, and that new dangers, and perhaps new demands, awaited them.

"Dear Mr. Arbor," said she, with a double proportion of the pathetic, "do let us off as easy as you can; do let me see my boy, and know that all is right, and you shall have the money."

"Madam," replied Alek, "you shall have sufficient security

that I shall fulfil my engagements. Mr. Marshy knows very well that the family of Deacon Arbor, whose son I am, always fulfil their engagements; besides, I will call a gentleman, well known to you as a man of honor, who will take charge of the money, and return it to you unless the boy be forthcoming."

The Marshys assented, and Alek bade the boy run for Mr. Harry Boynton. They started at the name. They would rather not have faced their former neighbor, under present circumstances; but there was no help. Harry came and looked upon the crestfallen couple, but made no remark. Alek explained the business, and Harry consented to act as banker. Little as the Marshys could comprehend the nature or motive of honor, they knew it to be an indisputable quality of the Boyntons; and the money was deposited without much more delay, for the harassed and jaded couple had worn out much of their energy and power of resistance. All the faculties sink under long-continued excitement, and even avarice loosens its grasp when nature is exhausted. They were anxious to have the business ended, and to be away from the city, where the lady had vague fears of further trouble and expense; and whence Marshy, now that he knew himself known, had good reason to wish to escape as noiselessly as possible.

Alek wrote a note, and sent it off by the boy. He then took from a drawer a legal-looking paper, tied with red tape, and addressed Marshy thus: "Sir, your son will soon be here, and your wife will be free to depart with him. You will also be free to go when you have put your proper name to this document, which Mr. Grappler, a legal friend of mine, has prepared for your signature. He has also drawn up another document to which your attention will be emphatically called, if you decline this. You will infer from the paper that Bragly senior, of Wolfsden, is dead. This document," continued he, opening it and occasionally quoting from it, "this document, as you see, is already sealed, and, when properly signed and witnessed, transfers all the 'right, title, and interest,' which Simon Bragly, son and heir of the 'late Solomon Bragly, of Wolfsden, has in the property of which said Bragly was seized and possessed at the time of his death,' to 'Colonel Jacob Bowler, of Wolfsden, aforesaid, in trust,' for the support and benefit of Susan Barker and her son 'Jotham Barker, widow and son of the late Benjamin Barker, of said Wolfsden, blacksmith,' and to their 'use and behoof forever.'

"My motive," continued Alek, "for requiring this transfer, is that the Bragly here mentioned was the means of turning Barker the blacksmith into a sot, and depriving his family of their proper protection and support; and, therefore, his property should go to recompense the injury. I think I have said enough to bring you to that opinion; if not, I have a stronger argument, or, at least, one of more personal application."

Marshy guessed well enough the kind of argument which Alek held in reserve. Since the mention of Mr. Grappler, and the additional document drawn up for him in case of his demurring at this, he felt himself, to express it gently, in a delicate position.

CHAPTER XXXVII.

Marshy's delicate position may be briefly explained. Simon Bragly, left his paternal home in Wolfsden about twenty years previously, being then of age. He went to seek his fortune, and supposed himself well qualified to make his way in the world; for he had learned all his father's maxims of low cunning, and had no scruples of honesty to interfere with whatever chance of gain might fall in his way. He spent a year or two in Saco, then a year or two in Boston, and then a year or two in New York. In each city he gained practice and experience in his chosen line of life, so that, at the end of six years of advanced pupilage and practice, he self-complacently considered himself a finished villain.

He did himself no more than justice, so far as the solid qualities of such a character go; but he was somewhat deficient in the tact and adroitness which characterize the most accomplished professors of his school. His natural gifts were not equal to the greatest attainments in any line. Besides his lack of capacity, there was some deficiency in that earnest perseverance and singleness of purpose which is necessary to great results; for he had devoted himself occasionally to debauchery, which necessarily impeded his race for preëminence in the sublimer mysteries of knavery.

Having, however, tested his abilities and good fortune, by the success of some small villanies, he felt encouraged to venture on a larger enterprise. He forged his employer's name to a draft of considerable amount, and sent another person, — whether innocent or confederate is not known, — to present it for payment, with directions to bring the money to a certain place. Simon did not await his emissary at that certain place, but posted himself in sight of the bank to judge of his success. Omens were not auspicious. The emissary tarried too long. A boy came out of the bank, and ran to a police-station. A police-officer came to the bank. When the emissary reäppeared, the police-officer was also in sight. The emissary hastened to the place of rendezvous, and the police-officer followed and entered with him. Simon understood the manœuvre, and congratulated himself that, though he had not got the money, he had outwitted the officer.

Henceforth he wisely judged that New York was not his proper sphere. He had already abstracted a little sum from his employer, and put it with the other avails of his professional industry; and with this means he immediately absconded, and, though advertised, was not overtaken. He found his way to North Carolina, which he judiciously judged to be his proper sphere.

It is not worth while to track his crooked trail very closely. To evade pursuit, he changed his name to Marshy, and, after various fortune, sold himself to Tim Bateman's daughter of smutched reputation, for the consideration of a plantation. It was worse than a wooden-nutmeg speculation, for both parties got the worst bargains possible.

When Alek first saw Marshy at Newbern, he was struck with something in his face at once familiar and disagreeable.

"If Bragly had a brother," thought Alek, "this must be he; or, can it be his son? He looks too old for that, but his reputed habits when last heard from, and the Carolina climate, may have added to his age."

The more Alek studied his features, and expression, and voice, the more strongly he was impressed with the probability of the supposition. His inquiries at Washington concerning Marshy's previous history, of which nobody knew anything, confirmed his belief; for concealment is seldom sought but to escape infamy. He told Ike Bowler what he thought; and when Ike (whom the reader has recognized as Dr. Pollywog) visited Washington and saw Marshy, he said there could be no mistake, — Marshy must be a Bragly, for nature would never fashion two families on such a shabby model. Alek, therefore, upon consulting Squire Grappler, who happened to know young Bragly and his history when in New York, had the papers referred to made out in preparation for his appearance; for it was judged that, upon the whole, the ends of justice would be better subserved by inducing the rogue to part with his property for the benefit of his father's victims, than by his arrest and imprisonment.

We have seen that when Alek in effect charged upon Marshy his identity with Bragly, he showed no surprise. He saw himself detected, and did not venture on denial. He had supposed that after the lapse of so many years he should not be recognized in New York. His wish now was to retreat with as little loss as possible; for his arrest and conviction as a forger would not only hurt his feelings, but, what was worse, would endanger his fine prospects as planter and guardian of Bob's patrimony, and perhaps also as future legislator, representative, judge, governor, or president, — for all which offices he thought his talents and qualifications to be of the kind most in request.

Therefore, when Marshy understood that by resigning his own patrimony for the benefit of his father's victims he might be allowed to escape the present dreaded danger, he accepted the compromise as a lucky chance. He acknowledged himself to be the identical Bragly junior; and went with Alek and Harry before Squire Grappler, who at once recognized him, and by whose legal aid the deed of transfer was duly authenticated.

When they returned to the office, Dr. Pollywog had already brought Bob, who was very dirty, and very sulky, and received his mother's caresses, coaxings, and promises, with a very ill grace. He "did n't want none of their doggin' arter him," and wished his "mother and Old Sneaky" (meaning his honored father) to — a place unnecessary to mention. He swore he would stay in New York "where there was something of some 'count, — music-grinders, military soldiers, and monkeys."

The reader, though regretting the perjury, will be gratified to know that he was finally persuaded to go back with his mother and "Old Sneaky;" and that they still continue very creditably to fill their place in the upper circles of society in Washington, North Carolina.

CHAPTER XXXVIII.

Alek wished to return to Mr. Boynton the two thousand five hundred dollars, plundered by Marshy and borrowed by himself, but the generous merchant would accept no part of it. After consultation with all parties, it was finally determined to apply the whole three thousand dollars taken from Marshy for the benefit of the slaves at Oakridge, whom Harry had determined to emancipate, and to instruct in the use and advantages of freedom. Harry, therefore (accompanied by Ike), returned to Oakridge; and, after consulting the wishes and capabilities of the slaves, brought most of them to New York, where, being scattered in different families and employments, they soon acquired ideas and habits of self-dependent industry and economy. Those who remained in Carolina, being superannuated, or otherwise incapacitated for freedom, were allowed a small pension for their support.

Ben Blacksmith found employment in an iron foundery connected with Messrs. Greening & Russet's establishment, where his strength and dexterity commanded high wages, so that he soon saved a considerable sum; and then, to the surprise of his employers, asked for his discharge. He made no explanations, but, having settled his small affairs, silently disappeared. He was not heard from afterward till the account of the capture of the brig "Creole" electrified the nation, exciting in the friends of freedom the highest admiration, and in the lovers of slavery the fiercest indignation.

How came Ben Blacksmith again in slavery, and compelled to achieve his freedom by desperate strife against armed kidnappers and keepers? He returned voluntarily to the land of slavery, but with no motive of again submitting to its boasted institutions.

He returned to the region of slavery from the same motive which led Orpheus to brave the horrors of the infernal regions; which urged Menelaus to ten years of strife and danger on the plains of Troy; which brought Samson to the Philistine's house of bondage; which impelled Don Quixote to encounter dreadful dangers; which betrayed Antony to a bloody death.

It was love! Of life's voyage, the tempting siren, the hidden rock, the faithless quicksand, the wrecking hurricane, the fatal whirlpool.

Of life's battle, the ambushed foe, the unsuspected mine, the treacherous ally, the fatal destiny, the overwhelming enemy, the Waterloo defeat.

Of life's economy, the wild extravagance, the sanguine folly, the misplaced trust, the desperate venture, the reckless loss, the inevitable bankruptcy.

Of life's pilgrimage, the enchanted ground, the slough of despond, the vanity fair, the doubting castle, the dire Apollyon, the giant Despair, the city of destruction.

Ben Blacksmith went back to the south that he might rescue his dark Virginia bride from slavery. While in concealment awaiting his opportunity, he was betrayed by a false friend, surrounded by an armed force, and loaded with fetters. He was sold, with others of his acquaintance, including the wife whom he had come to rescue, to a slave-trader to be carried to the Louisiana sugar plantations, where the avowed policy is to work men and women, and boys and girls, to death within six years, and to replenish their gangs by new purchases.

How the slave-trader, after completing his purchases, shipped his freight of human beings for New Orleans on board the brig "Creole," fastening them with fetters and under hatches; how, on the voyage, Ben Blacksmith and Madison Washington, with other heroes whose liberty-loving devotion redeems the land of slavery from the reproach of utter degeneracy, burst from their confinement, and inflicted just vengeance on their truculent keepers and kidnappers, but spared those who submitted, and then, with a prudence and skill unsurpassed in heroic history, navigated the vessel to a British port, and there maintained their own and their companions' just independence, is told by the "protest" of the owners of the vessel in New Orleans, who, though compelled to record the glorious deed, worthy the tallest monument on American soil, yet suppressed much that adds to the honor of the victors.

They did not tell of the wanton cruelty and insult which wound up to desperate valor the unarmed slaves, till, braving every disadvantage, they rushed upon their armed guards, and bore them headlong to the deck, or over the bulwarks.

Nor did they tell how, in the plenitude of their irresponsible tyranny, they tortured the husband by cutting with the merciless whip the quivering flesh of his wife — his wife, dearer to his heart than its own life-blood.

And how, when her little child besought the cruel wretch "not to whip mamma," he spurned the beseeching babe with his boot, and sent it headlong and stunned against the wall of their floating dungeon.

Then the electric spark darted forth from the overcharged brain of the husband and father, and strung his nerves to deeds of matchless valor. In vengeance the volcano found vent, or the brain would have burst with accumulated torture.

With superhuman strength he wrenched the irons that bound his wrists, and dealt the wretch a blow that needed no repeating. It was the crisis of fate. Then the outbursting spirit of the hero inspired congenial spirits around. Madison Washington, a man of milder mood and less feared by the captors, had just been unfettered that he might perform some laborious service for his masters, and he now sprung to the side of Ben, and shouted "Liberty!"

"Now for liberty, boys!" they shouted both, and sprang through the hatchway upon the deck. Their first onset decided the fate of the day. They wrenched the muskets from the vainly-struggling sentinels, and shouted to their companions, now fast emerging from the unguarded hold, and in a few moments the victory was won.

With what consummate skill the fruits of victory were secured; with what vigilance they guarded against treachery and surprise, and compelled their tyrants to become their servants, and to pilot them to a haven of safety, in spite of their wish to betray them; with what forgiving mercy they abstained from all retaliation for cruelties received; with what heaven-trusting faith they threw the deadly arms overboard, relying upon British justice and the God of the oppressed to protect them,—all this may be gathered from the story even as told by their enemies in the "protest" of the owners; and if such was their defamers' story, in what glorious words might their eulogist record their deeds!

What stirred the blood of these submissive and all-enduring blacks to such deeds of matchless valor? It was the controlling energy of the master spirit Ben, communicating itself like the electric current to the sympathizing hearts about him. What was the power that strung his own spirit to that pitch of frenzied valor — to that desperate encounter with adverse odds, where prudence would have counted success impossible?

It was that power which bore Ulysses through a thousand dangers again to his long-deserted Ithaca, and his long-widowed Penelope; which sustained Jacob in his twice seven years' service to the faithless Laban; which inspired the gentle spirit of Petrarch in strains of deathless song, and prompted the heroic Tell to deeds of deathless fame.

It was love,—which dares all things for its devoted object, and snatches victory even from opposing Fate.

It was love, — of life's battle the invincible champion, the heaven-sent aid of chariots and horses of fire, the sacred banner, the palladium of power, the inspiring watchword, the tocsin of victory.

Of life's economy, the cheap luxury, the elevating dignity, the gain counterbalancing all losses, the insurance covering all risks, the guarantee of ultimate success.

Of life's voyage, the unerring compass, the leading star,

the hopeful anchor, the protecting flag, the directing helm, the welcome port.

Of life's journey, the flowery path, the pleasant companion, the refreshing fountain, the cheerful sunshine, the sweet return.

Of life's pilgrimage, the interpreter's house, the greatheart guide, the delectable mountains, the embosomed roll, the key of promise, the helping angel, the celestial city.

CHAPTER XXXIX.

A VISION.

LET the heart be pure, and the faith be clear, and the soul be strong to pierce the bounds of earthly knowledge, and learn the wonders of the spirit world. We are on its borders. We are in its midst. The soul has eyes to see a million surrounding, sympathizing, kindred souls. But the film of mortality curtains the spiritual vision, and we grope in spiritual darkness, though surrounded by spiritual light.

So the man born blind walked the streets of Jerusalem, but saw not its holy temple, nor its glorious sunlight, nor the faces of his brethren; for his eyes, though formed to see, were darkened by a film, and he saw not the wonderful and pleasant things of the world wherein he walked. So the film of mortality shuts our spiritual eyes from the inward world wherein we walk, and we see not its spiritual glories, nor our spirit companions.

But when the Lord of light appeared and touched the blind man's eyes, though all things else remained as before, he was ushered into a new world, of glories inconceivable. So the Lord of light has power to open the spiritual eyes of mortals. This grace he has shown to some, but not to all. Of the many blind men of Judea, but few were healed.

O, deep, unfathomable mysteries of our being! Why do men say that the age of miracles is past? Each man is a miracle. Each new discovery of the laws and powers of matter is a revelation. God still speaks to man in the thunder's crash, and the ocean's roar, and the whispering breeze, as once in the Eden garden-walk.

In visions of the night God's angels have talked with men; or on the holy mountain, or on the desert plain, or in the wilderness, or in the crowded streets.

Frances was ever, while amongst us, but as a visitant from some brighter sphere. Native grace and loveliness surrounded her as with a more ethereal atmosphere. Always pleased and cheerful, she threw the sunlight of her own happy disposition into every place where she entered, and her presence was always an assurance of pleasantness and peace. Where she came, even the rude affected gentleness, the overbearing became affable, and the selfish learned to be generous. Human nature, however degraded, never becomes blind to the attractions of unaffected goodness. Happy Frances! the favorite companion of angels, even while in mortal life. Happy spirits! who now, with the angel Frances, rejoice in immortality.

There seemed no failure of Fanny's health or strength; — her eye was bright, her step was free, her voice was clear, her cheeks lost not their lovely glow. But she talked to her mother of heaven, as a home where she soon should go; and spoke cheerfully and happily, as though it were not a matter of regret, nor even of solemn thought. It had become familiar to her mind, as if it were but a removal to a new and better tenement, where the same loving friends would still be about her, or would soon follow.

There was a heart which throbbed with anguish then, when her true words told of its coming bereavement. It throbs with remembered anguish now, though so many years have passed. But, away with selfish regrets! She said that she would still be about us, and love us; and it is so. Soon the veil will be removed.

THE VISION, AS TOLD BY HERSELF.

It was a moonlit night, and Frances had retired to bed alone. The door which opened into her mother's room was shut, but not fastened. She lay quietly, thinking only of common affairs, when, without the slightest feeling of alarm, she became conscious of the presence of other persons. There were three of them, and all unknown to her. One was an elderly lady, looking much like her mother, but more slender, and dressed in Quaker fashion. Another appeared as her daughter, and looked much like Frances herself, but dressed like the mother. The third was an elderly man, looking benevolent and happy, but rather staid and precise.

The little girl approached the bedside, followed by the mother. Their faces were radiant with goodness and love. "Will you go with us a little while, and see the new home?" said the daughter.

The invitation was so gentle and winning, that Frances thought not of refusing, but gave her hand in confidence. Instantly her relations to the things about her were changed. She was no longer confined to her bed, nor to the room, nor even to her bodily form. Neither the curtains, nor walls, nor any of the surrounding world of matter, obstructed her sight or her movements. A vast and delightful plain of waving groves and winding streams and charming flowers opened before her. Thousands of radiant beings, with looks of love and social joy, thronged the delightful region, and seemed to expect and welcome her approach. She felt the attraction of mutual sympathy, and hastened to join them. To one, even more than to the others, her soul was linked in love.

"I have long been your guardian angel," said the bright being; "and now I will show you the delights and the duties of immortality. Here we are free from earthly hindrances and infirmities; and here duty is ever a delight, because our minds are moulded in the love of duty. The world of infinite progression is before us, and every step is a new joy, higher and better than mortals know. The march of improvement has no limit, and its resources of delight are inexhaustible. Millions of happy spirits have progressed for millions of ages in these paths of peace, and are ever filled with new wonder as worlds of new and varied happiness are unfolded before them. How impossible is it that mortals should comprehend the idea of infinity! Not even seraphs can compass the thought.

"Yet it is not that the soul travels far to its heaven. It is only the awakening of new powers; for the more the soul is developed, the more it is capable of appreciating and enjoying. Creation has no limits, either in extent or variety, when the powers have become expanded and refined to survey it. But mortals are like the beasts which grovel upon the earth, and know nothing but its grossest gifts. The dull ox grazes in the meadow, or basks in the sunshine; but feels not the beauty and fragrance of the flowery green, and has no ear for the warbling melody of the grove, and no eye or thought to pierce the wonders of the starry heavens. Of all that Heaven bestows, only the herbage and the warmth of the sun is within the scope of his capacities. Mankind have faculties a little more expanded and refined to embrace the things about them, yet theirs is but a slight advance toward the high progression of spirits.

"Creation has no limits. These spiritual bodies which we have, and this wonderful landscape which surrounds us, though invisible to mortal eyes, is still as much a part of creation as the grosser substance of earth. In this wonderful creation you also continually move, though your eyes are not open to behold it. Unimaginable beauties and angel companions surround you; and they often influence your minds, and communicate thoughts of which you know not the source. But it is only to those who bring themselves near to the spirit-sphere that we have power to communicate.

"Not all who enter this world are capable of enjoying its happiness. They who have nourished the passions of avarice, of envy, of hatred, or of low sensuality, are unfitted for heavenly joys. What are delights to the good are plagues to the evil; and the tastes which they have formed find no food. See, afar off, at the foot of that unsightly mountain, an unhappy group. Their faces show their discontent. Even now they are in contention. Vulgar taste ungratified, or, if gratified, unenjoyed; sour disdain, gnawing envy, soul-racking hate; ignorance, which scorns truth; jealousy, which repels confidence; cruelty, which feels no sympathy, — these are the kindred cankers of earthly life: they are the devils, self-begotten, who guard the infernal gates; for these gates are only perverted wills. They herd together, though not in peace.

Theirs is the affinity of baseness, and they are repelled by inward antipathy from the good.

"Let us partake of these surrounding fruits. You have tasted nothing on earth so delicious. But their excellence is, that they nourish not only our spiritual bodies, but also our souls. Observe the fragrance of these flowers, and their variety, each with its own delightful perfume. How refreshing are these fountains! — how grateful the breezes!

"Now, let us ascend the empyrean heights; for, in whatever direction we move, we equally ascend; or, rather, the distinctions of height and depth, in the earthly sense, do not prevail here, but only in a moral sense. The highest-ascended angels stand by our side, or dart with us through space; their loftiness of ascent is within them, and they gladly help us to rise toward their eminence.

"Yonder bright being is my guardian angel, as I am yours. See! he kindly proffers to accompany us, and invites us to a circuit among the infinite heavens. Together, gently or swiftly, with one mind they fly."

The worlds of wonders opened to Frances' sight were inconceivable; as if the vast concave sky were filled with floating, sparkling bubbles, and each bubble magnified into a world of surpassing size and beauty, each filled with its own peculiar wonders and delights, yet all uniting in one grand whole, through which the happy dwellers might pass at will. Such seemed the opening panorama of heaven.

"Yet these," said the guide, "are but the beginning of scenes of which there is no end. The archangels of uncounted ages know that these wonders are without limit. They are the works of an infinite God; and he has made them also infinite, even as he has formed us for infinity."

"But, where is the heaven of God's throne? and where is Christ the beloved Son?" asked Frances of the superior spirit.

The angel smiled sweetly, and laid his hand upon his breast. Heaven and Christ were there.

"Think you," said he, "that God's throne is afar off, or that his kingdom is confined to place? Through all the incomprehensible vastness of infinity there is no place where his glories dwell more than in your own heart, nor any other place where you could approach and dwell among them. The loftiest seraphs who stand in his presence are but those whose faculties are most nobly improved, and who thus come into nearer unity with his will. They then dwell in the immediate brightness of his glory; for his glories are unfolded within them. Learn, then, and understand what Christ told you long before, that 'God's kingdom is within you,' and cease to form ideas of a local heaven, — as though He who is omnipresent could be less in one place than in another. His highest and happiest angels are ever drawing nearer to him, and more clearly beholding his glories; because each, within his own heart, explores and ascends, and receives the inward light. Yet, though they ever advance in wisdom, and goodness, and happiness, the way of progression is still infinite.

"To you, as to us, it is given to partake these heavenly fruits around us. Often have you unknowingly been refreshed by them. The fragrance of heavenly airs, wafting good desires, hopes, and resolutions, has revived you. Heavenly streams of confidence, resignation, faith, forgiveness, charity, and love, have refreshed and strengthened you. When you have been startled by new triumphs of your own thoughts, and when spiritual light has unexpectedly filled your mind, it was then that you had unconsciously been refreshed by heavenly fountains, and partaken of spiritual food; and when you now return to your earthly sphere, where your pilgrimage will be brief, your soul will be strengthened by what you have seen and tasted with us.

"Behold a sign by which you may know that you have seen realities, and talked with angels."

Frances looked, and saw her brother Alek, seated at a rude table, in a rustic and roughly-furnished room, and surrounded by wild and unwonted scenery. One other person, of refined and intellectual appearance, accompanied him; and these two were attended by strange-looking persons, of various complexions, and savage though submissive aspect. Before him lay a parcel of letters just written, one of which was directed to herself, informing her that he was then in South America, whither he had gone suddenly, in company with a son of one of his employers, on business which would require extensive journeys, and consume much time.

Frances clearly saw and studied her brother's countenance, and admired his air of sagacious resolution and deliberate self-confidence. But, while she looked, she felt herself rapidly receding from him; and in a moment the vision had passed away, and she found herself in her own room, and alone.

The strong assurance expressed by Frances that she had indeed conversed with spirits made a deep impression upon her parents, and others who shared her confidence. In a few weeks a full confirmation of the spirit-intelligence was received in a letter from Alek. He was indeed in South America, — having been sent by his enterprising employers, in company with Mr. Sylvester Russet, son of the junior partner of the firm, and, like his father, strongly devoted to the science of agricultural husbandry. And here I cannot but express my regret that so few young men of talent and energy like his are led to engage in a field of enterprise so healthful and remunerative, and giving scope for the largest activity of body and mind.

Young Mr. Russet, having received all the advantages of a scientific training in the best schools, devoting himself especially to those departments of natural science pertaining to agriculture as a profession, formed a plan of exploring different regions of South America, to transplant to the soil of New York such of its productions as might appear worthy of the experiment. His father, though he approved the plan, would not consent to his son's attempting it except on condition that Alek should accompany him; for Alek's good conduct and good fortune had by this time gained him a reputation for energy and sagacity equal to any emergency: and it was in this way that he was introduced to a new field of adventure, well adapted to his nature, and favored with the advantage of cultivated and scientific companionship.

It belongs not to this history to pursue the adventures of these utilitarian travellers; but it may be said, in passing, that to their active and successful researches and selections the magnificent gardens and plantations about New York owe some of their choicest embellishments. Their stay was prolonged to nearly three years, during which they visited most of the semi-civilized countries of the southern continent, examined their productions and resources, and rendered substantial services to their employers in a commercial view, besides adding much curious knowledge to the public stock.

CHAPTER XL.

THE full story of a single life would fill many volumes. How briefly, then, must we note events who attempt the history of a whole town in a single book! Matters which were a month's wonder in Wolfsden must be compressed in a single line; and, like the school-girl's genealogical sampler, one little page must suffice for all that is important in many lives,—their births, marriages, and deaths, with moral reflections, rejoicings, and regrets,—an epitaph, a tree, and a tomb.

The Wolfsden Philharmonic Society, after snapping many strings, and exploding much wind, and setting many teeth on edge,—and many tempers, too,—at length composed all its differences by the expulsion or voluntary withdrawal of all its members, who colonized into new harmonical associations, borrowing names from Handel, Haydn, Mozart, and Beethoven, but manufacturing music independent of all masters. Squire Noseby's oft-resounding hall is now silent as the cave of Fingal. Squire Noseby is silent, too. Dropsy did it. Brandy began it. Snuff and tobacco aided it. Squire Noseby has blown his last twang.

Squire Chinby still flourishes. We cannot pause now; but we must again visit Chinby, if but for his blue-eyed daughters, as bright and cerulean as ever.

Time's wheel revolves, and brings many changes; but the pivot stands still and unchangeable. Lucinda Boreman is still the same sweet slender siren as in other days, — her curls still captivating, and her everlasting net-work purse, like Penelope's web, still perplexing her lovers. But Lucinda has seen the sorrow which comes nearest a faithful daughter's heart, the loss of her mother. Her smile is sadder than before, but not the less sweet.

The good old parson has received an added dignity. Before his bereavement it would have been a glory and a triumph. Even now it adds a solemn grandeur to his presence. He is made a doctor of divinity. No parson better deserves the degree than he. No town better deserves a doctor of divinity than Wolfsden.

Ax is a faithful servant — faithful to his patron and to himself. He has grown to be a likely lad of sixteen, and tall as some boys at twenty. He perseveres in his resolution to be a schoolmaster, and the very resolution has already given him the air of one. Besides, he has really gained much knowledge. He has made the most of district school advantages, and has devoted all leisure hours and holidays to study. Lucinda has been his teacher; that is, she has heard him recite lessons, spell, abbreviate, and parse, and has taught him to guess riddles and make acrostics. She has set copies for him, and with her pretty fingers showed him how to hold the pen. She sometimes bends over the slate to show him the sums, and her captivating curls wave near his cheek, — possibly they may once or twice have brushed against his budding whiskers. Ax loves to write and cipher — who would not?

The good old parson, who has thus given a home to the

fatherless in his own house, forgets not the widow. He comes often to Colonel Bowler's to see poor Susan. But Susan is no longer *poor*, in any sense. Her comfortable residence, since Bang's death, has much improved her appearance, and she is plump, cheerful, and good-looking. Her accession to Bragly's property (for she has the benefit of it while Ax is a minor, and he says she shall always have it) has made her quite wealthy. Whisperers say that the parson's attentions to the widow have been more regular and particular since her good fortune than before. The insinuation is not becoming, if intended to reflect upon the good minister's motives, as though they could be mercenary. Charity thinketh no evil, — especially of a doctor of divinity.

Major Murray and his wife miss Margaret much. As monotonous time moves slowly on, they miss her more and more. They are in the uncomfortable position of people who have nothing to plague them. The old lady cooks, and pampers the hired man and the cat, but cannot find half enough employment in that way. She has knit a trunk full of stockings; but there is nobody to wear them out, and no darning to be done. If sometimes a moth makes a hole, she is thankful for the favor, and makes the most of it; but such good luck comes seldom, for she beats and brushes her hoarded stores every week, which happily passes away some supernumerary hours. She sweeps her house twice a day. Once, in her palmy days, she could have made a glorious dust; but now nothing comes of it. She taught the major long ago to clean his shoes as he entered the house; and now, though he seldom goes in the dirt, he is tediously scrupulous, and makes no tracks to give occasion for mop or broom. Poor madam is puzzled what to do; yet, as the mill-stone still revolves though the corn is all ground, so the busy lady still goes round, and tries to make a comfortable clatter.

Colonel Bowler still reports himself as fit for service. The spirit of Seventy-six sustains him. He says the campaign is a pretty long one, but he trusts that it will end honorably, and that he shall be promoted into the great army above, where every soldier is greater than conqueror or king. The "Adjutant" is still the colonel's favorite "staff," and by this time a pretty stout one. The boy loves his grand'ther more than all other playmates, — so permanent are the affections which are fixed and fostered in childhood.

Amy is as sweet as ever — sweeter, for there is more of her, and she is all sweetness. She has grown up from a pretty child to a more than pretty maiden, but still is as artless and unpretending as in her bread-and-butter days — the same generous, impulsive heart, the same sincere, overflowing affections. The instinctive love of truth and goodness, and the antipathy to wrong; the care and regard for others' welfare, fearless for herself; the nice sense of propriety which nature gives to those whom she chooses to be known as ladies, wherever they may be found; all the loveliness of childhood, with the added dignity and worth of womanhood — these were, these still are thy qualities, dear sister mine. From infancy till now, thy life has been a continual lesson of goodness, and thy presence a reward.

CHAPTER XLI.

In reverent silence let us approach the chamber where the soul prepares to change its earthly garment for the robe of immortality.

Pale as the pillow which supports her feeble form, mournfully beautiful as the white rose which even now withers by her side, with failing breath and fluttering pulse, the young Frances awaits her summons to the spirit sphere.

A hectic glow at intervals passes over her cheek, and her eyes dilate with unusual brightness. It is as if the curtain were lifted, and the soul's vision looked beyond mortal things, while a rosy gleam of immortality illumines her face. But the hectic glow passes away, and the eyes are closed. Not yet is the spirit victory won.

Sometimes she has strength to speak a little. When her friend knelt at her bedside, and took her thin, transparent hand, and pressed it to his lips, she faintly smiled, and said, "It is but dust,—soon I shall have a form better worth loving."

When a companion asked her if she suffered much, she cheerfully answered: "No; my body has pain, but no more than I can easily bear; and my soul has no pain, but is filled with peace and joy. How good was the Saviour, to teach us that these little pains are but the birth to a better life, and to show us how to bear them!"

It was wonderful to observe how constantly she considered the soul as distinct and separate from the body, and as the only essential interest. In speaking of herself, she did not include the idea of her outward being. "I seem," said she, "to perceive my gradual separation from the body, and often to watch the progress of my new birth. Yet I neither wish to hasten or delay it. God has ordered it aright. The bud swells and the flower expands by his rules; it is so with us."

To one who read a hymn referring to

"The faithful Saviour, who shall come
Our dust to ransom from the tomb,"

she replied: "O no! not the *dust*. We shall be done with dust. Nothing which goes to the tomb returns. The body belongs to the tomb. Our Saviour came to raise us *from* the body."

Another read or spoke of the death of the righteous as a blessed sleep, and she replied: "Not *sleep*, but a blessed waking. We are not fully awake while in the body, but when we leave the flesh we shall have spiritual bodies, which will not retard the soul with sleep, nor with other infirmities. God has given us these bodies only to prepare us for better ones."

To her mother she said: "Think of me as with you still. God will permit me to minister to you, and others whom I love; and it will be a part of my happiness to commune with you, and to sustain you till you also shall be free, and we shall be sister angels." — "Only remember," said she, playfully, "that *there I* shall be the *eldest*."

As the moment of her dissolution approached, she seemed mostly insensible to outward things, but her countenance often expressed the soul's communings, and a radiant smile passed over her features. Through the thin and broken veil of mortality, she may have seen and talked with the happy ministering spirits in the angel sphere.

When the last earthly hour approached, there was a struggle of bodily pain, severe, but short, and then she breathed calmly, but more and more faintly, till daybreak. As the light dawned she rallied her strength for a moment, and wished to speak. Her sister Helen bent over her to catch her words, but could distinctly hear only the word "SEE." The expression of her countenance explained the rest. It was some beautiful sight of which she wished to speak. . . . .

How beautiful was that mortal body which we consigned to the grave! — O! then how surpassingly beautiful must be the spiritual! We cannot conceive, but, when *our* spirit victory is gained, then we shall "see."

Let us bravely bear our earthly lot, our burthens and bereavements, rejoicing in the treasures of love which shall surely be restored to our faithfulness. And let us not mourn that those whom we love are sooner advanced to the blessed sphere. If death were indeed dreadful, its most dreadful form would be a long-protracted earthly life, with the successive loss of all our joys, and decay of our powers. But to the truly enlightened death in no form is dreadful; it is but the sudden or the gradual awakening to a new and glorious life.

Yet it was mournful news to pass from house to house in Wolfsden, when the young Frances, so lately the fairest, loveliest, and most welcome, wherever she appeared, was now departed from our sight.

The young and old, from far and near, came to take a last look of the form no longer animated by the spirit which moulded it in such grace, and to learn anew the lesson of death, so often learned, yet so little understood.

In little scattered groups, with hushed voices, they spoke of how she looked when they saw her last — so blithe and beautiful; or told what they knew of her patient sickness, and how it was believed that she had talked with angels, and foreknew her early death; or they spoke of the absent brother — how dearly he loved her, and how he would grieve.

The scripture which she selected was read, and her chosen hymn was sung. They expressed consolation and triumph.

Over the flowery turf which her fairy feet had so often trod, beneath the spreading elms where her play-ground had been, past the green grove where she loved to wander, through the field and by the hill-side where every picture of the scenery is blended with her presence, silently, reverently, mournfully, the long procession passed, attending her body to the grave.

Yet the robin sweetly sang, and the sparrows blithely twittered, and the flowers expanded their various beauties and sent up their sweet fragrance; and all nature smiled as if to assure us that God's laws were even now, as ever, harmoniously working out their happy results of mercy and love, — only our eyes were too dim, and our spirits too sad, to receive the grateful truth.

CHAPTER XLII.

ANOTHER year has unfolded its lessons of duty, of patience, submission, and improvement; and another spring brings its tokens of faith, hope, and love. Affection's wounds may not heal, but we learn to endure them. Departed delights may no more return, but we hasten to overtake them.

New duties demand our attention. Life, like the historian's page, still hastens on. We may not loiter in the field, for the harvest demands the sickle, and the reaper Death follows close behind us. Let us hasten our work while the sun still shines. Hasten your deeds, ye heroes of destiny! Glide glibly, fair pen of history!

It was near the close of a pleasant day of June, 18—, when two travellers pursued their winding upward way along the wildly romantic banks of the Saco. One of them, gentlemanly-looking, and in the early prime of life, rode in a well-varnished "rockaway," whose easy luxury might have served a softer frame. The other, a stout and spirited horse, trotted briskly along the uneven way, and drew the shining rockaway, as gay and well pleased as his master; and as they journeyed he who rode mused thus:

"Here am I and my good steed pursuing our winding way along the banks of this romantic river; and why are not we and our fortunes fit matters for romance? Were the wonder-writing JAMES apprized of our position, how quickly would his genius install us in the long ranks of his renowned heroes! Little thinks that mighty master of rigmarole what a quarry he misses by not following on our track. Let us cast a retrospective view.

"Seven years have I wandered from my native home, driven by unrequited love and unrelenting fate — (so the story should read, though the plain fact is, I went of my own free will). Many perils have I encountered, and many achievements have I performed, some of which might deserve at least a ballad, if a cheap poet could be found; but Willis has taken to prose, and Holmes to pills, and the others are probably above my price. These scenes bring back early lessons of economy. If I buy a whistle, it must be a small one.

"Beneath yon beechen tree, by the side of that rippling rivulet, I met the first peril of my travels, which came near to prove the last; but I killed the rattlesnake that threatened me, and hung him for a warning on that very thorn-bush which still guards the wayside.

"My first adventure in New York was worthy of Quixote's fame, and something more; for my impulse was as good as ever warmed his chivalrous bosom, and my success better than he often found. I beat the rowdies who would have mobbed the women, and suffered no damage in the encounter.

"I shall not omit to credit myself for my flight from Count Flummery's palace of seduction. That flight was my most praiseworthy deed, for it was my most difficult one; and, if recorded at all, it shall be compared to the retreat of Xenophon with his ten thousand Greeks.

"Also I preached morality to poor Fitz-Faun; but I could

not save him, and therefore I infer that he was a predestined reprobate. It is of no use to contend against the decrees of destiny.

"But I helped to save the splendid Erycina, who so dangerously imperilled me. She is now a good and happy matron, with a lot of pretty children. I claim the whole family as stars in my diadem of good deeds.

"What a knight for distressed damsels and widows I have been! Sophia Greening may thank me that I put her deliverer on the right track for rescuing her and winning her; and widow Simperkins owes the recovery of her 'hunique' to my sagacity; but we 'll offset that against the snowdrift 'haccident.'

"But Bang's widow and son owe me full credit for my labor of love in their behalf; though Ike must come in for his share of merit in the management of Marshy, which was very adroit, and perfectly justifiable. Wretches who ignore all honorable principles and rules of conduct cannot claim protection by them. Vermin are out of honor's pale.

> 'Who ever recked where, how, or when,
> The prowling fox was trapped and slain?'

"Ike writes me that our old minister, now a widower and doctor of divinity, pays extra attentions to the widow Susan since her fortunes have mended. All very natural, and very characteristic. It is prudent to befriend those whom Providence befriends; it proves our piety to be on the same side with Providence. I hope she will profit by his ministrations.

"But I forget to complete the summing up of my own good deeds. No matter, — they are all recorded, and will appear in the final reckoning; but possibly may not figure up so favorably as I am disposed to make them. It is unsafe to reckon without our host.

"I have, however, served my employers faithfully, besides services rendered to others, including myself; and I believe that I have wronged no one wilfully, either in mind, body, or estate; so that between myself and my fellow-men I have a clear conscience, which is doubtless an essential part in the great account. And in the great struggle between right and wrong, which in a thousand forms is ever going on in the world, my sympathies, at least, have always been on the side of truth and humanity; which, however, is no matter of boast, for it was not in my nature to be otherwise.

"And now, after my seven years' apprenticeship in the world, I return to embrace my beloved parents and brothers, and to see the grave of my sister. She left word for me that I should not weep, but rejoice, for her. If my soul were as pure and elevated as her own, I might perhaps be able to obey her request; but, O, how much of the loveliness of home has departed with her! Yet the dear remembrance of her presence will ever be a bond of attachment to the scenes of my youth, and I doubt if ever I shall be enough of a philosopher to regard any other place with equal interest. How beautiful is the image of her life and death as pictured in my mind! How elevated and unselfish her thoughts, and how fond and strong her affections! Her last message to me, through sister Helen, was to bequeath her share in my heart to her dear friend Amy. Dear little Amy! how fond was she of Frances, and how much attached to me! I remember that I left my home at dawn of day, to spare her the pain of parting. But she is now no longer a little pet. How many of the sweet charms of home I shall miss! Yet my father and mother still remain in health, and this is much to be thankful for; and Billy and Tommy I hear are stout and good boys, and ambitious to emulate their brother Alek, whom they have set up as a pattern. Well, we shall see what they can do."

Thus, musing and soliloquizing, our romantic traveller in the rockaway communed with himself, while his horse trotted steadily along, making speedy progress, pausing not in the upward or downward waving, bending way, — now through cool valleys, arched by the overhanging forest and dusky from the declining sun; now over knolls rising into the smiling view of approaching sunset; now turning by sharp angles around insurmountable ledges of precipitous rock, and now in graceful bendings by the base of some near encroaching hill, till at length they came where a road turns abruptly from the river, and a guide-board pertinaciously directs the traveller to Wolfsden, as though there were no other place in the world where travellers need to go.

Our travellers obeyed the intimation, and, ascending a hill, soon emerged from the woody solitude to scenes of livelier interest.

Behind, stretching far to the south and east, lay the shadowy vale, threaded by the winding river, along whose banks hitherto for several hours they had journeyed, meditated, and soliloquized.

Before and on either hand, near and remote, high on the hill-sides or deep in the shady valleys, on the level plains, by the border of wood-encircled lakes, and along the fertile meadows, where slow-winding streams loiter lazily along their level bed, — by the wayside, or in remoter retreats, threaded by green lanes, and obscured by orchards and scattered trees, a hundred homes fill and adorn the pleasing panorama; a hundred homes, recalling a thousand familiar faces, and ten thousand associations of early life. Even yet the apple-trees were in bloom, and gave their fragrance to the gentle breeze. The rising corn had just begun to mark the fields with slender lines, and green patches of various grains displayed their young luxuriance. Cattle of every color and degree — gentle cows, majestic oxen, and defiant bulls; mares sedate, and frisking colts; quiet ewes, and bleating lambs — harmoniously shared their green pastures, and helped to fill the faithful picture, and recall the realities of rural New England life.

Every farm-house, every family, every human heart, has its history, — its joys and sorrows, its thrilling hopes and trembling fears, its anticipations and disappointments. Life's drama is everywhere in progress; its curtain rising and falling, ever closing and ever renewed; and, however high or humble the stage, still the story is of humanity. Human hearts throb with all that humanity can feel, and learn what experience alone can teach.

Here, a newly-married couple have just begun life's career. Themselves, their cares, and their young dreams, are enough to people and fill with ample resources their home and their time. There, a maturer pair are surrounded and overshadowed by a rising family: striplings confident of untried powers; young maidens with timid steps entering upon life's stage, each needing and receiving the correcting and supporting aid of parental experience; while, lingering among the busy bustlers of life, the gray patriarch and ancient dame, with silent care, perform the last duties, and await the closing event of mortality.

Half hidden in the distance toward the left, among the

hills and the trees, the searching eye obtains the outward view of an unpretending yet independent home,—the home of three living generations, as of other generations which have passed away, and perhaps of generations yet unborn. There, at this moment, the flower of them all, a lovely maiden, stands at her little glass, and arranges her simple toilet. Her daily routine of duties done, she prepares for an evening walk. Though untaught by fashion, she is educated in all that nature, truth, and innate delicacy, can teach. Her neat and dextrous hands easily supply all the ornament her native beauty needs. Her wavy auburn hair is combed with a gentle downward curve, slightly covering her fair temples. Her muslin kerchief protects, yet not quite conceals, her beautiful neck. A well-chosen and well-fitted fabric of light material displays the symmetry of her form, moulded and rounded in the fairest proportions of perfect womanhood. Her eyes, radiant with intelligence and good-humor, but softened with modest diffidence, look approvingly upon the faultless form and features reflected in the little glass. She turns this way and that in every direction, but finds nothing amiss; and, calling "Champion," the strong and watchful house-dog, who gladly obeys her summons, with gentle caress and light elastic step, she leaves the house.

She trips along the green path, bordered by the lilacs, their gay plumes now bending with superabundant fragrance. High over head the tall old pear-tree showers down its white blossoms, half covering the turf, and giving a brighter yellow to the new-coined dandelions which thickly bedeck the green.

She passes through the gate and adown the road by the old stone wall, over which the blackberry waves its flexile branches, and displays its snowy blossoms, in token of luscious pickings to come.

She pauses but for a moment where a narrow grove of beeches, fresh in the light green of their young leaves, fringes the field, and gives to the wayside traveller in sultry noon a grateful shade. Here, each year, when October frosts open the rough burrs, has she gathered ample hoards of nuts for winter evening's hospitality, but left to the squirrels and wild pigeons their larger share.

The road descends and crosses a little brook, which gurgles and glides and eddies along, among mossy rocks, and over shining sands, and in deep pools, where the speckled trout loves to hide, and dart upon the luckless grasshopper betrayed upon the treacherous tide.

From the thick alders which border the brook a partridge springs and whirrs away to securer depths. Champion jumps to chase the escaping prey, but soon ceases the fruitless pursuit, and only wishes he had sooner been there.

The ascending road, fringed and encroached upon by ferns and whortleberry-bushes, at length discloses a by-path, — the hypothenuse of a distant angle. It is a shorter and prettier way, and leads through a grove of maples, where but lately the dripping sap filled the shallow troughs of rifted wood, and, thence transferred to the boiling kettle, became by rustic alchemy transmuted to the yellow nuggets which juvenile mortals love.

At length the path emerges upon a broad road, with well-built walls of stone on either side, enclosing and protecting far-reaching fields, now springing in green promise, and soon to glow in gorgeous array of gold, and silver, and crimson, and purple, such as Solomon in all his glory could not reach,

— but soon again, alas! to be despoiled by the unsparing scythe, — relentless emblem of the fate which awaits all flesh, which is but grass.

But youthful beauty moralizes not thus. She trips along and enjoys the lovely scene and balmy air of June, and thinks not of despoiling autumn. Champion, as regardless as herself of the destiny of dogs and men, now scours away in long excursion, scaring blackbirds and robins from their grassy hiding-places, and now trots panting by her side. Happy mortals! No objects or cares perplex them. They go forth without expectation, and, therefore, meet no disappointment.

But events meet those who do not expect them. Whether unawares or anticipated, the fate which destiny decrees will find us. The fair maiden had already sufficiently prolonged her walk, and was about to return, when a carriage came suddenly in sight. It was a shining rockaway, occupied by a single traveller, and drawn by a handsome horse. She could not well turn to go back till she had passed the carriage, for that would look like an uncivil avoidance of the stranger. She saw that it was a stranger, and such a one as youthful maidens do not often shun.

The carriage approached, and the stranger, with deferential grace, bowed, and, with apologizing politeness, begged to be informed whether Colonel Bowler lived in the vicinity. His look, and indeed his motives, were sincere, but his words dissimulated; for he already well knew where Colonel Bowler lived. It was something else he wanted to know, and which his penetrating eyes seemed already to find in the maiden's countenance.

The maiden replied, unsuspiciously, but with a flutter in

her heart which she could not understand, nor quite repress, that Colonel Bowler was her father, and lived less than a mile distant. It was the first house after turning the first corner to the left.

"If you are Colonel Bowler's daughter," said the handsome stranger, "you must be Amy, whom I have so often called my daughter."

Amy looked up with surprised recognition.

"Do you not know Alek?" continued he, alighting from the carriage, and offering his hand. "Recollect who found you in the woods, and whom you used to call uncle."

The maiden's eyes sparkled and suffused with artless and earnest welcome. It was Alek, — altered, indeed, but still impersonating the image cherished and venerated from childhood. Alek saw his advantage, and, seizing her hands, pressed them to his lips with many kisses. Her cherry lips, and blushing cheeks, and radiant eyes, looked as if they had at least equal claims. Amy forgot for the moment that she was not still a child. Alek seemed to forget it too; for he clasped her in his arms, and repaid to cherry lips, and blushing cheeks, and radiant eyes, their well-deserved tribute of a hundred kisses.*

But her self-forgetfulness was but for a moment. With gentle dignity she disengaged herself; and, giving her hand, told him that she would accompany him home — "Where," said she, "your father and mother, and Billy and Tommy, will be gladder to see you than I am."

She got into the carriage, and sat by his side. He asked a thousand questions, not one of which was prompted by the

* Amy, who has got a peep at the manuscript, insists that this is an exaggeration by ten-fold.

interest uppermost in his mind; for his heart and brain were filled with new-born thoughts and emotions, — too immature for present utterance. What were they? A glance at his present position may explain them.

He had just returned, after years of absence and enterprise, to the calm and congenial scenes of his youth. His mind, so long given to the pursuits and projects of busy ambition, was now turned into a new channel, where early feelings, affections, and sentiments, cherished, though repressed, were waiting to resume their sway.

His heart was filled and expanded with tender emotions and ardent affections. His love of home beat stronger in his bosom as the distance lessened. Even inanimate objects shared his regard; — the dumb animals seemed like familiar friends, and the birds in the branches gave notes of welcome.

Attentive readers, who have retained the philosophy as well as the facts of this history, already understand the moral anatomy of the human heart; how, when the warm emotions — filial, fraternal, and social love — friendship, patriotism, and their kindred train, crowd into and fill their respective places, then the whole sentimental system expands, and opens to every generous impression. Then the connubial cell, before described, and now accessible through a thousand enlarged channels, is prepared to receive its occupant. If at this auspicious moment the destined one comes by, the indwelling spirit recognizes and invites the life-long guest.

Thus, surrounded and swayed by the unseen destinies which direct and control the actions of mortals who fondly fancy that they move with unbiased free will, Alek drove on, and the fair Amy sat by his side, — by the side where his full heart lay the nearest and beat the strongest. He asked a hundred random questions of things he thought not of, that he might look in her radiant face and hear her sweet voice in reply. He saw — for his quick-discerning mind could trace the true signs which mark the abode of a heavenly-gifted soul — that the face whose beauty delighted his eyes was also lighted with the deeper and rarer radiance of refined and expansive thought. The features and form which must attract all eyes was invested with grace and dignity compelling respect from all. He saw what a precious prize awaited some happy adventurer in life's lottery, and pondered how long the golden moments of opportunity might last.

The idolized though forbidden image which had so long been shut up in his secret heart, excluding every other tender impression, was now suddenly obscured; for a brighter vision filled its place, and sweet hope rejoiced in the change. He rode on, and held joyful converse with his fair partner; but not of the subject which filled his mind.

And what were Amy's thoughts? Tell, ye who can fathom the female heart. The looks and words were those of undisguised gladness and frank welcome, — such as a sister might bestow. Was there a deeper and secret sentiment? Who can know, — or, knowing, would presume to tell?

Their carriage moved slowly, but the moments passed quickly; and, in a space which seemed miraculously brief, they came to the paternal door. Alek announced himself to his parents with fond embraces, and introduced Amy as a lady whom he had picked up astray, and brought to be identified.

"You could not have brought one whom it gives me more

pleasure to identify," replied his mother, welcoming Amy, though a daily visitant, as warmly as if she had been absent a month.

Billy and Tommy, stout, red-cheeked, rough and ready youngsters, full of youthful spirits and green promise, were quickly present to share the reünion; and even Lion, now in his dotage, by degrees recognized his old master, and rejuvenated himself with reminiscences of the fights and frolics of his days of glory. Joy, thankfulness, and deeper emotions and remembrances, mingled their sweetness and sadness in the full fraught hour

CHAPTER XLIII.

When Alek and his mother were alone, and after other matters had been sufficiently treated, she asked him what he thought of Amy. Alek, with assumed indifference, replied that she had grown finely, and seemed a clever girl.

"She is a precious girl," replied his mother, earnestly. "I have never seen one out of my own family whom I should so much rejoice to call daughter."

To Alek's excited mind the remark had a meaning perhaps stronger than was intended; and he blushed, — not with confusion, but with pleasure.

"Surely," said he to himself, "I shall not be so undutiful as to deny my mother so reasonable a wish, if it shall be in my power to fulfil it."

Thus, the first day of his return from enterprise abroad became the era of more important enterprise at home.

But the enterprise was not difficult. It is provoking that such fine materials for romance should be spoiled by the perverse kindness of fate. Never was wooing, and winning, and wiving, so quietly done. Like the boy's whistling, it did itself. Everybody saw that it was an inevitable event, and therefore helped it along with hearty good-will; and those who might be most suspected of secret envyings were most forward to manifest their magnanimous approbation. Before the principal parties had proper time to interchange a word on the subject, their wedding-day, with all its circumstances and ceremonials on a most liberal scale, was debated, arranged, fixed, and proclaimed, all over Wolfsden. Under these circumstances, an explicit understanding between the primary parties became essentially expedient.

"Dearest Amy," said Alek, one day, after several weeks of closely-cultivated companionship, with mutually increased esteem and attachment,—"dearest Amy, our kind neighbors have not only given us to each other for life in anticipation, but have actually appointed our wedding-day for next Thanksgiving. If you will be but as kind as they, I shall be still happier in your society than now, for I shall feel secure of not losing it."

Amy was silent for a few moments, as if endeavoring to comprehend the meaning of what she heard; then, with a trembling voice, though trying very hard to appear natural, she replied,

"You know I love you very much; but—indeed—really—I—this is an important matter, and—very sudden—I—"

"Sweet Amy," said Alek, stopping her broken speech with a kiss, "you shall not be hurried; we will delay the subject till evening; and now let us take our morning walk."

They walked through the orchard, where the new-mown grass gave a smooth, soft carpet to their feet; along by the embowered hedge, bending with ripe raspberries; through the grove where the birds sang songs of love; across the field, and adown the cross-road to the Morgan estate, now possessed by Jacob, the elder brother of Amy. Before they reached the gate which led to his house, Amy stopped, and pointed, —

"That," said she, "is the tree under which I left my basket of berries, when I went to gather flowers, just twelve years ago yesterday. This is the anniversary of the day when you found me, and made me —— yours forever."

She looked up in his face; her own was full of blushes, and her eyes suffused with starting tears, but love shone resplendent and triumphant through them all.

"Mine forever! — and may God make me worthy of the gift!" said Alek, with deep emotion, as he clasped her to his bosom, and kissed her blushing cheeks and tearful eyes.

They prolonged their walk; but minded not whither they went. There was no need; to them the world was everywhere full of beauty and sweetness. The loving skies encircled the peaceful earth, and the peaceful earth reflected back its smiles of love and joy.

Come, ye who find the world a dreary abode of moody discontent, of harsh discord, and pining grief, and learn how it may become a home of heavenly peace and delight. Let it be filled with love. Heaven is full of it, and is free to bestow it upon the earth in fulness, would mortals but receive it.

When Alek went home, he told his mother of his engagement to Amy.

"Now," replied she, "my fondest wish for your happiness is granted. She is worthy of your best affections; for she has the heart to reciprocate your love, and the mind to comprehend and associate with your own. Nothing is more essential to the happiness of a man of refined understanding than that his wife should be able to appreciate and respond to it. The sweetest tribute to superior talent is that paid by a beloved wife. But when a man of high endowments marries a woman of common or vulgar mind, mutual dislike is sure to follow. The husband naturally expects the deference due to conscious superiority; while the wife, so far from acknowledging, or even seeing it, probably considers him inferior to the common kind, who belong to her own level; for them she can understand, and him she cannot. Your love will be lasting, for your wife will have the good sense to perceive and take pride in your intellectual powers — to enjoy them, and even improve them; for a woman of good natural endowments will aid to improve her husband's mind, though his endowments and attainments be superior to her own. There is a delicacy and refinement in a true woman's genius, whose influence is essential to the highest point of man's culture, as her approval is to his highest triumphs. It is the foible of men of genius that they scarcely prize even love itself, unless accompanied by respect and honor."

Alek announced the matter to his father, who warmly expressed his approval.

"It is now more than thirty years," said he, "since I was united to your dear mother, who was then more beautiful than any girls we see nowadays, though Amy comes nearer than any other I know of. I hope she will prove as true and as good, and then you will have the best blessing earth can give — one whose price, as Solomon says, is above rubies. I am truly thankful that you are to come with so good a girl to make your parents' home brighter in their old age. You are much richer than your father ever was, or desired to be; but you are above pride in wealth, and therefore are not in so much danger from it. I hope you will always be content with the home place. You may improve it as much as you will, but I wish that my children may always possess the home that has been so dear to their parents, and so signally blessed to us all."

"It will ever be the dearest spot in the world to us all," replied Alek, "and when Billy and Tommy shall have finished their apprenticeship in New York, and seen enough of life there, they will return to settle about us, so that we shall all have opportunity to help and enjoy each other while we live."

It should here be explained that it had already been arranged that Alek should take the home place, and that Billy should accept a place in Messrs. Greening & Russet's agricultural establishment, and Tommy should go into Mr. Boynton's counting-room. Alek's good conduct and successful services had opened the way for these valuable situations, with peculiarly favorable circumstances; and it may be mentioned, in passing, that hitherto they have justified the expectations raised by their brother's honorable career. But we cannot pursue their fortunes. Our history must pause, and end where it began — in Wolfsden.

CHAPTER XLIV.

TIME moves swiftly on golden pinions. Many a youth and maiden, looking upon Alek and Amy, see a more attractive grace in their devoted though dignified and unostentatious affection than they had before imagined, and sigh for equal bliss. Their sighs mingle, and the soft contagion spreads. There will be more weddings than one, next Thanksgiving. Parson Boreman, or rather the Rev. Dr. Boreman, will be in request.

But the Rev. Dr. Boreman's gracious head has already pondered and arranged a matter which must intercept, for his own benefit, the benedictions with which he has blessed so many couples for so many successive Thanksgivings. He means to be blessed himself. But so important a matter must be announced in his own words.

It was of a Sunday evening, while the reverend doctor was still invested with the dignity of his pulpit dress, his robes and bands redolent of sanctity, and his face radiant with his own eloquence, that he sent for Lucinda to his study, and, with an air which indicated matter of unusual weight, thus addressed her:

"My daughter, it is now two years since your departed mother left me a mourner. During that time, as ever before, you have been all to me that a daughter could be, and I have been resigned, as it behoved me, to the divine will. But, considering your solitary condition, without the help and guidance of maternal counsel, my mind has been led to reflect upon the fitness and propriety of changing my condition. I have, therefore, taken counsel with a very worthy woman, and it is appointed that she shall dwell in my house as — as — as one of its united head. I refer to Mrs. Susan Barker. I trust that you will be prepared to receive her as a mother; and I doubt not that the — the visitation — or rather the — the dispensation, as I may say, will be sanctified — that is, profitable to us all."

Lucinda, as already hinted, had read romances, and well knew how such announcements should be received by dutiful and sentimental daughters. She therefore gracefully advanced, and, kneeling by his chair, kissed his hand, and in a pretty speech prepared for the occasion, which she had long been expecting, wished him every joy in his new relation.

The reverend doctor was delighted at what he considered the happy conclusion of this embarrassing part of the business; but, as his own impatient congregation had too often found, there were more "last words," even after the conclusion. Lucinda still kept her position — *she* had "a word to add."

"My dear father," resumed she, "I — I have something on my mind to say; I — I hope, as you are so good as to give me a new mother, you will not object to — to receiving her son; that is, Jotham, as your son — that is, I mean, we have thought of being — being — a 'united head.'"

"What! you marry Ax?" exclaimed the doctor, hardly believing that he had heard aright.

"Yes, father," meekly replied the daughter.

The reverend doctor was dumbfounded. Here was an unexpected catastrophe. He had not imagined an emergency so out of the common order of events, and it took some moments to calculate the consequences.

"This is a crabbed text," thought he. "She pays me back in my own coin. Who would have thought of such a plot where all seemed so quiet! But it is the way of her sex, ever since Eve. Truly the apostle observes, 'Woman was first in the transgression;' and some able commentator says, that 'women sometimes lose their wits.'"*

Reflecting, however, that it was best to put a good face on it, since opposition would provoke trouble all round, and that Ax, though but a boy, was well grown and a serious lad, he gave his paternal consent; and Ax (who was, by Lucinda's contrivance, listening in the adjoining entry) being called in, the clerical benediction was bestowed, and the business comfortably concluded.

* This remarkable saying is quoted in the Arabian Nights by the Caliph Haroun Alraschid, who declares that he does not know who is its author. Dr. Boreman's quoting it proves that his reading was not exclusively canonical.

CHAPTER XLV.

Time may have lagged with the impatient lovers; but it shall not so with the reader. Thanksgiving day came in its appointed season, with all its budget of good cheer. To Col. Bowler's hospitable house it came with even more than its wonted preparation. Ike had proclaimed his resolution that Amy's wedding should be celebrated in grand style. Nobody dissented, and all the younger fry applauded the resolution, and joined in the preparation. The colonel expressed himself gratified that the spirit of Seventy-six was still extant. The Adjutant volunteered to muster the company. George said that he would screw up his fiddle once more. The guests were invited, and the auspicious day came in with glory.

Elder Kraken (the same who presided at the reformation meeting, where Harry was mistaken for a convert) performed the priestly office; for the Rev. Dr. Boreman had two weddings on his hands at home — his own and Lucinda's; but the Elder did it with zeal, and gave good satisfaction to all concerned.

We cannot stop to enumerate the guests, nor describe the various entertainment, the sports and the solemnities; but the reader may depend upon it that it was a great wedding, just as Ike had resolved.

Harry and Margaret were there. They came a month before, with a brisk little curly-pated, bright-eyed imp of their own, who, being a prodigy, everybody had conspired to spoil. The grandparents—that is, Deacon Murray and wife—were there. The deacon's gravity was as an ounce of ballast to a whole cargo of gayety. The Chinbys were there. It was thought that much of the motive of Ike's enthusiasm for a great wedding was to get the Chinbys; for, by his contrivance and Amy's coöperation, he and the eldest of the blue-eyed daughters were groomsman and bride's-maid. Dr. Drinkmore was there. He came all the way from New York, at Harry's and Margaret's invitation, to try the air of Wolfsden. He finds it agreeable to his constitution; and Harry remarks that the water will prove no less so. He and Margaret have resolved to make a teetotaller of the doctor. Mrs. Simperkins was there; having timed her annual visitation so as to include all such occasions. It was well enough. The wise ancients hung up a skeleton in their halls of festivity, to remind them of their mortality.

Some were merry, and some were serious; there were laughter and sighs, mirthful jests and solemn reflections; every room had its congenial circle, attracted by mutual affinities. All tastes were accommodated. Major Murray, and others who had a character for gravity to maintain, took the little parlor furthest from the kitchen, where the festivities of the young folks, as ultra in their levity as the others in their gravity, became at times uproarious. The large sitting-room was filled mostly with the middling or transition class,—many of whom sympathized and sometimes joined with the rantapoles in the kitchen, where George, with his violin, somewhat restrained and regulated their wild spirits with musical harmony.

The happy bridal circle, including the principal parties and their closest intimates, and some others, inquirers or converts to the institution of matrimony, were generally grouped together. Old times and events were recalled with new interest, and the beautiful things of the past, culled from its asperities and garnered up in memory, were reproduced. Margaret, with matronly soberness, reminded Alek of their last merry meeting; and, looking significantly at Amy, archly inquired whether the hero of his "Match Story" had not found an estate with not only a better title, but also a prettier prospect. Alek was half confused by the reminiscence and the application, but owned that his hero (meaning himself) had profited by the suggestion with which she so ingeniously finished his story.

When the more active sports subsided, psalmody was suggested. The colonel brought out his bass-viol, George brought in his violin, and the soul-stirring strains and fantastic fugues of Billings and Holden were performed with the lofty energy of old days. The spirit of Seventy-six was roused. Harry and Margaret led; Alek and Amy seconded; Squire Chinby and his blue-eyed daughters, with Ike by their side, and all who had voices and lungs, joined in full chorus. There was a tempest of music.

When this was abated, match stories and other stories were told. We have not room to repeat them, but will give one to fill up this chapter, and attract juvenile tastes. It was told by Aunt Deborah to a group of young and attentive ears. Aunt Deborah always found a time to please and instruct children; and Parson Boreman, when, after exhausting his subject, he finds a page of his sermon left blank, generally fills it with "a word to the young." Philoprogenitive readers will not censure us that we follow their example, and devote a page to the juveniles.

AUNT DEBORAH'S STORY.

"A generous youth once met a warm-hearted maiden. A gleam of sunshine, brighter than common sunshine, shone upon them and the things about them, and made the flowers gayer, and the fruits sweeter, and the birds more melodious, and themselves more attractive to each other, than they had before imagined; and when they separated, the common sunlight seemed dim, and the flowers faded, and the fruits tasteless, and the birds mute, and themselves unhappy. So they again met, and resolved to live always together; and the gleam of bright sunshine illuminated their dwelling and shone about their path, and the flowers were again bright, and the fruits sweet, and merry were the songs of the birds.

"As they continued to live together, the gleam of sunshine took various forms. When *he* cultivated his fields, it ran along and smoothed the way, and made his task easy; and when he was tired, it made even weariness pleasant, and rest refreshing. When he drove his team, it made his steers docile and obedient, and his colts gentle and willing. His trees grew thriftily and bore abundantly; his house was filled with plenty, and his heart with peace.

"And as *she* performed her household duties, the bright gleam of sunshine ran along and made them light, and prevented all vexations. The cows gave their milk quietly and abundantly; the sweet butter came quickly from the rich cream; the hens laid eggs with liberal hearts, and cackled to give notice of their timely tribute; her stores of comfort increased, she performed offices of charity, and her heart was filled with peace.

"But the demon of discord passed by, and envied their happiness; and he came in disguise, and hid by their hearth, and breathed forth a vapor that clouded the gleam of sunshine, so that it could not illuminate the house, and the walls of the dwelling were filled with gloom.

"And as the man went forth to his toil, the cloud went with him, and his way was rough, and his labors hard, and his rest gave no refreshment. His oxen were unruly, and would not obey; his horses were vicious, and would bite and kick; his trees forbore to grow, and their scraggy branches were covered with canker-worms, and yielded only hateful moss; his prosperity declined, and his heart was filled with discontent.

"And as the woman toiled at her household tasks, everything went wrong. The cloud followed her from pantry to dairy, and from chamber to cellar. The sheep shed their fleeces among the briers; the cows held up their milk, or kicked over the pail; the butter would not come, and the maggots spoiled the cheese; the hens scratched the garden, but refused to lay; her cakes were heavy, and so was her heart.

"And they went out from their house by different ways. The man took the road that went upon the hill, and the woman took the road that went into the valley. And the man saw an eagle soaring and screaming among the cliffs as he guarded his nest; and he listened to the voice of the eagle, which seemed to say, 'I am the king of birds, and the companion of Jove. I rule my house in fear, and discord dares not to disturb my rest.'

"And the man said, 'I too will assert my prerogative, and compel the obedience which is my due, and discord shall not disturb my dwelling.'

"And the woman walked in the valley, and saw a raven upon her nest, watching her young. And the raven croaked, and seemed to say, 'I dwell in silence and gloom, and, though I am weak, yet my voice has power to chill the heart with omens of ill, and I am feared by those who are mightier than I.'

"And the woman said, 'I too will dwell in silence and gloom, and nurture my powers to repel and assail.'

"So the demon of discord rejoiced, and made strong his dwelling in the hearth of the once happy home.

"And again the man and woman went forth by different ways, and the woman went upon the mountain, and the man went into the valley. And the man saw a dove by its nest, and the dove cooed, and seemed to say, 'I bow my spirit in meekness, and rejoice to give joy to others, and therefore my breast and my nest are filled with peace.'

"And the man pondered long, and various thoughts arose; but at last he said, 'I am not a dove, and I cannot bow my spirit in meekness.' Yet he sighed for peace.

"And the woman who went upon the mountain saw at a distance the gleam of bright sunshine which rejoiced her early days, and her heart yearned for it to come nearer; and she ran toward it, but it seemed to recede, and she was fearful and faint; but she stretched forth her hands, and cried, 'O, beautiful sunshine, come and warm my heart!'

"And a voice answered and said, 'I am the spirit of LOVE. I dwell only with those who subdue their spirit in meekness, and who seek reconciliation for offence, even though self-justifying pride oppose it. You have chosen the demon of discord, and therefore I have departed.'

"But the woman cried aloud, and said, 'O, beautiful spirit of sunshine and love, come back and drive the demon of discord away, for I will subdue my spirit in meekness!' and her heart trembled and was sore, but the weight and gloom which oppressed it passed away.

"And she hastened home, and the gleam of sunshine went before her, and her house was filled with its light, and the demon of discord was dazzled and blinded, and fled from the door.

"And while the man pondered in sadness, he looked up and saw his dwelling bright with the sunshine of former days; and he hastened home, and his companion came to meet him, and said, 'O, my husband! I have subdued my spirit in meekness, and the demon of discord has departed, and the sunshine of love fills our house; and even now shines upon your face, and makes it beautiful.'

"And the man answered, 'O, beloved of my heart! you are indeed my better half, for you have by example taught me what I should do. I will also subdue my spirit in meekness, and the demon of discord shall no more enter our dwelling.'

"And the man went forth to cultivate his field, and the sunshine went about him, and his work was easy and his rest sweet. His oxen ploughed their furrows deep and straight; his horses came at his call, and rejoiced to do his bidding his trees put forth thrifty branches, and bore abundant fruit, his garners were filled with plenty, and his heart with peace.

"And as the woman went about her house, the bright gleam filled every room, and her duties were easy and delightful. The pretty lambs frisked in her path, and gave their finest wool. The cows gave overflowing pails of milk, and sweet were the treasures of her dairy. The hens cackled to give notice of new-laid eggs; her bread was light and sweet, and so were her heart and her life."

CHAPTER XLVI.

WHERE are the heroes of my story? Like the fleeting shadows thrown by the magic lantern, they have flitted over the disk of romance into the shade of obscurity, — into the retreats of domestic life, or into the spirit sphere.

From my favorite window in Alek's house, which sister Amy's careful prudence and cheerful affection make so pleasant, I look upon a merry group of children playing beneath the trees. One, a "toddlin wee thing," is Amy's pride and everybody's wonder. I myself think him a "remarkable child." Of the others, the two biggest are Boyntons. Harry and Margaret are responsible for them, and will soon be here after them. Harry has found out that his genius is for farming, and the major has given up the farm to him. The old lady's influence brought it about. She could not have been satisfied otherwise. Too much ease was her disease. She was oppressed with too little to do. Quietude was killing her. Now that trouble is effectually remedied. Harry and his two boys and the baby would banish the quiet of a churchyard. Besides, Dr. Drinkmore is still their guest. He helps plan crops and improvements. Harry holds his opinions in high estimation. They are "book-farmers," and it must be owned that they produce some noble crops, and raise fine cattle, though neighbors say that, were Harry's resources limited to the proceeds of his farm, his genius would soon fail for want of funds, — but the sale of Oakridge supplies the sinews of enterprise, and the Boynton farm, with its cattle and crops, gets honorable mention in the "Agricultural Reports."

But there is no time for details. We are all to be at the wedding at Squire Chinby's to-day. Ike has won the eldest of those cerulean daughters to be his bride, and he wants us for witnesses. All of us are to be there, — Bowlers, Arbors, Boyntons, and the rest. Just now a carriage comes over the hill; it is Harry and Margaret. Dr. Drinkmore is with them; they are to call for the children, and we are all to go together. Alek's colts are harnessed, and impatient for the excursion. Lion, — yes, here comes Lion with the children. His faculties have lapsed into second puppyhood, and he judges himself still fit to partake in wedding festivities. Well, come along, Lion; you are not the only overweening dog in the land.

Hullo, Harry! Good-morning, fair Margaret! Still as fair and bright as in your girlhood, and a good deal happier, — with your pretty babe in your arms, and your rantapole boys spreading themselves around. Good-morning, Dr. Drinkmore. Here are all the children flocking to be taken into the carriage; and here comes Amy with her cherub, — a match for anybody's. Ah, doctor! these pretty sights sometimes make us regret our bachelorhood; but it is too late to sigh — THE HISTORY OF WOLFSDEN IS ENDED!

APPENDIX.

A.

The story of Mrs. Simperkins, being omitted in its proper place, for reasons there given, is here appended by virtue of permission contained in the following letter :

"Respected Sir : I received your polite letter, and take up my pen to inform you that I approve of your printing the history of Wolfsden; for when all the families have their names and connections printed, then everybody can tell who is who, and there will be no mistakes in generations. In the old country, everybody that is anything has a coat of arms, which is the same thing. As you propose very kindly to put my name in (which I consider very proper, being in some sort a daughter of America, as I adopted this country from affection, and not for profit), I send you my coat of arms, which you may put in the book, as it tells all about my family ; and you can get some Englishman to explain it, as I do not exactly remember the meaning of the signs, only the figure on the top is a 'vampyre rampant,' which signifies that we descended from the nobility.

"As you ask for leave to put in my story, I am willing, being in some sort bound, as an adopted daughter of America, to do something for the literature of the same ; and I shall feel that I have some part in the book, which I hope you will acknowledge.

"I shall spend the winter paying the visits I am owing in Wolfsden, at Deacon Arbor's, and Major Murray's, and Colonel Bowler's, and good dear Doctor Boreman's, whose family are all thriving nicely ; for Lucinda has got a fine boy, and her husband, whom we used to call Ax, is the best schoolmaster in Wolfsden. I mean to spend a few weeks at Mr. Harry Boynton's, and Alek Arbor's, and Josiah Brown's that married Ann Bowler, and Isaac Bowler's that they called Ike. They all used to be wild young men, but are now very steady and sober.

"I hope you will send me some of the books as soon as they are printed ; and also send a bottle of Dr. Diddler's Hair Dye and Remedy for Wrinkles, which is wanted for a friend ; and when you see Mrs. Greening, ask her to send any female medicines which she finds best. And so I remain your friend, respectfully,

"ANN AMANDINA SIMPERKINS."

The following is the substance of Mrs. Simperkins' story, so frequently crammed into our ears against the stomach of our sense ; though, as several years have since passed, it is not possible exactly to represent from memory her peculiar graces of delivery :

"When I resided in Lunnun I became hacquainted with a great gentleman, who came into hour shop in Cheapside. I say hour shop, because I used to be there hoften when Mr. Simperkins was haway ; and it was dull sitting in my parlor halone, and so I used to run hover to Mrs. Snubs'. And when poor Mr. Simperkins died I took hup my habode there, and elped to tend shop. Mrs. Snubs was a werry genteel lady, and her shop was the genteelest in Cheapside, and Cheapside is the genteelest street in Lunnun — next to Pall-Mall and Covent Garden. The nobility and gentry do hall their business there, and hit 's a grand thing to see the coaches, and the coachman hon the box, with his powered wig and white gloves, and the lords and ladies getting hout to do their business. And when the nobility walk through Cheapside, it is a grand sight ; for one can halways tell a lord by his hattitude and hair.

"I was one day sitting in the shop, when who should come hin but one of the most helegant gentlemen my heyes hever beheld. He had a star and ribbon, by which I knew he was a lord, and he hasked for some gloves, and tried hon a pair ; and O, such ands ! as delicate as a lady's, and covered with diamond rings. He hordered a dozen pair worth twelve crowns, and threw down three guineas and his card, and said he would send his servant for them ; and when I hoffered change, he refused it, and made one of those fine speeches which the gentry so love to make, but which I never would listen to.

"I appened to ave hon a werry fine bracelet which my usband left me. He had been hunfortunate in business, but the bracelet was werry waluable. Hit was left for security by a werry great lady, who borrowed money; for my usband was a pawnbroker, and the bracelet was presented to the lady by the Prince of Wales. He said hit was a hunique ; and certainly hit was something wonderful. Hit was made of the most waluable stones, set in gold. The centre was a brilliant diamond, with rays made of different gems and pointed with diamonds.

"I noticed that the count seemed to hadmire hit werry much. I won't say but what, being werry young, — for that was ten years ago, — I was a little wain. When he was gone I looked at the card, which was engraved with a coronet, and COUNT FLIPPERTON hunder it. In half an hour a spruce footman in livery came with his master's card, and took the gloves.

"Hin a few days Count Flipperton called again when Mrs. Snubs was hout, and bought some lace ruffles, and paid as liberally as before. And about a week hafter he came again in a coach with two smart footmen behind, and led in the prettiest lady you hever set heyes hon, and hintroduced her as lady Flipperton, and said to her, 'My dear, this is the young lady I praised so ighly;' and her ladyship gave me a werry polite bow, and hobserved that she was werry appy to be hacquainted with me. She was much pleased with hour goods, and made the greatest purchases we had sold for a long time. Hevery beautiful and rich thing she saw she hadmired, and the count hencouraged her to buy heverything she hadmired, so that the bill amounted to a undred pounds.

"When the goods were ready, the footman took them to the coach, and the count wrote a draft hon his banker for the hamount. I was werry much hembarrassed, for Mrs. Snubs had told me to take nothing but gold or silver; and I told im I oped he would hexcuse me on that haccount. 'Perfectly right,' said he; 'my servant shall take the draft and get the gold, and we will wait. I felt werry much hembarrassed, but lady Flipperton said to the count, 'My dear, there is a undred guineas in the pocket of the coach, that Dobson paid for rent this morning. You left it hon the table, and I hordered hit put hin the coach for safety.' 'My dear,' said he, 'you are hover careful; but it 's lucky just now.' So he sends for the bag, and counts hout ninety guineas to pay the bill, and gave me two more; one, as he said, for my good looks, — I was young then, — and the other for my good behavior.

"Just then the lady hasked to look at my bracelet. I held out my harm, and she hunfastened the clasp, and turned to show it to the count; who praised it ighly, and then she put it hon my harm again werry condescending.

"When they went away, I was werry much pleased with making so large a sale, till Mrs. Snubs came; but when she looked at the money she said it was hall false coin; and, sure enough, I could ave told it for bad money in the dark, if I ad not been so much hembarrassed by their genteel ways. Mrs. Snubs hasked me hall habout what they said and did, and when I told about the bracelet, she looked at it, and said they had hexchanged it and left a false one made of copper and glass; and sure enough it was so. Hon hinquiry at the police, we were hinformed that there was no such lord as Count Flipperton; but they took the description, but did not bring back any goods, nor money, nor my hunique bracelet."

B.

The account of Ben Blacksmith is derived from different sources, the best known of which is the protest of the officers and crew of the brig Creole, published in the *New Orleans Advertiser*, December 8, 1841, of which the following is a brief abridgment:

"By this instrument of protest be it known that on the second day of December, 1841, before me Wm. Y. Lewis, notary public in the city of New Orleans, personally appeared Z. C. Gifford, master of the American brig Creole, of Richmond, who declared that the said brig sailed for New-Orleans on the 13th day of October, laden with tobacco and slaves.

"That when about one hundred and thirty miles N. N. E. of Hole-in-the-wall, the slaves rose on the officers and crew, killing one and severely wounding others, including the captain and first mate.

"The conspirators then compelled the crew, under pain of death, to navigate them to a British island. Ben Blacksmith, Madison Washington, D. Ruffin, and Elijah Morris, were the ringleaders. These four assumed command, and watched the compass constantly by turns. So close was their watch, that it was impossible to rescue the brig. When they saw Merrit mark on the slate the latitude he was taking, they compelled him to rub out the writing and make only figures, for fear that they might communicate by that means. The conspirators threw all the arms in the vessel overboard.

"When we made the light of Abaco, and the brig approached Nassau, the pilot came on board. He and his men were all negroes. They told the slaves they were free, and could not be carried away.

"On Wednesday following, three civil magistrates came on board and set free the slaves, against the protest of the captain, and gave them their wearing apparel and blankets.

"And, therefore, the appearers do solemnly protest," &c. &c.,

Signed by officers and crew of brig Creole.

C.

To prevent misconception, it is proper here to repeat, that the lines attributed to Margaret were really written by that lady, and also that a few of the flowers of rhetoric which adorn the heads of some of the chapters were culled from Lucinda's album. Except for these, and what belongs to Mrs. Simperkins and others, the responsibility rests with

J. B.

www.ingramcontent.com/pod-product-compliance
Lightning Source LLC
LaVergne TN
LVHW020912110826
845150LV00004B/650

* 9 7 8 1 4 2 5 5 5 7 0 0 3 *